春风吻上我的脸

Spring Breeze Kisses My Face

赵舒娴 著

By Zhao Shuxian

Billson International Ltd.

Published by
Billson International Ltd
27 Old Gloucester Street
London
WC1N 3AX
Tel:(852)95619525

Website:www.billson.cn
E-mail address:cs@billson.cn

First published 2024

Produced by Billson International Ltd
CDPF/01

ISBN 978-1-80377-107-6

Hebei Zhongban Culture Development Co.,Ltd
Wanda Office Building B, 215 Jianhua South Street, Yuhua District, Shijiazhuang City, Hebei province, 2207

About the work
作品简介

This is a more realistic version of the marriage and love theme, describes the life of men and women in the choice of partners, some of the life, marriage, economic views, consumption views are different, the heroine Qin Ying has experienced three different versions of men as the object, the choice faced at different times. In the novel, there is a man Deng Cheng character to fight for the pursuit of love with action, a Cheng Mo is the pursuit of love with mouth sweet words, and want to occupy the assets that consume Qin Ying.

The heroine Qin Ying in the novel, after experiencing the failure of her first love and Su Yong, became cautious and careful, in the treatment of the two men she met later, she analyzed the exploratory observation from every Angle, and gambled on finding the perfect love and marriage happiness in the future half life!

Saw the true state of mind of the two men, the false heart of the false man out, will sincerely love her men choose to communicate as a partner, and strive for happiness.

Deng Cheng true feelings touched Qin Ying heart, this life Deng Cheng is the only woman engraved on my heart. Two people love each other meet running-in love, with sincere feelings, more firm walk together!

The novel advocates the correct three views, only truly cherish the lover around, life will be valuable! A sense of belonging to be loved.

这是一部比较现实版的婚姻爱情题材，描述了男女在选择伴侣的生活中，发生的一些生活、婚姻观、经济观点、消费观点不同，女主角秦瑛对经历了三位不同版本的男士为对象，进行了不同时期面临的选择。小说中有一位男士邓诚人物用行动去争取追求爱情，一位程默是用嘴巴甜言蜜语追求爱情，并想占有消耗秦瑛的资产。

小说中的女主秦瑛，从经历过初恋与苏勇的失败后，变得谨慎小心，在对待后来遇到的两位男士，女主从各个一个角度去分析试探观察中，为未来半辈子的生活中，去寻找完美的爱情婚姻幸福，赌了一把！

看到了两位男士的真实心态，将假心假假意的男士出局，将真心实意爱她男士选择为伴侣交往，为奔向幸福而努力。

邓诚真情打动了秦瑛芳心，此生邓诚是女主刻骨铭心的唯一。两个人相爱相遇磨合中的爱情，以真心相待感情，更加坚定走在了一起！

小说提倡正确的三观，只有真心珍惜身边的爱人，人生才会有价值意义！有被爱的归属感。

Contents
目录

Spring Breeze Kisses My Face

Preface

The spring breeze gently brushed, kissed the face of the years, leaving a gentle mark. At this moment, we are about to explore the warmth and sincerity hidden in "Spring breeze kisses my face" . This work created by Ms. Zhao Shuxian, with its delicate brushstrokes and deep emotions, let us feel the power and beauty of love.

In the book, we meet the heroine Qin Ying, a woman full of energy and pursuit. Through her emotional entanglements with three different men, she went through twists and turns and honed, and finally realized the meaning of true love. In this process, Qin Ying's image has been shaped into a real and three-dimensional, she has been confused, hesitant, but always maintain the persistent pursuit of love, choose to understand her, cherish her partner.

In addition to the heroine, the other characters are also lifelike, each with its own characteristics: the hypocritical Cheng Mo, the sincere Deng Cheng, and the kind-hearted Shen couple. The emotional entanglements and conflicts between these characters make the whole story full of twists and turns and surprises. Every emotional conflict is heart-wrenching, and every turning point makes people happy. Especially the love line between Qin Ying and Deng Cheng, the author, with his keen insight, digs deeply into Qin Ying's inner struggle and growth, and shows the complexity and beauty of love through the love line between Qin Ying and Deng Cheng. From acquaintance to acquaintance, from acquaintance to love, every detail is described incisively and vividly by the author, so that we seem to be in the story, and the characters experience those joys and sorrows.

This work not only carries forward the correct values and views of marriage, emphasizes that only by treating lovers sincerely can we get sincere love, but also reminds us to bravely face the difficulties and challenges in life, and actively pursue our own happiness and dreams. In this world full of changes, we need to be like Qin Ying and Deng Cheng, firm faith, love, courage.

"Spring breeze kisses my face", let us, along with the hickey of spring breeze, embark on this journey full of love and hope! I believe that in this journey, we will be full of inspiration and inspiration, and will cherish the love and happiness around us more.

Editor of Huiwen Book: Qing

March 2, 2024

Chapter 1 :Encounter on a Rainy Day

July in Zhuhai is the most unpredictable season of Marine climate, the weather changes as it says, the cloudy sky suddenly begins to storm, and the torrential rain pours down on pedestrians.

At that time, Qin Ying was near the seaside scenic spot fish female stone, saw the heavy rain, she did not care so much, rolled up the pants Angle with the crowd of people lying in the rain. Panic, Qin Ying stopped, looking across the road "love bar book bar" , hesitated for a while, or hurriedly ran over.

"Love Bar Book Bar" interior covers an area of 160 square meters, divided into two floors, the front door has a courtyard of 100 square meters, placed six sets of stone tables and benches, weekdays for guests to drink tea and read. There are large trees planted on both sides of the door, and the thick leaves cover some of the rain. There are many passers-by who come here to take shelter from the rain. Qin Ying plunged into the gate standing, casually stomp up the moment saw a familiar figure. Qin Ying heart startled: "Is he? How did he end up in Zhuhai?"

Not far from the man named Su Yong, Qin Ying is looking for years of lover. Su Yong also seemed to see Qin Ying, two people suddenly froze in place. Soon, Su Yong bowed his head into the "love bar book bar" , Qin Ying quickly chased up. She was anxious to find Su Yong to ask clearly, ask him where he went in the end these years, and now what is the relationship between them.

Qin Ying looked around after entering the book bar. Behind her came the familiar bass voice: "I am behind you." Qin Ying suddenly turned around and saw that it was Su Yong standing behind her, she dragged Su Yong's arm with her hand, deliberately pressed down anger and asked him: "How did you leave without saying a word?" Do you know I've been looking for you like a fool all these years?" Qin Ying wronged like a child, but can not loudly accuse Su Yong, she said while pulling Su Yong to the quiet corner of the book, want him to immediately say understand.

It seems that Qin Ying is familiar with the environment of the love bar, in fact, the decoration here is designed by her - she is the boss of the love bar, and there are not many people who know this matter.

There was no one nearby, Qin Ying's voice was louder, she asked Su Yong: "Where have you been these years?" Why didn't you leave me without telling me? After a few years, you may have forgotten me long ago, I will not pester you, but you must tell me the truth!"

Su Yong did not avoid, but also appeared particularly nervous, do not know where to start, he hesitantly answered: "That year I left in a hurry, the thought of Guangzhou after settling down to tell you." Then a series of things happened, and I was so busy that I put it off. Then my female boss divorced, she took a fancy to me, we slowly walked together... Now that I'm married to her, her daughter from her first marriage lives with us. I have failed you, so I dare not go back to you."

Hear Su Yong answer, Qin Ying calm down, she finally waited for an answer. She felt silly to have waited so long. In fact, she has long thought that Su Yong has given up himself, after all, Su Yong is handsome and considerate, it is easy to attract women to fall in love with him.

Su Yong continued, "My friend also came today, right over there. She and her daughter are coming towards us." With that, Su Yong waved in the direction of the door.

Qin Ying turned his head and saw a woman of average appearance come to the front. The woman had a square face, a large mouth, short shawl hair, and large but unattractive eyes, clearly cross-eyed. She pulled a girl about ten years old to Su Yong. When she saw Qin Ying clearly, she suddenly shouted, "Are you Qin Ying? We went to high school together, do you still recognize me?"

Qin Ying also recognized it: "You are Ma Ting, commissary in charge of studies!"

Why are you here?"

Ma Ting pointed to Su Yong and said, "Our family is here to travel." Ma Ting's daughter called directly to Su Yong: "Dad, how did you run here, causing my mother and I to look for you in the love bar book bar!" Dad, there are so many books here. I love this book. Have you found a place after all this searching?"

Su Yong pointed awkwardly to an empty seat that happened to appear next to him: "I only found this empty seat at the small table. Too many people came in to take shelter from the rain. There is not much space here.

Ma Ting took Qin Ying's hand and said, "I forgot to introduce you, this is my husband Su Yong, who is the general manager of my company in Guangzhou, and this is my daughter Yuan Yuan." Remembering that we haven't seen each other since graduation, it's rare to meet here, let's have dinner together."

Qin Ying unwilling to lose to the high school classmates, she also curious Su Yong later experience, so agreed to Ma Ting's invitation. The four sat down at a small table and ordered what they liked to eat. Then Qin Ying excuse to go to the bathroom, he went to the front desk to settle the account first.

After a while the waiter put the dishes on the table, Ma Ting ate one of the snacks called vegetarian meatballs, and praised Qin Ying: "Old classmate you really know how to order food, this meatball is so delicious!" Qin Ying secretly looked at Su Yong, found that his face was a little unnatural. Speaking of this vegetarian meatball, there is a story about him and Qin Ying.

When the two were together, they had eaten a vegetarian meatball made of glutinous rice flour at a shop in the county, and Su liked the taste, saying it was the most delicious vegetarian food he had ever eaten. After eating, Qin Ying specially asked the owner of the shop, asked her how to do this dish, also bought another 50 balls to pack away, said to share with relatives and friends in the city. When Qin Ying went back, she said excitedly: "In the future, I will also open a small teahouse in the original retro style, and the snacks in the teahouse must have this sticky rice flour vegetarian meatballs, and they are accompanied by books and magazines, so that people can read while drinking tea." I believe the business will be better than the small shop just now." Today's "love bar book bar" is almost the way Qin Ying described to Su Yong at that time, I don't know if he will guess that this book is Qin Ying opened.

Ma Ting said to Qin Ying, "You are still so beautiful now, not at all like me." By the way, have you got a family?"

Qin Ying smiled a little reluctantly: "Which is like you have a blessing, the children are so big, sensible, her husband is handsome." I've been messing around, and I haven't met the right guy, but I want to get off my bill. Seeing how happy you are, I want to marry myself soon."

Qin Ying said this or said to Su Yong listen to, suggesting that he should put down this relationship. Meet Su Yong family today, Qin Ying completely gave up waiting for Su Yong fantasy. She can not accept Su Yong for his career, would rather give up her Qin Ying love. Did not think that Su Yong is also a very realistic man, in order to pursue the so-called goal of life, willing to be Ma Ting's husband, do the stepfather of the child. Su Yong and Ma Ting obviously do not match, but it can be seen that Ma Ting is very confident, humorous, can talk, will coax men like, which is Qin Ying does not have the ability.

Love bar book bar put a gentle quiet music, sitting here will feel the heart will be quiet down. The atmosphere of this book bar is suitable for anyone, you can read quietly alone, you can sit by the window with a pot of tea, look at the direction of the sea in a daze, and you can whisper together with three or four friends. On weekends, it is the norm for young couples to come here with their children for tea and books.

Ma Ting said to her daughter, "Yuan Yuan, you seem to like it here. The boss of this book bar is really creative, the decoration style is very careful, simple, but it looks very comfortable. It seems that the boss has good taste and I really enjoy the atmosphere here." Said, she also lovingly looked at Su Yong, Su Yong can only nod to agree with Ma Ting words.

Ma Ting then turned to Qin Ying and said: "By the way, ask the waiter to bring a pen and paper, let's leave a mobile phone number, or leave here, how to contact you?"

Qin Ying dont want to participate in the life of Su Yong, but not good directly refuse Ma Ting, she immediately got up to check out the bar for a while. She said a few words to the waiter and went back to the table: "I've paid my bill. Now that the rain has stopped, take your tea and get some rest. I was supposed to meet a friend today, and she just called to rush me, but now I have to leave, so excuse me."

Ma Ting did not have time to write his mobile phone number, Qin Ying suddenly left, she was a little unprepared, there are many people in the book, loudly called Qin Ying and appeared impolite, can only watch Qin Ying hurried away. Su Yong is mixed taste, also dare not chase up. Can not get Qin Ying's mobile phone number, it seems that his life with Qin Ying fate has done, today's encounter is to say goodbye to Qin Ying completely.

Recalling the happy days with Qin Ying in the past, Su Yong is very nostalgic, but he clearly knows that he loves himself more, between love and material, he will choose the latter. Think of or he lived up to Qin Ying, feel very guilty in the heart. He remembered that in the days of their relationship, he had only given Qin Ying an old-fashioned silver ring as a gift, which was all he could give Qin Ying at that time. Su Yong inadvertently touched the pocket, found the silver ring in it, must be Qin Ying secretly returned to him. Thought of this, he was sad again.

Qin Ying escaped from the book, deeply relieved, she walked quickly to the sea. Before she escaped, she quietly took off the silver ring from her hand and put it into Su Yong's pocket when Ma Ting wasn't paying attention. This move is to tell herself that she decided to put down Su Yong. People have a family, where there is their own place? Qin Ying feel really ridiculous, in order to wait for Su Yong spent his youth, now she has 39 years old. Waiting for so many years of love, or nothing. Her heart was cold, but she woke up!

Chapter 2: Man is Not a Plant

After leaving Su Yong couple, Qin Ying straight to the seaside rambling walk, feel himself is put down, but after all, love waiting for so many years, still some can not think. They have been in love for so many years, almost did not choose to talk about marriage.

Qin Ying did not consciously think of their past: when they were living in the small town of their hometown, Su Yong worked in the bank, the current director of the Taiwan hall; Qin Ying at that time in the commercial bureau under a wholesale station of non-staple food work, every day sales fell in Qin Ying is responsible for depositing into the company's account, fixed bank linked business is Su Yong responsible for the branch. Over time, Su Yong noticed Qin Ying, and Qin Ying was attracted to this handsome Su Yong. His every move, she will be very careful to watch, every time can not help but blush, afraid to look up and see Su Yong, but hope Su Yong can be on duty at the scene. She knew that this time suddenly there was a feeling of love, pure unrequited love, because at that time there was no mutual confession, just slowly say hello from familiarity.

One day shortly after she went to work, Qin Ying slept too much in the morning, walked too fast and did not stay at home too early, and there was no business in the morning, so she ate breakfast in a special beef powder shop opposite the bank. It is said that it is a ten-year old store, the taste is not said, as long as the guests will return to patronize. This is true, Qin Ying is a frequent customer who loves to patronize this store.

At that time, Qin Ying was eating beef powder and a deep-fried dough stick, suddenly Su Yong walked into the shop, as if familiar with the boss: "I came to a bowl as yesterday, refuel a bar, put some spicy soup." The original Su Yong also like to eat this beef powder, the taste is exactly the same as Qin Ying. Qin Ying heard Su Yong's voice, head dare not lift, head down did not hear to eat, a magnetic voice behind Qin Ying ear rang: "Hey, Qin Ying you today how this time to eat beef powder ah?" She knew it was over. Su Yong had seen her. She looked up sheepishly and said, "Well, I'm late today."

Su Yong: "Are you here too early?" I eat here every day and I love the taste."

Two people began to talk casually, Qin Ying always forget the first time so close to a handsome young man to talk, Su Yong seems to be better than the time at work.

Qin Ying later knew that Su Yong's father was the head of a very famous troupe in the city, and his mother was the heroine of the troupe, his parents' love passed for the story of that era, Su Yong was handsome like his father, very handsome and heavy, but did not take the class of his parents, take the road of literature and art, but engaged in the financial industry. Because of his outstanding image, Su Yong became the front desk lobby manager of the bank. I heard that Su Yong was as a training object in the line, as one of the candidates for promotion.

It seems that time passed very quickly, and Qin Ying is very happy to go to the bank for these businesses, looking forward to seeing Su Yong every day at this time. And Su Yong as long as listen to Qin Ying at the front desk to talk to colleagues, he will walk into the front desk from the background to receive Qin Ying. The two gradually get to know each other and naturally establish a love relationship.

Later, after understanding just know, Su Yong colleagues as long as see Qin Ying to line deposit, intentionally let Su Yong out to say hello, they all want to contribute to the two of them become a pair, a not married a not married, it looks really well-matched pair.

This affair is not publicly exposed, at that time Qin Ying is sitting after Su Yong bicycle, smiling happy woman, their time together is so good, no worldly distractions, no interference, Qin Ying smiled brightly, can be a public Su Yong are deliberately to avoid letting everyone know he and Qin Ying love. Because Su Yong has not thought of marriage, just feel very relaxed and comfortable with Qin Ying. Although there is no mouth to Qin Ying clear confession, but can not let go of this good woman Qin Ying. He believed that men should put aside their feelings for the sake of their career, and he would not talk about marriage until he had achieved his goals.

Su Yong intentionally or unintentionally made such a suggestion to Qin Ying, when he had a successful career to marry Qin Ying. In order to stabilize Qin Ying, Su Yong will grandma gave him a silver ring as a token of love to Qin Ying.

Later, Su Yong was transferred from his home town because of his work and moved to a private company in Guangzhou. After that, Su Yong could not be reached. Since Su Yong left without saying goodbye, Qin Ying also did not intend to continue to work in the original unit, every time to the bank will think of Su Yong shadow and voice, also feel Su Yong colleagues will talk behind her.

This kind of touch thought people's day, really let Qin Ying can not stand, a few years of love because Su Yong play missing and completely shattered, too big blow to her. She had to change that, and the only way to do it was to do it.

In this way, Qin Ying made a decision to change his own, resign into the sea. She made further investigations in Zhuhai and Zhongshan, Shenzhen, Guangzhou, Macao and Hong Kong, and finally decided to develop between Zhuhai and Zhongshan.

Qin Ying first found a place to settle, is a yoga studio in Zhuhai physiotherapy center service company. She was hired by a service clinic, working as a physical therapist during the day, and running her own "Love Bar Book Bar" on weekends and weekdays in the evenings after work.

The staff of the book bar are two distant relatives recruited from their hometown, and these two country girls keep the book bar in good order.

The business model of the book bar is very simple, based on the operation model of the library reading room, there are some hot tea and snacks service items, which is also for people who love reading books, can stay in the book bar for a whole day.

Love bar book bar business slowly made famous, book bar and did not draw her much energy, Qin Ying put this business investment as a spiritual enjoyment and comfort.

Wealth income is just equal to rent and utilities and two staff salary expenses, weak income some thin profit.

This is what Qin Ying most want to do, the usual holidays, colleagues will go to travel, and Qin Ying will dive into their love of the book, reading and dealing with some daily affairs.

Never say that this love bar book bar is opened by itself, and it has been explained to employees, no matter what the situation, do not call her boss, so no one knows who the boss of the book bar is after staying here for many years. This is also Qin Ying low-key, in order to protect their best way.

In the first few years to Zhuhai, Qin Ying listened to the advice of real estate friends and decisively chose a place between Zhuhai and Zhongshan that was not expensive.

Fortunately, as early as 2015, Qin Ying seized the last opportunity to invest in real estate, bought a property on the border between Zhongshan and Zhuhai, a green plant garden residential bungalow, three rooms and two rooms 130 square meters, the total price of more than 580,000 yuan, after renovation, only after more than a year, immediately promoted to double.

Qin Ying in order to invest to make money, first sold this profitable property, and then put some of the profits into the sea, the same developer, the development of seascape apartment duplex.

In this way, when the first investment house quadrupled, it was sold and the capital invested was reinvested in financial management.

Compared with her peers, Qin Ying gathered all her scattered funds together, grabbed the tail before the price rose, and obtained the first bucket of gold for settling down in Zhuhai.

In order to the appreciation of this house space, maximize the interests, Qin Ying immediately to carry out decoration, is in the sales department beauty small Yi recommended to find the decoration of the couple Shen total and autumn sweet. It is under their influence that Qin Ying fell in love with the city of Zhuhai and its simple and kind people.

In the process of decoration, Qin Ying will always remember the autumn sweet and Shen to help her. As a stranger from a foreign land to venture capital, Qin Ying did not expect to become friends with them. Qin Ying felt that if there was no help from her husband and wife, she did not know where to start in many aspects.

Qin Ying with autumn sweet like old friends, the first time to her company to talk about decoration, autumn sweet as far as possible to save costs, planning simple installation repair heavy decoration program, suddenly captured the heart of Qin Ying. Only talk about a few back and forth, Qin Ying will rest assured that the house to autumn sweet decoration.

Beginning to Zhuhai here, Qin Ying has been accompanied by autumn sweet enthusiasm, took her to the hotel, the choice is to stay in the affordable hot spring hotel, close to the autumn sweet decoration company.

Qin Ying remember the initial scene of staying in the hotel, the hotel price is reasonable, the developer's sales department returned to the hotel to stay in the most preferential recommendation card, as long as 168 a night, bought the room owners can also enjoy discounts.

There is an open-air hot spring pool on the roof of this hot spring hotel, which corresponds with the sky and stars. Soaking in the hot spring pool makes you feel like entering a fairyland. Breakfast is free, and guests staying in the hotel are also free to soak in the hot spring. Each owner stays in the hotel during the renovation period, which is like a romantic trip to this holiday tour. There is no owner who does not like this place, Qin Ying is from here more like the city.

This is accompanied by autumn sweet credit, for a long time, Qin Ying also know clearly where the sea has seafood to eat. Qin Ying like to eat crab fish shells, autumn sweet to Qin Ying recommended local famous seafood restaurant "Cliff mouth family seafood restaurant". Qin Ying very like this shop, every time Qin Ying to see the progress of house decoration, will go to cliff mouth people to eat; When her girlfriend comes from other places, she will take her to the cliff mouth to taste seafood. There is also a shop specializing in fish, called "boneless fish shop" , a fish to eat more, fish bone soup, fish skin, fish slices, fried fish pieces, braised fish pieces, etc., there are foreign friends on the wall to take photos with the chef.

Time is the best medicine to cure love, to Zhuhai so many years of entrepreneurial struggle, life is busy and full, Qin Ying slowly forgot the pain of love, but did not expect to meet Su Yong so.

Still wandering in the seaside Qin Ying can not help but look at his left ring finger, there also vaguely see the traces left by the silver ring. Silver ring has been returned to Su Yong, her feelings between Su Yong completely ended. She told herself that since she had moved on, she should stop thinking about it and move on. Qin Ying took a deep breath, as if the inner depression had been loosened.

Qin Ying has been very accustomed to their own personal life, so slowly have already forgotten the love of this thing, a person life is very good.

Qinying in Zhuhai has no other friends, so as long as free to go to the autumn sweet decoration company sit.

It was another sunny weekend, and the employees of Shen's head office were busy preparing lunch for Shen's birthday.

It's better to be early than lucky, and when you hit a birthday party, it's a good sign.

Shen will arrange to eat three cups of chicken with the staff in the company, this time by the autumn sweet personally cook, for Shen deliberately burned three cups of chicken.

Autumn sweet saw Qin Ying arrived, happy to close the dragon's mouth: "you have come just right, I let you taste three cups of chicken today, this is the real taste of Zhuhai people, you guarantee to eat after want to eat."

This company activity, deepen Qin Ying on the autumn sweet good impression, did not think in addition to work, autumn sweet will be so much, no wonder Shen so care about the autumn sweet.

This kind of partner on the work, life is a husband and wife partner, doing things like a friendship partner, more and more let Qin Ying envy.

It was the happiest marriage she had ever seen, a happy, happy, ordinary life in pairs.

See the husband and wife in the company behind the stove busy look, Qin Ying looked stayed, in Zhuhai originally can also be half fireworks, half fairyland life, this oil rice firewood salt ordinary people's life, should not be like this?

That evening, Shen's brother-in-law also invited autumn sweet and Shen to their own guest, did not expect Qin Ying was also invited as a welcome guest, together.

Qin Ying is a little embarrassed: "You are a family banquet, I will not go."

Qiu Tian said: "No, no, no, no, no, you go to your sister's home, you will be the most popular." In this way, Qin Ying made an exception and went to Shen's sister home to eat a rich dinner.

After the family dinner, Shen's brother-in-law was happy and went to karaoke together, and the box was set.

Qin Ying really found that the first love song is Shen and autumn sweet chorus "husband and wife also home" singing so well, especially Shen, a popular singing method behind, but also simple voice like the original, autumn sweet is not bad up and down.

Qin Ying looked at the couple with appreciation, and what could be happier than them at this time?

Everyone asked to sing, of course, Qin Ying is no exception, finally Qin Ying was also infected by the lively atmosphere, point three of her best songs, "Shepherd song" , "I love you, the snow in the North of the Saibei" , "Love is priceless" ...

Autumn sweet clapped and praised the people said: "Look, the tai drama is Qin Ying ah, you are really versatile ah, believe in your evil, but also so modest, to know that you sing so well, how I also dare not sing!"

Until autumn sweet finished, Shen said: "Real people do not show!" Qin Ying has no boyfriend too pity, we must help Qin Ying to find a good man quality stock, I think of a person, very matching Qin Ying!"

After saying this sentence immediately attached to autumn sweet ear quietly say a name, autumn sweet after listening to keep nodding and saying: "Yes, you can, you can, next time you arrange for them to meet, really match yo!" It was a great night for everyone.

Qin Ying in addition to work, is the weekend to love the book bar, is always a two-line life. So autumn sweet and Shen always know, if you want to find Qin Ying, to love the book will be able to find.

Another weekend Sunday, autumn sweet and Shen after finishing the decoration work, will be with Qin Ying in love bar book bar for a while, listen to light music drink a cup of hot tea, brag and shake mouth.

But this weekend, Love Bar book bar, Shen Zong brought a rare guest! The bearer is not others, it is Shen always quietly mentioned that quality man Deng Cheng.

Chapter 3: Past Encounters

Deng Cheng into the love bar book bar, Shen always brought Qin Ying table for a moment, Qin Ying and Deng Cheng at the same time, can not help but laugh out, the world only such a coincidence, also happened in Deng Cheng and Qin Ying they two people, it is incredible!

Two people suddenly laugh, let Shen and autumn sweet wonder? Shen pointed his finger at Deng Cheng and said, "Do you all know Deng Dong? When did you meet her? Why haven't I heard you talk about it or seen you together?"

Autumn sweet in a confused stare at Qin Ying said: "Really have you, secrecy work done so well, have not heard you say it?" Haven't seen you two moving around, either? This is your fate, and if you don't hurry to attract it, tell me what happened."

Autumn sweet to urge Qin Ying, Qin Ying smiled and looked at Deng Cheng without a word, Shen total signal quietly with a finger to sit down and talk, he would like to hear Deng Dong and Qin Ying two know the story: "Please tell the truth."

Deng Cheng sat down to take a look at Qin Ying, embarrassed to scratch a few heads, smiling to face everyone like telling a story about their own situation in recent years.

At this time Qin Ying saw Deng Cheng in front of the opposite sit, talk about the scene, can not help but think of 5 years between the three contacts with Deng Cheng...

That year, before Qin Ying left his hometown, completely changed himself, and the picture of a new face emerged in his mind... Qin Ying rushed in Shenzhen to medical beauty micro plastic surgery, under the advice of the dean, spend 200,000 yuan to create the whole face! This is a fashion revolution. We all know that the best show of wealth is today's micro plastic surgery, after 9 hours of surgery, Qin Ying carefully looked at himself in the mirror, feel stimulating excitement and pleasure, the operation returned to normal, in the eyes of outsiders, only feel Qin Ying became beautiful, young, good-looking, but can not see any traces of change, this is the effect of micro plastic! The most beautiful years of life is to keep a happy mood like this forever, appearance for Qin Ying is a love of life attitude, she wants to come out of a change.

When Qin Ying checked in to Zhuhai Hot Spring Hotel again, the lobby manager did not recognize her. When he saw the name of the ID card, he looked up at Qin Ying again and cried out in surprise: "Really you?" My sister is becoming more and more beautiful and younger! I was afraid to recognize it, but I thought who does this person look like?"

The lobby manager happily continued: "Welcome, or give you the standard room No. 6, I know you like 6, things can go smoothly!"

Qin Ying once said that she chose to buy a house like the house number, did not expect the little beauty lobby manager still remember so clearly.

Through the stairs to the room on the third floor, Qin Ying light and graceful hair fluttering with the wind, looking at the bright sunshine in the afternoon, Qin Ying felt a sense of fatigue to her. She lay down on the soft and comfortable bed, and slept with the sun, and fell asleep in the warm bed. I don't know how long later, the lobby manager called to wake her up to the first floor lobby for dinner.

Qin Ying slowly back to carry a small bag, slowly into the restaurant to eat, because it is a person to come, Qin Ying chose a window position, tonight the guests are not a lot, so Qin Ying is not urgent, she just have time to think about tomorrow to go to the sales department to see, or to the sales department small Yi recommended decoration boss Shen Qinying temporary driver and guide.

It was nearly evening, when Qin Ying was full, she took a walk on the covered bridge around the hotel, enjoying the green trees and colorful flowers in the surrounding environment, as well as the night sky full of stars. Qin Ying couldn't help but stop by the wooden bridge and sit down on a stone stool, as if she didn't think about anything, quietly listening to the rustling of leaves in the wind and looking at the distant scenery. There are mountains, water and the sound of birds, as well as the sound of frogs in the pond, interdependent animal world are so happy to communicate, when Qin Ying is very curious to imagine, peripheral light let her feel that someone approached her...

The restaurant has been closed, the hotel and out of a handsome and calm man, from the other end of the corridor also walked to the near Qin Ying, in Qin Ying's line of sight, two people at the same time eyes at each other, and naturally spread out, each look at the sky up, and finally the man could not help but also sit next to Qin Ying, looking for words: "You live in the hotel meeting?" I'm at the same meeting."

Qin Ying watched warily before saying, "I came here to have a look." Qin Ying this answer is equal to not say.

The man began to introduce himself: "My name is Deng Cheng, is here to study and participate in the development trend of the insurance industry conference, my peers went to the hot spring on the roof, I want to take a quiet walk, the city, especially the hotel environment health and good air." We choose to meet here every time! You're not from around here, are you?"

Qin Ying: "You can also see this?"

Deng Cheng smiled and nodded, and then Deng Cheng euphemistically and carefully asked: "What occupation are you doing?" Can you tell me?"

Qin Ying did not answer directly, just smiled and said, "Aren't you a half-fairy who can guess?"

Deng Cheng self-mockingly said: "Can't guess!"

Deng Cheng did not know when, gave his business card to Qin Ying: "Here is my contact information, hope to add me!" If you need my help in Zhuhai, please contact me, see you later!"

The weather in Zhuhai in September is pleasant, although it is night, but the quiet around and the natural leaves exude the smell of green plants, so Qin Ying took a deep breath, looked at the back of Deng Cheng who had entered the hotel, opened the business card, and Deng Dong, an insurance company group, put it in the bag.

Since then Qin Ying busy looking at the house, ready to open a "love bar book bar" area, and please Shen total husband and wife decoration house, but also writing, also for a busy living to apply for physiotherapist work rush, by the medical beauty of small xia recommended, finally stable, this industry in the coastal city most popular! Life turns up almost forget the Deng Cheng of the one side.

One day, Qin Ying was working in the physiotherapy room of an upscale club in Zhuhai when she walked into a man who had met Deng five years earlier. Their eyes met and they were surprised and delighted.

The front desk is Qin Ying on duty, too late to avoid, had to smile and said: "Did not think of it?" Shall we meet again here? Do you need physical therapy? What's wrong?"

Qin Ying site, a series of inquiries, let Deng Cheng for a while will not know how to answer.

Deng Cheng some pain stammered and said: "I decorate lifting things, the waist strain!"

Qin Ying did not say much, hurriedly opened the moxibustion infrared instrument, to Deng Cheng waist irradiation, Deng Cheng before leaving and handled the treatment of the recharge card 6800 yuan.

Later because Qin Ying self-study and got a professional physiotherapist professional teacher certificate, was another medical beauty clinic high-paying employment, the most important is only on the day shift, two days on weekends, every holiday have holidays, since then have never seen Deng Cheng, this is the second time met Deng Cheng.

The third encounter with Deng Cheng is the weekend before, Qin Ying as usual, every weekend will come to "love bar book bar" to read, do some novel creation idea outline! Busy up to the point of forgetting to eat and sleep, this is an important part of Qin Ying's spare time life.

Qin Ying has recently published two books and is replying to readers who bought the books on her mobile phone. Qin Ying has been used to this detection of authenticity to identify friends, just like the waves, leaving friends must be worth Qin Ying friends of the bottom line and principle, her false friends elimination system.

This kind of people more to go, Qin Ying is very ordinary mentality to face the people and things in real life, so there will not be too much disappointment, because do not expect to look forward to anything, life is particularly simple! Qin Ying buried in the book, mobile phone if there is information to reply, suddenly a familiar voice into her ears: "Really you?" What a coincidence? Can I sit here?"

Qin Yingxin Xi looked at Deng Cheng, embarrassed to smile! Two people are so destined. Qin Ying nodded, the body moved to the inside a little position, Deng Cheng sat down side by side, picked up the table Qin Ying read the book, opened a look, found that the author introduced the picture is only Qin Ying photos, then turned the catalog, looking at the beginning and the end, only with an appreciation of the eyes looked at Qin Ying said: "This book is a novel you wrote, the book is sold?" I want to take it home and read it."

Qin Ying said: "You are serious, how many copies do you need?"

Deng Cheng said happily: "Buy ten copies first, I can give them away."

Qin Ying looked at Deng Cheng so support, of course, some different, did not want to meet three times Deng Cheng, than some of the classmates, colleagues, peers Wenyou teachers for decades. Really make her feel a little warm, but also mixed with a variety of difficult to tell the cold, a kind of has been ignored countless times, false fudging, perfunctoriness, refused sadness, and those who do not want her good people, what people in society have, all kinds of character relations, really is not as simple and beautiful as it seems. Oh, Qin Ying this book planning promotion activities, at a glance to understand what is the world, cold and warm know it.

Can really not think of sincere friends or some, like the present Deng Cheng, an instant let Qin Ying Deng Cheng sit up and take notice. It seems that the relationship between the two people have the opportunity to win better development, Qin Ying's mood is much better now, there are still human feelings in the world, she wants to these years, Deng Cheng has not found her? At this moment, it is Qin Ying to Deng Cheng some good feelings and curiosity, seems to also look forward to what? She told herself to stop thinking and just go with the flow!

Did not think of a week later in love bar book bar to see Deng Cheng, and he is Shen sum autumn sweet to introduce her friends. Deng Cheng sat opposite Qin Ying, told everyone about his life in recent years.

The reason why Deng Cheng did not disturb Qin Ying in recent years is that he is facing a divorce judgment with his wife, that is to say, he is ending his marriage. At that time, Deng Cheng only wanted to devote himself to work, and used non-stop working hours to reduce the loneliness after divorce!

Divorce property should be half of the husband and wife, but Deng Cheng gave a large villa and luxury car to his wife, a downtown apartment for his adult daughter. He left a set of suburban very have not been decorated rural farmhouse, this is still when the inadvertent visit in the village to inspect the suburban residents of the villagers, for insurance market research, found a desert no one living with a yard 1000 square area of flat floor house.

Village director told Deng Dong, the house is his nephew, a family of three into the city to do business development is very good, the house has been idle, they are eager to buy shop in the city, hand money, want to sell the house, but no one to take over. At that time just Deng Cheng want to buy a house like this can live for the aged, inadvertently LiuliuChengyin, Deng Cheng took over and spent 460,000 yuan to buy this country house with a yard, there is nothing valuable in the house. The village director is very grateful to Deng Cheng for his timely help to solve the funding problem of his nephew.

Deng Cheng bought the house has been empty, until after the divorce, need a place to live, just think of this place. Every weekend, I find Shen to arrange the decoration master to redecorate the house, keep the red brick on the external wall, remove all the wall panels between the rooms, and change the Windows into floor-to-ceiling glass Windows with better lighting. He likes this simple design that is transparent to the eyes! The courtyard is just a large circle on three sides with the bamboo purchased by the villagers planted around the courtyard, leaving one side to enter the place where six vehicles can be parked. Several stone and wooden chairs are designed beside the corner window, placed symmetrically on both sides, with tables, chairs and benches for people to rest. Several steel tubular concrete structure shelves are set up on the top, which makes full use of the spatial value visually. After the overall construction, it looks like a rural architectural villa.

There is no decoration in the house, just a simple ordinary ceiling fan above the roof beam, the ground is all cement road, the wall is also a corresponding layer of cement wall and then coated with a layer of clear paint, adding a bit of nostalgia, a strong atmosphere attracted many villagers praise: "The people in this city are smart, the whole of such a shabby house like a tea shop, but also a bit like a farmhouse, can also be a B&B hotel, can also be a display shop selling agricultural products, flower shop." Because of the large space and high plasticity, we can add cabinets and soft decorations needed for some projects according to the needs of the future.

Speaking, we do not want to interrupt Deng Cheng, like listening to the story, Deng Cheng witty talk about rural customs and worldly.

Qin Ying listen to secretly glad, this may be the fate of the arrangement, the right time, the right person, met the right opportunity, really have such a magical feeling, God Shen and autumn sweet Deng Cheng brought into the life of Qin Ying.

Tonight's love bar book bar, because Deng Cheng arrived, two people have unlimited imagination space. Shen sum autumn sweet two than who are happy, a strong to Deng Dong to discuss wine: "I see, you two are destined, see what I said?"

Autumn sweet rushed to say: "Yes, we do not know you two first know the case, coincidentally think of you two very well matched ha, really, at that time Shen has not said your Deng Dong name, said to introduce a boyfriend to Qin Ying, I think of you Deng Dong, you two are too suitable!"

At first, Deng Cheng heard that the two kept recommending his girlfriend to him, and his heart was still very resistant. Did not think that the original is only five years ago to see Qin Ying. Secretly happy in the heart, fortunately tonight was Shen forced to drag, Deng Cheng has been embarrassed to refuse directly, push again. It seems that there has always been the shadow of Qin Ying in mind, in addition to work in life, there are no other women, he wants to marry life in the future, the other half must choose themselves, he does not want to see the wrong person, and do not want to waste time on a woman who is not interesting.

So from the beginning to avoid Shen's girlfriend introduced, so did not ask the woman's name? Where are they from? What does he look like? What occupation? Didn't ask them all?

And Shen also want to mysterious surprise two people, the situation of both sides did not reveal anything, Shen patted his chest and said: "You see you see, this is fate!" Ha ha ha!"

Deng Cheng explain say almost dont come to see girlfriend episode, suddenly opened Qinying knot, Deng Cheng like know Qinying mind, hurriedly add the reason to see tonight.

Deng Cheng: "Tomorrow is a special banquet for Shen General autumn sweet two, thank you for introducing the grace of holding the red line, and invite Qin Ying to accompany to the 'Yachou family' to eat seafood dinner." Deng Cheng blurted out that he would go to "Yachou Family", which is the most famous and delicious seafood city in Zhuhai.

As soon as Deng Cheng finished speaking, Shen almost shocked his jaw: "My mother, you two eat the same like to eat the same food, haha too predestined!" His eyes smiled.

This night until nine o 'clock love bar book bar to close, we were reluctant to part, that night is Deng Cheng and Qin Ying fourth special reunion.

Shen total autumn sweet two excuse to go first, before leaving to Deng Cheng make a look, to give Deng Cheng the opportunity to drive Qin Ying back, Deng Cheng drove a Land Rover Jeep, Qin Ying safe to rent the seaside community in front of the building, just rest assured secretly happy up, like to get the baby as happy to drive away!

Chapter 4: Half happy, half sad

Qin Ying let Deng Cheng drive away first, then turned into the community, this is Shen sum of autumn sweet actively recommend the rental of high-end apartments, because their new house in this community, has not been decorated! She does not want to explain too much personal life private information, the most sensitive is the specific residence! Also do not want to prematurely expose their own life circle, of course, including their own love bar book bar shop! For this special told Shen sum autumn sweet two, do not say love bar book bar she is behind the boss, also do not say in Zhuhai this high-end residential area there is a personal property. Because Qin Ying these two house decoration is after Shen and autumn sweet arrangement.

In Zhuhai Qin Ying only trust Shen total husband and wife, this couple is Qin Ying to Zhuhai to know, become the most trustworthy friend, life in the big things are consulting them both, husband and wife in Zhuhai can be really know-it-all.

Qin Ying personal marriage problems, Shen total husband and wife very recommended Deng Cheng, see tonight, it is the same person who has met several times. In fact, the first impression to Qin Ying also have a little fantasy to become a partner feeling, but this idea in the brain, was forced to stop, that moment of good impression by Qin Ying's rationality replaced, she does not want to become a fool, also dare not casually to men emotional, that is, the reason for these sensitive character, Qin Ying can be quiet for so many years, she learned to be alone with themselves, Living an ordinary life, she felt that her life was very good, very full and independent. If in the decision to choose a partner this lifelong event, she has to choose her own grasp, she can no longer look at the blind eye, must be careful and strictly responsible for their own future.

Marriage for her this is a very serious thing, the first love has made her heart suspicious of men, at the same time in more than five years, although no one has talked about love, but she vaguely felt that there is a man to show her good, the recent period of time this man more frequently told the pain of missing, Although only on the wechat network to talk about Qin Ying's good feelings! But those proper care and greetings, in the dead of night, often accompany her to sleep.

Because the man was not in the same city, Qin Ying and the man who had never met could only communicate on wechat, and the man said that he lived in a northern city, while Qin Ying had chosen to live in the coastal city of Zhuhai, and the two people had been talking for more than seven months, and there had been no substantive progress.

The mysterious man is Qin Ying submission on the Internet called Editor-in-Chief Cheng Mo, know the editor-in-chief Cheng Mo, Qin Ying to the author's pen name added wechat, the way of communication with the author, in wechat transmission. One after another, Qin Ying's article was published in the provincial newspaper with the help of Cheng Mo, the chief editor, and was gradually recommended to be on the monthly and published in the magazine.

I remember once talking about publishing a book on wechat, the editor-in-chief actively asked Qin Ying: "Can you write a novel to me first, if the content is suitable, I can help you recommend the publication."

At that time Qin Ying has not seen the chief editor Cheng Mo, only know its name did not see the person! In the notary number, and the provincial newspaper magazine editor is Cheng Mo phone number, micro signal, through the introduction of writers, just know Cheng Mo editor is a great writer of literature, there are many titles, what provincial writers Association editor, Chinese Writers Association member, short fiction member secretary president, etc., Qin Ying was this sudden advent of good news, a little surprised, she would not think, Publishing a book with the help of Cheng Mo Editor-in-Chief recommendation is only so easy, this consultation asked the right person. So Qin Ying will just write the serialized manuscript, after finishing and revising, summary sent to Cheng Mo chief editor. In fact, before meeting Cheng Mo editor-in-chief, Qin Ying has two publishing house editor teachers scheduled a good novel publishing matters, just want to compare several book methods, since the book manuscript is completed, it is appropriate to choose the publishing house.

Qin Ying has been with Cheng Mo on the Internet wechat exchange manuscripts and such topics, and then gradually familiar with it, you can talk about some love and marriage topics, and then encouraged by Cheng Mo, Qin Ying on the manuscript frequency is very high, almost every issue has a short story on the manuscript, because Cheng Mo editor-in-chief is the executive editor, the author on the draft as long as there is Cheng Mo recommended, will be published directly in the newspaper, Therefore, Qin Ying has become a prolific writer, slowly in the literary circle of the industry, a firm foothold, behind Qin Ying and Cheng Mo actively recommended the publishing house cooperation, is also a natural thing.

Qin Ying's first book, written in biographical style, describes a woman inspirational moving novel, after three reviews and three schools of modification, finally published as scheduled! With the joy of sharing after the publication of the book, there is an emotional resonance between the writer and the chief editor, the chief editor Cheng Mo seems to have several times through the content of the novel, judging that the characters in the novel have some of Qin Ying's life and growth trajectory, since then, Cheng Mo began to talk about work, friendship, and a certain thing in life on wechat every day, in this Cheng Mo guided Qin Ying many ideas.

Two people chat in many areas, the emotion quickly heated up, sometimes Qin Ying creation will forget the time, even in the middle of the night suddenly think of writing inspiration, want to talk about some plot ideas, Cheng Mo will patiently listen to Qin Ying finished the story line inspiration. In this way, the two people seem to have not talked about love, but always say the words of the heart.

Cheng Mo asked Qin Ying three times: "If you can, you will marry me?"

Similar to this hypothesis, this way of testing, Qin Ying has felt the blatant Cheng Mo in the near future! One night, Qin Ying wechat Cheng Mo more than a dozen messages unread...

Cheng Mo to Qin Ying wechat voice sound came out to open the first message: "Oh, these last few days why go?" I miss you every day, you can not think of me, but you remember I miss you every day, only I this stupid man, always miss you, you remember me..."

The second message: "If you that day, see Cheng Mo naked, unkempt, like a madman, mouth called Qin Ying's name, that is over, remember I think you are almost crazy."

The third message: "Really, can we video? Don't ignore me! But remember I'm thinking of you!"

The fourth message: "You remember what I said, you are a fairy writer, if you identify with me in the future, I will make you a famous writer, a prolific writer with high exposure."

Qin Ying listen to Cheng Mo sent her wechat voice, there is joy, but some incredible, thinking in the heart, not so exaggerated? What the hell is that? They never even met? Aych! Qin Ying sighed, shook her head silent down, and did not reply to Cheng Mo information in time.

Deng Cheng about the second day of the treat, it is Sunday in the cliff mouth people seafood city meet, Qin Ying saw Deng Cheng again, or the original team, Shen and autumn sweet take Qin Ying together, because with living in a community. At 5 PM, Deng Cheng arrived here early and waited for a long time, and the restaurant location was set!

This dinner with Deng Cheng, restaurant midway Deng Cheng to Qin Ying generous care, do natural considerate, just right, not at all unnatural, like a long lost friend, relatives, anyway, that feeling let Qin Ying at ease, Qin Ying began to cant help but Deng Cheng and Cheng Moby, this comparison does not matter, there is a puzzling feeling in Qin Ying's heart, She hopes that if the two men are the same person, it is good, because Deng Cheng is only lukewarm to her, and has not yet given her any language confession, and Cheng Mo, although he has not met, but the smiling photo of the writer's profile on wechat is a very kind and modest person from the appearance, the photo is smiling into a slit small eyes, with a very sexy thick lips. A pair of dimples, looks very satisfied with a simple and confident man, Cheng Mo wechat voice left numerous warm and concerned greetings, every word beautiful.

Qin Ying began everywhere intentionally or unintentionally take Deng Cheng and Cheng Mo comparison, just like Deng Cheng is warm fire, and Cheng Mo can light the fire.

Qin Ying in the half happy half worry between wandering, she did not have time to make any choice, only two men have not launched a direct action on the pursuit, this time if you want to choose who for life partner, it seems too early, Qin Ying today have to observe the performance of Deng Cheng, see Deng Cheng for her busy up with dishes and tea pouring, the heart is warm.

Shen and autumn sweet secretly made faces with each other up, autumn sweet quietly to Shen ear root said: "See Deng Dong Qin Ying very like the initiative, they have a play, is it!"

Shen said: "Still have to let Deng Dong close up, the man should take the initiative, I will let him work harder."

Qin Ying looked at Deng Cheng's eyes also became gentle

Deng Cheng gentle and humble for everyone at the table to provide intimate service, this seafood dinner for more than two hours, each fresh seafood Deng Cheng let the waiter recommend the ground, Deng Cheng in the middle of an excuse to make a phone call, the single to buy, and quietly sat beside Qin Ying, Qin Ying is a bright person, she from Deng Cheng today's performance, Deng Cheng to people to friends is real, That night Shen said, "Let Deng Dong spend money!" Set next Sunday, let Qiu Tian cook three cups of chicken in our home for Deng Dong to eat, ah! The same people, okay?"

Deng Cheng thought for a moment, turned his head to Qin Ying, Deng Cheng's eyes have a kind of expectation swept to Qin Ying shot, meaning to say: "Let's go together!"

Qin Ying smiled and nodded, autumn sweet took the opportunity to take Qin Ying hand and said: "This time I give you back to expose two food, you both must like!" That's settled, Mr. Shen and I will go back first. Deng Dong, you can accompany Qin Ying to walk on the beach and see the night view of the town. It's very beautiful."

Deng Dong from the heart grateful to autumn sweet husband and wife secretly help, smiling to everyone said: "OK, must do it, I am happy!" Don't worry!"

Qin Ying with Deng Cheng side by side along the water, looking at the distant lights, like the stars flashing night, Qin Ying said from the heart: "did not think there is so beautiful here."

Deng Cheng said happily: "Please go to my country house next Sunday, the air is also very fresh, very suitable for quiet and concentrated writing place, if you are free during the day, I will come to pick you up, first visit the country house decoration, give me some suggestions, and then go to Shen's house for dinner in the evening, what do you think?"

Qin Ying took back the distant look at the water and said to Deng Cheng: "You have thought so thoughtfully, can I not go?" Just like I also want to see Shen head office is how to give you the design and decoration of rural house with courtyard."

Curiosity made Qin Ying promised Deng Cheng's invitation.

Deng Cheng continued the topic and said: "I originally wanted to install the house and bring my old mother to live with me, but my old mother said that she was used to living in the city, everything is convenient, haircut, food shopping, and all aspects of life are very convenient, and she did not want to come to my remote village, and also said that she liked to be busy when she was old, so this country house was dragged until now to think about the creative design and decoration of my vacation residence. Slowly add the furniture you like."

Qin Ying listened to Deng Cheng talk about his mother's story together, listen to listen, feel Deng Cheng to take good care of the elders, the mother is very healthy, Deng Cheng to the mother's home invited a cooking and cleaning aunt, life care is very thoughtful, so usually Deng Cheng work work is very at ease, weekends will go to the country house to see the progress of renovation, encounter situations or whim, I can do some temporary work on my own.

Qin Ying looked at the front of Deng Cheng, there is a feeling that the man is very real, and dare to dare to do, is a strong hands-on ability of men. If you really live with this man, should Qin Ying enjoy some happiness? After all, Deng Cheng is much more capable than she is. Thinking about thinking about Qin Ying could not help but smile...

Deng Cheng saw Qin Ying suddenly secretly happy, but also thought that his words were wrong, nervously asked: "What are you laughing at?"

Qin Ying saw Deng Cheng this nervous cute serious look, intentionally pointed to the direction of the city in the distance to make Deng Cheng said: "Your mother heard is saying her bad?"

She chuckled and laughed again.

Deng Cheng reaction, Qin Ying has gone to Deng Cheng parked the car, Deng Cheng see time is not early, is to send Qin Ying back! The two quickly got on the car, the sight of the jeep looking forward is good, Qin Ying sat on the passenger seat, looking forward, the speed passed a row of roadside trees, a scenery along the way, has been open to the center of the city, looking at the front of bright high-rise buildings, glittering lights, Deng Cheng looked at Qin Ying with affectionate eyes said: "How do I feel the time passes so fast?" Don't you think?"

Qin Ying shyly pointed to the front of the car and said: "Well, now you hurry to look ahead, drive well and pay attention to safety, OK?"

Deng Cheng immediately replied: "Well, my eyes are looking at the road, also look at you, no delay!"

And they both laughed! The car floated out of the light music saxophone tune home, has been repeatedly put...

Chapter 5: Silly Talk

Qin Ying every Monday day work in a high-end club physiotherapy room to work, busy will not look at mobile phone wechat information, Qin Ying occupation has been used to a work to set the mobile phone to silent, such as busy a day after the old habit of dinner back to love bar book bar to solve, eat a vegetarian dumplings and a bowl of millet porridge, or cook a pot of fruit tea, while looking at the book, Sometimes there is no writing update!

Remember that three months before the publication of the book, the entire completed manuscript has been sent online to the chief editor of Cheng Mo, Qin Ying has a lot of creative inspiration during that time, just finished publishing the manuscript, encouraged by the chief editor of Cheng Mo, let Qin Ying write a perfect middle-aged love story, and even asked the prototype of life Cheng Mo male No. 1 and Qin Ying female as the theme, to create ideas, Qin Ying has written 31 chapters of the story line, the central idea, everything is ready, the beginning of the first to two chapters are written very smoothly, when the Spring Festival is approaching, all the trivial things at home too much to delay the writing process, this down did not start to write, the kind of fantasy love marriage happy happy story, In real life, Qin Ying seems unable to find a character prototype who pursues love, and there is no substantial progress in her novel creation! Qin Ying can not write out, also do not want to deceive others to write down, the heart is empty, think or write the first two chapters, temporarily precipitate for a period of time, to give themselves a charging learning process.

Qin Ying continued to look at the phone behind a few cheng Mo past information: "For your book before the end of the year to sign with the publishing house, you must play the full payment, the contract is only upgraded, the publishing house officially began the third review three school procedures, I did not wait for you three days later to play the balance, I have paid the balance of 30,000 yuan, so you do not worry about the progress of the book."

The second message: "Anyway, your business is my business, I will do it!"

Article 3: The screenshots of the cushion, as well as the screenshots of the dialogue between Cheng Mo and the editor of the publishing house, and the publishing house contract signed by Cheng Mo for Qin Ying!

After listening to see these, Qin Ying heart a warm flow of heart, language can not express their own mood at this time, so hurriedly put the mobile phone state set regular bank account payment back to Cheng Mo, wechat transfer 30000 yuan, see has shown the transfer success, only immediately reply to Cheng Mo wechat message: "Thank you for considering these details for me, you paid this money without saying, really thank you for your trust and help, now please check this payment in time, in addition, in order to thank you, I want to send you a gift!" But I don't know your height, weight, dress size, can you send me your dress size and address?"

Did not think of Cheng Mo second back: "See, the money of the publishing mat has been received, the clothes are free, we two don't have to say thank you, I should do things for you, I am happy, you don't talk to me polite, I am poor, there is not much money, but I have a heart, like your heart!" I have nothing, just like to engage in some literary creation of this hobby, and then meet you are a talented woman, help you should be!"

Qin Ying see after the information is want to return the favor, after all is not a relationship between male and female friends, can not be used, the favor can not owe, have to return immediately, this is Qin Ying life style of doing things! So Qin Ying sent several messages without thinking: "Please send me a photo of the brand behind the collar, which has the size sign you wear, and send me the address in time!" Please cooperate!"

This move really works, Cheng Mo according to the requirements of the information content sent to Qin Ying.

A few days later Qin Ying to Cheng Mo bought nine pieces of various styles of men's first-line brand clothes, the same day after the mail procedures, screenshots sent to Cheng Mo to accept, Cheng Mo for her to do these things, Qin Ying in contact with men, the most afraid of debt, so later work to deal with the relationship between men and women, also a little easier, she dont want to give Cheng Mo misunderstanding, This Cheng Mo initiative for her to pay for the things, let Qinying more and more relaxed for men to show caution, she imagined Cheng Mo and kind a lot!

Near the Spring Festival is coming, Cheng Mo received Qin Ying mail to his clothes, happy to Qin Ying reply: "Clothes received, really fit, did not expect to wear which all fit, thank you, in addition to this year's Spring Festival if you want to keep love bar books do not come back, New Year's Eve I must give you a red envelope, remember to receive ah." Have been used to, a person outside the Spring Festival, because of special reasons, entrepreneurship is not easy, the more holiday love bar book bar more people, the sixth day will be open! So Qin Ying will not plan to go back to the New Year, Cheng Mo promise this voice message, let Qin Ying feel a trace of warmth, she felt this time there is a person, thinking of her is very satisfied, although the two people do not have a clear relationship between male and female friends, such a person is concerned about ambiguous language, especially in the quiet night in a different place, it is particularly provocative. Cheng Mo from time to time warm words, like a warm current hit the heart of Qin Ying. New Year's Eve red envelopes to Qin Ying mobile phone wechat, but Qin Ying saw red envelopes and did not open did not receive, has not received. The first day of the New Year did not pick up, she did not want to accept Cheng Mo for no reason these small money, she took the heart. She does not wish to spend men's money, although she does not know how much the red envelope is? But she did not receive open, just want to tell Cheng Mo, the two people had better be clear in the economy, and the two people have not indicated what relationship, at this time a lot of information on wechat silent sent: "You do not pick up red envelopes, hurry up to accept, this is my heart money is not much, but you must pick up, otherwise I will be angry." Did not accept the red envelope 24 hours on the automatic return to Cheng Mo account, because of this matter Cheng Mo seems really a little angry, in wechat and to Qin Ying sent a lot of messages: "Although I am poor, but this is my mind, I remember there is a person far away, worthy of my care in this way, I anyway say, I will be in the Spring Festival, your birthday, these two major festivals will give you red envelopes." Take it." In this way Cheng Mo and persuade Qin Ying, if not accept is look down on him and so on some words, in the sixth day and find a reason, 66 Dashun Qin Ying sent a ¥600 red envelope, to Qin Ying accept, said this is a map and auspicious! This figure is very good, Cheng Mo know Qin Ying superstition this figure is a lucky bar, open the door. Good luck! I thought I'd give it back sometime. Like this kind of care about their own people, really not. Let Qinying feel Cheng Mo is in return, she knows that the several brands of clothes are not cheap, worth thousands of yuan, so accept 600 yuan red envelopes, perhaps Cheng Murray calm. That day remember Qin Ying is watching TV, suddenly Cheng Mo sent a message: "What, what at home?"

Qin Ying is watching TV series while soaking feet reply: "nothing, relax bubble feet." Then Cheng Mo replied: "In the future, I am willing to give you hot water feet every day, really, I will wash you every day, although I am poor, no other wealth to give you, but I will give you the most true love." I would do that for you." This word wechat, amused Qin Ying some dreamy heart warm. She thought, if this is the life, if the future met true love, maybe so ordinary life like a poem romantic, thinking about Qin Ying embarrassed to laugh, may be the reason for hot blistering feet, the body heat, that feeling as if he shy did something wrong, in fact, in addition to Qin Ying a person in the room, No one saw what Qin Ying was thinking in her heart?

Cheng Mo is still continuing to use the words of the younger sister Qin Ying listen, at this time the ear Cheng Mo described so warm words: "You don't come to my city, in fact, this feeling I originally told you, if you come, I see you, there may be tears in my eyes, you too dont understand people, I know who I want to?" I know who I want, you know? So when you came to see me, we have been in contact online, from the Internet to now this long time have not seen each other, this time I can see you, I will be excited, will be excited, my eyes will be red, I am such a person, I know myself, I do not know what you think? I am sure I know myself, and I cannot lie, and I have no lie to tell, for it is the expression of true feelings." A moment of love, Qin Ying dun feel blush hot dry.

Qin Ying in love bar book bar, quietly read these messages sent by Cheng Mo, the mood is contradictory. Looking at the stars in the distance outside the window, my heart began to think of Deng Cheng's invitation to go to the country house on the outskirts of Deng Cheng on Sunday, and I could not remember what kind of clothes to wear that day. This is like an official first private date, right?

Chapter 6: A Trip to the country

Sunday morning arrived, this is the first private contact between Qin Ying and Deng Cheng, by Deng Cheng's last invitation, Qin Ying walked to the gate of the community at 7 a.m. on time. Deng Cheng has been flashing lights in the jeep, prompting Qin Ying to hurry up on the car. Along the way, two people opened the music in the car, opened the Jeep's skylight, the scenery along the way is so wonderful, the air mixed with the green sea breeze, make people breathe smoothly, bright sunshine shining between the woods a flicker through the gap, the light is bright and dark, where the sun passes by, it is particularly bright, Deng Cheng drove the car to sit in the co-driver Qin Ying face to see, under the sun, It is particularly moving and beautiful, the car galloping on both sides of the road trees and flowers houses, quickly moving on both sides of the front, Deng Cheng smiled and asked Qin Ying: "Do you like this morning?"

Qin Ying said: "I have never been so early, riding in an open jeep, like a joyride."

From time to time, Deng asked, "Do you like the air here and the sea breeze on the road?"

Qin Ying nodded, looking at Deng Cheng said: "Like ah, if you do not like it is impossible to walk with you, because like, really, did not think I almost miss such a beautiful morning, the morning sunshine is really beautiful."

Driving to the countryside every weekend is forty minutes back and forth, Deng Cheng is familiar with the terrain and landform, and continues to say excitedly: "If the countryside is a very suitable place for living and leisure, think about this life, very comfortable, when there is nothing to plant fruit trees and some flowers, and then turn the front and back yards of the house into a place where flowers bloom, you will love it."

Deng Cheng couldn't help but be happy, today only took about 30 minutes to arrive, Deng Cheng got off the bus and teased Qin Ying and said: "I brought a bento, you can also eat a little, cushion the stomach, taste my cooking, and when we get to the countryside, I will make some local special snacks, we will eat there at noon today, you will certainly like to eat my fish, as well as the fruit from the trees in the village, all the fruit is now in the season, it is really fresh, the cost of living here is really cheap," Just start planting fruit trees and you'll eat enough."

Qin Ying said casually: "I like to eat apples, lychees, oranges, cherries. Also like osmanthus trees, gardenias, is like the kind of spring wind to smell the green aroma, the nature has green plants all year round, I like a lot, I like the sound of birds, but also like squeaking birds singing, although I do not understand the birds, but feel they are talking, as interesting."

When I got to the countryside, I began to get busy, but unconsciously the time passed quickly, and the workers were already there. I did not expect the workers to be waiting in the front yard of Deng Cheng's house so consciously on time, and the workers arrived earlier than they did. Contractor directly in the yard began to work, Qin Ying followed Deng Cheng into the yard to see a vacant steel, cement bags, floor tiles and other building materials, cement workers, painters, has been in the yard floor and wall construction brush. As Deng Cheng walked into the room, I felt that as Deng Cheng said for the first time, the general situation of his country house was only more practical than what he said. Deng Cheng pointed to the hall and said his future plan, and then went to the second floor when he said: "There are three rooms upstairs and two bathrooms, which turn the middle into a large study, set up two long book tables, with Chinese furniture partition screen in the middle, can be like an open study, open the door to both sides of the design display cabinet, bookcase, all literary works can be placed on the above display."

Deng Cheng yesterday pointed to both sides of the study window and continued to think and said: "Qin Ying, if you like you can write in the study, put two computers, do anything without disturbing." Deng Cheng said this, quietly glanced at Qin Ying's reaction, Qin Ying listening to the heart inexplicable feeling of a racing heart, the words did not answer, the heart can be happy, and then looked at the wall around the empty, put ready to hit the cabinet of wood asked: "You are ready to do the wall to the top of the bookshelf and display cabinet?"

Deng Cheng replied: "Yes, Shen's carpentry master workmanship is very high, more practical and durable than buying cabinets, and this can make full use of the area, I think it must be very nice to do, I use the original logs, the nature is moved here, you should like."

Qin Ying really didnt expect Deng Cheng decoration planning also put Qin Ying like also take into account, treat her as a hostess. Qin Ying heart palpitate, the man standing in front of this look, feel Deng Cheng is really very real, Qin Ying want to think of the sense of security came instantaneously, there is a feeling of practicality. Involuntarily with Deng Cheng knowingly smile, mischievously thinking: you have arranged so well, also did not ask people have not married you?

Deng Cheng in the mind, do not know how to think of Qin Ying, the design plan are arranged so thoughtful, consider Qin Ying used to quiet writing, avoid disturbing each other, the Deng Cheng will use space, design style, and can see each other at any time, and do not disturb each other.

This is the kind of space Qin Ying she also wants, she does not want to be very reserved, Deng Cheng's life is like transparent glass, at a glance to see the bottom, this arrangement is right for her, but she is also in the murmur: my idea, why Deng Cheng will be so understanding, why he knows he likes these? Did he feel the same way? How else to explain it? After only a few meetings, he took me into account as the mistress of life, even the way of living. It seems that this man is serious about her.

Qin Ying could not control his thoughts, went to the balcony of the second floor, looked out to the backyard, where there were far away mountains and rural roofs rising smoke, a smell of rural burning crenel, the nose, very good smell, Qin Ying closed his eyes and breathed deeply, the ear heard the chicken, saw the villagers picked baskets into the vegetable field, The kind of scene like the countryside in the 1980s, where people are pure and simple, so quiet ah, from time to time the chicken cry let Qin Ying imagine, this is a big rural nature, compared with the noisy downtown, can enjoy such quiet, it is really too difficult!

Deng Cheng was called down by the workers to ask what things, Qin Ying called Deng Cheng: "You hurry to busy it, I casually look at the walk, casually stroll." In the surrounding small village there are commissages, that is, the kind of small supermarket between the rural stalls, Qin Ying listen to Deng Cheng came to introduce, you can go to see, as long as before 12:00 noon can come back here.

Deng Cheng: "At noon I will take you to a village farmhouse, where the food is very delicious, so it's settled." Said Deng Cheng and Shen head office workers to the yard, the wood bamboo painting, busy.

Qin Ying is very happy with this arrangement, did not regard her as a guest, as if she is a hostess like walking and looking, and then with Deng Cheng pointed to the outside meaning, is to tell him that I go out for a turn, Deng Cheng knowingly smiled and said: "Go, go, I am here."

Walking outside the village, Qin Ying saw that although the front and back yards of this house were not very large, they could park six cars in the front yard of the gate, and there were two stone tables, surrounded by three kinds of saplings with bamboo, two fruit trees on both sides of the stone table, and two benches placed on both sides. In this setting, when you grow tall in the future, you can enjoy the cool under the tree in the summer, and you can sit down and drink tea, which is a long-term scene in the future, and this arrangement is really meaningful. Qin Ying knowingly smiled, really, did not expect her to bring himself into, has imagined that he is the hostess here. Small supermarket carpet to the village, there are more than 30 families, are ordinary life, there are a lot of antiques on the village street, the ground with potatoes, peanuts, seasonal oranges, pears and small apples, hawthorns, fruit everything, Qin Ying can not help but, squatting down to talk with the villagers aunt, go empty-handed, the result comes back, full of harvest, Each buy a catty also has enough for her to carry, the things on the hand have become more and more heavy, but also saw far away there are two farmers happy one is to eat fish banquet, authentic fish, there is a farmer called roast chicken stew.

Walked to a stool in the kind of roadside hut with a shed, Qin Ying felt tired, sat down to buy a pot of tea, Aunt is a 50-year-old, holding the home of peanuts, broad beans, peas placed three small POTS, let Qin Ying eat, a pot of tea with these snacks, this is a matching buy one get one, Qin Ying embarrassed to smile, look not delicious but very delicious, Peanuts and dried melon are very sweet, the original flavor is not fried food, there are broad beans fried rice cake, small peas are also a bite on the fried flower, full of fragrant feeling, snacks in the countryside than snacks in the city are delicious. People who never eat snacks, this time feel how mouths so greedy, it seems that people here are good to feed themselves. She seemed to be drunk and felt that the villagers were very friendly, and the aunt of the cottage said to her: "You are from other places, right? We often have tourists come to see us and drink afternoon tea." The second time I brought a wave of friends over to play, like you are not very busy in the morning, and there are many people in the afternoon."

Further on to the lake, there are old farmers touch small fish, Qin Ying could not help but stop, watching how old farmers catch fish touch shrimp, because like to eat this small fish. The city also can not buy, the farmer to Qin Ying divided into two bags, on the package, each bag has five or six catties, a total of more than ten catties, plus when also bought some fruit, she can not carry. When I was worried, I did not expect Deng Cheng to drive his jeep along the way to find it.

"Hi, Qin Ying, you are really here, I went around every place, thinking that you must have walked almost, should come here."

Qin Ying said happily: "How do you know I am here, come quickly to help me get on the car, I bought something I like, or you can do something to eat at noon."

Deng Cheng put all the bags on the ground into the car, and said: "noon has been arranged, this fish to the yard, I will help you wash, take it to the city and put it in your refrigerator, enough for you to eat for a week, if you like to eat fish, then we come every week, package you eat enough." I'll take you to the farmer's and buy some vegetables in season. You won't have to buy any for a week. Come on, I'll take you to dinner."

Old farmer: "So it is your friend ah, this fish is your friend to buy ah." Let me know once a week, and I'll get it ready for you in the morning. Don't wait long!"

Deng Cheng is very familiar with the old farmer said hello, mouth also intoned: "I am glad you like here, I am afraid you are not used to it, this is pure countryside, today we eat fish with the foreman, as well as rice porridge, can be delicious, every time I come to eat a few bowls, I ask aunt today specially add a few dishes." Is that good? Shen's workers like to work with me, the village they like to eat the fish here, said it is much better than the box lunch in the city, so you rest assured, the workers are very good, don't be shy, I hope you fall in love with this country, I am still short of a mistress! I want a mistress who likes the place as much as I do, and I'll give her the key. ' Then he looked at Qin Ying mischievously and laughed: "I am telling the truth, you can't laugh at me."

Qin Ying mouth did not refute, in the mind to think this Deng Cheng popularity is very good, with him invisibly have a kind of relaxed, even easy to bring Qin Ying into the future imagination planning, as if Deng Cheng has put her as the most reliable hostess, think of here Qin Ying himself embarrassed to lower his head, carrying the small stone on the road, to Deng Cheng said: "That's what you said. Don't regret it."

Deng Cheng smiled: "How, I like it too late, happy to die, I don't know why?" Monday to Friday after the work is finished, the nerves in the company are very tense, but once back here I am very relaxed, as if I was here decades ago, I know almost every family in the village. Come with me and you'll be a celebrity."

Say he laughed, Deng Cheng do not know what to laugh at? Infected with laughter, Qin Ying also laughed out of tears, wiped his hand and said: "I did not expect you to be so naughty, then you will be here when the village director."

Deng Cheng pucked his lips and smiled at Qin Ying and said: "You don't say, here the village director said, the construction plan of the village, have to come to ask me to talk with him, privately as brothers, in fact, he is an elder, but the village director to me every word is the fine idea of making money, this is not before in the city, no one has ever known to buy insurance?" As a result, after the village director knew me, almost every family of these villagers bought our company's insurance, and I did not spend any effort is the village director credit!"

"This also has to start from a child who got sick, asked me if I could claim medical expenses, after I had advised the villagers to do the insurance, only did three months of illness, our insurance did the claims procedure, the money to the villagers' home, so we passed ten, ten hundred, the result within a year the whole village bought our company's insurance, and also increased the insurance project year by year." From the original family only to do an old man, to the result of doing children, sons do, and do daughter-in-law, especially universal insurance, here the elderly and children do, now almost all villagers have medical insurance, life insurance and accident insurance. I have become their savior here, the villagers said that I am a noble person, my life is the deepest feeling is, as long as to think for the villagers, give them the heart. I never talk about insurance, but the villagers come to me for insurance, you know? The feeling of accomplishment is better than winning the lottery."

Looking at Deng Cheng tells the story of the villagers from the bottom of his heart, Qin Ying feels like Deng Cheng's joy at that time. Qin Ying was infected by Deng Cheng's bright spot, like his kind wisdom simple, and hard work would rather suffer for others for the sake of tolerance. She found Deng Cheng very manly charm, and a sense of intimacy. It feels like where Deng Cheng is, the atmosphere is very active. Qin Ying has felt, not only Shen total couple like Deng Cheng, and today saw the villagers are also supported towards him, no wonder Deng Cheng do things so smoothly, as if not successful are difficult. Qin Ying also began to slowly also have a good impression on Deng Cheng, began to produce telepathy, Qin Ying face turned red.

This village lunch let Qin Ying eat too full, Qin Ying quietly said to Deng Cheng: "you don't add food to me, you eat more, drink less, dinner must continue to go to Shen's house."

Deng Cheng: "Can't miss, today we bring Qiu Tian home some fresh fish, eggs, green vegetables, they also like!"

After lunch, the sun shines on their faces through the leaves, Deng Cheng and Qin Ying walk along the edge of the village into the courtyard, pointing to a room on the first floor: "You go to the sofa lunch for a while, I will go to the small fish to open and wash, salt salt into the flavor, you take home only fried can eat directly."

Qin Ying is really a little sleepy, nodded, not polite, straight into the room to walk!

Perhaps rest well, such as Qin Ying wake up, found the yard sun Deng Cheng has bought all the things on the car, two categories, a package is given to Shen, a package left to Qin Ying. This man really takes care of people, must be a good man to live!

Deng Cheng's performance, suddenly let Qin Ying think of an emotional expert said: "No action of love, nothing, the right people spoil you into a child, the wrong people make you crazy, full of eyes are your talent worthy of all your love, a lifetime of love, is forever accompany!"

Deng Cheng met Qin Ying and said: "We can go to Shen's house, these fish have to be sent early, put long will not be fresh, get on the car yo."

Qin Ying side car side carefully asked: "You did not rest for a while, busy these, a little tired today, I will drive it, you get on the car and lie down for a while, squint for a while!"

Deng Cheng looked at the understanding and considerate Qin Ying, the hand car keys to Qin Ying: "Then I am not welcome, good, a little tired, on the car to make up a sleep, to Shen house call me."

Qin Ying smiled and said: "People are iron, rice is steel, good health should pay attention to rest, have a dream.

Chapter 7: Falsehood is hard to hide

Time flies, during the publication of Qin Ying's works, Cheng Mo's novels were also recommended to another platform by Qin Ying; This Qinying submission has also been actively recommended by Cheng Mo in the provincial publications frequently reported, each issue has published short novels. Qin Ying feel in Cheng Mo encouraged to help, into the peak of creation, two like-minded hearts go closer and closer. Although thousands of miles apart, but there are endless topics between each other, so talk to the southeast, northwest, but one day to talk about another voice...

One day Qin Ying opened Cheng Mo's voice message: "In the future your thing is my thing, I said you are a genius writer, as long as you identify me, I will make you become a famous writer, you must be able to do the ideal full-time writer!" A woman's voice mixed with laughter called out, "Come out for dinner!" Then Cheng Mo raised his voice, it seemed intended to let the woman hear: "So, your article I first review, the next time to discuss the specific content of the layout, I go to dinner first, there are questions to give me a message." The content of Cheng Mo's speech is like talking about business tone with a wechat call person.

Qin Ying began a little wondering, why is the topic of love will suddenly become a businesslike tone, and the voice of the phone voice that came from the woman's voice, Cheng Mo is a family man?

Qin Ying has some doubts, then why sometimes in the middle of the night he can also reply to wechat at any time, or even directly answer the second back message? Several why Qin Ying himself confused. Voice second half, it was closed, she felt Cheng Mo there must be a hidden situation.

Qin Ying thought for a while and replied with these messages: "Listen to your voice message, understand your mind, but I feel that you are a family person, a woman in the voice call you to eat is your wife?" I always thought you didn't have a wife, you were single. If you have a family, why can you respond to messages in the middle of the night? Never mind. It's hard to ask you about this. I hope I'm not disturbing you. I really thought you were a free man! But now I've guessed. You can eat first, you don't need to reply."

Qin Ying from that moment to think, as long as Cheng Mo is a marriage and family relationship, you should cherish the maintenance of their own family life, do not think more about some things! Qin Ying's bones hate this kind of woman, Qin Ying in the novel did not write less of these women inserted into other people's families, so the life of Qin Ying is definitely not to play this role, her view of marriage does not allow these things to happen.

She thought in the following days will suggest Cheng Mo to look at the extramarital affair in the story plot of the novel she wrote, the work shows his view of marriage, world outlook, life outlook. She would never break up a home or accept the advances of a married man. She was looking for the one true relationship, worthy of all those years of waiting.

Qin Ying is a very assertive woman, although eager to get love, but the bone that love should be single-minded, the selection of men's standards for quality ranking first, career economic aspects are also very important, she is no longer an 18-year-old girl's feelings, she has to face the reality, life has taught her a lot of judgment of people's keen thinking ability, She is not easily carried away by the so-called sweet love story.

Is already in the dead of night, if in the past Cheng Mo will reply Qin Ying information in time, and even say "miss you" these words. If the morning walk on the road, Cheng Mo will require and Qin Ying video, but this requirement Qin Ying only meet the only one time.

Cheng Mo is not happy, but later several times, Qin Ying rejected Cheng Mo open wechat video chat habits, she wants to let Cheng Mo know, they are only the relationship between the author and the editor, compared with other authors, Cheng

Mo Qin Ying only some more good feelings and trust, they are still in each other to understand the test. She didn't want any further embarrassment, but tonight it was clear to her that she had been right. A woman's sixth sense is very keen, Qin Ying is also a super sensitive woman, and some details in the communication between the two people have also revealed some clues.

Cheng Mo every time when walking outside in the morning will be very relaxed chat video, the only video chat, Cheng Mo chat to very happy, suddenly take a breath spitting, Qin Ying saw suddenly feel a little sick, but out of politeness, and just know soon online, Qin Ying did not show disgust expression, just find a simple reason to end the video: "Sorry, the water is boiling, I have to make breakfast, can't talk, hang up!"

Another time Qin Ying opened the video sent by Cheng Mo, that is he participated in the activity to see the mountain scenery red leaves in the process of shooting, the video shows that are some male old writers, Cheng Mo said similar activities are all monks, without a woman, but ignored the video recording of the voice of a woman, when there is a woman is talking and laughing with the men in the shooting, the atmosphere is relaxed and happy. Needless to say, that day, Cheng Mo took his wife to participate in the activity of seeing Maple Leaf literature friends.

These scenes in Qin Ying mind repeated appearance, Qin Ying suddenly feel Cheng Mo is really not simple. Some time ago, when Qin Ying and Deng Cheng met again, Qin Ying will also compare Deng Cheng with Cheng Mo, will also consider if they choose a partner between them, how she wants to choose. At that time, Cheng Mo and Deng Cheng are equally important in Qin Ying's mind, and now she is disappointed in Cheng Mo, some antipathy and resistance.

Cheng Mo saw Qin Ying on wechat, asked about the essence of his marriage, thought about it to answer: "Yes, I have a wife, we are a son and a daughter family, but I do not have a common language with her, sleep is a separate room to sleep, only eat in a pot, usually do their own." My wife has my monthly pay card, I earn 4,000 yuan a month, and I only keep 1,000 yuan in change. We don't interfere with each other's life and work, and the property certificate only contains the wife's name."

Qin Ying replied: "Then you still have a very emotional basis, should cherish everything you have, the real love is the person who can always accompany you, have a good life."

Cheng Mo seconds back: "Before meeting you, I have never been tempted to any woman, I am serious about you, if you walk with me, I will give you a name." Of course, for love I will leave the house, I hope you bravely and firmly move forward, believe that I am the man who can give you future happiness, because I have a kind and love you sincerely."

Qin Ying speechless, also dont want to immediately contradict back, after all, just confirmed Cheng Mo is a family man, think Cheng Mo for a few months to help her, in the literature actively recommended in the enthusiasm to help, can not help a little sad. Why didn't you ask him about his marriage sooner? Now how awkward, forward is not back is not, in a dilemma. So Qin Ying in do not know how to answer him, only to keep silent, thinking about putting a period of time to think about it! It would be wise to wait and see what happens!

Qin Ying indifferent attitude let Cheng Mo some impatient, the next few days, and Cheng Mo's wechat message: "a few days without your information, you are driving me crazy, I miss you, I tell you I miss you, please reply to me." I want you to know that no man in the world is more serious about you than I am. You better stick with me. Believe me, we're gonna be so happy together, and I'm gonna make you the most famous writer, and I'm gonna support you in whatever you want. If you don't want to go down this road with me, just pretend that I never said these things, that I will never say them again, and that I understand you. I promised you things, I will still help to do, you rest assured!"

Qin Ying see this news just a little rest assured, are adults, experienced so many things, Cheng Mo should understand what they should do, what not to do. Qin Ying can also accept such a relationship between the two - the pure relationship between the editor and the author.

In the following days, Qin Ying, in order to repay the kindness, also actively asked the literature teacher to recommend Cheng Mo's books to foreign libraries for Chinese readers to read, and also played a role in improving publicity for Cheng Mo's works! Let more readers see the books written by Cheng Mo. In the field of literature, Qin Ying also tried to help Cheng Mo - as long as no personal feelings are mentioned, this friendship is still very good.

More than seven months have passed, Qin Ying has been avoiding too much contact with Cheng Mo, if there is no discussion on literary works, try not to contact.

Chapter 8: Getting Caught

Early in the morning, Qin Ying is very skilled to make breakfast, a fried egg and boiled a pear six red dates, plus a piece of lemon cooked a bowl of fruit tea, made a packet of cereal milk! After a simple breakfast, he picked up his carry-on bag and went to work.

To the unit is just Tuesday, the physiotherapy people see more, Qin Ying booked a lot of guests, enter the door to change work clothes put into work busy up, this busy busy to the time off work. I have two customers on hand, and I'm gonna have to work two hours overtime today, and I'm gonna finish at 8:30! Midway rest is only half an hour to eat time, casually fill the stomach will continue to busy, Qin Ying feel time is really fast, here is a private high-end club, high wages, but will not raise lazy people, all rely on good technical skills, good service to be competent for this job, the guests here are high-end people!

No slacking off at work! This is the foundation of the development of private entities!

Qin Ying came to Zhuhai in the past few years to put in the work time, pay a lot more than other women, otherwise, investment in self-housing, need to return bank loans, love bar rent and staff wages, need her own to solve, a job income to maintain the normal housing decoration repayment expenses, love bar book self-financing, maintain staff and rent payment, there are some profits every month.

In addition, the duplex apartment investment of the sea view room is a one-time payment, waiting for the opening of the Hong Kong and Macao Bridge, which is the investment environment of Qin Ying to Zhuhai real estate industry to do the most beautiful two real estate project investment! Only in this way can Qin Ying appear stable and mature, not to lose to any man in this respect, of course, this also formed her strength, in the future of the choice of a mate to choose a partner, improve their own value. With the older the single longer, the choice of boyfriend at the same time, will be comparable to the economic strength, so it is more difficult to match her conditions, she will never marry a man who is worse than his own strength! This is why Qin Ying spelled so much.

After a busy day and a little late from work, Qin Ying drove home directly, feeling a little tired, washed warm water feet and went to bed early. Wake up to Wednesday morning, but also get up at six o 'clock, unhurriedly prepare the old three early to eat, and then look at the wall time is still early, Qin Ying feel these two days in addition to busy work, life is very quiet. At this time, I found that her mobile phone was charging in the room, so I quickly opened the mobile phone to see.

"My God, there are so many missed caller ids and wechat messages!"

Qiu Tian wechat message: "Beauty, I know you are busy, but please take the time to reply, something to discuss with you."

Qin Ying to autumn sweet a reply: "Autumn sweet, forgot to bring a mobile phone, something please leave a message!"

There are 3 Deng Cheng did not answer the phone, Qin Ying also gave Deng Cheng the same reply: "forgot to bring the mobile phone, something please leave a message on wechat, read the reply in time, thank you for your concern."

Cheng Mo has 4 wechat: "The more I miss you, but the more I miss you."

Cheng Mo: "I'm out walking and I really want to talk to you. You know what? I have won another novel and would like to share it with you to tell you my joy. I am thinking of you."

Cheng Mo: "If we live together in the future, you take the car to the city where I live, I learn to drive when your driver." We'll start a paper together, and you'll run the business and contact the advertisers. With your cleverness, we are sure to earn money and make this newspaper better and better. Then you will have achieved your ideal life."

Cheng Mo: "Why don't you talk?"

Qin Ying Zipped her mouth to breathe, and felt surprised, was not already understanding each other no longer "over the line"? Why did Cheng Mo bring this up again? Moreover, these ideas of Cheng Mo are too much, call yourself to bring a car to him to learn to drive...

Qin Ying thought about it or could not help but respond: "If you are free and single, I will consider going to you, you say that you can give me future happiness, I will ask you today, if I really go to you, where do I live?" We can't use the sky as our house and the earth as our bed, can we? Got to have a place to stay. Let's be realistic, you said you can give me happiness, you now have a family, you are not a free person, how to give me happiness? For the record, I will never be a mistress."

Qin Ying never answer like this, suddenly by Cheng Mo a few information content made angry excited, she instantly understood Cheng Mo for her good is something.

Qin Ying intentionally leave these words, want to let Cheng Mo have self-knowledge, is also intended to stop him from saying the so-called true love, obviously, Cheng Mo already family, have a wife and children, even fall in love qualifications are not, can also talk with Qin Ying about the future? Cheng Mo can't even give the name, but can still talk about the truth? I really don't know what Cheng Mo has the confidence to say these words.

Then Cheng Mo explained, he not only said he was poor, but also said he was stupid, he was stupid, will not do business, do newspaper all money, just want to wait for Qin Ying, with Qin Ying IQ to the newspaper this platform do live to make money. We should wait for Qin Ying to make the literary press bigger and stronger.

Specific measures are not, are some big talk, if this matter in Cheng Mo has not spoken to Qin Ying before those ambiguous words, perhaps Qin Ying is willing to do a career, but also really will invest human and material resources, the newspaper platform industry to do well.

Unfortunately, Cheng Mo no patience to wait, the intention of the heart gradually exposed, if not for the original language chat exposed the flaw, Qin Ying really will jump into this pit.

Now Qin Ying brake still have time, after all, nothing happened. To tell the truth, how can such a talented man say these things so naked? And he doesn't seem to understand that everything he's saying now is just wishful thinking.

Qinying hope Cheng Mo understand her attitude, but she will never accept a family man's emotions, dont think. Qin Ying kicked the ball to Cheng Mo: "No free body, nothing to talk about!" Want to let Cheng Mo quit, put this crooked reading pressure down.

Cheng Mo there second back: "I'll tell you straight, I told you I was a poor man, if I want to give you now, the future bride like a young man, buy a car, I really can't do it." My heart may not be worth much, but if you recognize my love for you, you can create the ideal conditions of life, and you are now able to buy us a place to live. If you are not willing to give, then it proves that we are not destined."

Cheng Mo a speech confidence to the extreme. Qin Ying feel funny at this time, Cheng Mo sent her these words feel speechless. At this time, my heart suddenly jumped out of a word: what is the truth? Qin Ying also heard the deeper meaning of the words.

Qin Ying repeatedly understand Cheng Mo's phonetic meaning, repeated to listen to a few times. Began to think that it is a misunderstanding to hear wrong, the result over and over again to hear clearly, Qin Ying's heart is also cool, she thought Cheng Mo is really appreciate her literary talent, and then gradually moved the truth. Really did not think that these months of online emotional communication, the original is such a real purpose.

Qin Ying if have not heard these voices, may fantasize and Cheng Mo walk together, live an arcadian romantic life of the literati. Qin Ying is not dislike Cheng Mo often on the lips of the poor, she looked down on a man is not at all, did not want to pay a responsibility for love, for the cause to fight for the determination of hard work. When he had nothing, he said that he was content with this easy and comfortable life.

From beginning to end is to say that he will wait for Qin Ying to rush to fight, he to assist. It's beautiful. It's a fantasy.

Qin Ying's mind brought out a sentence: "really dare to think!"

Qin Ying really didnt think, Cheng Mo not only forget himself or have a family man, even love other women are not qualified, what is true to Qin Ying talk? And how can you be happy with him? Where is happiness?

Qin Ying carefully and carefully reply, otherwise it will misunderstand more, and then harm others, wrong family relations. In any case, since knowing that Cheng Mo has a wife, Qin Ying thought Cheng Mo will be like her, some words can not be said, it seems that Cheng Mo has forgotten that he is already a family...

Qin Ying think, or give Cheng Mo a chance to be the perfect man, before there is no real confirmation of Cheng Mo's intention, or want to express a little tactfully, give Cheng Mo a little face, so politely reply to wechat: "I know you have a family, I know we can not, so it is impossible to think in this regard." I haven't thought about these future things, and I can't! I hope you understand. We're all adults. There are things we can do and things we can't do."

Chapter 9: Whimsy

Qin Ying reply Cheng Mo information, just want to calm down, she hopes to have a transition period between each other, do not want too embarrassing situation.

Qin Ying think, between them only when the relationship is good, never mention feelings in this aspect of things, she can pretend that nothing happened between two people.

A week slowly passed, during this period is really quiet, Qin Ying thought so to keep calm or, understanding each other, can also maintain friendship in the circle of literary exchange, a long time she and Cheng Mo subtle relationship will slowly disappear. The two of them had nothing happened, but Cheng Mo in emotional expression has derailed, fortunately has not caused substantial impact. Nip this feeling in the bud, is the wisest way to deal with it.

However, one day Qin Ying on the way to love bar book bar after work, heard the mobile phone constantly ringing, because the car did not pay attention to answer immediately. To love the book bar to deal with things in the store, Qin Ying sat down quietly to read the book, the result of the phone constantly and have the sound of information reminder - Qin Ying set to "shuttle" voice.

Qin Ying recline on the sofa, looking at the wechat Cheng Mo sent her information: "These days I have been controlling myself to try not to think of you, do not look at any of your wechat, but did not think that you did not send me wechat." You can ignore me, but I can't ignore you and not think about you. I'm never gonna talk about it again, and the more I think about it, the worse it gets, because there's still something I want to say to you. In recent days, I have figured out that I am a toad who wants to eat swan meat, I am wishful thinking, I know that this matter is impossible to develop into the closer relationship I want, and you will not go to that step for us. I can already see how much I mean to you. I'll pretend I didn't say anything, but I'll do what I need to do for you, and I hope you'll continue to recommend my stories for the newspaper, and I hope we'll continue to help each other."

Qin Ying see Cheng Mo said to this paragraph, is nothing more than to express their inner feelings. Cheng Mo words between their own cynicism. Some words Qin Ying has been held in the heart did not say, Qin Ying really feel Cheng Mo mind is whimsical. Cheng Mo in disappointment with the "wishful thinking" to laugh at themselves.

Qin Ying did not immediately go to explain what to say, anyway, Qin Ying know as long as this period of time, Cheng Mo for her that feelings will recede with the passage of time. Because Qin Ying understand himself in Cheng Mo heart is actually an illusion, that is not true love.

Emotional experts have said such a paragraph: when a man really loves the woman, he will not cry poor in front of a woman, nor will he play machismo in front of a woman, so that the woman will pay all the wealth to prove his love. Otherwise, the man never loved this woman, in the man's heart this woman is worthless, and also use the excuse of love to kidnap a woman to pay for themselves.

This emotional test, blocked in Qin Ying's heart like a fire, burning. Qin Ying thought, Cheng Mo not only did not have the strength to contend with her a little economic conditions, but also asked for a room and a car, naked asked Qin Ying with wealth to pay to prove true.

Every word of Cheng Mo shows macho domineering, showing inexplicable swagger of confidence. Qin Ying feel sad, Cheng Mo actually has not been seriously invested. Is it so hard for Qin Ying to find true love? She had to give up her wealth to prove that her feelings were true love?

Qin Ying lack of security, in the emotion she appears cautious and careful, before not to determine the authenticity of love, she is indeed not impulsive. Because every penny she earns is earned by her own wisdom and hard work, her life trajectory is to think twice before you move. If feelings must be measured by economic money, even if their feelings fall in love, they will stop awake in an instant.

She is dedicated to her feelings, sincere, and is to give practical action, rather than just the sweet mouth, she is no longer an 18-year-old girl feelings, she has spent most of her life in order to get true love, have entered the ranks of older leftover women, but also at all costs to wait. Her character is destined to the other half, must pay sincere feelings for it, she can be moved by it.

As a partner, Cheng Mo can not reach the standards of Qin Ying, if in accordance with the relationship of ordinary friends to maintain, Cheng Mo good, anyway will not consider and Cheng Mo have a further relationship.

One day a week later, Qin Ying just finished revising a novel manuscript, which is Cheng Mo had promised to recommend to the publishing house works.

Qin Ying dont want to find Cheng Mo trouble, the work was sent to the other two editors teachers, the recognition and support of the two teachers. One of them is Qin Ying's hometown, the editor teacher gave comments and suggestions in the review, changed the age of the characters, set the career of the characters to a higher level, and will write a younger love and marriage work. In this way, the whole work is to recommend to the film and television platform, which is some pure commercial marketization, the theme of the novel has lost the original intention of Qin Ying's writing.

Qin Ying thought or want to stick to their ideas, dont want to make big changes. If we blindly meet the needs of the market, it is equivalent to losing the original true story prototype that the novel works want to express, losing a lot of objective things, if the authenticity is changed, Qin Ying is worried about changing beyond recognition, out of the original environment of life. Qin Ying also believes that if you write unfamiliar people and things, the work will certainly have no vitality, and you will not write feelings for the characters in the story. So after careful consideration, I decided to write according to my own wishes, in addition to the modification of the writing style, the main line of the story is maintained on the original theme, so that I can only choose another publishing house that can accept the original work.

At this time Qin Ying want to listen to Cheng Mo from the side, by the way to see if he is willing to help publish as in the past. After all, the content of the entire novel manuscript Cheng Mo clearly wrote what content, easier to communicate.

Wechat Qin Ying will publish the editor teacher on the publication of the problems listed out, Cheng Mo talked about their own opinions:

1. Let Qin Ying or wait for the suggestion of the editor teacher in the same township, modify it first, and then wait for publication.

2. Because of the connivance of his peers, he is not in a position to interfere in anything related to this publication.

3. In addition, since the choice does not want to develop into a partnership, Cheng Mo also shows his attitude and will not be a confidant.

Cheng Mo information tell Qin Ying, he is not going to help Qin Ying. At the beginning of Cheng Mo with Qin Ying said: "I should help you in the future, or will continue to support you, the thing must do!" These have now proved to be false pleasantry.

Qin Ying heard this information, feel that some words really should not say, try should not try. This communication down, Qin Ying Cheng Mo last thought have no.

Qin Ying some lost, this is the Cheng Mo of her "soft spot deep impression"？The man who had spoken so passionately about how much he loved her?

Cheng Mo performance before and after comparison, how all let Qinying feel is her own too naive, or Cheng Mo too dare to think, really some whimsical.

Chapter 10: Instant Insight

Qin Ying see wechat ChengMo reply, in the heart already thought is such a result, she just want to demonstrate whether their judgment is correct, and then do rational processing is not hasty.

Now Qinying comfort himself to Cheng Mo give up, she dont want to believe Cheng Mo really refused to help. On the one hand, she hopes that Cheng Mo's mind is magnanimous, and she has unconditional love for her purpose; On the other hand, some worry that it is their own wishful thinking. If Cheng Mo really to her selfless generosity of good, will not say those naked greedy words, her heart is very messy very complex at this time.

Sure enough, three days later, Cheng Mo sent a message in wechat: "I mean, if the publishing house editor teacher you contact has no specific contract, no specific time for publication, or no specific plan for publication, you tell me directly, and I will help you solve the rest of the publishing problem." I said ignore you regardless of you, in fact, I am angry with you, because I know your works are very good, but did not meet a good bole. I found you, I admired you, and then you rejected me. I pointed out the way, you do not follow, as I am your spare?"

Qin Ying understand that there is no love for no reason in the world, there is no hate for no reason, she knows Cheng Mo to help her is purposeful, and this purposeful has been obvious, she can not use the happiness of the rest of her life in the future, to gamble on the fate of the master power. She had heard a lot of shows from relationship experts about how the fate of intelligent women would cope with these problems in life, and she knew the relevant countermeasures.

So Qin Ying politely replied: "First of all, thank you for your help and support as always, and thank you for your understanding." As for the publication of the novel, I am still focusing on comprehensive revision. In addition, I have sent the revised version to other agencies willing to publish and distribute it. I have a plan to publish the book in cooperation, and I am waiting for their reply. I am satisfied with your concern for this publication, and I will not bother you with this publication, thank you here."

See Qin Ying reply information so polite, Cheng Mo heart suddenly all tastes, Cheng Mo heart and gave birth to a plan.

Cheng Mo has two members of the literary hobby writing group, Qin Ying has been silent diving, did not send their own works, generally never interact with anyone in the group, only look and learn.

In the next few days, the group frequently appeared a lot of new female author articles and author profiles, the whole group is morning greetings and good night blessings, the group became the author to Cheng Mo editor-in-chief of the morning request and evening report phenomenon. Cheng Mo enjoyed this kind of treatment like the emperor, the satisfaction of spiritual vanity, has made him more and more confident, and the attitude of arrogance is unprecedently active and high.

But no Qinying flattery, a message did not appear, which let Cheng Mo again suspicious.

One morning Qin Ying opened the mobile phone wechat, and saw the wechat content sent by Cheng Mo: "Never met wechat friends, if there is something to ask, I am willing to help, if you do not want to stay in the group, you can also freely quit." Qin Ying transfixed, this is Cheng Mo which tendon is wrong? Why always backtrack, agreed to maintain the status quo, why began to set up a defense? Qin Ying did not want to directly issue six words: "What do you mean?" Is it to withdraw?"

Then the mobile phone rang up, Qin Ying a look at wechat voice call show is Cheng Mo, connect listen to Cheng Mo how to say, save a sentence reply.

Cheng Mo wechat this head explained: "I don't mean that, I can't find you in the group, I am anxious, I want to use this way to ask what you mean, how did you quietly withdraw from the group?"

Qin Ying explained: "You have two groups, I quit one of the groups, I remember telling you earlier." The other group I did not retreat, I just silent no voice. If you want me out of the group, just say so. If you do not want me to see something in the group, I can immediately leave the group, you can do what you want to do. There are a lot of new female writers in the group recently, and I just don't see anything. I still want to emphasize two points, why I still keep in touch with you, one is that your book is on the way to the mail, you asked me to put the book in the library, for people to read, to increase your popularity and publicity use, if I finished these, I want to let you know? Second, I have another story that I'm supposed to publish in your next issue, so if you do it, will you let me know if you do something good? After all, it's the best way for us writers to keep in touch with our editors."

Cheng Mo listen to hurry to explain added: "I do not mean this, I will not want you to delete my wechat, my meaning is very clear, or that sentence, your thing, I will help, you want to leave the group by you decide, I have nothing to hide." You see a lot of female writers, they come from all over the country, all love literary writing, although the works are not as good as you write, but give them more encouragement, give them more opportunities to show their works. To tell you the truth, there are several female writers who love me, and even willing to buy a house in my city to accompany me, I did not agree. There is also a woman writer who is abroad, has a villa and a car, and wants me to join her, but she doesn't want anything but me. Do you understand? You don't like me, but a lot of women do. You give a word today, OK, let's continue to work towards this goal; No, I'll never mention it again."

Qin Ying instant see through Cheng Mo, forced her to say, Qin Ying stopped a few seconds later: "We don't mention this topic?" I don't want to bother you with the book thing, because I can't give you the life you want. Some things are our common interests, such as the house and car you said, but the difference is that these wealth I rely on their own hard work to get, and you have these things tied together with love, to women for your so-called sincere love to pay to meet your needs, but also to prove that this is true love? If you must do so, so test my bottom line, honestly, today I also say the truth, our relationship is impossible to be as simple as at the beginning! You are a man, you should be in the family life to pay for your women and children, and provide this wealth. Instead of asking for it from the woman you love?

You say that you love me and miss me very much, but I would like to ask you, what have you done for your 'true love'? If you can't even give me the basic conditions of life, how can I expect you to give me a happy life in the future? I don't know why you can still have the confidence to say it, you can't even give a promise. You say that you are poor at present this is the reality, the only thing that can change is that in order to love you will leave the house; And the condition is that I must first buy a house and a car for your love before I can have a place for you to live, is that the understanding?"

Cheng Mo made a laugh, interrupted Qin Ying with self-deprecating words: "Well, I just tell you, as long as you promise me to develop a partner relationship, I will be clean for you." But today you make me feel like you're not willing to do these things for our love. Well, I'm sorry you lost the chance to meet a good man like me, so go ahead."

Qin Ying suddenly feel some unreasonable, some emotions directly put the words out: "Chief editor leadership please don't interrupt, let me say what I want to say in one breath, so as not to misunderstanding each other delayed life." I have seriously considered before answering truthfully, let's stop here and never talk about this topic again, otherwise even wechat friends can't do it. No, I must be busy."

Two seconds later, Qin Ying tried to send a picture reply instead of what she had to say, and the result showed a red exclamation point! Failed to send this message.

Qin Ying wechat has since reduced a lot of noise, she laughed at herself, buried herself in wechat to make a big clear, leaving no trace of her and the Cheng Mo editor-in-chief once talked about traces, out of sight for net, to screen pull completely clean.

Qin Ying deleted Cheng Mo more than once affectionate expression. Unfortunately, the words have not been fulfilled, has been completely cut off contact.

Obviously, Cheng Mo heart think you Qin Ying dont give me what I want, help you in vain that is impossible. Although Cheng Mo always said: "I help people, never ask for anything."

Can women believe what comes out of this man's mouth? What about Qin Ying? Qin Ying secretly glad, this time would rather give up the so-called vanity of fame and fortune, also have to cold treatment, know people really can not be too face, the subtraction will have to decisively give up selfish thoughts, no desire. Some love really can not accept, this affair can not develop. She has the bottom line and looks down on men who are disloyal to love. Qin Ying how to stick this kind of man, once she saw through, she will have the patience to look at this person, automatically find the steps, walk away honorably.

Qin Ying lucky bet Chengmo can not calm, first "shield" her, otherwise she really not say tough words: "pull it down!"

Sometimes this writer is full of nonsense, there is a famous saying, "Time is the test of truth!"

There is no pie in the sky, and there is no free lunch. Sometimes "money" is good. For both men and women, money can tell the difference between true love and fake love. Cheng Mo know with Qin Ying will not play, know to slip first.

Qin Ying is indifferent, about Cheng Mo's good or bad, never mentioned to anyone. She knows that some people are passing by, can only be regarded as a passer-by in her life, to the point of the next station, as the first understanding of the good, is an illusion.

Chapter 11: Tugging at the Heartstrings

As the saying goes, "day to think, night to dream," Qin Ying's dream gave her a very obvious reminder: Cheng Mo out. Cheng Mo give is not Qin Ying want emotional life. The words she remembers most clearly in the dream "Who can accompany you for the rest of your life?" Perhaps it is to suggest that his love object is definitely not Cheng Mo, but a man who needs to continue to wait, a man who can let Qin Ying entrust his life.

Qin Ying in this period of time did not hear the news of Deng Cheng, Deng Cheng is busy what? Qin Ying suddenly thought has half a month no Deng Cheng, what happened to him?

Qin Ying called her friend Qiu Tian before going to work: "Hello, Qiu Tian! What is Deng Cheng busy with these days? I hadn't heard his voice in almost two weeks and didn't dare ask him. I'd like you to contact him and let me know."

Qiu Tian on the other end of the phone said: "You two really have a connection, two weeks ago Deng Cheng's mother suddenly died of cerebral hemorrhage, he was busy dealing with the aftermath." Because this kind of thing happened too suddenly, he only called and told my husband Shen before the temporary, and told not to tell you, afraid you worry. He said he may have to take his mother's ashes back to his hometown mountain, stay in his hometown for a while to deal with some things, and has not come back yet. Listen to Shen said, it seems that he will come back next month, after all, his company has a lot of things to decide. Deng Cheng told us that if you need help with anything, let's try to tell him first."

Qin Ying quietly listening, suddenly the phone came Shen Zong's voice: "Qin Ying ah, just I am in autumn sweet side, by the way to tell you a message, you have to have psychological preparation, about the beach you rent that love bar book." A friend from the planning department told me that it is within the scope of demolition, and the rental contract you signed will not be renewed. You will receive a notice from the government in the near future, so make preparations. But you also don't worry too much, I have put this information and the actual situation of love bar book management to Deng Cheng said - just that day Deng Cheng called to care about you, I did not consider it directly to Deng Cheng listen to. Deng Cheng told you not to worry, he will come back and work out a solution with me. Now you have to be steady, and until you receive the official demolition office notice and the landlord does not talk to you, you must operate as usual."

Qin Ying after hearing all dont know what to say, seemingly calm two weeks but so many changes, if not for Shen and autumn sweet these two good friends, Qin Ying really dont know how to do. The urban planning department is lucky to have Shen's friends, otherwise, once the demolition and resettlement of large items is a very difficult thing.

Can Qin Ying not worry? Love bar, book bar, where to move? Do you still need to operate? Give up a job and a lifestyle you love? To know that this is not only a part of Qin Ying's life source, the most important part of her spiritual sustenance.

There is a small town called Nanlang near Zhuhai, which belongs to the planning of the Greater Bay Area. The state has given a lot of good policies and measures. Especially in recent years, with the growth of China's economic development level and the completion of the construction project of the Hong Kong and Macao Bridge, there should still be development prospects for the development and operation of the service industry in Nanlang Town. Qin Ying is very optimistic about Zhuhai, a tourism city with development potential, so the nearby urban and rural tourist attractions must also be suitable for the development of supporting service industries. With these general directions, Qin Ying has a goal in her heart, she is no longer anxious.

In the spiritual world, Qin Ying is no longer entangled with the relationship with Cheng Mo, there is no love in this world, but there must be no career, Qin Ying understand what kind of life they want.

Qin Ying as usual, during the day in the club physiotherapy room work, work and weekends will be in love bar book to take care of business matters, quietly waiting for the formal notice of the landlord, know not to panic not to mess - she also made the worst plan, a big deal temporarily shut down not open love bar book, it is not terrible, while there is still time to go nearby to find a place suitable for opening a new store.

Another weekend, Qin Ying in the love bar book bar thinking about what things can stay, what things can be moved, in the memo book wrote a item to prepare for the matter, a voice interrupted Qin Ying's thoughts: "What is a person writing?" So serious, the message is not back."

Qin Ying surprised to look up, see Shen sum Deng Cheng together came to the table. Just that sentence is Deng Cheng said, he showed a worried expression. Shen added: "I told you, Qin Ying is fine, she will be here, Deng Dong still do not believe, must drag me together to see you."

Qin Ying pointed to the sofa beside the table and said: "Sit down, come at the right time, there are two things I want to ask Shen, this love bar book bar cabinet, which parts can be unloaded and removed for use?"

Shen smiled and said to Deng Cheng, "Let me add your own suggestions."

Deng Cheng confidently said: "That day to hear Shen talked to me about this love bar book bar is you in business, learned that the policy will be the regional planning demolition information, I took into account that this is a big project, I also discussed the matter with Shen." Let me start with my opinion, and if you disagree, you can make a suggestion. My idea is that we do not take laborious things, strive for a one-step arrangement, I put the plan out for you to choose:

1. If Love Bar Book Bar wants to continue to relocate and operate, it is suggested to move to an area with potential development of rural tourism. There is a floor space in my place, which has not been specifically designed and decorated.

2. The decoration style of Mai tea is still designed and decorated by Shen as a whole, because Shen always knows the style you like.

3. This arrangement can reduce the cost of decoration, reduce the waste of resources, and create conditions for long-term work environment. The advantage is

that the development of this industry in the tourist attraction area will be supported by policies and will have broad development prospects.

4. I am very optimistic, so I will always support your long-term operation here, and I will benefit. Don't think I'm helping you, but I'm helping myself.

I'm done. Let's see what you think. Let's hear it."

Qin Ying a face surprised, do not know what to say. She knew that Deng Cheng wanted to help her, but she was still a little worried, she really didn't want to owe a favor. Cheng Mo is also actively help Qin Ying at first, and then know that failed to become a partner to develop a relationship, and finally even failed to do friends. She really doesn't want her emotional life to get worse and worse, and her requirements are not high: she just wants to find a man who can understand and love her for a partner, rather than confuse friendship and love. She needs to be calm, on the one hand, she needs to develop her career, on the other hand, she can't accept friendship support for no reason.

Qin Ying is very entangled, at present she is willing to become a good friend with Deng Cheng, but she thinks must learn the lesson of Cheng Mo. Qin Ying help to Shen looked at, Shen always understand Qin Ying concerns, immediately explained: Qin Ying you rest assured, I as your mutual friend middleman, I help Deng Cheng draft a formal lease contract, the time according to Deng Cheng's will, can be signed for 10 years, the first 5 years of rent can be delivered according to 5% of the turnover, no turnover can be directly free of rental costs, because of the new regional business can enjoy preferential policies. You can give three months decoration time, all in accordance with the normal procedures to sign the contract, so you two see OK?"

Qin Ying after listening to Shen total supplement, but more uneasy, which is to sign a contract? This is clearly a free gift, and does not give Qin Ying any pressure way, this is more inappropriate?

Deng Cheng seems to see Qin Ying's concerns: "Oh, Qin Ying don't think too much, if my country house is well decorated, then the good space is not more wasted, and after my mother died, I will live in the house in the city, that is, I will return to the house in the country on weekends." Oh, and I just chose to stay on the second floor for my personal space, and Mr. Shen helped me think about it, opening the door from the backyard directly to the second floor, without occupying the business space on the first floor, without any impact, Mr. Shen designed the layout is very humane, I think this plan is beneficial to all three of us."

Qin Ying see Deng Cheng and Shen total two people said so, also understand that there is no better way than this, this idea may be the two of them have agreed, see this help her sincerely, for a while she really have no reason to refuse this kindness.

Qin Ying outside business is also very not easy, can not deal with Cheng Mo relationship is not good, and doubt any well-intentioned people. Although Deng Cheng did not communicate with Qin Ying for long, but Deng Cheng each time to her friendly are not pretend, and feel very practical, is to help Qin Ying.

A house is a place to live in, otherwise it's a waste of resources. Deng Cheng is Qin Ying understand that, deliberately say easy, let Qin Ying agree.

Shen is always a very good person, immediately said to Qin Ying: "Don't hesitate, today decided to come down, I will go back to the company to plan the rental contract, or tomorrow to sign the contract here, I will arrange the specific design and decoration materials ready, to try to get it all right before the end of the year, otherwise the night long dream, the relocation of the demolition office will not be too long, at most half a year, we have to hurry."

Qin Ying looked at the two of the serious energy, really not joking, had to nod and keep saying: "Thank you, really thank you for my consideration so thoughtful, OK, we will settle down here tomorrow."

Deng Cheng smiled at Qin Ying and said, "That's right, don't let us all worry about you, I also like to have such a quiet place to read."

General Manager Shen patted Deng Cheng on the shoulder and said: "We can rest assured that we can go to my company to draw a specific rental contract."

Qin Ying looked at them out of the back of the door of the love bar book bar, only to catch the reluctant eyes, warm in the heart, she leaned back on the sofa, some red eyes. It was a grateful sad, this feeling only she deeply understand.

Chapter 12: Clear

After going out, General Manager Shen said to Deng Cheng, "Deng Cheng, honestly, do you know what this decision means today?" Let alone half the rental income, you can consider well, the next gang will be ten years ah!"

Deng Cheng said to Shen: "After the company I will tell you the truth."

The car opened to Shen's company, get off into the company when Deng Cheng began to ask: "Shen, when you chased the autumn sweet, is not also from giving her a sense of security?" You have bought a room at that time to write her name, otherwise how can autumn sweet follow you so bent on entrepreneurship? You have many difficult times, autumn sweet did not leave you, this is you find the right partner, you must give her enough security. Since I choose to be good to Qin Ying, I don't let her think about things, I also want to learn from you, I also want to take out my sincerity, silently do something for Qin Ying, don't let her look around and ignore my true feelings, I must use action to learn from you."

Shen smiled and said: "You do not know how difficult it was to start a decoration company, autumn sweet a girl can work with me this divorced man with a son to struggle with the company, silently followed the most difficult three years, I can not give her a sense of security?" Of course, you and Qin Ying are in a much better situation than we were at the beginning, wealth this thing, as long as it is given to the right person, leave the closest person, let her heart at ease, follow you for a lifetime, this wealth is not in your home? I regard wealth very lightly in this regard, as long as the beloved person goes on with you through thick and thin, my wealth is shared, because as long as the beloved person is in, the wealth will only increase, you are not this reason?"

Deng Cheng: "So, today I want Shen to help me a favor, so that when the contract is signed tomorrow Qin Ying will leave a copy of the ID card, please leave a copy for me, my village compound house can also do a division of property rights certificate immediately, I want to bring Qin Ying's name, the name of the first floor are written to her, the second floor is my own residence, I want her to operate love book in peace in this decade, But I'd better not tell her until I've done it, and when the time is right, I'll choose the occasion to tell her. What do you think?"

After listening to Deng Cheng's voice, Shen smiled and said, "I believe in your vision, I wish you everything you want to come true, I support you."

The second day of love bar book lease contract completed as scheduled, at this time for Deng Cheng this is just let Qin Ying settle down a ceremony, Shen always Deng Cheng good deeds with. Qin Ying did not know!

This side of the operation time to wait for Shen total rural renovation speed and relocation time.

Shen said in public: "Fortunately, three months ago Qin Ying high-grade apartment room fine decoration, now you can move in at any time, the next time, I will step up the country love bar design decoration plan, such as decoration design renderings approved, we can sign the decoration contract."

Qin Ying: "I am looking forward to this rural love bar book bar program design, my idea is to advocate all natural style, not only spend less money but also carry out practical design style without formality, but also transform old things, which can increase the difficulty for Shen." Please Shen more trouble, thank Shen first, you work I rest assured."

Deng Cheng then looked at Shen said: "Shen can be the first floor of the front yard all the design layout of love bar book bar area, my second floor you will be designed from the back yard straight up to the second floor, and the business scope is not contradictory, you can bring two different living areas and business space, first decorate all the first floor of the business site, my second floor later decoration."

Shen added: "I also mean this, first decorate a floor, will also consider the design of an office and lounge bathroom suite, available for living." If Qin Ying is running late, do not want to return to the city toss, you can rest in love bar book bar. Rest assured, I will do the best I can with the required features."

Qin Ying: "Shen, please call a moving company car, I will start to move into your installed house 6-606 next week, has been ventilated for three months, the room should have no odor."

Mr. Shen: "No problem, you just need to call a business car, pack some of your daily necessities, the rest of the furniture matching."

Deng Cheng volunteered to say: "This good thing I want to count as one, rejoice, housewarming is worth celebrating!" I can carry some things in my car, too."

Qin Ying smiled and nodded, and Shen said, "Let's meet at six o 'clock next Sunday morning at the downstairs of the community." Wish us all the best in our new house."

Qin Ying at this time in the mind suddenly emerge Cheng Mo those self-righteous voice message, with standing in front of the real work of Deng Cheng can not be compared. Deng Cheng is everywhere for the sake of Qin Ying, consistent with words and deeds; And Cheng Mo mouth sweet words, but also just ask, people have not seen, but the conditions opened to Qin Ying.

Qin Ying is glad to be able to find Cheng Mo selfishness in time, stop loss in time, is also a very good thing. She believes that everything she sees in front of her, life is still a real experience, in order to really distinguish between true and false, and Qin Ying will not expose the beginning of online love, completely put down, it is time.

She has to start again, can not miss the good people around, feel Deng Cheng is also good for her, she really look forward to further understanding Deng Cheng, both men and women are single, nothing can not go to contact, compared to Cheng Mo, Deng Cheng can really be a diamond king five. And Cheng Mo even pursue their own qualifications are not, have a family and talk to other women about love. Think of here, Qin Ying suddenly feel a little tacky, material, but this is the real idea of Qin Ying. Is she easy? This way to find true love, never care about personal gains and losses, not only paid emotion and money, there are so many years of time and energy, that is, never care about money with men, the result also hurt themselves, became an old leftover woman. Are almost 40 years old, she can no longer pretend to understand with confusion, must shine your eyes, and want to be a partner of the man, talk about a love, talk about money, talk about career, talk about life trifles, to see if it is really suitable.

She does not want to be limited to the surface of the good, she asked to find a person who can accommodate her good and vulgar, she does not want to find a person who makes her uncomfortable uncomfortable together, that kind of marriage life, she Qin Ying would rather not.

Qin Ying see time to noon, immediately told the staff, put on the local chicken yam soup brought from home, please Deng Cheng and Shen two people to eat, and also with the hometown of spring glutinous rice flour vegetarian round, and Deng Cheng last village to Qin Ying prepared small fish, all fried until both sides golden, let them eat quickly, back to the autumn sweet prepared some, I also prepared some for Deng Cheng to take home and prepare a packing box.

Qin Ying's love for friends is also with a grateful heart, she did not express what words of gratitude, she can only use action to return friends to her help and care, she is willing to do more for them. Seeing Deng Cheng and Shen do not give in, eat with relish, Qin Ying's heart has unspoken happiness, smiled and said: "You like to eat more, I can eat more for you in the future, Deng Cheng seems to have lost a lot of weight recently, to make up more nutrition."

Shen said with a smile while eating: "haha, love dearly Deng Cheng." Qin Ying embarrassed to take things away in the kitchen.

Back to the table, Qin Ying hands have two bags of packaging boxes packed with good food bags, handed Shen sum Deng Cheng hands: "Put in the refrigerator, want to eat how much, get a hot wave stove heating for a few minutes can eat." Take it, and keep it with you when you're done, knowing you two have a lot to do."

Deng Cheng ate and drank enough, smiled with satisfaction and said: "This chicken soup is the best soup I have ever had in my life, it tastes delicious, and this glutinous rice noodles stuffed with vegetarian vegetables, and this fried fish, I love to eat." Mr. Shen, I eat more than you."

Shen still lowered his head and drank all the soup in the bowl: "Look at me, eat all of it, it's delicious, I can really grow fat if I eat like this." Hey hey, smug, thank you Qin Ying, then I am not welcome, this for the autumn sweet thank you. Deng Cheng, let's go to the country house scene to see it, put you want to account for the site office, I'm ready to decorate the next step to implement."

Qin Ying looked at the back of them to eat and leave, happy to continue to stay in love bar book bar, with two employees busy up. This day, Qin Ying seems to have something to look forward to, all the problems with the help of friends to arrange, things are not as complex as imagined, there are friends who can help do things, it is really the blessing of Qin Ying repair. She secretly like Deng Cheng work style, work reliable execution, always feel Deng Cheng is her blessing star, always in Qin Ying very difficult time, and then the difficulty seems to be solved. In the impression of Qin Ying, always Deng Cheng for her to pay more, at this time Qin Ying heart warm. She is thinking that on the day of moving next Sunday, she must do a better table of delicious food in the new home, share the good specialties of her hometown, show her skills, and eat enough for Deng Cheng and her friends.

Thinking of this, Qin Ying's mind has been filled with recipes from his hometown.

This week Qin Ying mood particularly bright, carefree, single-minded three line physiotherapy room work, love bar book, go home. Every time I go home, I also prepare to pack daily necessities and prepare for the move. People meet the spirit of happy events, time is really fast, and the day of moving is here.

The season is about to enter the summer, spring flowers, the environment of the high-grade community is very good, a piece of green grass and branches along the path, the faint fragrance of flowers, birds fly over the treetops jump, the air is filled with a thick osmanthus fragrance, the sun is shining and falling to every place.

Deng Cheng, Shen total autumn sweet have already come to Qin Ying rented the building door, the original purchase took a look at this good community, because the community environment is mature and convenient, but also take into account the new house decoration after convenient relocation.

For a building is Qin Ying choose 6-606 room, really don't say, a residential relocation, the choice of auspicious day auspicious time at 6 o 'clock on June 6, this is called Shunshun.

Qin Ying is happy to welcome everyone in, the packed luggage has been arranged for everyone to move into the car, the two cars are installed, three hours all unloaded and installed to the new home, the room No. 6-606 in the middle of the door, the living room is large and bright, the living room terrace is against the green belt of the community, Qin Ying and autumn sweet plus love bar two employees Xiaoxue and Xiao Bei, All in the kitchen busy cooking, Qin Ying specific will love bar book bar listed in advance for a holiday for two days, at ease to do a big meal to move friends to eat, today to a local chicken hot pot, the most important is to struggle for many years in a foreign land, there is no feeling of home like today, friends are together, this seems to be the first time in a family dinner, Relax without feeling inhibited. The midday sun was shining brightly into the living room from the terrace. The kitchen design is large, four people are very handy in busy spinning together, and the functional area is planned and designed very well. This is the credit of autumn sweet and Qin Ying.

After a while, Qin Ying patted Qiu Tian and said, "There is nothing for you here, you should take charge of the wine and start to serve the food for dinner, it will be ready soon."

In the living room, Autumn Sweet asked everyone: "Are you drinking red wine, or beer?"

Only listen to Deng Cheng said: "We still choose the red bar, ladies and beauties can drink together."

Shen smiled and said: "Or by the hostess Qin Ying, come and joke together, you say two words."

Qin Ying greeted Xiaoxuet and Beckham, sat at the table together, and then pressed his voice and said: "Listen to Deng Cheng, we all drink red wine." This first glass of wine, I would like to express my gratitude to everyone, thank you for your help and love for me, I will do it first for respect. Drink well, I wish everyone a better life! Cheers!"

The day's lunch stretched into the late afternoon, when the sun was setting and everyone was still talking passionately. Deng Cheng look at things to do, while from the living room end empty plate into the kitchen, while will cut the fruit plate on the table, while the good tea will be placed on the coffee table, for the wine run lung fire, see the scene Deng Cheng also understand health.

Qin Ying see Deng Cheng dont put themselves as outsiders, do housework than Qin ying also quick. Her mood at the moment really want to laugh, Deng Cheng this is to help her, clean up the dinner plate for her to clean everything, really like the master, think here or did not refrain from laughing, immediately restrained, looking into the living room. Here Xiao Xue Xiao Bei watching TV drama "romantic love house" , autumn sweet and Shen also seem to talk about the decoration of the house, Deng Cheng sat beside the sofa, sometimes add tea, sometimes give some of their own ideas, talking about the topic is the overall decoration of the house in the countryside.

Looking at this group of friends so concerned to do things, Qin Ying's heart finally put down. With these good friends, career, life, work will be better and better.

Chapter 13: Single-mindedness

Qin Ying let Deng Cheng on Monday, every afternoon to the club physiotherapy room to do moxibustion conditioning body, Deng Cheng membership card has not been used, recently do more things, the body always feel very easy to fatigue sleep.

Qin Ying from Deng Cheng recent times to her help, she saw Deng Cheng did not take care of their own life, inevitably some distressed, she can only remind Deng Cheng has a healthy body, in order to live better.

Deng Cheng as long as he can see Qin Ying, he is happy to listen to Qin Ying, Monday morning after dealing with the work, at one o 'clock in the afternoon knocked on the door of Qin Ying physiotherapy room.

Qin Ying has prepared the red ultraviolet instrument, with from the spring Li Shizhen hometown moxa leaf paste, the sore parts of the waist and back respectively warm moxibustion physiotherapy. Lying on the physiotherapy bed, Deng enjoyed the warm feeling and soon fell asleep. An hour later, the sound of the meter stopping woke Deng Cheng up.

Deng Cheng extended a stretch, patted his belly, pushed off his legs, and said shamefully: "This moxibustion warms my body, it's really comfortable, I will insist on coming this week." It's good to take a nap to catch up."

Qin Ying gently answered: "Yes, good health is the capital, while I am still working here in these two months." I have passed the certificate of training instructor. I will apply for quitting this job to the company in the second half of the year and work as a lecturer in the company's training center, because it is more suitable for me. Working hours only three days a week, wages and benefits according to the number of students to be given commission. I have the option of preparing from home and working flexible hours so that it doesn't affect my writing process."

Deng Cheng happily listen to Qin Ying talk, he from the heart more admire Qin Ying enterprising spirit, Qin Ying inspirational diligence, has been Deng Cheng to her one of the reasons. Her quiet and stubborn are two different sides, sometimes presented in Deng Cheng's dream, Deng Cheng knows that is the reason why he misses Qin Ying. Today listen to Qin Ying say the work plan, he is more happy than Qin Ying. Qin Ying is trying to change towards her ideal goal, she has done it, she can not change the social environment and others, she can change herself and do a better self.

As Deng Cheng witnessed Qin Ying, Qin Ying has two roles, and wants to live a better life in order to help his family. Qin Ying is very self-discipline, what is the most should do at the moment, Qin Ying is very independent.

Just like personal marriage problems, she will not waste time on men like Cheng Mo, and she has no time to spend in the hypocritical world. And the fake love and hypocrisy of Cheng Mo did not have the patience, the last time to send Qin Ying such wechat content: "To your heart you do not want, the membership group you have returned, then you will delete our wechat!" If you don't have a relationship, then we won't be wechat friends."

See this message, more proof that Cheng Mo heart of egotism and selfishness, no trace of Cheng Mo once said infatuation, the man's face can really be faster than the book. Fortunately, I have not met, and fortunately Qin Ying has not had time to start to end this "online love" for a few months.

Deng Cheng goodbye interrupted Qin Ying distracted comparison, Qin Ying accompanied Deng Cheng to the stairway, looking at Deng Cheng left, turned to his physiotherapy room. She has to tidy up the instrument, there will be a new appointment customer arrival, in this medical beauty industry, Qin Ying has become the backbone of the company.

Qin Ying has also cared about the eyes of others, after all, he likes to face the public as a writer, how decent ah, is a woman with knowledge and culture. Face is said to be good, but in a foreign land development, you must have the ability to support yourself, think about it or listen to the girlfriend's recommendation to study research. The construction and development of the motherland has made the development of this coastal city more rapid, which is a good era for the development of medical beauty.

Qin Ying in order to make more money, it is necessary to pay more efforts, the pie will not fall in the sky, only people who continue to work hard to put into action, in order to harvest wealth and happy life. This is the most profound experience of Qin Ying, a woman's backer is himself. Life can be without love and marriage, but never without career and work.

When there is no strength, when there is no choice, only to do the service work that you don't like - the original choice of this medical beauty industry is to solve the problem of supporting yourself, making money quickly, accumulating entrepreneurial costs as soon as possible, and then transiting to the cause that you like.

Deng Cheng Qinying's good feeling increases day by day, Deng Cheng heart has a more perfect plan, he wants to do the rural house property rights, to Qinying a surprise. He wanted to fill his heart with the future Qin Ying needed.

People in this life will encounter a lot of coincidences, the more you want, the more you can't get. The more you don't care about things, they will happen around you inadvertently. Life is like this, when you don't expect anyone, as long as you work hard in the direction of your planned life intention, to learn to find business opportunities, do what you like, even if it is temporarily far away from the goal, step by step and strive hard, after all, one day unconsciously came to your side.

Qin Ying sat in the physiotherapy room, recalling the life experience of the past few years, looking for a job, renting a house to open a business, buying a house, and has always insisted on writing and publishing, publishing essays, novels and columns in the literary world on municipal and provincial journals, and has serialized three novels. Back to think of some admire their own self-discipline and perseverance, time witnessed Qin Ying's initial heart began to take root and sprout and blossom, although this day came a little late, but she believes that women's career success, economic independence, not afraid of good partners object, she believes this, because love is a beautiful moment of emotion, And a marriage needs a balance of values in order to go long, and what should come will come.

Deng Cheng after this week of physical therapy, coupled with Qin Ying every day also bring some different nutritional meals to him to eat - today old duck soup powder, tomorrow's pork liver soup, the day after tomorrow braised pork chops, put on different delicious things every day, but also really put Deng Cheng gas tone good, spirit and spirit restored to the original look.

Before leaving on Saturday afternoon, Deng Cheng said to Qin Ying, "I have been eating your nutritious meals this week, and I have gained weight. Tomorrow Sunday, let's go to the country house to meet with Mr. Shen, and we will discuss the renovation plan face to face."

Qin Ying heard this sentence, immediately remembered one thing, let Deng Cheng wait, turned to the desk to bring a letter to Deng Cheng, is the demolition office notice: Please complete the relocation before December 30 this year.

Qin Ying said: "You don't have to rush, this time is still too late."

Deng Cheng said: "This matter sooner rather than later, we have to be ready first not to panic, tomorrow morning I will pick you up at your door at 8 o 'clock."

Qin Ying heart also know, rural house decoration is a big project, is to seize, but she dont want to let Deng Cheng worry too much. She was very grateful that she could rent such a good place to her and specifically make room for her to continue to run the Love Bar book bar.

I like this environment! Even live for the elderly! She likes them all, and the courtyard, the whole floor area, rented to her for ten years, which is a big help to her. This is the most suitable for Qin Ying's favorite lifestyle, half fireworks and half Xianqi. Qin Ying can open love bar book, can also plant four seasons flowers! Where the traffic conditions are good, and with the suburbs of the countryside border! At the end of the year to be able to move to this rural tourist spot, in their favorite living environment for a long time, engaged in their favorite work, it is really Deng Cheng to help her realize her wish.

Before eight o 'clock on Sunday morning, Qin Ying went downstairs to the gate of the community a few minutes early to wait for Deng Cheng and Shen. Do the cause of efficiency of people are very punctual, Qin Ying down to see Shen has been sitting in Deng Cheng's car talking, the three people's breakfast passed to Shen hands: "You and Deng Cheng two people's breakfast, home glutinous rice dumplings, is mince, and the hot soybean milk from the ground, and I do dough sticks, eggs, make do in the morning."

Mr. Shen smiled and said, "I will wait for you to send us food while I am hungry." Hey, Deng Cheng I am not wrong, see Qin Ying more virtuous, you know will prepare a delicious breakfast."

Deng Cheng took the food, quit the main driver's seat, Qin Ying got on the car and said: "You two eat while it's hot, I'll drive."

This way two men eat while talking, Qin Ying drive smoothly, less people on the road less car, breeze blowing through the window, very cool!

40 minutes soon arrived in Nanlang town and countryside, Deng Cheng and Shen said in unison: "Let's start from the yard layout."

Qin Ying followed them to listen, Deng Cheng took out Shen design drawings, ask a place, Shen will explain, no opinions, have better suggestions immediately on the project to make a mark, if Qin Ying has a better idea of inspiration halfway, will also participate.

Seeing the plan of the courtyard designed by Mr. Shen, Qin Ying excitedly pointed to three places and said: "If apple trees, osmanthus trees, orange trees are planted here, it will be more perfect, in August when osmanthus flowers are in full bloom, the rich aroma is overflowing, and guests will enjoy reading and drinking tea and chatting in the sunshine outside." When apples and oranges bear fruit, I make applesauce, orange cake, and osmanthus tea, and make full use of the fruits. Do you think it's okay? The cost of planting the trees will come from me and will be included in the renovation budget."

Deng Cheng listened to Qin Ying say so, Epiphany came over: "This idea is good, Shen, I also want to plant these three trees in the backyard, simply this kind of tree project is counted together, all count my funds, the front yard and back decoration layout civil construction integration are counted as my, so it is settled."

Shen always know Deng Cheng's mind, Deng Cheng want to help Qin Ying, so with Deng Cheng said: "Of course you Deng Dong's territory you said." The first floor of all indoor counts Qin Ying, outdoor counts Deng Dong you, I decorate the budget so separate fair? I'll just go ahead with the budget, and if we can work out the general plan now, we can make the budget tonight."

This day three people around the graphic design, around a floor house from the outside to the inside, discussing, discussing, compared to drawing, the key matters recorded on the plan, it seems not long to more than five o 'clock in the afternoon, the project has finally completed the check, the on-site office is very efficient.

Shen said: "Well, today is here, the rest of the work is me, the next time I take the decoration contract to sign, will begin to implement."

Deng Cheng said with one hand akimbo: "Let's go, can we go to the farmhouse to eat?" Qin Ying's breakfast really worked, and she didn't feel hungry until now."

Qin Ying said: "Yes, yes, during the renovation, I will be the minister of life, how about eating and drinking?"

Shen joked: "Then I want to eat more, tube full."

The meal served a large pot of spicy dishes, dried chicken stew, three people drank a case of beer, talking and eating, until the moon climbed the treetop sky, the stars were shining, or Qin Ying said: "It is time to go home, I will drive, you can squint in the back seat for a while."

Deng Cheng looked up at the sky and said, "The moon is really round tonight!"

Shen added: "This means that our things will be a complete success, tonight I go back to work overtime to draw up the budget contract, rest assured, I will not drag you down, will be ahead of the end of the year to complete the renovation plan."

Shen sent the outdoor decoration contract to Deng Cheng's office to sign at ten o 'clock the next day. Deng Cheng said: "The interior decoration contract can be signed to Qin Ying, but the decoration payment is written and installed. I'll pay for all the decorations in advance, and you'll pay only me. You only said to Qin Ying that this is your company's regulations, let customers rest assured and satisfied, do word-of-mouth publicity."

Mr. Shen: "Then I will also give you a contract with Qin Ying, Qin Ying is just a procedural form?"

Deng Cheng looked at Shen and said: "No one can understand my mind better than you, so it is, since I have chosen to care for Qin Ying this good woman, identified her, I have to let her peace of mind, until she is willing to be my bride one day." I will give her whatever I can. These things are not as important as Qin Ying, and I should devote myself to treating her well and solving her problems."

Shen always nodded and waved the contract in his hand while withdrawing from Deng Cheng's office and said: "Then I went to find Qin Ying to sign the contract, see you in the countryside on Sunday."

Qin Ying see Shen prepared the contract, just a glance, immediately signed, and directly asked: "The decoration money should be transferred to you, you have to enter the materials need capital turnover, first transferred to you 200,000 spare how?"

Mr. Shen: "No, I want to install the acceptance of the payment method."

Qin Ying surprised a big mouth looking at Shen: "No? How much does it cost to do business like your decorating company? No, no, we can't do this!"

Shen smiled and said: "You will give me a chance to my company, when you help me do advertising, more business can be introduced." What? This is your bonus package! Come on, I will start preparing materials tomorrow, rest assured!"

Qin Ying looked at Shen's back, thought of outdoor decoration contracts are paid by Deng Cheng. She Qin Ying how virtuous, worthy of friends so great favor to her. She really do not know how to repay these friends, at this time and think of Cheng Mo said, "He is true, but not valuable." Qin Ying thought, what is the truth?

Deng Cheng did not say too many sweet words to Qin Ying, but the action has given a shoulder to rely on. Qin Ying from the heart is full of warmth, she has realized what is the true sense of love, she felt who she can rely on for the rest of her life. He was right next to her. How could she not have seen it before? I almost missed someone so good again.

Chapter 14: The Truth

The next days Deng Cheng and Qin Ying to a week together, only in the weekend village house there to have the opportunity to meet, Shen total decoration progress as planned orderly development.

Three months passed, Qin Ying passed the self-study exam, and the company approved her application for a lecturer position. Qin Ying successfully turned around and put the focus of her work on her favorite writing, while having time to earn some money part-time to solve the slow pace of rural life. She fell in love with the state of life in the country. She had a strange feeling in her heart. The air here, the villagers and the simple friendship of friends, she liked this feeling of relaxation. There is no fake perfunctory, only mutual tolerance and mutual understanding of support and encouragement, where she can open her heart to the experience of doing what she loves.

Deng Cheng is not idle, Monday to Friday to deal with the company's business, two days on the weekend with Shen to provide financial support for the renovation.

When planting grass and flowers in the last part of the rural renovation project, Deng Cheng said to Shen: "I put the rural property rights private property division certificate down, a floor of building property written in the name of Qin Ying, such as love bar book bar migration, we choose a good day, and then tell Qin Ying." I won't be at ease until I get this done. Mr. Shen is happy for me first. We have arranged to plant the trees in recent weeks. I have selected the saplings and grass seeds with the landscaping company, and bought the trees and flowers that can bear fruit in the second year after transplantation."

Shen said to Deng Cheng with admiration: "Support you, cooperate with you, and say what good things, let me be happy!" Qin Ying finally waited for her happiness, and Autumn Sweet and I wanted to drink your wedding wine."

Deng Cheng smiled and said: "This must not urge Qin Ying, I wait for her to marry me willingly, I want to wait until this love bar before and after the garden of spring, fruits, osmanthus blooming, birds and flowers, that time is the best."

Shen saw Deng Cheng to Qin Ying so heart of some true feelings, as a common friend, he also want to help Deng Cheng a love. He stood in the man's point of view, he is also proud of Deng Cheng's broad mind, can be said to be admired, he believes Deng Cheng will be able to find his love and the perfect partner, Qin Ying will fall in love with this lover. Deng Cheng is the good man who can prove true love with practical actions.

Good days, time feels fast, a blink of an eye has reached the last two weeks of the end of the year, this weekend is extraordinary.

Qin Ying, Deng Cheng and Shen total, autumn sweet meet together in the country house, set a relocation auspicious day, plan a grand ceremony, make a noise, these are Deng Cheng Qin Ying do everything.

Deng Cheng also invited the village director, to 9 o 'clock in the morning, the village director could not help but first announced: "On behalf of the whole village villagers, welcome you to share your knowledge with everyone, this friendship we will always benefit a lot, thank you for bringing surprises to our village."

Then Deng Cheng expressed his heartfelt words: "I would like to thank the village director for the strong support of the villagers in time, and thank Shen for his great help in implementing the renovation project." At the same time, welcome our village hostess Qin Ying to officially join the rural revitalization project, operate the love bar book bar, and settle the spiritual knowledge and culture exchange in your village. I wish the event a complete success!"

This day is December 16 9:9, Qiu Tian said: "It means everything goes well, a long time of happiness."

Qin Ying first listen to Deng Cheng so some of the words, village mistress? Deng

Cheng shouted, "Welcome our hostess to speak." The turn of Qin Ying hostess speech, this sudden scene, let Qin Ying have a little surprised and unprepared. Fortunately, Qin Ying has experience as a lecturer, which is not difficult for her to deal with. Qin Ying immediately calm the first 3 seconds, autumn sweet quietly attached to Qin Ying's ear said: "Deng Cheng has put the scope of business area property rights to write your name, you are a real hostess."

Qin Ying was a little surprised, these sudden happiness came to make her feel too surprised, can not help but send out the true voice: "How can I enjoy everyone to give me so much trust and grace?" I don't know where to begin... This trust and valuable gift, I can only repay this truth with action in the future. Here I would like to thank all the blessings and friends for their company, thank you for your help and encouragement to me. What I want to say is in my heart..."

Qin Ying some cant go on, some throat choked, she dont want to cry in this happy and peaceful day. Perhaps it is the feeling of gratitude, the love for Deng Cheng beyond words, perhaps it is glad that they finally wait for the man who loves themselves. She could no longer restrain her joy and tears welled up and blurred her eyes. This situation was instantly seen by Shen's sharp eyes, and quickly took over the words: "Everyone now follow me to see our hostess's love bar book, please accept it together!" Come and visit with me."

Autumn sweet with Qin Ying, gently patting shoulder and back with his hand said: "Should be happy, this is a good thing, Deng Cheng so sincere to you, can really be solid in the face of you, such as love bar book bar began to open, later we are waiting to drink you two wedding wine." Wipe the tears off your face before you look like you're being bullied."

Shen always with everyone a group of people, from the country house after the courtyard began to introduce, Deng Cheng accompanied the visit before and after, to see the autumn sweet accompanied Qin Ying around together, it is assured, but Deng Cheng from time to time to the direction of Qin Ying and move concern.

Qin Ying saw that the courtyard has realized the beautiful scenery on the planning map, she said with emotion: "Thank you and Shen have realized everything I want to do, it really seems to be in a dream." I really want to thank you for all this. Thank you for doing so much for me and Deng Cheng. I really don't know how to repay you and Shen for your help."

Qiu Tian laughed and said, "I told Shen that drinking your wedding wine early is the happiest thing for us, do you know?" As the saying goes, the beauty of life increases the seven blessings of life."

Qin Ying nodded and looked at the distance of Deng Cheng to autumn sweet said: "listen to you, such as Deng Cheng himself said to marry me, then set auspicious day!"

Deng Cheng did not know when he had gone to Qin Ying's side and asked, "Is it what you want?" Are you satisfied? Let me show you the interior layout first. It has been slightly modified to add some living space."

Qin Ying took the hand of autumn sweet, together with Deng Cheng walked into the love bar book bar hall, a look is Qin Ying like a great pastoral nostalgia style, both simple and natural, the materials are all natural stone and abandoned wood, the wall has red brick decoration also has cement wall decoration, together is to look particularly comfortable and warm, there is a warm, warm feeling, The two employees of the book bar XiaoYing Xiaobei played the light music of the old record, and said to Qin Ying: "Sister Qin, this is the most suitable music for the book bar, like the sound of floating from far away, it is quiet, and it will not disturb the guests to read, and the melody of meditation is beautiful, all the sounds given by nature, like our hometown."

Then Xiao Bei also said: "Sister Qin, come and see, Shen has helped us solve the rest room, which is great, we don't have to run back and forth anymore." You see me and Xiao Ying live together, there is a bathroom cloakroom, on the right is our standard room, better than a hotel, on the left is your single lounge, also a small suite, everything."

Deng Cheng hurriedly opened the faucet said: "This is Shen sum autumn sweet credit, autumn sweet afraid you after the business late tired dont want to go back to the city, specially designed this suite."

Qiu Tian smiled and said, "Do you like it? Shen said, this is like a five-star hotel bag check in."

Qin Ying saw love bar book bar will be the previous boutique cabinet, can use things moved over, put on new paint, refresh the results like a new cabinet, it appears to be so coordinated, the overall tone is only three, brown, light gray, and black series. It looks stylish. Shen can really save decoration costs as his own home.

Shen just took the village director together with friends to the hall looked at, here Qin Ying and autumn sweet things discussed with Deng Cheng muttering a few words, all the people after the visit, Deng Cheng shouted to everyone: "Now everyone please take a seat, we Qin Ying to say a few words to you."

Qin Ying, encouraged by Autumn sweet, walked to the center of the hall, said hello to every friend who came, and then said: "In order to thank you for your support, today, as an operator, I officially trial business to you, and officially renamed our original Love Bar Book bar as ' Love Bar Book Bar ' , to recommend to you friends the flavor of our hometown food and snacks, and provide all the books to read, to bring readers a pleasant visual enjoyment, taste delicious hometown snacks." Finally, please eat and drink well and have a nice and happy weekend in the comfortable environment of Love Bar and Book Bar."

After everyone took their seats, under the guidance of Qiu Tian, Xiao Bei Xiaoying served the tea prepared in the morning to the friends after they took their seats, and the glutinous rice flour dumplings, bobbin bone Tommy noodles, boiled peanuts, boiled broad beans, marinated chicken eggs, marinated chicken feet, eight treasure congee, osmanthus sugar cake, green tea and wheat tea, osmanthus tea, jasmine tea and the new tea of the season.

David put up a sign on the bar with today's activities: "If you have a special variety you like, you can handle discount card activities today. Welcome to visit, buy and book various varieties later."

This free trial tea time, from noon to 6 p.m., for promotional activities recharge card 18,000 yuan.

I did not expect that the soft opening was so successful and loved by so many friends. Everyone said well, here can not only relax reading and rest, but also choose to bring friends to the outdoor sun umbrella to drink tea and talk business, and friends to chat together. There are only three tables of stone benches and three tables of old anti-corrosion wooden chairs outside, it is really a pleasant climate here, like spring all year round, Deng Cheng helped Qin Ying make a detailed walk census data show that outdoor seats will need to be developed to be booked seat business.

After six o 'clock, such as friends have left, Qin Ying let Shen and autumn sweet stay, the decoration accounts.

Did not think of Shen said: "Deng Cheng has all settled, the interior decoration part only labor costs, demolition, installation and purchase of new small electrical equipment and other costs a total of 160,000 yuan Deng Cheng fully paid."

Qin Ying looked at Deng Cheng and said: "Do you still want to let me at ease to manage this rural love bar book?"

Deng Cheng smiled and said: "It does not affect, you see we signed a ten-year contract, this is just the trial period, when you get on the right track, have earnings and then pay me, it is also in time." I'm not waiting for money now, you need money to open a shop."

Qin Ying looked at the Dengcheng in front of this, the heart poured into a lot of sudden dark comparison, what can she say at this time?

Experienced three different periods of different forms of love, Qin Ying full of brain flashed a vague green first love, draw and Cheng Mo flash a few months of virtual online love, and then think of Deng Cheng for her to do so many practical things, silently for her to share all the problems. Standing in front of Deng Cheng, Qin Ying felt steadfast from the heart, the sense of security was Deng Cheng's true feelings, no little rhetoric, all substantively for her to solve problems.

The truth can be seen everywhere.

Chapter 15: The Village Retreat

When being loved appears, Qin Ying feels happiness, fullness, protection, acceptance, calm, attention, and ease. This is what it feels like to be loved. These feelings are Deng Cheng to Qin Ying, she also want to put these ordinary and beautiful gentle pass to Deng Cheng, she already know how to cherish the love now have, she wants to spoil their men peace of mind. Qin Ying, in front of the matchmaker Shen and Qiu Tian, asked affectionately, "Deng Cheng, do you want to marry me?"

Deng Cheng looked at Qin Ying unabashedly and said: "Yes, but I will wait for you to be willing to that day, I give you these are not enough, in my heart you are more important than money."

Qin Ying walked to Deng Cheng, looked at the scenery outside the window and said meaningfully, "You know what? You gave me a platform to do business, and I love everything here. You helped me realize my literary dreams and inspirations ahead of time, and now you have finally made it possible for me to have them ahead of time. I never dreamed that this beautiful day would come so early, so today I express to the friends present that I am willing to live a long life with Deng Cheng and live a secluded village life. There is you, there is the love we built together, the book. And thank you to me and Deng Cheng's matchmakers for introducing me to Deng Cheng. It was a privilege."

Shen total autumn sweet to see them express love to each other warm scene, immediately clapped, pushed Deng Cheng Qin Ying, loudly said: "Deng Cheng rushed up, say it!"

Deng Cheng seriously excited and wooden told everyone: "I have long wanted to wait for the osmanthus trees open, orange, apple tree harvest bearing fruit garden season, I marry you here, hold our wedding ceremony."

Aiba Book Bar is located in the countryside here, with unique natural resources and environment, west of the Wugui Mountain, looking east of the Lingdingyang sea, natural Marine hot springs, 300 acres of natural mangrove ecological area and a large wetland park. The surrounding transportation is convenient, there are Beijing-Zhuhai expressway, western coastal expressway, Shenzhen-China channel, eastern outer ring Guangzhucheng rail, provincial road, community direct bus. Here is close to Zhuhai Tangjia, belongs to Cuiheng New District, home ownership in one step.

Qin Ying think well, Deng Cheng here has laid the foundation of the business all paved the way, the real estate certificate are done in her name, she can not accept it, she has to make good faith for Deng Cheng's pay.

So she prepared two sets of business plans for Love bar book bar:

First, all the profits of the ten years of contract operation are divided into 5:5 to Deng Cheng, and the money invested by Deng Cheng to buy a house and decorate the house is used as the investment cost. It is a form of cooperation for managing technology and management personnel to invest in shares.

Second, the annual operating income of 5:5 is divided into all parts as the cost of returning the investment in the real estate purchased by Deng Cheng, as self-financing, excluding staff salaries and all water and electricity expenses, the net profit of ten years is first used to pay off the house. In short, she can't ask for Deng Cheng's gratuitous support for nothing. Either of the two ways can make the normal development of love bar.

She also knows that writing cannot support herself at present, but Love Bar Book Bar has the right to use this land, which can enable her to build a platform for the development of her entrepreneurial and literary dreams. I believe that she will live up to expectations, she will love the book bar business, become her and Deng Cheng future common business planning happiness harbor.

At present, writing only enriches Qin Ying's life, but running love bar and book bar will make Qin Ying realize her literary dream of being a full-time writer. At that time, it was not clear whether writing supported her, or whether she used the joy of writing to achieve a good life.

Qin Ying did not directly answer Deng Cheng wish, the supplementary terms to Deng Cheng looked at, pointing to his and Deng Cheng common bank account that column blank both formally and mockingly smiled to Deng Cheng said: "After reading please put your account number, name, fill in, so that you will regularly receive dividends into the profit." I agree with what you just said about the idea of the wedding, and I think the scene will receive more blessings at that time."

Deng Cheng saw the supplementary contract, in the heart of a nervous mood, he did not want to be so clear with Qin Ying. Shen always see frozen in place waiting for do not know how to reply to Deng Cheng, take a look at the supplementary project, including Shen witnesses signature column, just to sign, this contract supplement is very formal, Deng Cheng has economic benefits.

Shen always seems to understand Qin Ying's good intentions, she does not want to owe Deng Cheng too much, she wants to separate the love and money, so there is no pressure, she does not want to let the people misunderstand her is in love with Deng Cheng's wealth, and she also has the ability to make money.

Of course, as a woman, in Deng Cheng's mind she is the only satisfied. Qin Ying thought, so she and Deng Cheng really become a family, what can be shared together, but now can not accept such a big gift. If she takes it all, she'll feel uncomfortable. She hopes that marriage must give each other enough balance value, she has always advocated equality between men and women, economic independence, you have the strength, I am also excellent, each other have the potential to earn money, or there is a sense of family, only to make her more practical.

After seeing this supplementary clause, Shen played a round game: "Take a pen to me to sign first, Deng Cheng, you fill in your information and name." That's a good thing. Why are you so stupid? If you sign, you can prove that you recognize Qin Ying has this strength, and manage the love bar book well."

Deng Cheng in Shen and Qin Ying signal, obediently put their bank account to write up. Shen joked: "So good, you can get dividends every month profit." Look at the joint account."

Deng Cheng took out the real estate certificate to Qin Ying, Qin Ying smiled and said: "I understand your mind, or you keep it first."

Qiu Tian smiled to Qin Ying and said: "I was like you at that time, in fact, as long as the person who loves you has this heart, we women are happy." What we women want is a man's undivided love, treating you as if you were his only woman. It goes to your heart."

Qin Ying kept nodding: "Yes, as long as it is serious to me, I am willing to share all the wealth with my lover."

Deng Cheng see Qin Ying is very assertive, at this time said nothing will change Qin Ying's decision, it is better to accept. He understands Qin Ying at this time of the inner thoughts, he is more willing to give Qin Ying a lifetime of peace of mind. Looking at the lover standing beside him, Deng Cheng understood that he had found the right lover in his life. Qin Ying also recall the past experience of emotional objects, they are just passers-by, in front of Deng Cheng is her waiting for years of true love.

Qin Ying heart like a mirror, see clearly, who is true, who is false. She will cherish this solid and sincere good man Deng Cheng.

After Shen finished joking, Deng Cheng naturally signed a supplementary agreement. Think in the mind is to Qinying pre-stored happiness, give Qinying reserves, the income account password, later will be set into Qinying birthday plus shop date numbers, then tell her the password. This is good, Qin Ying has entrepreneurial responsibility may be more able to tap the potential of opening a shop, so that wealth growth unlimited, let its development.

Give Qin Ying more free space to do as she pleases, which may be the most suitable love for Qin Ying to accept, but also make Qin Ying no pressure, and create a bigger life stage for her literary dream.

Deng Cheng thought, as long as Qin Ying is willing to settle down in this village, step down and work hard, Qin Ying put forward any plan, any supplementary agreement he will fully cooperate, so that he will always support closely. His and Qin Ying's love will sow, blossom and bear fruit on this hot land.

Think of here Deng Cheng signed the nib, brush brush brush signed in one go, solemn hands will supplement the contract to Qin Ying: "to you, I want to sign you for a lifetime."

Deng Cheng's words, made everyone laugh, Qin Ying very shy said: "OK, you wait."

Chapter 16: Romance Full House

When there is the love in your life that you have been waiting for, you will feel that everything in your life is so good. Qin Ying felt Deng Cheng to himself is true love, she also chose to believe. Every Monday, Wednesday and Friday, she goes to the city to complete her work as a lecturer, and the rest of the time, she focuses all on the management of Love Bar book bar.

Qin Ying a free with small Becxiaoqin production of natural plant crafts, the use of waste, add beautiful colorful waterproof paint to the country house comprehensive dress up. The outer walls, the large and small stones under the ground, the tree trunks that surround the three sides, the arches and pillars of the courtyard, etc., as long as the eyes see, Qin Ying will paint the passion for life with colors. It is afraid that just passing people will be infected by this romantic warmth.

Two hometown brought out of the girl Xiao Bei and Xiao Qin has deeply realized what is meaningful things, they thank Qin Ying from the heart to them as the master of the village love bar book bar, they admire Qin Ying talent from the bottom of my heart, with her learned a lot of way of life. They never felt that Qin Ying taught them with a lofty attitude, and they volunteered to participate in these transformation work. At first, it was just fun and fun, but after experiencing it, I found that I really enjoy doing these things. To be able to live and work in this picturesque place all year round, they are extremely lucky, because they are always happy and feel that time passes very quickly.

Qin Ying almost to the degree of obsession, every day there is a little unexpected surprise change, triggered Qin Ying more imagination, keep tossing out their favorite design concept. Qin Ying from the heart to the bone are grateful to Deng Cheng to give her so much space to display the stage of life. Qin Ying has realized that a person who really understands himself can give her the happiest love. This is the strength of her confidence in life, but also the true meaning of her revel, she really found her own true love, the love of life is the essential feature of all good things.

Deng Cheng or Monday to Friday time to go to work in the company, a weekend on the initiative to do Qin Ying assistant, Deng Cheng is happy to be Qin Ying ordered to drive to the city, with a list of all kinds of paint and paintbrushes and other tools, and then cooperate with Qin Ying on the rural outdoor plant replanting, physical labor, the ground uneven construction and finishing, to ensure that water and electricity can be used normally.

With the help of Deng Cheng and Shen, the transformation of the rural house exterior progressed more smoothly and quickly. In the twinkling of an eye, in the autumn of the second year, the wall made by the young trees has slowly grown tall, surrounded by flowers, and the transplanted fruit trees have been flourishing.

Looking at this slowly becoming beautiful rural scenery, more and more like the TV series to see the romantic full house as beautiful, the tall and upright several fruit trees, osmanthus trees, has grown new green leaves. Qin Ying by their own hand-built home, let her love this place more. Qin Ying often stood under the apple tree to pray, hoping that the autumn of the next year can realize Deng Cheng and her wishes: we will be here waiting for fruitful, harvest season in sight, the weather is fair, the earth testifying, we will be better and better, happy life.

Another weekend, Shen and Deng Cheng talked mysteriously, while Qin Ying and two employees are still in the love bar book bar, after sending off the last table of guests, Deng Cheng smiled happily and said: "Qin Ying, we can see the miracle moment tonight, you must truly tell us how you feel."

Xiao Bei Xiaoqin took out the prepared staff meal food on the table: "Qin sister sit down quickly, Deng and Shen always have something to say, eat it together."

Qin Ying was shoved to the table to sit down, Shen said: "Now we eat first, busy for a few months, tonight can see the effect, and I can shoot several groups of videos in autumn sweet." Qiu Tian took the camera in the car and went to enjoy our masterpiece later."

Deng Cheng also only smiled and said: "hurry up and eat, after you press the switch power for the ribbon-cutting ceremony."

In Qin Ying single-minded creation of wall painting, Shen and Deng Cheng is not idle, in order to give Qin Ying a surprise, especially in the position to put the light line, let the autumn sweet Qin Ying. The road lighting design outside the whole roof garden is all Deng Cheng wants to increase the charm of the whole love bar book bar at night. Deng Cheng than anyone is looking forward to the arrival of this moment, this is the most romantic gift he gave Qin Ying, he hopes she will fall in love with everything here, including his own such a person.

Qin Ying, like everyone present, finished her food in a moment. Everyone said in unison, "I'm done." Then everyone burst into laughter. Everyone mysteriously please Qin Ying quickly go out, standing under the apple tree, holding Deng Cheng handed over a wireless button. Everyone shouted in unison, "123!" Qin Ying pressed the switch, and first the street lights of the small courtyard lit up along the foot, then the bulbs on the roof shone like stars, and then the stars flickered along the wall to the branches of the trees. At a glance, the saplings around the fence along the small yard are covered with green and red light bulbs, and the small trees look like a group of fireflies jumping and shining. The whole view is a shiny world, where the night scene is surrounded by people who love life. Qin Ying was shocked, she only casually said to Deng Cheng, want the beautiful things in the fairy tale world. That is just the plot of the novel she wrote, really did not think that Deng Cheng but remember in my heart, when she did not know the low-key completion of these things. After months of hard work, Deng Cheng can finally have a good rest tonight.

Shen said, "Qin Ying, is this your romantic full house?" For this, Deng Cheng often recite the words in your novel, Deng Cheng can recite the full text."

Qin Ying was still immersed in the fantasy, did not answer, just smiled stupidly at the sky, a moment to sweep the head of the branches, and then touch the light on the fence around the saplings in the courtyard, as if in the fairy tale world. Qin Ying was moved to say: "Thank you Deng Cheng, thank you for giving me such a good gift, I like good love ah..."

Qin Ying tears, is happy tears, Deng Cheng wooden a little distressed to hug Qin Ying joke: "You guess I see a what light?"

Qin Ying immediately restrained his emotions and asked: "Where? What light? Let me see."

Deng Cheng happy happy laugh: "I said you really believe, your tears ah!"

All the people present were laughed by Deng Cheng's answer, and laughter floated in the air here. In this field, another star-lit country house has been built.

Chapter 17: Creative Peak

Deng Chengyin weekly Monday to hold a company meeting, tonight and Shen completed the courtyard light line, the evening also tried normal power, see the lighting has achieved the desired romantic effect. After everything is ready, although said some reluctant to part, but still have to go back to the city with Shen total husband and wife that night.

Qin Ying's work arrangement is every Tuesday, Wednesday, four, five four days in the company to do training instructors, weekends two days plus Monday can stay in the countryside. Since moving to the countryside as the main day, Qin Ying has stayed in the rural living space is larger than the urban environment. See the quiet countryside scenery, the air filled with thick fragrance, Qin Ying to Deng Cheng left, how also can not sleep, inspiration came, that night suddenly and write another novel at the beginning.

Qin Ying soon entered the writing state when she calmed down in the country house. Several months have passed, many of Qin Ying's essays and short stories have been accepted for publication by short fiction magazines, and the finishing of the second long novel manuscript is almost completed, and new chapters are injected. The third novel is being serialized and updated.

A dazzling has come to the second half of the year, Qin Ying has been the peak of creation, almost one after another have a publishing house editor appointment to talk about publishing matters. Qin Ying really did not think of his novel without Cheng Mo's care, also recommended by other publishing house editors and teachers. My second novel, which has been written for five years, has passed the review draft and is entering the proofreading process for publication. Qin Ying's third novel has been completed, and has been serialized in the paper media to the end of the chapter, and the editors of three publishing houses have made an appointment with her to discuss the specific matters of publication.

This kind of creative efficiency is the life state Qin Ying wants, she likes to write when inspiration comes, Qin Ying's work and life are busy and orderly, happy days feel passed quickly.

Sometimes Qin Ying would rest for a while on the wooden chair in the courtyard, looking at the blue sky, smelling the fragrance of flowers and plants, always let her eyes close for a while, enjoying a daze for a while, and her mind would flash up like a movie in the plot of the novel, a certain paragraph to express the essence or inspiration. At this time, Qin Ying would bring a small book and pen with her hand. Open and record a passage, a scene. Qin Ying maintains the good habit of diligent and persistent literary creation, in addition to the company's training and preparation, leave some time to use in the management of love bar book, the rest of all scattered time, all Qin Ying free play writing golden time. I often wake up at three or four in the morning, and start to write a dream of a clear story idea, and record it with a sentence intentionally on my mobile phone. When I write, I am passionate about creating stories in the novel in a orderly manner, with rich and rich remarks materials. This is the reason why the content of Qin Ying's novels is grounded. In addition, the author wants to express the characters' ideological views and educational significance in the work, and integrates the correct three views into the work to move the readers, which must be higher than the effect of life. Qin Ying has fallen deeply in love with literary creation, which has become an important part of Qin Ying's life. Writing has been unable to give up the state of life, and Qin Ying can not distinguish it. Writing taught her what it meant to be alive.

Sometimes I will wake up naturally, immediately sprinkle water to the small garden flowers and vegetables, walk a few circles, stretch the body, wear headphones to listen to music and music for ten minutes. Then he walked freely again, touched the big fruit trees, osmanthus trees, looked at the vegetable seedlings, and admired the flowers he planted. There are many buds on the flower branches, smelling the subtle fragrance of plants, coming with the wind. She enjoyed the taste of the rain and dew moistening nature, ushered in the morning sunshine, ushered in the sunset dusk, really comfortable. The source of creative inspiration comes from the good times here. The romantic cottage she loved was full of flowers.

Back to the study a sitting at the table, with a cup of coffee, as well as a pot of refreshing tea, Qin Ying in this stay is all day. Only David or Qin can deliver a set lunch on the way, and there are do not disturb signs hanging on the door. The sign was made by Qin Ying herself with a small piece of wood. She drew a petal with colored paint and wrote "Do not disturb!" Four words.

Xiao Bei Xiaoqin knows that there is no need to knock on the door when delivering food, and every time gently put the tray full of food on the designated sofa coffee table, sometimes Xiao Bei will leave a small note of warm advice: Qin sister eat while it is hot, and drink the soup while it is hot.

It is autumn season, looking out of the window, osmanthus trees are covered with yellow osmanthus flowers. The fragrance came to blow Qin Ying's hair, wrote tens of thousands of words of novel content, eyes some distension, Qin Ying will be used to develop some eye exercises, rub the muscles around the eyes to relax. Then turn on the light music, close your eyes and sit on the sofa, after listening to two songs, casually tear the editor teacher mailed her a short story published in this season's publication, saying that it has been included in the cover nomination. A headline writer is a good writer.

Qin Ying is very pleased to open the magazine, selected on the cover to see the small novel "upstairs and downstairs" , this is a very early want to write a small story about the workplace, before the job when you want to write, has been busy survival without taking into account the literary creation of hobbies. I do not know why, to the environment of rural life, always inadvertently think of the past bit by bit, some inspiration from the past emotional stories.

After reading these works in a moment, Qin Ying has attracted the love of more readers, and there is a great happiness. She realized what is suitable for her other half, this person is very important. Isn't it true that many emotional experts have said such a paragraph: "A woman in marriage, if you choose a man as a partner, a woman must choose a man who can achieve your perfect life, give you the world you love, soul freedom, and understand your love."

Qin Ying feel she met, think about Deng Cheng this good man, Qin Ying heart will inexplicably laugh: Deng Cheng you listen, I Qin Ying not you do not marry. This kind of psychic connection and creative motivation is great.

During that time, Qin Ying herself could not believe that her works could be published one after another. The creative source of these periods all came from the support and understanding given by Deng Cheng. Qin Ying found that Deng Cheng understood her heart best, and Deng Cheng often took a road trip with Qin Ying on weekends to visit the historical sites around Zhuhai and Zhongshan. Deng acted as a tour guide, explaining wherever he went. During a tour of Sun Yat-sen's former residence, Qin Ying stood in front of the hall and watched Deng Cheng, a polyglot, patiently explain the story of Sun's revolution to her. Qin Ying to Deng Cheng and a little more worship and respect.

During the period of living in the country house, Deng Cheng and Qin Ying made an appointment to run and climb the mountain in the morning, go to the local town to taste the morning tea, take a walk in the seaside fish woman scenic spot, occasionally watch a movie like young people, and then drive back to the village to drink afternoon tea.

Take a rest in front of their sunny window, looking out the window at the fruit trees, which are slowly full of new leaves and colorful flowers, quietly blooming in front of the sun, and the green grass planted on the ground covers the trees and continues around the house. Qin Ying like and Deng Cheng here has been reading, drinking tea, talking to say endless. Until the evening outside the front yard street lights and tree lights are all lit up - a fairytale world, is the highlight of this rural bookstore. Opened for more than a year, it has been passed around by the villagers and attracted many tourists. When the tourists are tired, they will rest here for a while, drink a cup of tea and eat some rural snacks sticky rice noodles, and don't forget to buy a few more to take away when they leave.

The gift box is specially customized by Qin Ying, which is printed with the characteristics of the rural love bar, wechat signal, the exterior of the entire country house, and the picture of the starry night scene. The guests all like this kind of packaging bag, the publicity effect is very good, there are many guests through the wechat scan code online booking farm snacks. This publicity has also led to the trade of local markets in the local villages, as well as the catering business. Some tourists plan to stay in the countryside for a few days, which leads to the development of rural farmhouses. In order to expand sales, Qin Ying designed a semi-finished glutinous rice flour ball that can be easily heated and eaten with nutrition and vegetarian food as a selling point. This kind of product is in line with the healthy eating life concept at that time, and the product is recognized by customers.

This is a beautiful period of time, is the peak of Qin Ying's literary creation, is also the peak of the management of love bar book bar, but also the growth of love and wealth.

Qin Ying will be in accordance with the terms of the contract every month, to Deng Cheng's account to deposit all the profits, not only wealth, but also her love for Deng Cheng return. Qin Ying likes the process of giving love as she wishes, she enjoys the happiness of these gives, she feels the continuation of a woman's love, must also come up with value sincerity, respond to Deng Cheng's true love for her. Think about one day can and Deng Cheng into the rest of the marriage scene, love each other balanced and relaxed rhythm of life, that is not the ideal scene of Qin Ying love picture?

Qin Ying Meimei thought here, naturally knowingly smiled, she and Deng Cheng such a way of getting along really meet her expectations of love, no constraints, mutual trust, always thinking about each other. This kind of love in action is a hundred times better than just the three words "I love you" out of the mouth.

Deng Cheng feel Qin Ying love and kindness, every time Deng Cheng looked at the front side of Qin Ying face, there will be a kind of unspeakable happiness and satisfaction. "Qin Ying, let's get married now." This several times almost said export, and was restrained, just looking at Qin Ying giggle. Deng Cheng held his excitement, he wanted to give Qin Ying the best and most perfect wedding, he wanted to give Qin Ying a romantic surprise.

Chapter 18: The Unexpected

Deng Cheng lukewarm busy in the company, all spare time is used in the decoration of the whole second floor of the country villa, he wants to do not affect the company's work at the same time, with Shen with the decoration team to finish the decoration work. Deng Cheng present, Shen always meet things can be solved on the spot, so the construction period progress smoothly.

During the renovation period, Qin Ying love bar book bar for the decoration staff to provide working meals and services, in small private room food standards in accordance with Shen general requirements, so that manual labor workers eat delicious, two meat, one vegetarian soup and a little under the food.

Over the course of a year, the villa installed a central air-conditioning system, bought modern equipment such as washing machines and dryers, and customized all-wood furniture. The second floor living room is designed to be warm and comfortable, the two master bedrooms are designed according to the suite, two large vanity, extended on both sides of the coat cabinet, the living room on the side of the large room has an open study, and the two sets of second bedrooms can be used freely without disturbing the master bedroom.

During this period, Deng Cheng never delayed the progress of rural villa decoration due to work, and it was true that he earned money to start a business and build a family. Toward the end of the renovation, Deng Cheng felt tired and sleepy recently, and he planned to go to the hospital for a comprehensive physical examination.

After a morning meeting on Monday, Deng drove to a large hospital in Zhuhai for a thorough examination, only to be called out by a leading expert, Dr. Ye: "Do you have cancer patients in your home?"

Deng Cheng did not want to say: "No cancer relatives, father died naturally, mother died suddenly heart attack."

Dr. Ye said: "From the examination found that you have suffered from the second stage of gastric cancer, treatment should still be able to improve." You need to treat it quickly, or else it could get worse, metastases. You can choose chemotherapy or choose traditional Chinese medicine conditioning, and I suggest you decide on a treatment plan as soon as possible."

Deng Chengmeng, this period of time he felt uncomfortable without appetite, he thought that the body was just too tired, did not think that was actually got the second stage of stomach cancer. Deng Cheng looked at the medical report written on the diagnostic results, a little unsteady standing. Deng Cheng never thought that he will suffer from incurable disease, the doctor's words seem to imply that he can live for another two years, perhaps active treatment is still saved? He and Qin Ying have not yet gone to enjoy a good life, so wait for death?

Deng Cheng dont want to die in the pain of chemotherapy, imagine hair fall until bald, skinny body, he dont want to appear in front of Qin Ying in such a way. That scene is too cruel, did not give Qin Ying love, but on the contrary, his heart is very unwilling.

Deng Cheng did not answer the doctor's questions, holding the medical report silently out of the doctor's office. He trudged helplessly for an unknown amount of time, and sat down on a seat in the hospital flower bed. It happened so suddenly that he could not bear it for a moment, and he did not know who to talk to about it.

Deng Cheng just walked out of the trough of his mother's death, met Qin Ying, a woman who can spend the rest of her life and give him joy and love, happiness has not begun, and suffered such a heavy blow. Deng Cheng thought from time to time and Qin Ying together a pleasant sightseeing scene, such a picture warm and romantic. He promised Qin Ying the rest of his life to give her a better life, he promised to accompany her life, he can not be so gastric cancer was killed.

Slowly calm down Deng Cheng thought again, if his disease really can not be cured, he must cherish the precious time with Qin Ying before going to heaven, and he also want to let Qin Ying the rest of his life without worrying about life. Deng Cheng intends to deal with all things well, but also do something for Qin Ying, so that she can be happy.

Deng Cheng had a plan in mind, and he called the lawyer hired by his company. Lawyer Yan Daming is a trusted good friend of Deng Cheng for many years, Deng Cheng company and his own private legal affairs work, he will all be handed over to lawyer Yan Daming.

The call is urgent, also about to meet in the park near the hospital, Yan Daming thought there must be something important happened. He immediately came after receiving the phone call, see Deng Cheng sitting on a chair in the park, a preoccupied look.

The afternoon sun was fierce and blinding, and the city's autumn wind mixed with the damp smell of the ocean made Deng Cheng look gaunt and old on his face, as if he had not slept well.

Yan Daming went straight to the point: "Is there something urgent that Chairman Deng needs me to do immediately?"

Deng Cheng's voice cracked: "That's right. There are three things to do, and you need to do a notary. First, the company's insurance beneficiary added a name, her name is Qin Ying, is my favorite woman in this life. The second is to share 50% of the total profit of my personal company with Qin Ying. Third, add Qin Ying's name to the ownership of my rural real estate industry, including the property rights certificate of the entire second-floor building." Deng Cheng explained these after the appearance of a lot of relief.

Yan Daming cautiously asked Deng Cheng, "What happened? Can you tell me why?"

Deng Cheng said seriously and resolutely: "I just checked out the second stage of stomach cancer. Qin Ying is the woman I intend to spend the rest of my life with. We had planned to hold a wedding on National Day on October 1. Now that the wedding seems out of the question, I want to love her in this way and let her live for me."

Deng Cheng some choked to say cant go on, eyes red to look at Yan Daming, some topics and swallow back.

After a moment of reflection, lawyer Yan Daming said, "I have a suggestion for Deng Dong. Isn't the company going to hold an annual meeting of top elites in Sanya in September? You can bring a family member or a high-end insurance customer. I suggest inviting your fiancee to accompany you to Sanya this time to witness the development process and achievements of the company since its establishment. In addition, I also want Qin Ying to take good care of you. Handling the transfer of the company's total personal net profit dividends, as well as the property rights of rural houses, I think it is not too late to discuss after the company's annual meeting."

Without thinking, Deng Cheng said, "OK, I promise to do this after the meeting, but I must prepare the written report first, so that I can sign it when I am sober." In addition, please book two air tickets to Qin Ying's hometown Hubei. I want to go to Qin Ying's hometown after holding the company meeting. There is Li Shizhen's hometown, I will go there in the name of health to find some famous Chinese medicine to see a doctor, do conservative treatment. I want to spend more time with Qin Ying, and spend more time with her while taking a rest. I trust you to handle the company's affairs."

Lawyer Yan Daming said seriously, "OK, I will do it according to Deng Dong's opinion." I also think it is a good idea for you to go to Li Shizhen's hometown to look for famous TCM prescriptions. One of my friends suffered from a serious stomach disease and was cured by Chinese medicine. Deng Dong has a good constitution, and Chinese medicine treatment can also remove the root cause of the disease and restore health without any problems. I believe you and Qin Ying this time to Li Shizhen's hometown, will be fruitful."

Deng Cheng suddenly remembered a passage said in Inamori Kazuo's book, about what is the meaning of marriage, which is the most recognized answer he has ever heard: "Not to drag down each other, but to encourage each other in life." There's someone you can talk to about things. When life is tired, comfort and encourage each other. After work, I can have someone to eat with. When you are wronged outside, you can have a warm hug when you come home. Life is too long. You have to have someone to go through the rest of your life with.

Deng Cheng thought of here, he would like to adjust his mentality and actively start Chinese medicine treatment. If you want to marry Qin Ying this good woman, give complete love, you must pour out all. The first is to live well, his heart can not put Qin Ying, he wants to accompany her for the rest of his life.

Yan lawyer saw Deng Cheng full of eyes is Qin Ying that feeling really look, at this moment very hope to be able to meet in the company's Sanya meeting Qin Ying side, see that is how a woman can let Deng chairman give her all the love. In the eyes of Yan Daming lawyer, Yan Daming lawyer clearly saw Deng Cheng that love to Qin Ying sincere, in the critical moment of the disease into the body, Deng Cheng think not themselves, but first consider to solve Qin Ying's worries. No matter what age, appearance, family status, until now lawyer Yan believed that there is true love in the world.

Yan Daming lawyer in the heart is still thinking, if he has cancer, he is absolutely unable to bear, and will not first think about how to use the last time to take care of their loved ones. He felt ashamed for Chairman Deng's people and broad mind, and even unconsciously gushed out moved tears. He met true love for Deng chairman and moved, Deng Cheng to Qin Ying so sincere treatment, Yan Daming this life single, is not yet in love with the celibate, are so moved.

Lawyer Yan Daming was afraid that Deng Cheng would see him in such a tearful state, turned his head and did not dare to face Deng Cheng, turned and waved his hand, and issued a voice from his throat: "OK, rest assured, I will do it."

Chapter 19: The True Embrace

Deng Cheng company held in Sanya a year of high-end meeting time is coming, Deng Cheng conceals the illness after the company's work arrangement, decided to personally issue an invitation to Qin Ying.

This is a special weekend time, since Deng Cheng learned that he has cancer, looking at the familiar scenery in front of him, lamenting the twists and turns of life, how he wants to live without incident! He felt very weak, but did not know how to tell Qin Ying. He wanted to invite Qin Ying in the name of travel vacation to Sanya to participate in the annual meeting of the company, to announce his relationship with Qin Ying, he wanted to live with Qin Ying, will all the good to Qin Ying.

In the courtyard outside the village love bar, Deng Cheng paced around, and finally chose a wooden chair to sit down, looking at the romantic house full of all the good, the mood is difficult to calm, the sunlight makes him feel warm, at this time Deng Cheng relax and close his eyes, thinking of Qin Ying smile, scenes emerge in the mind, lingering.

Qin Ying recently also realized that Deng Cheng mental state is not good, words become less, a preoccupied look. Every time Deng Cheng returns to the countryside on weekends, he feels secure and secure. This weekend Qin Ying have half a day did not see Deng Cheng figure, busy after work followed to find into the yard, see Deng Cheng sitting in the yard.

Qin Ying quietly from the house to Deng Cheng behind, looking at Deng Cheng tired thin face, Deng Cheng closed his eyes to rest, really lovely, but careful Qin Ying feel Deng Cheng something wrong. Because recently watching him eat less and less, I feel that he is always very tired. Qin Ying has been worried that Deng Cheng work is too busy tired.

Qin Ying heart more and more love in front of this man, very want to hug Deng Cheng, so gently walk beside Deng Cheng, hands covered Deng Cheng eyes. At this time, Deng Cheng felt that it was a pair of Qin Ying's soft, delicate and smooth hands, conveying a kind of love between the touch. Deng Cheng's emotions like the upwelling up in his heart, he did not want to open his eyes, he wanted to Qin Ying so covering his eyes, he enjoyed this feeling. After falling in love with Qin Ying, he has never had such close physical contact, he and Qin Ying are deliberately restrained their desires, especially the kind of love and love revealed in the eyes when the line of sight intersects.

Deng Cheng want as long as can see Qin Ying he will be satisfied, because he knows to give Qin Ying the best life, not just a little touch of men and women's pleasure. He knows Qin Ying is a good woman, he understands Qin Ying self-discipline and stick to the emotional bottom line, more know they both belong to mature and stable people. Because of this, so they can understand each other's advantages, go closer and closer, physical and mental pleasure to enjoy that quiet Zhiyuan happiness.

Deng Cheng feel Qin Ying palm warmth, and want to open your eyes to see Qin Ying. Catch Qin Ying's hand stroked both sides of his cheeks, like covering his heart. Deng Cheng wanted to say to Qin Ying: "Dear, I really want to go on like this forever, I am in your world, I am in your heart, every day and every second, you are by my side."

Qin Ying's hand was kissed by Deng Cheng, prohibited from hugging Deng Cheng, wrapped around Deng Cheng's ear and gently said: "How can today be so quiet so nice?" Do you have anything on your mind or to tell me?"

Deng Cheng looked at Qin Ying affirmatively nodded and said: "Say you are a talented woman, you still do not believe, guess, I will give you what good news?"

Qin Ying smiled sweetly and said, "Dear, there is really good news, so tell me quickly."

Deng Cheng sold official language and said happily: "There are two good things.

First, I formally invite you to attend the high-level meeting of the company; Second, immediately afterwards take me to your hometown, visit your family, and look for a famous Chinese medicine cure for one of my sick friends. By the way, we also put aside our busy work and enjoy the natural scenery in the Princess Villa Hotel in your hometown. Do you accept the assignment?"

Surprised and delighted, Qin Ying asked, "Why did you suddenly promise to accompany me back to my hometown?" I invited you to check it out before, but you have a lot of work to do. What is it that wakes you up? Tell me anything else. It can't be that simple, can it?"

Deng Cheng was afraid of Qin Ying entanglement to break the casserole to ask, so Qin Ying said: "No, quickly get ready to go back to your hometown." You are about to meet your family, how can you introduce me?"

Qin Ying was embarrassed and smiled stupidly and said, "Me, just say that you are my big butler, how do you want to introduce?" Let's hear it?"

Deng Cheng did not think about how to introduce himself in front of Qin Ying family, just want to let Qin Ying promised down his invitation. Then let it go, as long as you can hide the illness, step by step. The current time is really too precious for Deng Cheng, he feels that life is fragile, he must race with time to do things well.

At present, he just wants to do more things for Qin Ying, silently praying for a miracle in his heart, and firmly believing that Chinese medicine can cure his cancer disease. The doctor also said that adjusting the optimistic and cheerful attitude will have a good impact on the treatment. And isn't lawyer Yim Daming's friend cured? Deng Cheng comfort himself at the moment, only believe, take active action, early to find a famous medical expert to treat, and then obey the will of God!

Qin Ying saw that Deng Cheng really could not ask anything, he pointed Deng Cheng's head with his finger and said: "You don't say yes, see if I found your secret, I must take care of you."

Say that, Qin Ying will Deng Cheng wound more tightly, hair was blown to Deng Cheng's face, just covered Deng Cheng has red eyes. Deng Cheng restrain his emotions, he knows he is not a liar, in front of his beloved woman, he saw Qin Ying innocent smile, more can not let Qin Ying know he has cancer. He couldn't bear to see Qin Ying sad for him, he thought he still had the chance to fight with cancer, and the last chance for Chinese medicine treatment. Less than a last resort, with Deng Cheng's character, he is in any case can not say to Qin Ying condition, he hopes a miracle.

With such an idea, Deng Cheng took back the sadness and helplessness in the depths of his heart, quickly turned around and hugged Qin Ying from behind, tightly and gently snuggled together. Taking advantage of Qin Ying invisible moment, Deng Cheng tearful face, deep in Qin Ying clothes back. He carefully wiped away his tears, and then slowly let go until he was calm again. Really afraid Qin Ying see his fragile side, dare not think Qin Ying will be how to face such things. Although Deng Cheng is a man, he can usually find the answer to everything in contemplation. When things happen to him, he also shows from his resume. He worried that the mind heavy appearance, will be delicate Qin Ying see what. Qin Ying is a writer herself, with a smart eye for capturing material in real life and a quick mind. In order to escape Qin Ying questioning, Deng Cheng really spent a lot of thought, he has been contradictory play to avoid Qin Ying long talk, afraid of a long time can not go down.

What happened recently really made him a little unprepared, but fortunately with the cooperation of Yan Daming lawyer, not only to take care of all the business of the company for himself, but also to do some important private affairs for him, almost his private secretary. The celibate Yan Daming, working around Deng Cheng stayed for more than 20 years, advocating not marriage he saw Deng Cheng to Qin Ying so infatuated, he also began to believe that there is still true love in the world.

Deng Cheng most assured trust Yan Daming lawyer, with Yan Daming's friend through the precedent of traditional Chinese medicine to cure cancer, Deng Cheng will have comfort and hope to live. He understood that to make time for treatment, but also from their own mindset change, career, work, money is more important than life. Everyone knows that in addition to life is their own, what else can not take away, wealth is zero.

If the fate does not care for Deng Cheng, he is also prepared to accept the status quo, he will be prepared for both hands, in the limited life more accompany Qin Ying, the happiness to her. All about the transfer of wealth called Yan Daming to do, in Deng Cheng seems to be normal. He should take good care of his beloved people, let Qin Ying happy, even if he really did not save, really want to go, to heaven he will bless Qin Ying can live happily. He believes that Qin Ying will always remember his true feelings, must be no one can replace the love, let her life without regret.

Qin Ying who is favored more and more feel Deng Cheng delicate and considerate care, she is also more and more dependent on Deng Cheng this unforgettable love, the two of them so quietly embrace, quietly feel the happiness of embracing love.

The two of them spent the afternoon in the country yard. Until the evening sunset, when the sun was fading away, smelling the fragrance of osmanthus flowers and grass leaves, they were intoxicated, you and I have you, two people in the courtyard chair side by side, holding hands, admiring the romantic house they had built, two people laugh from time to time.

This afternoon Deng Cheng mobile phone set mute state, Yan Daming made a lot of calls and sent Deng Cheng information he did not notice, do not know whether there is something tricky happened.

Chapter 20: Never Leave

Yan Daming see Deng Cheng did not answer the phone, had to leave a message on wechat: "Deng Dong, urgent interview, I have found the man who can cure stomach cancer." It is suggested that you fly to Hubei on the evening of the company meeting. I have booked the air tickets from Sanya to Hubei for you and Qin Ying. Now I will send the detailed address of the famous doctor to your mobile phone, please keep it. Qin Ying is a local, I suggest that you should explain to Qin Ying that she has suffered from the second stage of cancer, so as to facilitate the timely formulation of treatment plans with famous doctors and not delay the time. Please be prepared to attend the Sanya conference first and then fly to Hubei."

When Deng Cheng saw the mobile phone information, he was dining with Qin Ying in the book bar. Qin Ying see Deng Cheng recent appetite is not good, specially cooked chicken stew, want to give Deng Cheng supplement nutrition. Qin Ying see Deng Cheng take out the mobile phone to see is preoccupied, do not know what happened, he said: "Don't look at the mobile phone, quick peace of mind to drink soup." What is more important than your meal now?"

Deng Cheng immediately returned to his mind: "Qin Ying, the company just sent a message to tell me that you have arranged a plane ticket to Sanya with me for a meeting, and we will leave the day after tomorrow, let us prepare our luggage." Due to tight time, we will fly to your hometown Hubei on the night of the meeting. We have arranged personnel to pick us up at the airport and take us directly to the hotel. I'll head back to town today to get some information and personal luggage for the meeting. And don't forget to be ready for me to pick you up on the day of the meeting."

Qin Ying said, "I know, there are still two days left." Now you must eat well and drink soup, rest well, and have enough to eat and drink. You're usually not in a hurry, but you're so upset about this little thing. It's not like you. Eat the soup before it gets cold."

Qin Ying words let Deng Cheng realize his confusion, immediately adjust themselves, pretend to be nonchalant, very give face to eat up. A pair of Wolf appearance, amused Qin Ying. Deng Cheng see Qin Ying smile blossom happy appearance, seems to have forgotten his disease. If Qin Ying has been around, Deng Cheng's illness seems to be half better, how important is the spiritual pillar of people! Deng Cheng heart is like this, began to look forward to Chinese medicine treatment, the kind of want to live with Qin Ying power, formed a strong desire to survive. He thought he must fight cancer and actively cooperate with treatment. There is a strong desire to restore the body to health as soon as possible.

Three days later, the high-end elites who attended the conference gathered in the airport waiting hall on time. Deng Cheng early in the morning to receive Qin Ying, two people have been in the company's crowd, Deng Cheng arranged Qin Ying sitting on the nearest seat. There is still half an hour before the security check, Deng Cheng put his bag into Qin Ying's hand and looked at the time on the watch: "You look at the ticket and ID bag, I go to the bathroom first."

There were a lot of people in the hall, Qin Ying looked at Deng Cheng's familiar back, until she could not see it. This time Deng Cheng bag phone rang up, Qin Ying looked left and right to see Deng Cheng has not come out, the mobile phone has rung three times, it seems to be a very urgent thing. Qin Ying afraid of miss Dengcheng important things, so not so much, hurriedly open the bag to take out Dengcheng mobile phone press the key to answer the phone. Qin Ying did not have time to speak, the voice on the other end of the phone came over: "Deng Dong, I am afraid that you are busy forgetting, I took you back in the hospital, the expert diagnosed your cancer report and the film are put into your file information bag, and the information bag inside the contact information and detailed address of spring famous doctors." Our company has arranged the layout of the meeting venue in Sanya, waiting for the arrival of the meeting personnel. You can rest assured that the security check is about to begin. Your mobile phone contains the information I have sent you in recent days. If I see no reply from you, I will call you to talk about it. Hey, hey, hey? Are you listening, Deng? Why is it so noisy over there? Why didn't I hear you? Hello, Deng Dong, is the cell phone signal bad? Is it at security?"

Qin Ying heard obedient that came from the voice, she does not know who is, but know Dengcheng recently very abnormal reasons, the original DengCheng cancer! How can this happen, how I don't know at all, just feel that he is thin, I did not take good care of Deng Cheng, I also ignored him, how to do! What am I supposed to do now? Deng Cheng is still hiding from me!

Waiting hall has begun the ticket queue, Qin Ying quickly hung up the phone, and saw the name of Yan Daming lawyer sent Deng Cheng text message content: "In addition, Deng Dong you account for the transfer of Qin Ying's rural house property certificate, as well as your company's dividend insurance beneficiary Qin Ying notarial certificate, I have prepared the legal documents also brought, to the meeting free time, please look at and sign it." Please rest assured that the first task at present is to put down work, actively cooperate with traditional Chinese medicine treatment and conditioning, everything will be better."

Qin Ying swept a few eyes to see the information content, hurriedly put the mobile phone back to Deng Cheng handbag, eyes to the bathroom direction anxiously looked. Qin Ying mood at the moment like a roller coaster, suspended in mid-air, her heart panic, even dont know what can say after seeing Deng Cheng. Blame him for hiding the truth? Or can do something for him, such as clearly tell him: cancer is not terrible, with me by your side, no matter what happens, no matter how the future, I will never abandon you. Dear Deng Cheng, I will always love you, this is what I want to say to you. Remember, you still have me. As long as you can get better, I would rather not anything, I just have you, you are more important than money wealth! How can you still be so stupid? Still thinking about me at this hour. I met you in a foreign land, I only choose you in this life, I would like to be with you in this life.

These words in the mind of Qin Ying kept emerging, Qin Ying want to find a suitable opportunity to Deng Cheng confession, her heart only Deng Cheng, she does not care who should take the initiative to propose, she only knows that she wants to give Deng Cheng confidence, Deng Cheng will be better. I told you, good men live in peace!

Deng Cheng go to the bathroom, Qin Ying accidentally heard and saw Yan Daming to Deng Cheng information, Qin Ying found that things are much more serious than she imagined. Mr. Deng seemed reluctant to break the news to her.

At this time Deng Cheng more need Qin Ying around, Qin Ying determined to spend the rest of his life with Deng Cheng, accompany him to face life positively. The mood has a great impact on cancer patients, and many people face the fact that they have cancer and are overwhelmed by the pressure of reality. Qin Ying tried to take good care of him. Deng Cheng came back from the bathroom, still try to behave as usual, Qin Ying also pretend nothing happened. Both had something on their minds.

Queue to Qin Ying soon, Deng Cheng to catch up with the team. Qin Ying has let three of the company's people go through security procedures first, Qin Ying looked at the sweating Deng Cheng, busy distressed to take out paper towels, help wipe the sweat on Deng Cheng's face, restrain his inner waves, placate Deng Cheng ridicule: "I'm afraid you fell into the bathroom." There's still time. There's no hurry. You got diarrhea? Are you all right?"

Deng Cheng smiled and said, "It's not all your fault, eating soup every day must be too good." Nothing. It's much easier now."

The two boarded the plane and sat side by side in first class. Sitting on the plane to Sanya, they can finally have a good rest, the chase along the way, Deng Cheng felt a little tired. This trip is like two people on vacation, enjoying a romantic trip. Two people on the plane looking at each other, Deng Cheng found Qin Ying this white sportswear dress is so sunny and healthy, his thoughts myriad: his sick body can give Qin Ying happiness? So hide Qin Ying, but also want to marry her as a wife, so appropriate? Deng Cheng heart contradictions, dont know should not propose to her.

Fate is so absurd, finally met her, but he may not be able to accompany her down; However, it is possible to fully recover after treatment, when the illness did not happen, he then bravely proposed to Qin Ying of course.

Qin Ying found Deng Cheng face spirit dim a lot, body also thin. She looked out the window at the wide sky. The plane was flying high in the blue sky and white clouds. At this moment, the voice of the stewardess sounded on the radio: "Dear passengers, please fasten your seat belts, the plane has encountered tropical airflow and entered a thunderstorm and gale weather, please do not walk around, the bathroom is closed."

There was some commotion in the cabin and everyone was suddenly Shouting. "What to do? What's going on? Why are you so unlucky?" At this time, the voice of the stewardess came over the radio: "Everyone don't panic, please listen to the radio instructions quietly."

Everyone held their breath and listened quietly to the stewardess explain the escape knowledge and the impact of the air flow, and everyone's face looked very serious. Just like the plane is about to explode and crash, at this time the top of the plane came with the sound of impact friction with the air flow, and everyone clearly heard the sound of solicitation. Care about the external temporary, people will appear so small, the distance between life and death is calculated in minutes and seconds.

Qin Ying and Deng Cheng's hands were clasped together and they stared at each other. At the same time, they could not help but blurt out: "Dear, I have something to say to you." "Qin Ying, I'm sorry, I have to tell you something, I hid something from you."

Qin Ying covered Deng Cheng's lips with his hand, looked at Deng Cheng affectionately and said: "I say first, I don't want to make it clear before the accident." I love you, no matter what happens to you, no matter what happens to you, I will always love you, and I will always be with you, never part."

Deng Cheng also rushed to Qin Ying: "Dear, I love you too, I can spend the rest of my life to accompany you." If there is no accident, I will leave all the beauty and love to you. With you by my side, I feel nothing to fear, even to die together. Is this an act of God? I have no regrets in this life! There's something else I'm not telling you, and it's not too late, and I wanted to keep it from you my whole life. Now I have stage 2 stomach cancer, I never want you to worry about me, I just want to leave you with joy and happiness. So you don't blame me for keeping this a secret? Before I die, I tell you everything, and it's easier to have no secrets. What else do you have to say to me? You speak, and I'll listen."

Qin Ying has been in tears, Deng Cheng in turn to hug her: "Dear, don't do this, see you cry, I feel uncomfortable, almost cry." People who don't know, still think I bully you?"

Qin Ying beat Deng Cheng with a small fist on the body, sobbing, choking out: "You are a big bad guy, the worst bad guy, I hate you to hide everything from me, I hate you would rather a person to support these mental pressures." I want you to marry me, I want you to marry me, for the rest of my life, and we'll never be apart, okay? Promise me!"

Deng Cheng was blurred by tears in his eyes, he wiped away the tears for Qin Ying, smiled happily and said: "I promise you, I will marry you." We'll be all right."

Perhaps even the sky was touched by their love, the plane bumpy 15 minutes after passing through the stormy air, the system showed that it had returned to normal operation. On the radio came the voice of the stewardess: "Hello, everyone, we have passed through the storm air, everything is back to normal, but everyone do not move around." We only have one hour and 40 minutes to go to the beautiful city of Sanya in Hainan Province."

The cabin suddenly burst into cheers, Deng Cheng tightly hugged Qin Ying, they both experienced the test of life and death. See nestled in the arms of Qin Ying face of tears, two people laugh at each other. So they quietly waited for the plane to land safely.

Chapter 21: The Heart Follows the Heart

The plane finally landed safely in Sanya airport, Deng Cheng and Qin Ying out of the gate, saw lawyer Yan Daming waiting there to receive Deng Cheng. Yan Daming looked at the intellectual and elegant woman around Deng Cheng in surprise, nodded and smiled politely, walked next to Deng Cheng and quietly said: "This is the future sister-in-law Qin Ying right?" No wonder Deng Dong was obsessed. Now I understand. Let's go straight to the hotel, it's all arranged."

Deng Cheng unabashedly said to Yan Daming: "You not only matched the number, you also talked to her through the phone, which also have to thank you, my lawyer Yan." This is my fiancee Qin Ying." And to Qin Ying introduced: "This is my company lawyer Yan Daming, you have a good formal acquaintance."

Lawyer Yan Daming immediately changed the topic and said, "First go to the hotel to rest, and hold the meeting at 10:00 in the morning, in the conference room on the 16th floor of the hotel." I'll give you 10 minutes' notice."

Deng Cheng took the hotel room card in the hands of Yan Daming, handed Qin Ying a, two people followed Yan Daming came to the bus, the car then asked: "Shen and autumn sweet husband and wife arrived? We'll have to go and see them first, we'll have something to say."

Yan Daming smiled and said, "I know Deng Dong will not forget his friends, it has been arranged, right across the door in room 107, you are 106." The rooms are suites, one size."

Qin Ying could not help laughing and said: "Don't worry, take your time, there is plenty of time." I also happen to have something to say to autumn sweet, we love the book bar later a few months have to let Shen and autumn sweet two people more exercise dim sum. During the epidemic prevention and control period, the physical store is not open for business, do a good job of selling special cooked food products online, and rely on Xiaoqin Xiaobei two people, only do local old customers business. "We focus on online delivery services."

Yan Daming looked at Deng Cheng with a puzzled face, that meaning clearly asked: "Qin Ying know your disease?"

Deng Cheng patted Yan Daming's shoulder and said, "I went to the bathroom when you called me, and the phone was answered by Qin Ying." Thank you very much, finally let me breathe, otherwise I feel uncomfortable."

Yan Daming this only dare to respond positively to Qin Ying said: "Not have the intention to hide from you, because I have a friend is also got this disease, people really recovered through Chinese medicine treatment." We Deng Dong is also kind, afraid you know after one more worry, want to wait for the cure to tell you. Don't you, Deng Dong?"

Qin Ying calmly accepted the reality and said to lawyer Yan: "Thank you, Lawyer Yan. Deng Cheng has you as a friend, I am very happy, and very relieved. With you in the company, Deng Cheng can go to my hometown to have a good rest and recuperate, and he will surely recover."

The 20-minute journey along the way in the chat, soon arrived, the car stopped at the door of the beautiful villa hotel, where each villa balcony directly through the natural swimming pool, a night of hotel accommodation cost is 3600 yuan, a villa is divided into six large suites, we can share the hall, kitchen, bar. The indoor supporting facilities are perfect and complete.

Came to the hotel to rest for a moment, rushed out of the shower after two people in a much better state of mind, Qin Ying and Deng Cheng put on clothes to attend the meeting, and then sounded Shen and autumn sweet room. Three sounds, the door opened, autumn sweet thought is the waiter, did not react, see standing at the door is Deng Cheng and Qin Ying, surprise shouted: "Old Shen, is Deng Dong and Qin Ying come!" Come in and sit down. The meeting starts in half an hour."

Shen smiled to meet Deng Cheng and said: "This conference accommodation specification is more comfortable than our home, I just said to my wife Qiu Tian, I have decorated the house all my life, but I have never enjoyed such a high-end hotel, this is with Deng Cheng your light yo!"

Deng Cheng: "I am relieved that you and Autumn sweet are satisfied, so, there is not much time, we go to the conference room, while talking." I have something to ask of you both."

A line of four people together to the meeting room, Deng Cheng said with Shen total men to account for things, Qin Ying put love bar book can not put things account to autumn sweet. Of course, Qin Ying told the truth to accompany Deng Cheng back home for a period of vacation. She is not in the shop time, let autumn sweet more accompany to take care of the store of small celery small bey, two girls need to have a look after each other.

Qiu Tian said with emotion: "To see you can face it with such optimism, I am really happy for you, everything will be fine." It's okay. You can count on it. I got you. I think of it as my home, and I go there every day to be with them."

Autumn sweet can no longer say, say out the words, a listen to know throat choked. Although Qin Ying tone seems to be very relaxed, like comforting himself is also comforting autumn sweet, but the heart of autumn sweet is some panic and sadness. She thought Deng Cheng such a good friend, how can have stomach cancer second stage? The couple, whom she and Shen set up together, are preparing to harvest love and hold a wedding ceremony in the autumn. That way, there's no telling how long the wait will be. Autumn sweet worry they can still get married?

Qin Ying saw autumn sweet secretly want to cry, busy holding the hand of autumn sweet said: "How you think in your heart, I know." Don't worry about us. Deng Cheng and I have it all figured out. This time I don't want to go back to my hometown, that is, to take good care of my body in my beautiful hometown. With Chinese medicine treatment, it will be better. There is a famous doctor in my hometown who has already had friends who have cured him. So rest assured, don't worry about Deng Cheng, I will be at ease to accompany him, take care of him. When he recovers, he will return to our love bar and get married."

Deng Cheng dont know when to go to Qin Ying behind, looking at his love of the woman, hear Qin Ying comfort autumn sweet words, suddenly found himself the happiest man in the world. Deng Cheng full of eyes love the woman, not wrong at all, Qin Ying is a good woman, really deserve to have happiness. He must live a good and healthy life, must fulfill his promise, always love Qin Ying, give her a lifetime of companionship, not only wealth. Qin Ying needs the company of love, then this man is I Deng Cheng.

Deng Cheng did not disturb Qin Ying and autumn sweet talk, listen to the voice, his nose has been sour. When he was about to turn around and leave, Lawyer Yan waved to Deng Cheng and shouted: "Deng Dong, you can take a seat, the meeting is about to start, you are the first to speak, please come into the venue!"

This cry brought autumn sweet and Qin Ying back to reality, this time two talents found Deng Cheng on the other side of the column they were leaning against. Qin Ying thought, what she said must have been heard by Deng Cheng, or Deng Cheng how red eyes?

What can we do? Will you speak on stage later? Can you speak well in such a mental state? Qin Ying some remorse, should not say these sad things to autumn sweet at this time.

After entering the venue, everyone soon quieted down, and the host said a few words after asking Deng Cheng to speak on stage. Qin Ying has never participated in the meeting activities of Deng Cheng company, this is the first time to see Deng Cheng on the stage. Qin Ying looked at the prince in her heart a little infatuated: Deng Cheng a suitable dark blue suit, with a red tie, temporary blow hair. Although he has lost a lot of weight, his figure is tall and upright, and a man's gentlemanly demeanor is shown just right. Qin Ying looked at his sweetheart standing on the stage, and felt Deng Cheng walking to the front of the stage at first glance to look at himself, and paused for three seconds on his body.

Deng Cheng first expressed his gratitude to the audience, thanked everyone for their support and trust over the years, and wished everyone to find a new insurance type in the new insurance project organized by the company. This policy enables the insured to enjoy a lifetime of security. Finally, he wished everyone a good time during the meeting.

Deng Cheng's speech mobilized the atmosphere of the meeting, and the next meeting atmosphere was very warm, and it was time for lunch unconsciously. This is the highest grade of the ocean buffet for guests, there are hundreds of food patterns, to provide all guests with red wine, white wine, beer, and a variety of hot and cold drinks for guests to enjoy.

Qin Ying in the peripheral search Deng Cheng shuttle in the crowd figure, aftertaste Deng Cheng from the stage after the speech, directly went to her side, inch by inch, I can see Deng Cheng dont want to let Qin Ying feel strange. I am glad to have good friends Shen, Autumn sweet and Yan Daming lawyers around. Qin Ying can feel Deng Cheng's care, his careful and considerate warm Qin Ying's heart.

In the banquet hall Deng Cheng quietly told Qin Ying: "You eat more today, this is your favorite crab, male crab meat is more, you eat a few more, and drink more black chicken soup."

Deng Cheng only pay attention to Qin Ying like to eat things, all with Qin Ying walked around, introducing the name of the delicious dish. Qin Ying plate is full, Deng Cheng started to take their favorite food to eat. Shen sum autumn sweet in turn sitting Qin Ying table.

Outside the window, the sun is shining brightly, and the green plants and colorful flowers look beautiful in any way. Qin Ying know just stay one day, but feel very familiar with the environment here, like seen in a dream scene. She felt accompanied by Deng Cheng, where will feel kind, care, there is no Deng Cheng fear of strangeness. Qin Ying likes everything here, because there are no good friends here to talk about, and there is no sense of loneliness when staying with friends.

In this scene full of guests, Qin Ying suddenly relaxed a lot. See Deng Cheng sunny smile, she heart like and admire this can let her heart, can accompany her for a lifetime of men, she is glad that she is waiting to love his good man, with Deng Cheng infatuations, Qin Ying heart already have a sense of belonging.

Qin Ying is in a good mood at the moment, she is crazy for love Deng Cheng, with the feelings of a young girl, with a heartbeat, who says the girl is not in love, is a beautiful emotion will make the little woman cherish, but before not too embarrassed to say it. Qin Ying looked up, see Deng Cheng also staring at her, eyes honest and captivating, these two people four eyes line of sight has been electric, can not hide.

Chapter 22: The Capital of Qai

In the afternoon meeting, Deng Cheng only showed his face. In order not to alarm the other people who attended the meeting, the news of Deng Cheng suffering from cancer was not revealed, the company only Yan Daming lawyer know this matter. If someone asks why Deng Cheng left, he will cooperate with Deng Cheng to make a reasonable explanation.

After coming out of the conference hall, Deng Cheng met Qin Ying directly at the gate of the villa. Shen sum autumn sweet has helped Qin Ying Deng Cheng luggage on the vehicle to the airport, see Deng Cheng out hurriedly comfort said: "Rest assured leave, good fun, here I and autumn sweet." Have a safe trip, we are waiting for you and Qin Ying's wedding wine!"

Qin Ying reluctantly and autumn sweet goodbye, Qin Ying after the car buried his head into Deng Cheng's arms: "rest for a while on the road, we can finally take a good vacation, must be a good health."

Deng Cheng held Qin Ying's hand and said, "We are going to your hometown, which is also the hometown of Li Shizhen, the national treasure of Chinese medicine." I'm not sick, drink Chinese herbal soup, promise to cure me. Don't worry, I have the confidence."

Qin Ying took advantage of this topic and said to Deng Cheng: "Let me tell you a story, there is an old man named Starax, he was diagnosed with advanced lung cancer by doctors in the United States in 1976." The doctors told him he only had nine months left to live. Considering the high cost of medical treatment in the United States, he insisted on returning to his hometown to spend his last days. He refused all chemotherapy. After returning to the countryside, sleep to wake up naturally every day, eat what you should eat, drink what you should drink, optimistic attitude. Every day in the sun, do some fishing and planting flowers and vegetables, chat with the local villagers, walk and do some interesting farm work. The doctor was sentenced to nine months of time, alive and well. In this way, he lived until the age of 104, becoming the local longevity old man.

The family sent the old man to the hospital to check his whole body, only to find that the cancer cells had disappeared, but the doctors who diagnosed him had died early. The old man did not take any medicine or chemotherapy, he was just enjoying daily life, forgetting time, forgetting that he was a patient. This true story is available on the website. In fact, many of us do not die from cancer itself, but this fear and resistance to cancer makes them lose hope and lose their lives.

Scientists visited the old man's hometown of Decca and were unable to find out, except that the old man ate all natural, unprocessed foods, and the cheapest foods were the healthiest dietary remedies. The old man also has a good schedule, he has the habit of taking a nap, when the body wants to sleep, which is very important. This example illustrates everything, health depends on their own heart, to see what kind of mentality a person lives. To be less angry and more tolerant of others is to let go of oneself. Remember only the good things, you can find the meaning of your life in the ordinary life. I think you must also be in the patient to live to 100 years old, we have a happy mood together, enjoy the beautiful oxygen bar time, you will be better and better. You are not ill, but you have promised to stay with me all my life."

Deng Cheng listen to Qin Ying finished the story after, really from the downturn realized a lot of truth, the heart is much easier. Yeah, don't worry too much, live like a fool, go for it, as if every day is the last day, and the remaining time is a good day to earn. Deng Cheng advised himself, there is nothing can not, I have a good physique, the old man is late lived to 104, I am still young, still only the second phase, there is no reason not to live well.

Qin Ying heard Deng Cheng say so, repressed in the heart of worry no, Qin ying of traditional Chinese medicine to cure Deng Cheng disease is very confident. Talking along the way, I unknowingly arrived at the airport in Sanya. The sun was shining high here, and the wind under the blue sky and white clouds was hot on my face. Just in time, waiting in line for security and getting a boarding pass. Mr. Yan is so thoughtful. He booked the first class for two people. It's spacious and comfortable. This Southern Airlines service is very good, after the stewardess handed two towels blanket, Qin Ying told Deng Cheng before takeoff said: "After taking off, you have a good sleep, don't think nonsense, have a dream we are here." There is a hotel car service back home to pick us both up."

Deng Chengzhen obedient, after the plane started to take off, covered the towel blanket to close the eyes and rest, soon began to snore, sleep very sweet and solid.

Qin Ying can not be idle, do a good job in the effect of agistrodon wormwood data collection and sorting. When I saw the blog post of Li Shizhen's hometown introduction, I looked at it with more confidence.

Qin Ying intently stared at the contents of the computer: the world wormwood to see China, Chinese wormwood to see Qichun, the home has three years of ai, the doctor does not have to come. "Compendium of Materia Medica" recorded "moxibustion sickness".

Mention this millennium herbs, Qichun people are full of pride, in a short span of ten years, Qicai industry chain from scratch. A variety of Qidai health products, including moxa sticks, moxa velvet, moxa cake and other traditional raw materials; Moxibustion paste, eye paste, foot paste, neck paste, waist paste and other moxibustion paste; Chinese mugwort essential oil, Chinese mugwort foot bath, Chinese mugwort daily chemical and other products have been popularized in the lives of people in Qiqi Township, and the good prescription for the treatment of Dengcheng gastric cancer must be found in the blue sea of great health.

Qichun moxibustion treatment method originated from the medical sage Li Shizhen's Compendium of Materia Medica. It is a local moxibustion method with obvious regional characteristics and is based on authentic Qichun moxibustion material. Qichun's major health industry led by Qichun has developed vigorously, inheriting Qichun moxibustion therapy and spreading traditional Chinese medicine culture, which has been praised by international patients.

Traditional Chinese medicine characteristic treatment: moxibustion in the emperor - Dao pulse moxibustion. The median line of the back of the human body, that is, the distance from the cervical spine to the tailbone, runs through the main body of Yang. The ancients called it "the sea of Yang veins" . The pulse, as its name, is like the ocean, which gathers the Yang of the whole body meridians, and transports and disperses these Yang to the skin of the whole body surface, plays the function of warming the body and resisting external evil.

Moxibustion is the king of moxibustion! Moxibustion on the governor's vein, with the help of the governor's Yang, stimulates the body's own Yang, and transmits this warmth layer by layer to the whole body through the complex and orderly meridians system, restoring the body's self-healing power.

Moxibustion treasure, moxibustion smoke, moxibustion area is large, temperature control is convenient. A treasure in hand, can moxibustion Du pulse, can also moxibustion Ren pulse, very convenient. Patients can expel moisture from the body through moxibustion, because after Ai heat enters the human body, it can promote blood circulation and activate the meridian, remove moisture, and relieve back pain and various body discomfort. "Compendium of Materia Medica" has such a sentence: "Qimoxibustion all diseases."

Along the way Qin Ying consulted a lot of traditional Chinese medicine treatment of patients with a variety of true stories, more understanding of the Chinese herbal medicine culture to people's lives to bring help, saved countless patients suffering, saved has been diagnosed as not much time for cancer patients, they have overcome the disease to live to more than 100 years old people, this is the essence of Chinese herbal medicine 慱 . Qin Ying looked at the cultural inheritance of wormwood in her hometown, and a little comfort gave her confidence.

Qin Ying heard the voice of the stewardess announcing: "Passengers, the plane will land in 20 minutes, please fasten your seat belts."

Deng Cheng was awakened by the sound of the radio, this sleep is really deep. See Qin Ying just close the computer, concerned to ask: "You did not rest ah?" Writing novels again?" Qin Ying tender pulse silent, meaning you guess.

Soon the plane landed safely, and as soon as they left the lobby, they saw the hotel staff holding up a sign with their two names. Yan Daming arrangements really in place. The staff took the two large luggage boxes of Deng Cheng and Qin Ying, the two of them smiled and followed the hotel staff into the parking lot.

Along the way, Qin Ying saw the rapid changes in his hometown, feeling both familiar and unfamiliar. This was the city she was going to, known as the capital of Qichun, where Qin Ying grew up as a child.

Less than an hour's drive, quickly arrived Qichun Princess Villa Hotel, which is the most suitable for health of the local famous hotel.

Qin Ying did a lot of records on the efficacy of traditional Chinese wormwood on the plane, and also had a trip plan. She asked the hotel staff for help: "Can you take us to these places after breakfast tomorrow?"

Qin Ying does not want to waste time at all, go straight to the theme of doing things.

Deng Cheng is different, he wanted to take this opportunity to first visit Qin Ying's family. Deng Cheng kindly said to Qin Ying: "Not bad for these two days, or to see the parents and family first."

Qin Ying sulkily glared at Deng Cheng with a bad smile and said: "In my territory, I say yo, listen to my arrangement?" Charter a bus to these places tomorrow. If that goes well, there'll be plenty of time for us to stop by my house and satisfy your curiosity. Let your future son-in-law do his filial duty, ha ha, this arrangement is OK?"

Deng Cheng understand and admire Qin Ying's ability to do things, it seems that he can only listen to Qin Ying's arrangement here, there is no reason to refuse Qin Ying, as if Qin Ying said is very reasonable.

On this evening, Qin Ying and Deng Cheng chose a table of hometown dishes outside the hotel courtyard under the careful arrangement of the hotel. There is warm local chicken and yam soup, and some local snacks. Two people slowly product, slowly and whisper to each other.

After dinner they went for a walk together outside the hotel. The crisp evening breeze in my hometown blows two people's faces. Deng Cheng looked up to the respiratory tract: "Here is really natural aerobic air, really fragrant, you smell it?"

Qin Ying had closed her eyes at that moment and enjoyed the wonderful sounds of her hometown: the squeaking of birds, the rustling of leaves in the wind, and the moon peeking at them, revealing a soft light source against her and Deng Cheng's silhouetting.

Chapter 23: Selflessness

The next morning sunshine into Qin Ying room, white curtains through the light just shine on the wake up Qin Ying face. Qin Ying looked at the small alarm clock on the bedside table, it was five minutes past six, it was time to get up. I wonder how Deng Cheng will rest in the master bedroom next door? In order to let Deng Cheng rest well, she specially proposed to sleep in the hotel suite side bedroom.

Yesterday they said, next Deng Cheng listen to Qin Ying arrangement. Qin Ying clean up after knocking on Deng Cheng door, didnt think Deng Cheng already washed well, and so Qin Ying went to the east side restaurant on the first floor.

There are rich breakfast varieties in the restaurant, there are milk, eggs, fruit, rice noodles, noodles, fried sauce noodles, fried dough sticks...

Qin Ying asked for the lightest millet porridge with a small dish of pickles and vegetable fried dumplings, and served Deng Cheng a bowl of bean curd and a bowl of lean pork wonton.

The weather was perfect. It was a beautiful day. At the door of the hotel, the stone master of the chartered bus has been waiting for a long time, see Qin Ying and Deng Cheng two people coming to the car, busy and warmly welcome up: "You two are going to bridge town Tanshuling Mountain Resort to find a famous doctor to consult it?" Please get in the car."

Qin Ying looked at the person who spoke familiar home dialect: a face was sunburnt red skin, strong and kind and easygoing appearance. Qin Ying kindly responded: "Yes, you are the local famous know-all stone master, these days are going to ask you to be a mentor, thank you stone master."

Qin Ying and Deng Cheng on the master stone's car, master stone driving along the way, and said has made an appointment with the doctor's time, ranked third on the Deng Cheng treatment.

Master Shi went on to say, "You two don't have to worry, as long as you see a famous doctor, you will be assured." Take Chinese medicine seven times a week, and then return to the doctor after drinking, according to the condition adjustment and treatment, then open seven Chinese medicine, drink and see again. The patients sent by me were cured and went back happily. What if everyone came to see this famous doctor? The doctor is also strange. He never advertises or even gives his name. After the patient was cured, he became famous, and the people called him Ai Shen Doctor, and we called him that."

Talking and chatting, after a while, we arrived at the gate of the courtyard of the Ai God doctor that Master Shi said. Ai Shen Doctor lives in a small village on the edge of the mountains near the Taiping Villa, where only a dozen villagers of forest protection live. Later, because of the reputation of Ai God doctor, an endless stream of patients came to seek medical consultation, and the results made this small village of more than a dozen households famous. Many people know that here lives a Bodhisattva spirit doctor Ai, a kind old man.

Ai Shen doctors never charge for medical treatment, but only give the diagnosis and treatment methods, and use Chinese herbal ingredients to regulate the body. Another feature of this village is that almost every yard and ridge will be planted with pieces of wormwood. When the mugwort leaves sway in the wind, you can smell the fragrance of mugwort from a distance, the fragrance of pure plants.

The courtyard of the doctor's house of Ai God, there is a whole piece of wormwood. From the gate of the courtyard, the wormwood plants and plants are arranged and grown, forming a scenic wall of wormwood leaves. From a distance, it is really a natural beautiful scenery.

Deng Cheng and Qin Ying enjoy a variety of herbs and flowers in the yard, every corner of the yard can be basked in the sun, everywhere there are stone stools, wooden tree stools for patients and their families and friends to sit and wait, sometimes there are many people from different places, we do not know each other, but finally from patients to friends. Everyone sympathies with each other, comfort each other, overcome the disease together, and walk out of the shadow of cancer.

At this time, the baby Xiaochao beside the doctor called out to the yard: "No. 3 Deng Cheng please come in."

Qin Ying want to go in together, the result is small super blocked out: "Ai ye has rules, in order to take pulse phase accurate, not to let the patient distracted, set God take pulse to see a doctor, idle people do not enter."

In this way, Qin Ying had to wait outside for more than 1 hour, and the expression of Deng Cheng who came out seemed very dignified, holding a pot of soup and a bag of Chinese herbs. There are some herbs in the prescription to go to the county herbal medicine shop, according to the formula said to fry and drink, a week later to diagnose the situation.

Doctor Ai did not say how serious, but warned Deng Cheng: "Don't eat cold and spicy food, don't overeat, and don't be hungry." Eat light, eat small meals, sleep until you wake up naturally, and do what you usually do. Look down on everything, but love life, treat every day as the last day of the end of the world, to do what you like. Forget yourself, think more about others, care about others, this disease will go quickly. If you wake up and see the morning sun every day, you've earned it."

Qin Ying forward, let Deng Cheng first get on the car and wait for her, ask yourself a thing to come out.

Ai God doctor knew what Qin Ying wanted to ask at a glance, and quickly stopped: "Don't ask Deng Cheng about the cause of illness, you just need to accompany him." Drinking medicine every day is called tea, don't tell him to drink medicine, you should take him to the countryside to see more, play with him, eat well, rest well, in short, happy."

Ai God doctor's words gave Qinying spiritual comfort. Qin Ying see in the god doctor here no longer ask what questions, think about the vested is an, the next is to go according to Ai God doctor prescription with Chinese herbs, back to the hotel boil medicine.

After getting on the car, Qin Ying said to Master Shi: "We go to the town Chinese medicine shop, according to the prescription of Chinese herbal medicine." Master Shi, you must be familiar with this way, thanks for your hard work, let's go as soon as possible."

Master Shi then suggested: "After grasping the Chinese herbs, by the way, in the Chinese medicine shop to 7 days of Chinese medicine decocted into bags, back to the hotel refrigerator, three packages a day, hot water for a few minutes, you can drink." Patients have done it this way before, but it's easy."

Qin Ying said excitedly: "Is there still a medicine room? Great, how long will it take to cook?"

Master Shi immediately replied: "The queue number is about two hours, it doesn't matter, waiting for two hours, I will take you both around the Taiping Villa, see if you can still be transferred to the Taiping Villa hotel to live." In this way, you can walk to the Ai God doctor for a follow-up visit without having to come and go. Is this arrangement OK?" After listening to Deng Cheng think this suggestion is good.

To the Chinese medicine shop to grasp the formula on the medicine, stone master directly with Qin Ying and Deng Cheng will Chinese herbs to the decocting room, made a registration, get the number of the note. Just pick it up in two hours.

Really have a loss of stone master, otherwise how to have this ring set a ring of smooth, not to say that there is a friend outside is a treasure.

Master Shi will drive the car to the Taiping Villa hotel, ask at the lobby information desk, and know that there are suite rooms, you can check in today. In this way, Qin Ying let Deng Cheng rest and wait in the Taiping Villa hall, she and master stone to the original hotel check-out procedures, daily necessities let master stone transfer to the Taiping Villa. This series of operations is done, and it is just time to take Chinese medicine, and everything is going well.

Deng Cheng see Qin Ying busy for himself to finish these things that should have been done by him, the heart feels very warm. Master Shi saw Qin Ying busy after a little tired look, busy to two people said: "after drinking medicine today, early rest, I will come to the hotel at nine o 'clock tomorrow morning to meet you, to Xujiawan Qin Ying's aunt is it?"

Qin Ying and pleasant said: "Yes, we will take the day's medicine pack tomorrow, let Deng Cheng go to the countryside to accompany my uncle fishing, relax." I haven't visited my good family in years, and I really miss them. I called them yesterday and said I would visit them in a few days. They knew we were staying at the hotel, and they made me check out the hotel room. I don't want to cause them any trouble."

Deng Cheng happily said: "Really, tomorrow can go to the countryside to see fishing?" See the master tomorrow morning." Said can not wait to pull Qin Ying together to the hotel room.

This night, the two people may be mental effect, sleep to wake up naturally, rested very well. After breakfast in the hotel lobby, see time is enough, and take a walk in the nearby reservoir to breathe the fresh air.

Deng Cheng took the initiative to say: "I have a lot of ideas after yesterday's diagnosis, and Ai Shen doctor did not say any guaranteed treatment plan, only said that patients have this disease, there are two different results." The key is to depend on the patient's mentality, put down any pressure, calmly face, and actively regulate the body, then the disease will heal itself without medical treatment. If you take illness too seriously, you'll scare yourself to death. If I don't think about anything for one night, then I figure it out. The Ai God doctor is not treating a disease, but a disease in my heart."

Deng Cheng said these words, pointing to his heart, meaning that I put down, I can not scare myself to death, "Ai God doctors have said that everyone has cancer cells, defeat the disease is to learn to get along with cancer cells, non-aggression, peaceful coexistence." That sounds kind of interesting!"

Qin Ying and Deng Cheng Shi master's car to Xujiawan near Li Shizhen winery, bought a box of Chinese herbal tonic wine and seasonal fruit on the street, to aunt and uncle with gifts. Deng Cheng also let Qin Ying seal a big red envelope 10,000 yuan, that is Qin Ying's heart. You should know that this relative is Qin Ying's mother's half-sister.

Qin Ying early childhood to listen to her mother often recite, her own mother in the revolution was killed by the traitors, when Qin Ying mother is only one year old. Later on the organization for the father to arrange a life can give care of the small foot village girl, the village girl is the hostess of the new home, Qin Ying mother's stepmother, that is, Qin Ying aunt's mother. Qin Ying's mother left the village at the age of 16 to join the working class in the city and rarely returned home. After getting married with Qin Ying, every year before and after the Spring Festival or Qingming, will bring Qin Ying to see the half-sister born of Qin Ying, Qin Ying called her little Jane aunt.

Shaozhen aunt's husband called Xu Zhongjia, is an orphan, in the hometown agricultural machinery factory when the doctor, and Shaozhen aunt in the agricultural machinery factory work meet, natural love, after marriage has a son. Shaozhen aunt and uncle Xu Zhong family in Qai Township retired farming, now three generations live together harmoniously with their children and grandchildren, built a five-story country villa, live a happy pastoral life.

Far to see little Jane aunt and Xuzhong family uncle at the door to meet, Qin Ying and Deng Cheng get off into the yard gate, heard firecrackers behind, ringing non-stop. Shaozhen aunt said: "Today came a guest, small ying son, your uncle said to set off long firecrackers, let you long and happy."

Qin Ying after listening to little Jane aunt these words, suddenly saw little Jane aunt and uncle with white hair, the pair of rough hands, are out of the blood vessels, a show on the back of the hand, wear the clothes or Qin Ying a few years ago to. Qin Ying said: "Now life is so good, have built a building, Shaozhen aunt how to wear such simple clothes, soon lost it, for a new."

Shaozhen aunt said with a smile: "Nothing, nothing, this rural wear good, there is no one to see us, I do farm work really like to wear this dress, comfortable very close, there are a lot of small ying you give clothes in the cabinet, not the same every day, can not wear over, you don't buy, waste."

Deng Cheng has been sitting in the hall on a high-back wooden chair, and quietly looking at the Xuzhong family uncle for their arrival: in the wind blowing hair is still confused, but the dark face is red, full of energy, let Deng Cheng immediately feel the master's affability. Xu Zhong family uncle simple and loyal, everywhere for the sake of others, see him constantly see things to do, busy catching chicken and busy with a bamboo basket just picked fruit.

Deng Cheng heart gushing out a lot of moved, can not help but come forward to pull the hand of Xu Zhong said: "Please don't be busy, no wonder Qin Ying often said that you want to you, that you are the most close relatives in her hometown." When I met you today, I liked you both. It was like an instant connection. It felt so good."

Qin Ying interrupted Deng Cheng's words, grabbed to say: "Uncle ah, I bring Deng Cheng this time, may have to stay for some days, this back uncle fishing, farm work picking vegetables and farming, also teach Deng Cheng do, he likes the atmosphere here." Look at Deng Cheng's red eyes. He's even more excited than I am."

Qin Ying who said this is not talking about himself? She deliberately shift the target, can not cover up their own inner nostalgia and love for relatives, tears have already flowed out, only by saying Deng Cheng to make their tears into smiles.

Deng Cheng grabbed the words and continued, "You miss Shaozhen aunt and love them every day. Now come, in front of you, you have to say the love in your heart out loud ah! Aunt Jane, uncle, I'm serious. Qin Ying is embarrassed to say that she is such a person, with you for a long time, has become particularly honest, so I want to protect her."

Xu Zhong home stared at Deng Cheng, said a meaningful heart words: "At this time I understand your thoughts very much, you love small Ying, then you should accompany and guard your loved ones." Put down the pressure, cherish the people in front of you, and live happily every day. We must live to understand, to achieve the realm of selflessness. You can do anything, the sun will moisten your life, welcome the morning and watch the sunset every day as happiness, you are the happiest person in life."

Chapter 24: Selflessness

Deng Cheng took over Xu Zhongjia uncle's fishing rod, net, a pair of rain shoes, and a cotton fabric of dark blue work cloth! Deng Cheng dressed like a local villager in these outfits. Deng Cheng felt relaxed and winked to Qin Ying happily, meaning: "I went fishing, see you later."

Qin Ying also happily waved and said: "You and your uncle today more fishing small ginseng and crayfish, I want to eat shrimp balls in the evening." In addition, I learn to make glutinous rice noodles vegetarian meatballs with my aunt Shaozhen, and sell them by myself in Zhuhai Love Bar Book Bar in the future, saving the cost of mailing. Isn't that a good idea?"

As soon as Deng Cheng started to catch the fish, he grabbed the tail excitedly with his hand, and the fish slipped away. Xuzhong family uncle hand in hand to teach Deng Cheng, Deng Cheng quickly, and then the number of fishing quickly exceeded the uncle. This time Deng Cheng Coke is bad, laughing, he has not been so happy for a long time!

Qin Ying here step by step with little Jane aunt, while going to dig in the vegetable, this is a kind of natural green vegetables to do glutinous rice balls filling, many people like to eat it, used when the main side dish or under the hot pot are delicious.

Qin Ying walked from the east to the west, and kept digging wild vegetables on the earth ridge on the ground. In two hours, Qin Ying was sweating and dug out full of bamboo baskets. Qin Ying never out so much sweat, before always stuffy in the air-conditioned study writing office, this whole body activity, a stand a look down at the field wild vegetables digging, she dug more and more vigorous. Qin Ying closely follow little Jane aunt, catch up a look, little Jane aunt in the bamboo basket of wild vegetables than Qin Ying more than half. Qin Ying unconvinced said: "Shaozhen aunt how you so fast ah, I did not stop, can not catch up with you, what tricks can quickly and accurately dig to wild vegetables?"

Shaozhen aunt continued to dig vegetables, hands kept saying: "There is no trick, practice makes perfect." You have done little farm work, how can you be like me, who works in the field every day? This is the best natural oxygen bar exercise, the air is fresh, and my favorite thing in the morning is to go to the vegetable field and pick the dishes that the family will eat for the day. Sometimes more food can not finish, dig more and ride a motorcycle to the market to sell. I rented a fixed stall, and my food was so fresh that it sold out soon after I put it on the stall. The people who buy the food are basically our acquaintances, and I will agree with them to set up a stall two mornings a week. The dishes in my family are not pesticides, all green, healthy and fresh dishes, everyone knows that it is good."

Qin Ying said again, "You know what? I dreamed last night that you took me to fetch eggs. Then see the eyes are full of vegetables, I keep digging ah pick ah, can be happy ah. Then the sound of chickens woke me up!"

Shaozhen aunt smiled and said, "You have a dream every day, like when you were a child, but also like to play in our countryside."

Qin Ying looked at the little Jane aunt who smiled and spoke in red light, the skin is the healthy color of the sun, the whole makeup without makeup, the sweat is stuck to the face, the forehead hair is gently blown by the morning breeze, it is very beautiful under the sunlight in the morning. Qin Ying could not help saying: "Shaozhen aunt is really beautiful, you don't move, I use the mobile phone to take a photo for you." Click click click a few sound, Qin Ying became a photographer to follow.

"Ha ha ha, this is my old aunt, still beautiful?" Don't shoot me. Shoot more nature. Look at that orchard, and your uncle's natural chicken farm in the Back hills. I'm sure you like it better. Let's go home and make sticky rice balls. You'll learn how to do that later."

Qin Ying also feel in the countryside to do farm work like play, work sweat do not feel tired, also do not worry about food. Earthenware cooking is really delicious, there is no seasoning and attention in the city, but the soup stew on the stove is good to drink, no wonder after retirement Shaozhen aunt and uncle have not been sick, the body is better than before. They rested when they were tired, and at night soaked their feet in wormwood. Sticky bed fell asleep, a sleep to wake up naturally.

Shaozhen aunt at home while the fire said: "Xiaoying you and Deng Cheng agreed to leave the hotel room, moved to the home on the third floor to live, there are new household supplies, more comfortable than you live in the hotel!"

Qin Ying thought she had no problem at all, every time to the countryside Spring Festival, are living in little Jane aunt home. At the earliest, I lived in a flat floor house in Xujia village, warm in winter and cool in summer. I never installed air conditioning in rural areas, and only had a small hairdryer fan when it was hottest. At night quietly listening to the wind rustling on the leaves to sleep, very relaxed, there is a kind of contentment.

When it was lunch time, Xu Zhongjia and Deng Cheng walked into the courtyard of the villa one after the other, changed into slippers, sat on wooden chairs, sat around the stone round table, and waited for Shaozhen Aunt's sticky rice noodles balls and pure and authentic chicken soup. I smelled the food before it came out.

Qin Ying beside the stove, has been looking at little Jane aunt is how to eat lunch. Sticky rice balls are learned today, Qin Ying also want to learn to do guoba porridge, she likes to eat this rural to eat guoba porridge.

Shaozhen aunt added all the rice and put it into the rice basin, when she saw the burnt yellow rice in the pot. She copied the bottom and added a few ladles of water, braised the lid, and cooked it well using the residual heat of the stove. After opening the lid of the pot, the aroma of the pot porridge smells very fragrant, think about the people who have eaten the pot porridge, can not forget the temptation of this food. For so many years, Qin Ying just returned to the countryside here, drink rice porridge with local seasonal vegetables, can eat two big bowls.

Shaozhen's virtuous hard-working and simple and optimistic attitude towards life can infect people around her. Xu Zhong home is to see little Jane aunt's kindness and sincerity. Deng Cheng this morning learned fishing skills, but also learned patience, but also understand the responsibility of being a man. He also saw in the body of Xu Zhong family simple and unpretentious, silently pay for the family, asking for nothing in return. This kind of personality charm attracted Deng Cheng, he instantly found that the shining point on the original man is not how handsome and good-looking, but his inner personality charm. The couple is really a model couple, Deng Cheng and Qin Ying's heart worship the simple and ordinary idol.

Deng Cheng suddenly felt that he had lived in vain before, and he now understood the philosophy of life. Deng Cheng asked himself in his heart: Is it still too late?

Deng Cheng can not be idle, a idle down to think of his illness. Qin Ying understand Deng Cheng's feelings, see his deep worries. Qin Ying pretend not to notice the appearance, careless to Deng Cheng shouted: "Good hot ah, Deng Cheng come to help me, come quickly to take the stew of chicken soup can, I end the pot porridge." Guarantee you want to eat both, really good smell ah, smell good!"

Deng Cheng quickly got up to help take Qinying hands of the plate. Shaozhen aunt said thoughtfully: "I didn't do much food, today I will eat some simple staple food, brown rice porridge, sticky rice flour balls, mushroom stew in chicken soup."

Xu Zhongjia added: "Dinner is simpler, a big bowl of fish soup stew full of vegetarian dumplings. Deng Cheng must eat, delicious oh! In our country life, there are no high-end delicacies, but these home-grown things are available to ensure that you eat happy, nutritious, and healthy. Look at me. I've never had a cold in all these years since I retired, and I'm getting stronger. If you look at something like fishing, think of it as getting calcium in the sun. You don't need any supplements."

Qin Ying approached Deng Cheng side to help carry the dish, put on the plate, forced Deng Cheng taste first. Looking at Deng Cheng first bite a vegetable ball, then drink chicken soup, the lovely expression of smiling naughty, let Qin Ying rest assured, "delicious to eat more, this can be really delicious food."

Deng Cheng has just started to maintain a correct sitting posture, and later all ignore the image, but also learn Xu Zhong home with a bowl, a while to see the yard long flowers, while eating the food in the bowl. After a while finished eating, and went to add a bowl of rice porridge, also really eat not tired.

Qin Ying's soft voice sounded in Deng Cheng's ear: "My little Jane aunt let us return the hotel room, don't spend money, come here for a long time, are you willing to?"

Deng Cheng thought about it and said, "You decide. It's not about the money, if you don't listen to the invitation of your relatives, you are looking down on such good relatives. Besides, I understand your relationship. You used to live here. I can't be a villain, I want you to kiss and kiss, I agree to do whatever you want, I'm happy to leave the hotel and move here for a long time, hey!"

Qin Ying listened to Deng Cheng say so, happy to jump up and punch Deng Cheng's waist: "I am really happy that you did not put my relatives as outsiders, you like my relatives, I am really happy." Get your hotel room back when you've had enough to eat and drink today. It doesn't count until two o 'clock."

Deng Cheng joked: "If you punch a few more times, it is as if you beat my back and legs." Look how cheap you are, trying to save a day's room bill."

Qin Ying ran in front of Shaozhen aunt laughing happily said: "Shaozhen aunt, he promised to move to the house." I never thought he'd make this his home so quickly. Aunt Shaozhen, do you think Deng Cheng is reliable? If you think he is well and ill, we are ready to get married!"

Aunt Shaozhen expressed her thoughts and said, "Deng Cheng this man is very good, he has arranged his wealth in your name after his illness." He does this to you with affection, and only true love can do this. I believe Deng Cheng's illness will be cured, so let him live here and cooperate with traditional Chinese medicine to maintain his health. Let him learn your uncle's altruism, and all will be well."

Qin Ying nodded in recognition, "At the beginning is to feel that he is so stupid, he is suffering from cancer two, do not hurry to see a doctor, but the first time to think of my life in the rest of my life." At that moment, I felt that wealth was a number for me, and living well was more important than anything else. At that time, I wanted to marry him, accompany him and take care of him. I said to him, active treatment is the true love for me."

Qin Ying's inspiring method gave Deng Cheng a reassuring pill. In the difficult times, they realize the value of true feelings.

Qin Ying and Deng Cheng live in little Jane aunt home is seven months, during this time Deng Cheng see the effect of Chinese medicine treatment gradually emerged, Deng Cheng's mental state is better day by day. Such results really depend on the natural oxygen bar environment in the countryside, and also come from the meticulous care of Qin Ying's relatives and family. In terms of diet, Deng Cheng eats pure natural green food, coupled with taking traditional Chinese medicine every day to regulate the body, Deng Cheng's physique slowly improved, and the spirit also recovered. Deng Cheng has developed a eating habit of eating less and more meals, and the body's previous stomach acid, stomach pain, stomach bloating and hiccups have not been committed again.

In recent times, Ai God doctor see Deng Cheng came to take the pulse treatment when talking and laughing, when Qin Ying accompanied around when he appeared to be in a better mood. Once after they had seen the sick, before they left, the Ai God doctor Kua Qin Ying said: "Brother Deng Cheng can recover in this short period of time, you have a great credit, Deng Cheng in a happy mood, the body naturally can produce the ability to fight against the disease."

For a patient, the mood is very important, and the care of relatives around Deng Cheng is one of the important reasons for his improvement.

After living in Shaozhen aunt, Deng Cheng did not regard himself as a patient. Every day, Xu Zhong's family took Deng Cheng to a chicken farm in the mountains to pick up eggs, and drove the chickens to the grass to free them to eat worms and grass. In the afternoon in the orchard to pick the fruits of the season, there are citrus, peaches, apples, pears, dates, these with the city to buy fruit is not the same, although the look is not good, but the taste is particularly good.

Deng goes fishing once a week and warms up in the sun after lunch, squinting and enjoying a half-hour nap. In the evening, people would sit in the small courtyard and talk, singing at the top of their voices and humming little songs.

New Year's Day approaching, Qin Ying received small Bei Xiaoqin two blessings and love bar book bar business report: "Ying sister, everything is fine here, really thank aunt Jane sent us vegetarian stuffing sticky rice balls, soil yam, peanuts and 100 kilograms of taro." This time the sales of gift boxes are three times more than last time, so many customers buy online. Online sales have doubled in these months compared to the last few months, with sales exceeding 20,000, and some gift boxes can be sold after the year, and will not be out of stock. I'll transfer the proceeds to you tomorrow. Here, I wish Deng Chengge a speedy recovery, we miss Ying sister and Deng Chengge.

Here the physical store love bar book bar busy weekend, are the owners of the nearby bay community acquaintances, they will come to love bar book bar at the weekend to eat some special snacks, read. Shen sum autumn sweet sister they both will help on the weekend. Here, please Ying sister rest assured, thank Aunt Shaozhen for us, the gift box arrived in time! Thank you for your support and help!"

Qin Ying pulled Deng Cheng see complete information, Deng Cheng understand, little Jane aunt and Xu Zhong family couple Qin Ying gave them ten thousand yuan red envelopes to buy agricultural products sent to love the book bar, things are done without a word, do so many real good things. Qin Ying and Deng Cheng looked at each other, thought how can this human favor?

Two people looked up at the distant stove before and after busy Shaozhen aunt figure, in the soft warm yellow light, Shaozhen aunt quickly packed firewood. Xu Zhong home handed a cup of water, let little Jane aunt drink. Shaozhen aunt wiped the blue cloth on her body, took the cup and drank it down. Xu Zhong home took out a towel to wipe the little Jane aunt face of water, the kind of love eyes, looking at people envy.

Qin Ying in Deng Cheng ear revealed said: "Uncle is an orphan, since and little Jane aunt after marriage and children, willing to pay for this home." My uncle Shaozhen aunt said to me that he has been a son-in-law all his life, but he still loves this home, see Shaozhen aunt's relatives and friends visit, and treat people honestly. No one said Xu Zhong family uncle good, all praise him hard work and wealth. On weekdays, he and Shaozhen never spend money to buy clothes for themselves, wearing clothes from relatives and friends, and a dress can be worn for many years. They always say that wearing too good clothes is awkward, afraid of getting dirty when working. Only wear new clothes when visiting friends and relatives."

Deng Cheng's eyes did not turn away, quietly looking at the respectable relatives. The setting sun poured into the small courtyard, and the beautiful countryside scenery was as beautiful as a painting. Through the open hall, the wind blew the corners of Shaozhen's dress. That dress is Qin Ying five years ago to send a birthday gift, did not think little Jane aunt is still wearing. Aunt Shaozhen's figure is still so slim and beautiful, she really does not look like a country woman. Even wearing coarse silk, cotton and hemp blended fabrics, it still looks innocent, kind and gentle. No wonder Uncle Xu Zhong often said: "Shaozhen is the kindest woman I have ever met in my life."

Aunt Shaozhen's beauty is not only the beauty of the face, people who approach her can feel the tenderness and kindness of her inner world, which is her charm. People who come into contact with her feel very comfortable, and she will treat others with understanding and express it with actions.

Deng Cheng think of the ten thousand yuan red envelope, the intention is to give Qin Ying relatives some favors, did not expect less Jane aunt and uncle free food and shelter, unreservedly love them, take care of them. Did so many things for them, even the purchase gift box of the love bar book bar were replaced, and did not leave a name for good deeds.

Deng Cheng ashamed to Qin Ying said: "We are too self-righteous, always think that money can solve every thing." I really envy Shaozhen aunt and uncle, they have love in their hearts, richer than we can imagine, spiritual enrichment. Popularity is good, so good in the village that every villager praises them from the heart. It's a bit of a struggle. I got my fellow villagers to help right away. That's pretty impressive. I'd be happy if we had half of them."

Qin Ying mind thinking over and over again, dont want to let little Jane aunt suffer. Qin Ying could not help but say the idea to Deng Cheng: "You see me do this? Late love bar book bar all the special snacks sticky rice balls, we let Shaozhen aunt to provide investment shares, online sales income are attributed to Shaozhen aunt. We also provide a sales platform for Shaozhen aunt to create rural food for free, so that Shaozhen Aunt can work more and earn more, rather than just earn some manual production costs. I hope Shaozhen can also lead the spare villagers' labor force in the local area, make use of the rich local characteristics and cultural food to form an industrial chain, and make the agricultural and sideline native products as big as possible. We can try to do this, do some practical projects for Aunt Shaozhen and the villagers, what do you think?"

Deng Cheng listened to Qin Ying so said, staring at Qin Ying smiled and replied: "I did not expect that you are faster than my brain." It's a good way to help them, and they'll agree when they hear it's good for the villagers."

Deng Cheng steady his heartbeat, holding Qin Ying's hand on his chest, feel his heartbeat. Deng Cheng did not cheat Qin Ying, he is want to let Qin Ying know, he will be as loyal to love as Xu Zhong family uncle. To understand what Qin Ying wants, love Qin Ying love, can bring happiness to Qin Ying relatives, he Deng Cheng will go all out to support.

Deng Cheng forgot himself at this time, think of Qin Ying want to do things, he is duty-bound to do the benefit of others forget myself, starting from small things, from the action to do practical things. This is Xu Zhong family uncle influence Deng Cheng sentence philosophy, take this altruistic selfless road, the road of life will go more and more broad.

Chapter 25: A Beautiful Day

The Spring Festival is approaching, every household has begun to prepare New Year's goods, rural people pay special attention to the Spring Festival, everyone wants to make this festival lively and festive.

This morning, Shaozhen aunt with glutinous rice to make glutinous rice cake for breakfast, specially let Deng Cheng taste fresh food. This dish she made three kinds of patterns: first, put a few glutinous rice cake in chicken soup, added a few pieces of yam, delicious and not greasy, with pickles and radish leaves, make Qin Ying eat not tired of rice porridge. Second, the glutinous rice cake fried until both sides golden, sprinkle some sugar stick to eat. The third, cut a long piece of glutinous rice cake with the stove's residual fire slowly baked, the shell baked golden crust.

Deng Cheng saw three kinds of glutinous rice cake on the table, a big appetite, he smiled to Shaozhen aunt said: "We live here do not want to go, eat a good meal, not a meal of the same, even glutinous rice cake can be made into three kinds of eating!"

Shaozhen aunt put a bowl of soup in front of Deng Cheng: "Drink chicken and yam soup first, and then taste other things." The Spring Festival is coming, there are a lot of singing places have set up a small stage, every year from the first day to the fifteenth have the troupe to the town's park gate to sing Huangmei opera performance. Your uncle discussed with me, Deng Cheng or in the year to go to Ai Shen doctor that to take the pulse, let him open more conditioning of the body of Chinese herbs to consolidate. This year, you will spend the New Year in our village home and experience the New Year dinner in our village which is different from that in the city. Then you can go to the town and listen to the opera."

Deng Cheng said: "Well, I have this intention, want to see how lively the countryside." I want to experience the feeling of setting off firecrackers, try all kinds of fun, delicious food, and see the play. Qin Ying, do you agree to stay for the Spring Festival?"

Qin Ying with eyes toward Shaozhen aunt passed a glance: "Of course I am willing to ah, these down-to-earth life materials can be recorded when writing materials."

Qin Ying came back from Zhuhai Qai hometown, writing inspiration more from the people and things here. Qin Ying does not stop writing wherever she goes. During this period of her life in the countryside, Qin Ying has completed all the manuscripts of the second novel, and the third novel has been published in serialization one after another. Before the work is finished, she is already making audio novels. Qin Ying felt that there was an endless good story to write.

"I didn't think about going away during the Spring Festival," Qin said. "I certainly agree to stay and experience the beautiful scenery of the countryside and have a different Spring Festival."

Xu Zhongjia uncle took out two red scarves, put on a Deng Cheng body, and handed Qin Ying said: "You little Jane aunt two days ago and I went to the granddaughter's school to participate in the parents' meeting, the granddaughter and the first place in the class, the principal awarded us these two red scarves." It's a nice bonus. We'll give it to you. It's settled. Have a prosperous Spring Festival in our home. Spring Festival Zhuhai Xiaobei Xiaoqin also want to go home, we can meet here. I was also thinking that the countryside could start paying New Year's greetings after the second day of the second year, and then I would invite them to our home for the New Year dinner."

Deng Cheng took the red scarf, the heart is very warm, suddenly Xu Zhong family uncle put him as his family and children to take care of, give meticulous care. Deng Cheng recalled the happy memories of the past Chinese New Year. Now my parents are gone, and I am living alone in Zhuhai. If it were not for knowing Qin Ying, it is estimated that during the Spring Festival, the company still lived the life of two points and one line.

Deng Cheng became fragile, at this time like when he was a child, seeing his loved ones was wronged, and tears suddenly fell down. Deng Cheng this tears do not matter, can be frightened Shaozhen aunt: "Deng Cheng where uncomfortable ah?" Did you eat something bad, or did you feel sick? Show your uncle! '

Deng Cheng knows what is going on, see everyone mistakenly thought he was unwell, and quickly blocked his eyes with his hands and said: "Nothing, is choked by the glutinous rice cake, I go to the bathroom."

Deng Cheng clever enough, even Qin Ying are over the past, really think he is ciba eat fast choke. When Qin Ying was a child, she also had such an experience, choking on food and crying. Qin Ying supported Deng Cheng and whispered, "Like a child, take it easy, are you better now?"

Deng Cheng walked into the bathroom door, stopped to look back at Qin Ying said: "You still follow in?" Look at me, how can I go pee?"

Qin Ying see Deng Cheng this kind of simple and poor appearance, suddenly laughed: "Then I will wait for you to come out of the door, really funny, I can collect health fees."

Deng Cheng does not want to let everyone know that there are so many years of emotional backlog in his world during the holiday. It was like a child's emotional release when he sees his own parents. It had been many years since the elders loved him as a child, and on this day he felt the joy of his lost childhood and the presence of his parents, as if he had returned to the previous happy days.

Deng Cheng for so many years, did not meet such simple relatives, pure affection makes Deng Cheng feel cordial, Qin Ying in the side also let him feel happy. He thought that since he learned of the illness, Qin Ying's concern for him has emotionally exceeded the responsibility of the relationship between men and women. In the case of their formal marriage, Qin Ying has been accompanied to guard his medical treatment, and even dared to show his heart in front of his relatives, to go on with him forever.

Although he and Qin Ying have not lived a real husband and wife life, but they have an open love relationship, in the eyes of everyone is already a fact of marriage between men and women. Qin Ying for love, gave up the girls pay attention to the reserve and face, single-minded everywhere for him to seek famous medical treatment program, devoted himself to cure the root of the disease, launched relatives to provide him with a quality living environment, let him carefree to live down, overcome his heart and physical disease. Qin Ying gave him a great faith to survive, is with the idea of love, let him see the confidence that is really good to live. Qin Ying is a good woman that he can never meet in his life.

Deng Cheng thought that his ex-wife betrayed him that period of heartless marriage life, which has a direct reason for his stomach cancer. In those gloomy and angry marriage days, he always had a full meal and a hungry meal, and often came home to eat cold vegetables or cold rice or bubble noodles. There was no domestic warmth in that house.

Every New Year's Day, Deng Cheng sent a lot of gifts to his ex-wife's family, and it was the whole kitchen cooking. After the New Year's dinner, never let him eat the reunion dinner on the table. At that time, Deng thought that if he truly loved his wife and her family, he would get the same emotional response, but he did not. In the good age of young career, but his ex-wife because of his long business trip outside someone, and the object of the derailment is Deng Cheng most trusted college students, it is a painful past.

Deng Cheng looked at himself in the bathroom mirror frame, rosy complexion, face are long round, two eyes sparkle, these are Qin Ying to bring him the blessing. Deng Cheng meditating for a long time, he did not say to Qin Ying between his former wife, the heart like a mirror to know that two women can not compare, Qin Ying's kindness and the good quality of her family, is the atmosphere of marriage and love he yearns for. He at this time a heart to cherish the people, that is Qin Ying, when he is ill, must give Qin Ying the happiest life, he wants to give the no desire but can be in his despair when accompanied around the lover.

Qin Ying's shouts outside the door interrupted Deng Cheng's thoughts: "Hey, so long, did you fall in the bathroom?" Come on out! Aunt and uncle are waiting for you in the hall! Little Jane aunt will take us to visit the town to choose the Spring Festival couplet red paper. Buy more this year, you write couplets to the villagers, you can not shirk yo."

Deng Cheng finished the door, firmly grasped Qin Ying's hand, and whispered in her ear: "You are a good woman given to me by God, I must take good care of you for a lifetime, and after the Spring Festival Lantern Festival, we will get married when we return to Zhuhai, OK?" I don't want to put it off any longer."

Qin Ying touched Deng Cheng's head: "You don't have a fever? I want to see your performance, our relatives agree! Then it's up to you. Otherwise, you can just raise it here and be a farmer every day!"

Two people smiled and sat back at the table, uncle and little Jane aunt did not move chopsticks, waiting for Deng Cheng on the table to finish the breakfast together.

Deng Cheng did not want to compare the scene when eating at his ex-wife's home, but instantly uncle Xu Zhong home and little Jane aunt to him so kind and respectful, let Deng Cheng and can not help but surge of gratitude. He blurted out what he thought in his heart: "Relatives ah, I must love you well, and then I will walk around as my own relatives, accompany Qin Ying to visit you every year, don't be annoyed with me."

After saying these words, Deng Cheng pretended to be relaxed, to hide his inner bitterness, and to press down the cool emotions of the heart that had just risen. He could not cry today, he should be happy, let the past be past, and he would never suffer like that again.

The Spring Festival in the countryside is as good as Qin Ying introduced, Deng Cheng and Qin Ying in their own yard, set up two long tables, pour black ink, write couplets to the villagers. The villagers choose their favorite couplets in the book, and Deng Cheng writes them on red paper.

This is not next door Liu fat uncle selected this pair of couplets, Hengpi: good luck in the New Year, connected: spring breeze into the Xi money into the household; Next: years to renew the blessing of the door. Yu master is the most senior elder in the village, he chose this pair, up: reading breeze can read; Lianlian: Thinking of the moonlight also read. Shaozhen aunt chose a pair of couplets is written in this way: good luck; Shanglian: smooth sailing family prosperous; Next: All the best family photo. In the process of writing, Deng Cheng also felt the inheritance of Chinese culture, giving the festival of happiness and wisdom, Hengqi: everything goes well, Shanglian: peace and good days; Lianlian: people shun the home and everything. Xu Zhong family uncle fierce said: "Give my son super super to a pair of couplets, Hengpi, congratulations on making a fortune; Shanglian, gold and jade full house prosperity; The next united, the great fortune is the same as the heaven wealth long."

Unconsciously busy all day, this kind of self-selected self-writing couplets is really interesting, everyone participates in, everyone presents. Although this comes from rural farmers, the sentences of cultural customs and customs come to the couplet, it is really worthy of being a new type of socialist new countryside.

Deng Cheng and uncle busy after the red door affixed to the door, from the big yard into the gate affixed, the window also affixed paper-cut red window pattern. There are small red lanterns hanging on both sides of the main gate of the courtyard, which makes the atmosphere lively and peaceful.

Every household in the village will hang red envelopes full of ribbons tied to the branches of the courtyard in front of their homes, which are said to be reserved for children who come to visit their elders as New Year's money red envelopes. The amount of money varies, but all are new banknotes specially exchanged by the bank before the year, ranging from 1 to 10 yuan. This is simply a blessing of a lively welcome, and the custom of paying New Year's greetings to each other has been handed down. This time let Deng Chengchang see, now more understand why Qin Ying always remember the countryside here. Now Deng Cheng has fallen in love with the people here, the trees and grass here.

Deng Cheng's first such year, I believe he will never forget. He thought it might be because the person he loved was here, surrounded by the love of the family, he enjoyed being pure and innocent love. Deng Cheng relatives to his good and unrequited love, in the eyes, love in the heart.

Over the year and a half, Deng Cheng in Shaozhen aunt and Xu Zhong family uncle personally accompanied, in the lunar calendar sixteen day to visit Ai God doctor. Doctor Ai looked at the visit of this large family, looking at Deng Cheng's energetic complexion, or could not help but professional habits, pulled Deng Cheng's hand, took pulse auscultation and said: "Pulse is very stable, the body is already very good, but in order to consolidate, I prescribe more stomach prescription this time, or prepare some mild Chinese herbs to take back, and only drink three pairs of Chinese medicine a week apart." After going back, wait for three months to drink the medicine, and then go to the big hospital to take a thorough check, and report me after the results come out, so that my old husband can rest assured."

Deng Cheng raised his voice and replied, "That's for sure. I still have to come to see Dr. Ai in person."

Doctor Ai looked up and smiled loudly and said, "At that time, I don't want you to come to me again, this is my wish."

Deng Cheng made a 90-degree bow to the doctor, kowtowing three times in a row. Deng Cheng's gratitude beyond words, Deng Cheng some excitement from the throat of a choked voice: "Thank you Ai Shen doctor magic hand, gave me the faith of regeneration, you are not only using Chinese medicine to cure my physical disease, you also heal my mind."

Doctor Ai held Deng Cheng's hands and said, "Brother, it is your relatives who saved you, don't thank me, thank them." Thank you for this land, it is this endless nature to care for you. We all want to thank the villagers who work under this beautiful scenery. It is the love you give us. With love, our days are getting better and better."

Chapter 26: The Love Ladder

Deng Cheng in the heart there are a lot of words want to say, but that is not to export, looking at Qin Ying this honest family of good relatives, Deng Cheng dont know what he can say now. Qin Ying saw Deng Cheng's mouth tremble slightly, it seems difficult to say a complete word, hold in a long time or jump out of the mouth repeated words: "Thank you, thank you." I feel like home for the first time in my life."

Deng Cheng reluctant to part, the eyes are enough to represent Deng Cheng's mood at the moment, it is very happy and grateful. The emotion that stuck in his throat couldn't be expressed in just a few words. He forbearably turned his back to the Xuzhong family uncle walked, first put his hands together to respect the little Jane aunt, and then embrace the Xuzhong family uncle. At this time, Deng Cheng's tears came out, he did not dare to look up, had to bury his head deeply in his uncle's shoulder, and could not calm down for a long time.

After saying goodbye to Ai God doctor, Deng Cheng wooden ground Xu Zhong family private car, seven big car can put Qin Ying and Deng Cheng two big boxes and ai township land specialty. Qin Ying did not want to take so many things, but little Jane aunt said: "This is by the way to my sister, we also go to the provincial capital to visit your mother ah, if you do not take the flight for two days, we can not make this determination, I am carsick."

Qin Ying came only in order to rush the time to treat Deng Cheng, the Spring Festival has passed the half month, the plane back to Zhuhai had to take a flight from Wuhan Airport in Hubei Province, only the airport is closest to Qichun.

Qin Ying's mother has been living in the provincial city after retirement, where there are relatives of Qin Ying's mother's older generation, some of them in the province as provincial leaders of important positions, but every festival, no matter how big the officials will visit Qin Ying's mother, because Qin Ying's mother is the largest generation. A big family will get together, the day of this year's gathering is today's lunar calendar sixteen, Shaozhen aunt and Xu Zhong family uncle will not be absent, every year will bring a car of native eggs, native yams, native chicken, sweet potatoes, peanuts, vegetables, to the size of the provincial capital relatives.

Xu Zhongjia uncle said: "We touch your mother's light, these things, you can take on the plane to bring back; Anything we can't bring, we send to your mom. If you have many relatives, one point is not much."

Qin Ying added: "This is how we arranged to visit our mother and relatives in the provincial capital, and Deng Cheng should also meet his family." And the city's famous cancer hospital is next to Wuchang East Lake, since the way to do a comprehensive examination here, back to Zhuhai also know."

Deng Cheng in the car than usual less words, his heart was uneasy, he did not know suddenly to face so many Qinying relatives, do not know everyone on his first impression will be how. Today he knew Qin Ying family there are such a high-level leadership, the heart will inevitably be a little uneasy, think of meeting will be uncomfortable.

In about two hours, I arrived at Qin Ying's mother's home district downstairs. We moved the car things down, then directly to Qin Ying mother picked up the car, to the place of family dinner - Hongshan Square hotel luxury restaurant. Provincial relatives are here waiting for Qin Ying and Deng Cheng this car of relatives, we have been waiting here for a long time, this is a big reunion after the month and a half.

At the beginning of lunch, everyone was busy greeting, Deng Cheng saw this scene for the first time, instinctively feel that he is an outsider, he very consciously sat next to Qin Ying, did not dare to take the initiative to greet relatives, smiling face because of tension and slightly stiff.

Deng Cheng met the leading relative, he is 1.8 meters tall, looks like the old movie actor Wang Xingang, his face is kind and friendly and said: "Relatives, we have a good gathering today." Poor care, but eat well, drink well, and be casual." Speaking like nothing, he put his hands on Deng Cheng's shoulders and whispered kindly to him: "You are Deng Cheng, I have heard your family mention you, eat more ah." There are so many families, there is no time to take good care of each one, if not thoughtful, don't put it in your heart."

Deng Cheng wanted to get up from the stool to thank the approachable big leader relative, and the other side gently held him down with a pair of warm big hands, indicating that he did not have to see. Deng Cheng had to sit in his seat and say "thank you" , nodding his head excitedly.

This big family dinner before and after eating for more than two hours, after the happy end, everyone is still like the old rules in previous years, all to Qin Ying mother's house, sit together to taste the new tea sent by the countryside, and then each will bring less Jane and Xu Zhong local specialties point. Like ants moving bricks, we can take what we want, we are very casual, and we do not care about each other. We all like to eat the local specialties brought, every time in the past is so spectral.

Qin Ying's mother said, "You can take back everything you like, and the excess is mine." Don't mention it. It's a gesture from Jane and the loyal family, thinking of all of us every year, to serve these favorite foods from all over the country. It's a blessing that we can eat it. It reminds me of the New Year's food you used to eat when you were young."

Deng Cheng see Qin Ying family is so big, everyone harmonious love and help each other, even big official relatives are not a bit of officialdom, it looks like a good elder for everyone to serve, red face at any time to take care of every relative.

Deng Cheng found himself more and more not confident, at the moment he suddenly had an idea, it seems that he climbed Qinying, he does not deserve Qinying this good girl. To tell the truth, Qin Ying with such family conditions, in his hometown can certainly find a better person than him, more suitable for her family love marriage. He Deng Cheng failed to give Qin Ying more things, but feel that Qin Ying will be a burden.

Deng Cheng silence of the moment, or be sensitive Qin Ying aware, this is she has not taken Deng Cheng see family elders one of the reasons, she is afraid Deng Cheng have concerns to think too much. But today this scene is really caught up, some things have to accept the reality, this ugly daughter-in-law also has to see the in-laws!

Because of the large number of people, Qin Ying is also inconvenient to ask more. This day is really busy, from the morning to the reunion of the provincial capital, and to the greetings and separation of relatives. When they returned to their homes, it was evening, the moon had risen, Qin Ying and Deng Cheng quietly sat on the balcony chair looking out.

Deng Cheng looked at the sky stupidly and said to himself: "So suddenly quiet down, and think of you and I in Zhuhai, that day is your new house moving, we are sitting quietly on the balcony." In fact, as long as the lovers are together, life will have the best feeling."

Qin Ying feel Deng Cheng a little tired and tired, said: "You rest early today, we have to get up on time tomorrow, uncle arranged the driver to pick us up, can not delay, this is our important thing." The specialists at the hospital couldn't wait for us. We had to arrive early."

The next morning Qin Ying simply packed things ready to go, with a clean apple - because to check some items require an empty stomach, can not eat breakfast. Qin Ying accompanied Deng Cheng did not eat breakfast, check after we eat an apple, in peace. This sentence is what Qin Ying heard her mother say when she was a child, and later became a habit. No matter what you go away to do, it is best to carry an apple in your pocket, which means to think about the good side, and the meaning of safe and healthy. Qin Ying has been used to carrying two apples around for years.

Sure enough, uncle contact the driver is very punctual, Deng Cheng and Qin Ying downstairs to see the corridor on the parking of a black domestic old car, know that must be waiting for their driver to come. Sure enough, the driver flashed two lights to Deng Cheng and them.

After getting on the car, I went straight to the central South Cancer Hospital, although it was 8:30 in the morning, I did not expect to be overcrowded, the queue of registration is really as much as a cow's hair, men and women old and young, I did not expect that there are so many people to the hospital to see a doctor just after the lunar month.

The driver expertly led Deng Cheng and Qin Ying to the door of the expert clinic and put the medical records in line. After sitting and waiting for half an hour, the expert called Deng Cheng's name. The expert carefully looked at the front and back for half an hour, prescribing the test list and the test sheet, and took the physical examination sheet of seven items, X-ray, blood test, urine test, and other items.

Behind it has been thanks to the driver with them through different corridors, in different floors through the queue to wait for sampling detection, otherwise so many people, is a person waiting for the inspection results report, do not know how long to wait. It's not always easy to get these things done in one day.

It is already after 12:00 noon to finish several samples, and two items have been scheduled to be checked in the afternoon. The need for fasting inspection has been completed, Qin Ying and Deng Cheng together to ask the driver to eat in the small restaurant opposite the hospital. The restaurant is clean and simple, with crock soup and a few home-cooked dishes.

The driver said, "I'm used to just ordering soup." Deng Cheng would like a rice noodle soup, too. Qin Ying originally wanted to let everyone eat better, did not think of the time is still a little tight, but also to seize the time, so also called a soup under the rice cake and liver powder. Three people eat three kinds, all very nutritious, very light. The soup is not greasy and with some small pickles, this Chinese food is comfortable. Maybe everyone was hungry, didn't eat breakfast, and ate everything. The driver said, "As soon as we finish eating, we go to separate lines to get the finished results." I will accompany Deng Cheng to do a few projects in the afternoon, take the result of the film, Qin Ying can go to line up first, we finished back to find you."

Just go through it item by item and get the results. While waiting for the blood test results, Deng Cheng looked at the computer screen displaying his name and number in the window, and found that his ex-wife's name appeared in the next two lines across the screen. "Is it her?" Deng Cheng looked around and saw a familiar figure next to him. It was indeed his ex-wife!

Deng Cheng looked at each other one by one, thought it was an illusion, wanted to avoid but couldn't help but look up and stare at her. Each looks surprised, no one expected to meet here.

Deng Cheng heart at a loss, mouth slightly open, but did not speak, stay there looking at the people in front of the mind a little confused. "I haven't seen you for years, how can you be so thin? Seems sick, too? What are you getting? No one?" Deng Cheng's head turned quickly, he used to live with this woman for ten years! How did that happen? Didn't she run off with her boyfriend? How did it get to this point? What the hell is going on?

Curiosity and heartache suddenly poured into Deng Cheng's heart, blocked panic, although he is done all the project inspection, his situation also do not know whether it is good or bad, but to see his ex-wife like this, obviously his ex-wife's illness is much heavier than he.

Ex-wife also saw Deng Cheng, hiding is not hiding, she bowed her head embarrassedly. The window nurse has called the ex-wife's name "Ye Xiaolan" . She had no choice but to go to the window and get the list. I took it, and I left without a look.

Deng Cheng looked at the back of his ex-wife who was thin and not adult, and wore that kind of hospital gown on his body, knowing that his ex-wife must be ill. He found his list, and immediately followed his ex-wife as fast as he could, because he was afraid that his ex-wife would find out that he wasn't following too closely. Deng Cheng just wanted to see what ward his ex-wife went to and understand what disease she had.

Even if she had betrayed him, but by this time, it seemed that Deng Cheng had no hatred in his heart at all, he just wanted to help her. Deng Cheng also do not know why will suddenly hate her, this is clearly he wanted to see the most hate the result. How can I see my ex-wife like this at this time, but there is no feeling of pain and hatred. He really wanted to come forward and ask directly, he wanted to find an answer to the dens in his heart in these years, to a result.

Ye Xiaolan walked to the building of liver disease patients, Deng Cheng followed and chased to room 4, room 4 wrote Ye Xiaolan's name above the door. Deng Cheng did not follow in, at the door of the nurse's room asked the ex-wife's cause. Nurse asked Deng Cheng is her what person, Deng Cheng truthfully answer is her ex-husband.

The nurse told Deng Cheng sympathetically about the patient's situation: "She has advanced liver cancer, and none of her family members have come to see her, so we told her the result so that she could be psychologically prepared." She's pretty poor. She has to carry everything on her own. If only this liver disease had been detected and treated earlier, she took too long. When she got sick, her husband divorced her. She didn't fight. She always came to chemo alone. Not for long this time. The root of her illness is out of anger, blocked in her heart. The liver is an important detoxification organ of the human body, and this late-stage liver cancer really can't save her. She is suffering mainly from pain. You used to be husband and wife, and now she is like this, you still comfort her! We're going to start her chemo in half an hour."

The nurse was busy, Deng Cheng could not help but turn his head and walk directly to the door of Room 4. When the knock rang, his wife looked back: "How is it you? I thought it was a nurse!"

Deng Cheng: "It is not convenient to talk here, the patient needs to rest, can we say a few words in the corridor?"

Ye Xiaolan followed him out, closed the door behind him and said softly: "How can you be in this hospital today, are you OK?" You didn't think I'd end up like this. I brought this on myself. Are you treating yourself today to get the results?"

"I didn't get all the test results," Mr. Deng said.

Ye Xiaolan: "As you can see, the man is a liar, and he hid far away when he saw that I had hepatitis." He split up with me the year after I split up with you. He's out there with another woman, and I know it's not all his fault, because I have this infection. And I know it was early days, but I didn't have the guts to come to you, so let you hate me. But did not expect day to play tricks on people, just afraid of seeing people, just met. This is laughing at me. I was like that, and the doctor told me that this disease is a gas, to keep it. My heart tired, is life! The house you left behind is still in your name. I didn't transfer it. Half of the money you gave me is for treatment, and half is enough plus pension, and health insurance, but a life like this without quality... I'd rather get out of here than live like this. Soon, my days are numbered, and now that I have seen you today, it is providence, as I have told you."

Deng Cheng listened silently, eager to write down all the information in these years. This context is finally understood, at this time his heart is very tangled and sad, thinking of irritably stimulate the ex-wife, but found that the feeling of five taste at the same time attacked his chest, he has a little fast support of the feeling. In the face of his miserable ex-wife, he does not know whether he hates his ex-wife or hates his inability to save her.

Is there really no way? You're just gonna let her die? After what the nurse said, what else could he do? How did that happen? How did that happen? Even if Deng Cheng does not get the love of his ex-wife, he does not want her to wait for death. He had a sudden feeling of pity that made him forget what he was doing in the hospital. He wanted to do whatever he could to help his ex-wife.

Ye Xiaolan is very calm, indicating Deng Cheng dont be too close to her, will be contagious. Deng Cheng then stopped the footsteps of Ye Xiaolan close: "You need me to help you can do anything?"

Ye Xiaolan: "Thank you, no need. I'm used to being alone now, being in the hospital all the time, and this is my third year. I have not dared to tell you, several times I want to find you, to tell you something. I thought I'd say hello to you before I left, and I left you the house you gave me before my marriage, which was yours, and I didn't change it. I was a little small, but after I married that man, I saved my ass. If he doesn't treat me right, he doesn't get half in a divorce, so everything is still in your name. I was thinking about the house and writing your name and a promise. Sure enough, he abandoned me, we got a simple divorce, the property returned to the original owner. As long as you don't hate me, I don't ask you to forgive me, only blame yourself silly, I see the wrong eye, I lost you so good people, I am sorry for you. I know you also have a good girlfriend now, you love her! I couldn't help but sneak in to see you a few times, when you were in love, so I had to withdraw from your life far away. A woman like me doesn't deserve your forgiveness, and I have no choice but to leave you alone. This is the best thinking, the best love. I'm really sorry, I was wrong, I hope you are getting better now. I really wish you the best. Let's go. I'm about to get my shots and my physio. Don't ever look at me in this ugly state again, I despise myself."

Deng Cheng some stiff seriously listen to Ye Xiaolan these words, also do not know is to cry for themselves, or for her fate and cry. Deng Cheng childish had the idea of revenge ex-wife, when the bad results came today, at this time Deng Cheng listen to ex-wife constantly apologize. He let go from the sad, Ye Xiaolan for him these penitent words, has let the good Deng Cheng tears. He had expected to be glad to hear the news, but instead he was crying his eyes out and did not know what to say.

Deng Cheng stammered: "Don't say, everyone is at fault, I am also at fault." I didn't care enough about you. I ignored you. I'm sorry. Now don't say anything. Just focus on your treatment. Now medicine is developed, it should be able to save, yes, how about trying Chinese medicine treatment?"

The ex-wife also broke down in tears and said, "Silly, don't be silly, I can't be cured here, the doctor has given me a diagnosis, I can't survive three months." It's God's will, too. It's good to see you before I leave. I'm satisfied. I put the deed and all my valuables in the drawer of the old locker, you know. The passbook is still the old password you set up. I haven't changed it. If it comes to that day, you must go to our old house and get those things back. Now that I've told you, my heart is free. I'm a little tired. I'll go back to the ward and lie down. You go, I want to rest, really don't waste money to see my doctor, I have no hope."

Ye Xiaolan walked to the ward, and turned back to Deng Cheng anxiously said: "I am in pain now, still hard to live, I want to go to heaven early now." I'm going. I've said what I have to say. Don't come again."

At this time, only to hear the corridor doctors and nurses shouted Ye Xiaolan to do chemotherapy, this time all the visiting family members have to quit to wait. No, Deng Cheng was driven out by the head nurse, Deng Cheng's feet went limp and sat on the ground in the corner of the aisle for a while. I had to walk out of that infectious inpatient building to get the results. At this time, Deng Cheng edge walked out, eyes never left the direction of his ex-wife's building, and his mind was full of Ye Xiaolan's bent body, that thin back.

Out of the building, Deng Cheng suddenly thought, have to hurry back to take the results of the window, otherwise Qin Ying can not find his people, will worry. He stumbled into the elevator and out of the elevator to the downstairs elevator, shuttling in several corridors, the main floor of the second floor of the split-floor, and finally arrived at the first floor to take a single window. When he saw Qin Ying anxiously looking for him there, he looked as if he was crying and immediately asked, "What ails you?" Where have you been? Oh, it's really killing me. It's been a long time. Show me the bill quickly. The driver will pick up some items for us later. He told us to sit on stools outside the gate and wait for him. He told us not to go anywhere again."

Deng Cheng like a small puppet listen to Qin Ying command, but did not listen to a word, just follow her to go to the clinic outside the chair to sit down. Thoughts are a little confused, Deng Cheng does not know how to say to Qin Ying. He can not hide from her, must be honest with Qin Ying account. But he does not know how to say it to Qin Ying, what kind of impact will it bring to Qin Ying?

Deng Cheng thought what kind of way with Qin Ying open. First of all, tell the reason for staying and not going back to Zhuhai, and then tell it all when Qin Ying is alone tonight? Or do you want to start with a white lie?

Deng Cheng's head is not good, he feels that life is always difficult with him, so that he is not peaceful. Deng Cheng think Qin Ying so simple and kind, he dont know should hide Qin Ying, he only know this is not right and wrong stupid way. So what's to be done? Deng Cheng anxious to look up at the sky, at this time the sun under the light just slanted in Qin Ying's face, Deng Cheng eyes looking at such a beautiful Qin Ying, like in the landscape painting, can not help but touch Qin Ying's cheek, the wind blowing in the ear hair, one by one. At this time Deng Cheng did not think anything, but instinctively repeated the action.

Chapter 27: Reluctant to part

Night slowly dark down, little Jane aunt and Xuzhong family uncle after the reunion with relatives, only in Qin Ying mother's home stayed a night, the next day back to the countryside Qichun. They only stay for one day at a time, thinking about the farm work in the countryside, the chickens to take care of, the garden needs to be watered, anyway, every time they come is to send agricultural and sideline native products, and they will rush home immediately.

Qin Ying mother has gone to bed early. Deng Cheng afraid to wake up Qin Ying mother, two people sat outside the balcony, quietly looking out of the window of the sky. Deng Cheng want to tell Qin Ying what happened in the hospital during the day, but for a time I do not know where to start. Deng Cheng feel today's night is particularly hard, he looked at Qin Ying several times is afraid to open his mouth, blocked in the heart but can not tell.

Deng Cheng looked at Qin Ying affectionately, took a deep breath and then said, "Do you know who I met in the hospital today?"

"Who is it? Don't be coy, come on." Qin Ying near Deng Cheng urged. Deng Cheng hesitantly said: "I met my ex-wife, she got liver cancer, admitted to the cancer hospital here, has almost died." I should hate her, but I can't when I see her in that state. I don't know why, I feel bad. Her days were numbered, she confessed to me, she told me that she had been down and out all these years, and I listened to it with a inexplicable sadness. When she regretted it, she came to Zhuhai to find me and found that I was in a relationship with you. She did not deserve to disturb my life anymore, and quietly returned to Hubei. I don't know if this is the right time to talk to you about my ex-wife's past, but I want to tell you something, and I want to make her feel better and less sorry before she leaves. After all, she is about to die, I can't bear to let her go so sad, you know my heart? I'm not asking you to understand why I forgive a woman who betrayed me. To be honest, I don't know why I did it. I'm not going to fly back to Zhuhai with you tomorrow, I want to stay with my ex-wife for the last time, Xiaoying, do you agree?"

Qin Ying was this sudden real events upset, she is a writer of novels, often write other people's love stories, but did not think that she and Deng Cheng will happen between such a life story. At this moment Qin Ying thought of not themselves, she was silent for a while, the heart rose a burst of love: "I understand your sadness, I just love you, do not know how to help you."

Hear this warm heart, Deng Cheng was very surprised, did not expect Qin Ying like him, showing his sympathy for his ex-wife. He was touched by Qin Ying's kindness and magnanimity, do not know how to express their feelings, just silently turned around. Qin Ying took a cup of warm water to Deng Cheng and said, "I understand you, don't think about me, you stay." But tomorrow we don't tell mother the details, lest the elders worry. We can find a hotel near the hospital for a while. Can I accompany you to the hospital to visit her? Maybe I'll fly back to Zhuhai alone to deal with some emergencies, and you stay here to take care of your ex-wife at any time, do you think it's okay?"

Qin Ying words let Deng Cheng very moved, Deng Cheng did not think Qin Ying has such feelings and atmosphere of mind, he felt at this time said nothing to express their feelings. Qin Ying magnanimously shared Deng Cheng inner pain, but also let Deng Cheng release repressed feelings in the bottom of my heart. Deng Cheng found himself more love Qin Ying, he once again firmly believe that Qin Ying is the most worthy of his life to protect the woman. Deng Cheng silently put Qin Ying in his arms, afraid of others run away feeling.

That night, the two of them just sat on the balcony and looked at the sky. They leaned on each other quietly and clung to each other for a long, long time, and it would be a sleepless night.

The next morning, Qin Ying explained to her mother before leaving for the airport and Deng Cheng to visit a patient, and then directly to the airport to fly to Zhuhai. Qin Ying mother is an understanding elder, mother only to two people said a few words: "You are adults, I believe you will deal with everything." Some things, according to their own will to do, naturally, naturally, you will understand later."

Qin Ying mother did not say what, the elder in the heart is very clear, just did not say it. On the day of the family reunion, as the representative of the elders, he said a reassuring word: "You should also pay attention to your health when you start a business, and only a healthy body is the most valuable wealth in real life."

Qin Ying know mother full of exhortation, the old man is hoping that young people can live a happy life, not just to earn how much money. The elderly hope that their children give priority to health and strive for development within their ability; In emotional to live up to their conscience, worthy of their original intention.

Deng Cheng was very grateful to Qin Ying's mother and bowed deeply to thank her. Deng Cheng has felt Qinying mother's recognition, this is the best affirmation for him. Qin Ying's mother is the most respected elders, can get the support of Qin Ying's mother, this is Deng Cheng and Qin Ying into the marriage hall of reassurance.

The plane to Zhuhai takes off at 6:15 PM, it is morning now, many things still have time to deal with. Qin Ying and Deng Cheng hurriedly bid farewell to their families, immediately rushed to the chain hotel near the hospital and booked a standard room. Qin Ying arranged Deng Cheng stay in the hotel, ready to go with Deng Cheng, buy some nutrition to visit Deng Cheng's ex-wife, just then Deng Cheng mobile phone rang, Deng Cheng through after came an anxious voice: "Hello! Are you Deng Cheng? I am the head nurse you met at the hospital yesterday. Could you please come to the emergency room at once? Your ex-wife was dying, but she kept calling your name, wanting to see you one last time. Come quickly!"

Deng Cheng could not understand why the head nurse could get through to him on the phone, presumably his ex-wife had filled out Deng Cheng's number in the emergency contact. At this time Deng Cheng a little panic, hands and feet cold, slow response, at a loss. It's so sudden for him, isn't it, that his ex-wife, whom he saw only yesterday, suddenly says she can't? What happened to a few months?

Fortunately Qin Ying beside him, hurriedly said to Deng Cheng: "Hurry to the hospital to see, I go with you." Qin Ying will be important personal items immediately packed up, holding the hand of Deng Cheng even ran away rushed to the hospital emergency center room.

Hospital intensive care unit, head nurse guide Deng Cheng came to the ex-wife's bedside, Qin Ying followed the past, standing behind Deng Cheng.

Ex-wife see Deng Cheng quickly came, her heart mixed feelings, tears involuntarily from the corner of the eye along the face down, a little sobbing. She was trying to keep her emotions in check, a kind of gratitude that mixed joy and tears. She wanted to support her body to get up, Deng Cheng immediately grabbed her hand and said: "You lie down and say, I listen, we will always guard your side."

Deng Cheng's ex-wife Ye Xiaolan is two years older than Qin Ying, was still young, reluctant to leave, after seeing Deng Cheng, she seems to calm down a lot. She pointed to a letter and a set of house keys under the pillow and handed them to Deng Cheng in person, then slowly and calmly lay down, without leaving Deng Cheng for a moment, smiling softly and saying, "Can you help me comb my hair?" I want to clean myself up. You can help me. Even if I go to heaven, I want to be beautiful."

Qin Ying loosen hold Deng Cheng that hand, let Deng Cheng to help Ye Xiaolan comb hair. He quietly exited the room with the medical staff and prayed silently at the window outside the door.

Deng Cheng with tears while helping his ex-wife comb his hair while looking at his ex-wife's cheek, like saying: if you have liver pain, shout out, don't bear it, I am in, you don't have the idea of suicide.

Ye Xiaolan dont want to live, there is her reason, she dont want to waste these unnecessary treatment fees, so would like to see Deng Cheng before the final leave.

Ye Xiaolan seemed to shine, suddenly refreshed, and Deng Cheng explained one important thing: "Remember, you must read the letter I wrote well and do it." Please, you are the only family I have, and I have failed you, so don't hate me."

After that Ye Xiaolan some reluctant to part, to Deng Cheng calm smile serenely said: "I want to rest, you go to work." Stop worrying about me and love her. She's such a good woman. I've had no luck in my life. I'm going to rest..."

Deng Cheng looked at his ex-wife and stopped talking, as if he had fallen asleep peacefully. After a few minutes, the screen of the instrument shows that the heart pulse has no beating signal, and only the sound of ticking is heard. The whole ward was silent, a few minutes later, everyone consciously slowly retreated out, only Deng Cheng like appreciating a painting, guarding the side of his ex-wife.

Qin Ying was touched by Deng Cheng's love and kindness before his ex-wife died, and she heard Deng Cheng's ex-wife's words: "You should love her well, I sincerely wish you happiness."

Qin Ying wanted Deng Cheng to accompany his ex-wife quietly for a while, fighting back tears to the nurses said: "We don't bother him, his best comfort at the moment is quiet."

The head nurse said softly to herself, "We must prepare for the funeral."

Deng Cheng on the side, feel Ye Xiaolan just fell asleep. Deng Cheng said to her, "I have forgiven you, I don't hate you." Who hasn't made mistakes? Don't worry, I will do what you want, bury you on the mountain, under the tree we once planted, it is called a tree burial. You can bury all your troubles and let the tree be with you. You'll think of it in heaven as if you were at home."

Deng Cheng thought of here, has been sobbing, there is a kind of unspeakable sadness, eyes gushing countless tears, he kept using shirt cuffs to wipe. Deng Cheng Ye Xiaolan so sad to cry, but all this she can not see. Qin Ying saw, and was touched by Deng Cheng kind deep moving scene, she was sad and glad that she met a love man worthy of life.

Deng Cheng suddenly thought that there are the most worthy of his love. Where is Qin Ying? Deng Cheng gently stroked Ye Xiaolan's cheek and slowly put the white sheet over her face. Deng Cheng exits the room accompanied by the nurse, when the head nurse with the staff holding a stretcher will Ye Xiaolan lift into the stretcher, transferred to the hospital morgue.

Deng Cheng looked at his ex-wife being carried to the direction of the morgue on a stretcher, and his tears contained endless sadness. Qin Ying held Deng Cheng, feel like he is standing unstable, Deng Cheng need to rest, physical and mental exhaustion.

Qin Ying had to accompany Deng Cheng back to the hotel, want to talk to him, let him not so sad. Deng Cheng calm down after thought can not delay Qin Ying back to Zhuhai plane. He pretended to be strong, tried to endure sadness, and very rationally took Qin Ying's hand and said: "Ying Zi, return my ticket." I'll take you to the airport. You go back alone. I'll stay and finish all this. Don't tell your mother about these things, don't let your family worry about us, you know what I mean?"

Qin Ying said, "You don't have to send me. Don't you want me to do something for you?"

Deng Cheng said: "No, I can handle it, you concentrate on your own things." You also have a lot of things to be busy there, you have delayed for me for a long time, there can not be without you. I'll just stay, I'll finish up here, and don't worry, I may have to stay here for a while, because I'll sell the house and get rid of all the things she's used, like she wants. I'll get back to you when we're done. In the meantime, I can wait for my test results to report. We will make further plans depending on the situation."

Qin Ying understand if she stay in Dengcheng side will only let him distraction, can not handle everything at ease. She agreed to Deng Cheng's plan and flew to Zhuhai alone.

Deng Cheng want to send Qin Ying to the airport, Qin Ying see Deng Cheng this mind heavy state, understanding to Deng Cheng a hug, attached to his ear softly said: "Take good care of yourself, I will wait for you to come back, goodbye, take care."

Deng Cheng just nodded, stifled a sentence: "I want to take you to the car, this can finally?"

Deng Cheng with Qin Ying hand in hand to the hotel door, Deng Cheng Qin Ying big travel box moved to the car, say hello to the driver said a few words: "This is a taxi fare, you take." Drive slowly, safety first." Then he went to the back seat and said goodbye to Qin Ying: "After arriving at the airport, I will arrange for General Shen to pick you up at the airport." Text me when you get home, and I'll think of you every day."

The driver started the vehicle, Deng Cheng helplessly back, to Qin Ying reluctantly goodbye. Carrying Qin Ying vehicle to the main road of the city, until can not see, Deng Cheng went to the direction of the hospital, the end of all the past old accounts, Deng Cheng can be completely relieved.

Chapter 28: The Moon and the Morning (End)

Three days later, Ye Xiaolan's body was cremated. Deng Cheng in accordance with the instructions she left the letter one by one, the last one is to bury her ashes in the hometown of the mountain under the tree of two people.

Deng Cheng comply with Ye Xiaolan will, under the tree do not leave a name, do not erect arch. He dug a small hole under the tree, put Ye Xiaolan's urn in it, and set the letter on fire. The ashes mixed with the soil under the tree and buried the urn.

Deng Cheng breathed a deep sigh of relief and said to Ye Xiaolan: "You rest in peace, you have done what you want me to do." I will live well for you." He leaned silently against the tree trunk, gently closed his eyes, and the smile of Ye Xiaolan appeared in his mind, like telling Deng Cheng, "I have already arrived home, you go busy!"

Deng Cheng opened his eyes to look at the blue sky and white clouds, and heard waves of rustling leaves shaking in his ears. Deng Cheng's mood calmed a lot, he thought of the old Chinese saying, "Death is inevitable, or heavier than Mount Tai, or lighter than a feather." After experiencing the death of his ex-wife, he is no longer afraid of death, and he believes that it is good to live without regrets.

Deng Cheng remembered what Inamori Kazuo said: "All our lives, we are looking for two things, one is the sense of value, the other is the sense of belonging, the sense of value comes from being affirmed, the sense of belonging comes from being loved." People in this life do not careless two things. One is to find the right lover, and the other is to find the right cause, because when the sun rises, you need to devote yourself to the cause, and when the sun goes down, you need to embrace your lover. Who you are, you will meet. Perhaps the best life is the ability to love yourself, the power to love others, the time to accomplish what you want to do and dream, and the feelings to explore poetry and distance."

After Ye Xiaolan ashes are buried, Deng Cheng will Ye Xiaolan left his own property hanging in the intermediary agent for sale. He went back to the hospital to take the test report, and some indicators also showed a + number, indicating that the body has not fully recovered. The doctor said to Deng Cheng: "To be completely cured, or continue to take Chinese medicine."

Deng Cheng combined with the current situation, with Qin Ying proposed temporarily did not return to Zhuhai, continue to stay here to treat the disease, and deal with the sale of housing. Doctor Ai Shen has seen the test results and confirmed that Deng Cheng's body has improved significantly, but it still needs to continue to recuperate. He also gave Deng Cheng seven doses of Chinese medicine for a week. Doctor Ai said to Deng Cheng: "It seems that our climate here is very suitable for you, if you want to be completely cured, you need to stay for a long time, I wonder what Brother Deng thinks?"

Deng Cheng to Ai God doctor said his concerns, Qin Ying to develop his career in Zhuhai, if he is separated from Qin Ying for a long time because of treatment, will be unfair to Qin Ying, after all, he had promised to return to Zhuhai as soon as possible and Qin Ying married. On the other hand, Deng Cheng also hopes to be able to do something beneficial to the public during the period of recuperation, Deng Cheng's career are staying in Zhuhai, staying here Deng Cheng vaguely feel that they are wasting precious life time, can not play their own life value.

Doctor Ai Shen thought for a moment and said to Deng Cheng: "Have you asked Qin Ying about marriage?" Let her decide where to get married."

Ai Shen doctor's words hit the nail on the head, Deng Cheng thought for a moment and said: "I will consider explaining everything to Qin Ying, but I feel that I have not thought well, I don't want her to worry about misunderstanding."

Doctor Ai suddenly remembered something and said to Deng Cheng: "I saw a patient the day before yesterday, and it seems that they mentioned that their township is developing some policies for green environmental protection development, opening up green channels for contracting barren mountains to the outside world, and developing afforestation and planting orchard bases. If you want to stay here long term and develop a new career, you may want to consider this direction. I can get you some contact information."

Deng Cheng jumped up with joy: "I am interested! This is very meaningful. I want to stay and transform the barren mountains into fruit forests. I would like to do something for the benefit of future generations in my lifetime. This is a once-in-a-lifetime opportunity, please Doctor Ai Shen help me contact. You have not only healed my body, but also opened my heart."

Deng Cheng suddenly had a spiritual pillar, he excitedly said goodbye to Ai God doctor in a hurry, went straight to the little Jane aunt's home to tell them about it. Deng Cheng is a person who dares to challenge, whether it is for love, or for career work, say to do it. A few days later, Doctor Ai contacted Deng Cheng and introduced him to Director Zhang, who was responsible for contracting barren mountains.

Secretary Zhang carefully listened to Deng Cheng's suggestions and drafted planning plans, and asked Deng Cheng to come up with a specific plan that could be implemented a week later, and to determine how many acres of barren land to contract.

Deng Cheng humbly consulted the suggestions of Xu Zhong's family, went from village to household to collect opinions from villagers, and understood climate change, conducted in-depth and detailed investigation and analysis of various situations, and noted the distribution of human, material and financial resources in the copy. After a week of full preparation, Deng Cheng will transform the barren mountain into a green fruit forest plan successfully handed over to Director Zhang.

Director Zhang held a special meeting to discuss the project, and the important person in charge of the project unanimously approved Deng Cheng's plan to contract 500 acres of barren mountains. Township leaders specifically approved Deng Cheng's right to use six acres of wasteland as a living house. After the plan was passed, Deng Cheng immediately said that he would invest 10 million yuan in the early stage of infrastructure construction.

After the Xuzhong family uncle and Shaozhen aunt asked Deng Cheng whether they needed to sponsor, Deng Cheng was very pleased, understanding refused their funding: "I will solve the funding problem, I just sell some real estate, there are enough funds to use this project." I believe Qin Ying will be very happy after knowing this. This is our future home, we can enjoy the blue sky together, we can live together the end of time, and we will not have to choose a cemetery in the future, we will return to our roots here."

Deng Cheng happily sleepless all night, thought Qin Ying after hearing the news dont know what will be the reaction. He could not wait to tell Qin Ying the good news.

Qin Ying returned to Zhuhai after busy, every day to take care of love bar book, has always insisted on writing, with Shen and autumn sweet busy on endless. Fortunately, two employees Xiao Qin Xiao Bei are very skilled in the management and operation of the book bar, helping Qin Ying share a lot of work.

Qin Ying returned to Zhuhai in the first few days did not disturb Deng Cheng too much, let him deal with his ex-wife at ease. From his attitude towards his ex-wife, Qin Ying saw Deng Cheng's kindness, deepen love Deng Cheng. Although Qin Ying is already Deng Cheng's fiancee, but she will not give Deng Cheng bondage, she hopes Deng Cheng can be happy and healthy and happy life, love him not occupy him, two people love each other, miss each other from time to time is enough happiness.

To deal with Deng Cheng ex-wife things, Qin Ying as before with Deng Cheng to maintain frequent contact. But recently, Qin Ying felt as if Deng Cheng was dealing with something important and sometimes couldn't reach him for days at a time. Deng Cheng last call told Qin Ying he had something to go to the mountains to investigate, there is no network signal, may not be able to contact. Qin Ying doubts Deng Cheng will do what important things in his hometown?

This day, when Deng Cheng finally told Qin Ying frankly about his next career to do, Qin Ying as Deng Cheng expected that surprise and excitement.

Qin Ying seriously replied to Deng Cheng's message: I am very supportive of your project of contracting barren mountains to reclaim trees, where you can improve the rural economy and promote the development of your hometown, and you can continue to fight against cancer and gradually recover. Trust that this land will nourish your life. You do what I want to do, and the way you like to live is my ideal life.

Dear Deng Cheng, I am very glad and contented to have met you in this life. You don't have to worry about our wedding. It's just a part of the marriage process. I love you not just impulse, is you really to me, let me naturally feel deep love. Where is true love, my heart is concerned about where, in my heart, there are three places can spend the rest of my life with the sun rising moon Ming beautiful treasure: my hometown - the capital of Chinese medicine spring Li Shizhen hometown; And then there are Zhongshan and Zhuhai, where we met each other, a vibrant city, our second hometown. The best home, is because of you and have the soul to store, the most steadfast, safe and warm harbor, is the rest of my life can be entrusted to the rest of my life.

As much as I love the song "With Love," the lyrics are on my mind right now:

I've been on the wrong side of the road

Tired who to talk

Met how many infatuation will not know

But I know one day

I'll find something better

With love I believe there is a way out

With love feelings

In this moment with you can finally hug

Even if it's always bad luck

Life has no trouble

Have fallen in this high and low twists and turns

Just suddenly feel happy heart simple already very good

The most beautiful is still love with tears taste is still good

Not afraid of the ups and downs of life to accompany the old

With love I believe there is a way out

With love feelings are not old

In this moment with you can finally hug

Even if it's always bad luck

Life has no trouble

Have fallen in this high and low twists and turns

Just suddenly feel happy heart simple already very good

The most beautiful is still love with tears taste is still good

Not afraid of the ups and downs of life to accompany the old

Have fallen in this high and low twists and turns

Just suddenly feel happy heart simple already very good

The most beautiful is still love with tears taste is still good

Not afraid of the ups and downs of life to accompany the old

With love, only one life honed to the old

postscript

As for the original intention of writing this work, I wanted to write a contemporary love and marriage story about the standard of old leftover women's choice of a mate.

The novel records the process of the female protagonist Qin Ying's communication with three men. Through the comparison of three different experiences, Qin Ying deeply realizes the true meaning of love and marriage. Finally, she chooses the lover who can understand her and the love who can accompany her for life. This is a novel to promote the positive energy of marriage, only the true love for the true love, will be able to enter the heart of the lover.

This work was first named "mind Pill" , the original story line is Qin Ying and Cheng Mo help each other, two people gradually deep feelings, and finally cultivate love. In the middle of writing, I found that Cheng Mo's original character was a unreliable person. I am a writer accustomed to extracting material from real life, and changes in real life have influenced my writing direction. So I modified the direction of the story and changed the title of the work to "Whimsical" , writing the two sides of some false men in life, on the one hand, hiding their selfish greed, on the other hand, showing excellent popularity, enthusiasm, initiative, and kindness. In the later stage of writing, I restrained my critical edge and did not add too much personal subjective analysis to the character of Cheng Mo. I preferred to show Cheng Mo's actions truthfully and let readers judge this character by themselves.

Later, I changed the title of my work to "What is the Truth" , and published it in a weekly newspaper "Literary world" column. After the completion of the work, I re-tasted it and found that the theme of the work later improved a lot than the original idea. I want to promote the correct concept of love through this work: to treat the person who loves you sincerely, you will get true love in return. In the preparatory stage of the publication of the work, I discussed and considered with the teacher, and renamed the work "With Love" .

Due to the demand of international readers, this work is now entitled "Spring breeze kisses my face" in Chinese and English bilingual book for readers to read in both Chinese and English.

It is not easy to write a good work, and it takes the enthusiastic help of many people to get a work published in a book. Thanks to all the friends who helped me in the writing process, thanks to the professional guidance and help of Huiwen book editors!

Author: Zhao Shuxian

March 2, 2024

春风吻上我的脸

序 言

  春风轻拂，吻过岁月的脸庞，留下了一抹温柔的印记。此刻，我们即将去探寻那些隐藏在《春风吻上我的脸》中的温情与真挚。这部由赵舒娴女士倾心打造的作品，以其细腻的笔触和深刻的情感，让我们感受到了爱情的力量与美好。

  在书中，我们见到了女主角秦瑛，一个充满活力和追求的女子。她通过与三个不同男人的情感纠葛，历经曲折和磨砺，最终领悟到真爱的含义。在这个过程中，秦瑛的形象被塑造得真实而立体，她有过迷茫、犹豫，但始终保持对爱情的执着追求，选择了能懂她、珍惜她的伴侣。

  除了女主角，其他人物的塑造也栩栩如生，各有特色：虚伪的程默、真诚的邓诚，以及善良的沈总夫妇。这些角色之间的情感纠葛和冲突，使得整个故事充满了曲折和惊喜。每一次的情感冲突都让人揪心，每一次的转机都让人欣喜。尤其是秦瑛与邓诚的感情线，作者以其敏锐的洞察力，深入挖掘了秦瑛内心的挣扎与成长，通过秦瑛与邓诚之间的感情线，展现了爱情的复杂与美好。从相识到相知，从相知到相爱，每一个细节都被作者描绘得淋漓尽致，让我们仿佛置身于故事之中，与角色们共同经历着那些喜怒哀乐。

  这部作品不仅弘扬了正确的价值观和婚姻观，强调了只有真情实意对待爱人才能换来真心的爱情，更提醒我们要勇敢面对生活中的困难和挑战，积极追求自己的幸福和梦想。在这个充满变数的世界里，我们需要像秦瑛和邓诚一样，坚定信念，心怀热爱，勇往直前。

  《春风吻上我的脸》，让我们一起，随着春风的吻痕，踏上这段充满爱与希望的文字之旅吧！相信在这段旅程中，我们会收获满满的感动与启迪，也会更加珍惜身边的爱情与幸福。

汇文书联编辑：衔青

2024 年 3 月 2 日

第 1 章　雨天偶遇

珠海的七月份正是海洋气候最无常的季节，天气说变就变，乌云密布的天空突然下起狂风暴雨，倾盆大雨向行人当头淋下。

那时秦瑛正在海边景点鱼女石附近，看见下大雨，她顾不上那么多，卷起长裤角跟着躲雨的人群奔跑起来。慌乱之时，秦瑛停下脚步，望着马路对面的"爱吧书吧"，迟疑了一会，还是赶紧跑了过去。

"爱吧书吧"室内占地 160 平方面积，分上下两层，前门有一片 100 平方米的庭院空地，摆放着六套石头桌凳，平日里供客人喝茶看书之用。门前两边栽种着大树，茂密的树叶遮住一些雨水，来这里避雨的路人有很多。秦瑛一头扎进大门口站着，随意跺脚抬头的一瞬间看见了一个熟悉的身影。秦瑛心中一惊："是他？他怎么会出现在珠海？"

不远处的男人名叫苏勇，是秦瑛寻找多年的恋人。苏勇好像也看见了秦瑛，两人都一下子僵在原地。很快，苏勇低着头走进了"爱吧书吧"，秦瑛连忙追了上去。她急着要找苏勇问个清楚，问问他这些年到底去了哪里，现在他们到底算是什么关系。

秦瑛进了书吧后四下环顾，她的背后传来熟悉的男低音："我在你背后。"秦瑛猛地转过身，看到正是苏勇站在身后，她用手死劲地拽着苏勇的手臂，刻意压下愤怒问他："你怎么不声不响就离开？你可知道我这些年像个傻子一样到处找你？"秦瑛委屈得像个孩子，可又不能大声指责苏勇，她一边说一边拉着苏勇走向书吧安静的一角，想要他马上说个明白。

看起来秦瑛对爱吧书吧的环境很熟悉，事实上这里的装修是她一手设计出来的——她是爱吧书吧的老板，知道这件事的人并不多。

旁边没有什么人，秦瑛的声音显得更响亮，她问苏勇："这几年你都到哪里去了？为什么不说一声就离开我？几年过去，可能你早就忘了我，我不纠缠你，但你必须告诉我实情！"

苏勇没有回避，但又显得特别紧张，不知道从何说起，他吞吞吐吐地回答："那年我离开得很仓促，本想到了广州安顿好之后再跟你说。后来发生了一连串事情，我一直忙个不停，就把这事耽搁了。再接着我的女老板离婚了，她看中我，我们便慢慢走在一起……现在我已经和她结婚了，她和前夫的女儿跟着我们一起住。我辜负了你，所以我不敢回去找你。"

听到苏勇的回答，秦瑛平静了下来，她终于等到了一个答案。她觉得自己很可笑，傻乎乎地等了这么久。其实她早就想过苏勇已经放弃自己了，毕竟苏勇长相英俊性格又体贴，很容易吸引女人爱上他。

苏勇继续说："我的那位今天也来了，就在那边。她跟女儿向我们走过来了。"说着，苏勇向门口方向招了招手。

秦瑛转头，看见一位长相一般的女人走到近前。这女子长着方脸大嘴，一头披肩短发，眼睛挺大，但不好看，明显的斗鸡眼。她拉着一个十岁左右的女孩走向苏勇。当她看清秦瑛之后，她突然大声叫道："你是秦瑛？我们是高中同学，你还认得我吗？"

这样一说，秦瑛也认出来了："你是学习委员马婷！你怎么会在这里？"

马婷指着苏勇说："我们一家来旅游。"马婷女儿直接对苏勇叫了一声："老爸，你怎么跑到这里来了，害得我和妈妈在爱吧书吧找了你一圈！老爸这里有好多书，我好喜欢这个书吧。你找了这么久，找到一个位置了吗？"

苏勇为难地指着旁边刚好出现的一个空位："我只找到这个小桌空位，太多人进来避雨了，这里地方不大，现在没有什么空位。"

马婷拉着秦瑛的手说："忘了介绍一下，这是我的老公苏勇，在我广州的公司当总经理，这是我的女儿园园。想起来我们毕业后再也没有见面了，难得在这里有缘遇上，我们一起吃个饭吧。"

秦瑛不甘心输给这位高中同学，她也好奇苏勇后来的经历，于是同意了马婷的邀请。四人在小桌坐了下来，分别点了自己喜欢吃的东西。随后秦瑛借口说去趟洗手间，自己到前台先把账结了。

不一会服务员把菜端了上来，马婷吃着其中一道名叫素菜丸子的小吃，对秦瑛称赞道："老同学你真会点餐，这丸子太好吃了！"秦瑛偷偷望向苏勇，发现他脸色果然有点不自然。说起这道素菜丸子，还有一段他跟秦瑛的故事。

以前他们两人还在一起的时候，他们曾在县里的一家店铺吃一种用黏米粉做的素菜丸子，当时苏勇就非常喜欢这味道，说那是他吃过最美味的素食品。吃完后，秦瑛特意请教店里的老板娘，问她怎样做这一道菜，还另外买了 50 个丸子打包带走，说要给城里的亲人好友分享。回去的时候秦瑛兴奋地说："以后有机会我也会开一个原始复古风格的小茶馆，茶馆的小吃里一定要有这一道黏米粉素菜丸子，还配上书刊，可以让人一边喝茶一边看书。我相信到时候的生意一定比刚刚的小店铺还要好。"如今的"爱吧书吧"几乎就是当时秦瑛向苏勇描绘的样子，不知道他会不会猜想这个书吧就是秦瑛开的。

马婷对秦瑛说："你现在还是那么漂亮，一点也不像我老成这样子了。对了，你成家了吗？"

秦瑛笑得有点勉强："哪像你有福气，孩子都这么大了，还懂事，老公又帅。我一直瞎忙，没有遇到合适的人，不过我也想快点脱单。看你过得这么幸福，我也想快点把自己嫁出去。"

秦瑛说这番话还是说给苏勇听的，暗示自己该放下了这段感情。今天遇见苏勇一家，秦瑛彻底放弃了等待苏勇的幻想。她接受不了苏勇为了自己的事业，宁愿放弃她秦瑛的爱情。没有想到苏勇也是很现实的一个男人，为了所谓的人生追求的目标，甘愿做马婷的丈夫，做孩子的继父。苏勇跟马婷明显不相配，但是看得出来马婷很自信、幽默、会说话、会哄男人喜欢，这是秦瑛所不具备的能力。

爱吧书吧里放着轻缓宁静的音乐，在这里坐着会感觉心灵深处都会被静下来。这书吧氛围适合任何人，可以一人静静看书，可以一个人要上一壶茶坐着窗边，看着海的方向发呆，还可以三朋四友一起低声细语聚聚。到了周末，年轻夫妇带着孩子来到这里喝茶看书是常态。

马婷对女儿说："圆圆，看来你挺喜欢这里。这书吧的老板真有创意，装修风格都很用心，朴实无华，但看起来很舒服。看来这个老板的品位真不错，我也很享受这里的氛围。"说着，她又含情脉脉地看着苏勇，苏勇只能点点头表示赞同马婷的话。

马婷接着转身对秦瑛说："对了，叫服务员拿笔和纸来，我们互留个手机号吧，要不离开这里后，怎么联系你呀？"

　　秦瑛不想再去参与苏勇的生活了，但又不好直接拒绝马婷，她马上起身去结账吧台待了一会儿。她对着服务员说了几句话就走回桌前："账我已经结了。现在雨也停了，你们慢慢喝茶，多休息一下。我今天本来约了朋友，刚刚她打电话来催我，现在我要离开了，对不起失陪了。"

　　马婷还没来得及写上自己的手机号码，秦瑛就突然离开了，她有点措手不及，书吧里人多，高声叫秦瑛又显得不礼貌，只能眼看着秦瑛匆匆离去。苏勇更是五味杂陈，也不敢追上去。拿不到秦瑛的手机号码，看来他这辈子跟秦瑛缘分已尽，今天的偶遇算是跟秦瑛彻底告别。

　　回想起从前跟秦瑛一起的快乐日子，苏勇很是怀念，只不过他清楚知道他更爱自己，在爱情和物质之间，他会选后者。想起来还是他辜负了秦瑛，内心里感到很愧疚。他记得两人交往的日子里他只给秦瑛送过一枚老式银戒指当礼物，这就是他那个时候能给秦瑛的全部。苏勇无意中摸了一下衣兜，发现那枚银戒指就在里面，一定是秦瑛偷偷还给了他。想到这里，他又是一阵心酸。

　　秦瑛逃出书吧，深深地舒了一口气，她快步地向海边走去。她逃出之前，悄悄地从手上摘下那枚银戒指，趁马婷没有注意的时候放进苏勇的衣兜里。这个举动就是告诉自己，她决定放下了苏勇。人家已经成家立业，哪里还有自己的位置？秦瑛感觉自己真的可笑，为了等待苏勇耗费了自己的青春，现在她已经39岁了。等了这么多年的爱情，还是一场空。她的心凉了半截，但是梦醒了！

第 2 章　人非草木

离开了苏勇夫妇后，秦瑛直朝海边漫无边际地走着，感觉自己算是放下了，但毕竟恋爱等待了那么多年，还是有些想不通。他们曾经相恋那么多年，就差没有挑破谈婚论嫁。

秦瑛不自觉想起他们的过往：那时他们都在家乡的小城生活，苏勇在银行上班，当前台大厅主任；秦瑛当时在商业局属下的一部副食品批发站工作，每天的营业款都落在秦瑛负责存入公司账户，定点银行挂钩的业务就是苏勇负责的支行。久而久之，苏勇注意到了秦瑛，而秦瑛也被这长相帅气的苏勇吸引。他的一举一动，她会很小心的注视，每次情不自禁地脸红心跳，害羞答答的害怕抬头看见苏勇，但又希望苏勇能在现场当班。她知道这次突然有了恋爱的感觉，纯单相思，因为那个时候还没有相互表白，只是从熟悉慢慢打招呼。

刚上班不久的某一天，秦瑛因早晨睡过了头，走得急就没有在家过早，早上并没有什么业务生意，于是在银行对面的一个特制牛肉粉小店吃着早餐。据说那是一家十年的老牌店，味道没话说，只要吃过的客人都会回头再来光顾。此言不假，秦瑛后来就是爱光顾这家店的常客。

当时秦瑛正吃着牛肉粉加一根油条，突苏勇又走进这个店，跟老板好像很熟悉似的："我跟昨天一样来一碗，加油条一根，多放点辣汤。"原来苏勇也喜欢吃这家的牛肉粉，口味跟秦瑛一模一样。秦瑛听到苏勇的声音，头都不敢抬，低头装着没听到埋头吃着，一个磁性的声音在秦瑛背后耳边响起："嘿，秦瑛你今天怎么这个时间来吃牛肉粉啊？"她知道完了，苏勇已经看到她了，她不好意思地抬起头说："嗯，我今天晚了。"

苏勇："你也在这里过早？我每天都在这里吃，我也喜欢吃这家味道。"

两人就开始了随意交谈，秦瑛总忘不了第一次这么近距离地跟一个这么帅的小伙子讲话，苏勇似乎比上班的时候更善谈。

秦瑛后来才知道苏勇的父亲是在本市很有名的剧团的团长，而妈妈是剧团的女主角，他爸妈的恋爱传为那个年代的佳话，苏勇长得帅气像他爸，很俊浓眉大眼，却没有接爸妈的班，走文艺之路，而是从事金融行业。因为形象出众，苏勇当上了银行的前台大堂经理。听说苏勇被作为行里的培养对象，作为提拔行长备选人之一。

似乎那段时间日子过得很快，而且秦瑛很乐意去银行办理这些业务，每天期待着这个时间就可以见到苏勇。而苏勇只要听秦瑛在前台跟同事说话，他就会从后台走进前台接待秦瑛。两人渐渐熟悉，很自然地确立了恋爱关系。

后来经过了解才知道，苏勇的同事只要看见秦瑛来行存款，有意让苏勇出来打招呼，众人都想促成他们俩成为一对，一个未嫁一个未娶，看上去真的挺般配的一对。

这段恋情并没有公开曝光，那个时候秦瑛就是坐在苏勇自行车后，笑得开心的女人，他俩在一起的时光是那么美好，没有世俗的杂念，没有任何干扰，秦瑛笑得灿烂，可一到公开场合苏勇都刻意地去避免让众人察觉他和秦瑛恋情。因为苏勇还没有想到结婚，只是觉得跟秦瑛在一起非常放松舒服。虽然口里没有亲口对秦瑛所明确表白，但又放不下这好的女人秦瑛。他认为男人为了事业应该放下男女之情，在还没有实现目标之前，他不会谈婚论嫁。

苏勇有意无意对秦瑛作出过这样的暗示，当他事业有成时再来娶秦瑛。为了稳住秦瑛，苏勇将姥姥送给他的一枚银戒指作为定情信物送给了秦瑛。

后来苏勇因为工作的关系调离家乡小城，改行来到了广州某一个民营公司。之后就再联系不上苏勇。自从苏勇不辞而别后，秦瑛也无心在继续在原单位干下去，每次去银行就会想起苏勇影子和声音，也感觉苏勇的同事会在背后议论她。

这种触景思人的日子，实在让秦瑛受不了，几年的恋爱因苏勇玩失踪而彻底破灭，对她打击太大。她必须改变这个局面，而唯一的办法就是走为上计。

就这样秦瑛做了一次改变自己的决定，辞职下海。她在珠海与中山、深圳、广州、澳门、香港这些城市都进一步的考察，最后决定在珠海与中山之间发展。

秦瑛最初找到的落脚的地方，是珠海的一个瑜伽馆理疗中心服务公司。她被服务诊所被聘用，白天理疗师的身份工作，周末及平日下班后的晚上，就打点自己开的这家"爱吧书吧"。

　　书吧的员工是两位从老家招来的娘家远房亲戚，这两位乡村女孩将爱吧书吧打理得井井有条。

　　书吧经营模式很简单，在图书馆阅览室的运营模式基础上多了一些热饮茶水小吃的服务项目，这也是为了爱读书看书的人，能在书吧待上一整天。

　　爱吧书吧生意慢慢做出名气了，书吧并没有牵引她多少精力，秦瑛把这种经营投资当成精神享受和慰藉。

　　财富收益刚刚持平房租及水电费及两个员工的工资开销费用，弱创收一些薄利。

　　这就是秦瑛最想做的事情，平常的节假日，同事都会去旅行，而秦瑛就会一头扎到自己的爱吧书吧，看书并处理一些日常事务。

　　对外从来不说这个爱吧书吧是自己开的，而且对员工也有交代，无论什么情况，不要叫她老板，所以在这里待了多少年都没有人知道书吧老板是谁。这也是秦瑛低调，为保护好自己最妥的办法。

　　来珠海那头几年，秦瑛就听了房地产朋友建议，果断地在珠海和中山之间，选择了一处房价不贵尾盘。

　　幸好早在 2015 年，秦瑛抓住了最后房地产投资的机会，买了一套中山与珠海之间的边界线的楼盘，一套绿色植物花园小区洋房，三房两厅 130 平方米，房价总款 58 万多人民币，装修后，才放了一年多以后，立马升职为翻了一倍。

　　秦瑛为了投资挣钱，先卖掉了这套获利的房产，接着又将盈利部分资金又投入海边，同一个开发商，开发的海景公寓复式楼。

　　就这样把第一套投资的房子翻两番的时候，就卖掉了，将投入的本钱进行再次投资理财。

　　秦瑛与同龄人比，她所有的零散的资金归集在一起，在房价涨之前抓住了尾巴，为落户在珠海站稳脚跟，获得了第一桶金。

　　为了这套房子的升值空间，利益最大化，秦瑛立马要进行装修，是在售楼部美女小伊推荐下找到了装修的夫妇俩沈总和秋甜。也就是在他们的影响下，让秦瑛喜欢上了珠海这个城市和这里朴实善良的人们。

　　在装修过程中，秦瑛永远记得秋甜和沈总对她的帮助。作为一个异乡来创业投资的陌生人，秦瑛想不到会跟他们成为忘年之交。秦瑛感觉到如果没有她夫妻俩的帮助，自己有很多方面都不知道从何着手。

秦瑛跟秋甜一见如故，第一次去她公司谈装修，秋甜尽量考虑节省成本，规划简装修重装饰的方案，一下子俘获了秦瑛的心。只谈了几个来回，秦瑛就放心将房子交给秋甜装修。

开始来珠海此地，秦瑛一直由秋甜热情陪同，带着她入住酒店，选择的是经济实惠温泉酒店入住，离秋甜装修公司也近。

秦瑛记得入住酒店最初的情景，酒店价格合理，开发商售楼部还给了酒店入住最优惠的推荐卡，一晚上只要 168，买了房的业主还可以享受折扣。

这温泉酒店的楼顶就有露天温泉池，与天空星星互应，泡在温泉池中，仿佛进入了仙境，早餐免费，住酒店客人还免费泡温泉。每位装修期间来业主入住酒店，如同是来此度假旅游的浪漫之旅。没有不喜欢此地的业主，秦瑛就是从这里更喜欢上了这座城市。

这都是秋甜陪同的功劳，时间长了，秦瑛也清楚知道海边哪里有海鲜吃。秦瑛喜欢吃螃蟹鱼类贝壳，秋甜给秦瑛推荐当地有名的海鲜餐饮店"崖口人家海鲜餐厅"。秦瑛很喜欢这家店，每次秦瑛去看房子装修进展的时候，就会去崖口人家吃饭；自己的女朋友从外地来，她都必带到那家崖口人家品尝海鲜。另外还有一家专吃鱼的店，叫"无骨鱼店"，一鱼多吃，有鱼骨头汤、下鱼皮、下鱼片、油炸鱼块、红烧鱼块等，墙面上都有外国友人慕名而来与厨师的合影。

时间是最好医治失恋的良药，来珠海这么年的创业打拼，生活过得忙碌充实，秦瑛慢慢忘记了失恋的痛苦，却没有想到会跟苏勇这样相遇。

还在海边漫步流连的秦瑛情不自禁地看着自己的左手无名指，那里还隐约看到银戒指留下的痕迹。银戒指已经还给苏勇，她跟苏勇之间的感情彻底结束。她告诉自己，既然已经放下了，就不要再想了，要向前看。秦瑛深呼了一口气，好像内心的郁结松开了。

秦瑛已经很习惯自己一个人生活，这样慢慢地早已把恋爱这事都忘了，一晃一个人生活挺好的。

在珠海秦瑛没有其他朋友，所以只要有空就去秋甜装修公司坐坐。

又是一个阳光明媚的周末，沈总公司的员工正热闹地为沈总过生日准备午餐。

真是来得早不如来得巧，撞上了生日派对，就是好兆头，沾喜气。

沈总就安排在公司跟职工一起吃三杯鸡，这次由秋甜亲自掌厨，为沈总特意烧了三杯鸡。

秋甜看到秦瑛到来，高兴的合不龙嘴："你来了正好，我今天让你尝尝三杯鸡，这可是地地道道的珠海人口味，你保证吃了以后还想吃。"

这次公司活动，加深了秦瑛对秋甜的好印象，没有想到除了工作之外，秋甜还会这么多，难怪沈总那么在乎秋甜。

这种工作上伙伴，生活上是夫妻搭档，处事又像是友情的伴侣，越来越让秦瑛羡慕了。

这是她看过的最幸福快乐的婚姻生活，夫唱妇随，快快乐乐，成双成对的美好平凡生活。

看到夫妻俩在公司后面炉子上忙碌的样子，秦瑛看呆了，在珠海原来也可以一半烟火，一半仙境地生活着，这油米柴盐的普通人的一生，不就是应该这样的吗？

当天晚上，沈总的姐夫也邀请秋甜和沈总去自家做客，没想到秦瑛也被作为欢迎邀请的客人嘉宾，一同前往。

秦瑛还有一点不好意思："你们是家宴，我就不去了。"

秋甜说："那不行不行，没你不行，你去姐姐家，定是最受欢迎。"就这样，秦瑛破例又到了沈总的姐姐家吃了丰富的晚餐。

家宴吃完以后，沈总姐夫高兴，又一起去歌厅 k 歌，包厢已定好。

秦瑛真正发现，第一首情歌是沈总及秋甜合唱《夫妻双双把家还》歌唱得那么好，特别是沈总，后面一首通俗唱法，更是纯朴的嗓音像原唱，秋甜也不差上下。

秦瑛用欣赏的眼光看着这对夫妻，还有什么能比此时的他们更快乐的呢？

同去的每个人都要求唱歌，当然秦瑛也不例外，最后秦瑛也被热闹的氛围感染，点上三首她自认为最拿手的歌，《牧羊曲》《我爱你，塞北的雪》《情义无价》……

秋甜拍手叫好连连夸赞地对众人说："看看，押台戏是秦瑛啊，原来你真是多才多艺呀，信了你的邪，还那么谦虚，要知道你唱歌这么好，我怎么也不敢唱了！"

直到秋甜说完，沈总说："真人不露相！秦瑛还没有男朋友太可惜了，我们一定要帮秦瑛找到优质股的好男人，我想起了一个人，很配秦瑛！"

说完这句话后立刻附在秋甜的耳边悄悄说出一个人名，秋甜听后不停点头说："对，可以，可以，下次你安排他们俩见一面，真的很配哟！"这晚大家都很尽兴。

秦瑛除了工作，就是周末到爱吧书吧，永远是两点一线的生活。所以秋甜和沈总知道，如果要找秦瑛，到爱吧书吧就一定能够找到。

又一个周末星期天，秋甜和沈总忙完装修活后，都会跟秦瑛在爱吧书吧小聚一会，听听轻音乐喝杯热茶，吹牛抖嘴皮子。

但是这个周末，爱吧书吧，沈总带来一位稀客！来人不是别人，正是沈总曾经悄悄提到的那位优质男邓诚。

第 3 章　从前邂逅

邓诚一进爱吧书吧，被沈总带到秦瑛桌前一刹那，秦瑛和邓诚同时不约而同地，情不自禁地笑出来，世界上仅有这么巧合的事情，也发生在邓诚和秦瑛他们俩人身上，真是不可思议呀！

两个人突然的笑声，让沈总和秋甜纳闷？沈总手指着邓诚说："邓董你们都认识？几时认识的？怎么没听你们说过，也没看你们在一起呀？"

秋甜一头雾水地瞪着眼睛看着秦瑛说："真有你的，保密工作做得这么好，也没有听你说过呀？也没见你们俩走动呀？这是你俩的缘分，还不快快招来，快说是怎么回事。"

秋甜一个劲地催着秦瑛，秦瑛笑而不语地看着邓诚，沈总示意小声用手指着快坐下来好好说说，他很想听听邓董与秦瑛俩认识的故事："请老实交代。"

邓诚坐了下来看了一眼秦瑛，不好意思地抓了几下头，笑着面对大家像讲故事一样说出自己最近几年的状况。

此时的秦瑛见到邓诚就在眼前对面坐下，侃侃而谈情景，不禁想起 5 年之间与邓诚的三次接触……

那一年，秦瑛远走他乡之前，彻底改变自己，脑海里浮现改头换面的画面……秦瑛赶在深圳去医美微整形，在院长的建议下，花 20 万元全脸打造！这是一次时尚彻底改变。大家知道赶时髦最好的炫富就是当今的微整形，经过 9 小时手术，秦瑛仔细看着镜子中的自己，感觉到刺激兴奋和愉悦，手术恢复正常，在外人看来，只感觉秦瑛变美了，年轻了，好看了，但是就是看不出任何改变的痕迹，这就是微整形的效果！人生最美的年华就是像这样永远保持快乐心情，容貌对秦瑛来说就是一种热爱生活的态度，她想来一次脱胎的改变。

秦瑛再次入住珠海温泉酒店办理入住手续的时候，大堂经理并没有认出她来，看见身份证的名字时，再次抬起头看着秦瑛，惊讶地叫了一声："真是你呀？

姐姐变得越来越漂亮年轻了啊！我都不敢认了，只觉得这人长得好像谁？"

大堂经理高兴继续说："欢迎，还是把那间 6 号标准间给你，知道你喜欢 6，办事能顺顺利利！"

秦瑛曾说过，她选房买房喜欢的门牌号码，没想到这小美女大堂经理还记得这么清楚。

穿过楼梯上到三楼的房间，秦瑛轻盈飘逸头发随风飘动，望着午后明亮灿烂的阳光，秦瑛感到一阵倦意向她袭来。她躺在柔软舒适的床上，与阳光一同入眠，在暖暖被窝中一下子就睡着了。不知过了多久，大堂经理打电话叫醒她到一楼大厅吃晚餐。

秦瑛慢悠悠地背起随身携带的小包，缓缓地走进餐厅用餐，因为是一个人来的，秦瑛选择了一处靠窗位置，今晚客人不是很多，所以秦瑛也不急，她正好有空想着明天先去售楼部看看，还是托售楼部小伊推荐的装修老板沈总当秦瑛临时司机兼向导。

已经临近晚上，秦瑛吃饱了就在酒店的周边廊桥上散步，走走看看，一边欣赏着周围环境绿色大树和五颜六色的花朵，还有夜空满天繁星，秦瑛情不自禁地在木桥边停下，选一处石头凳子坐下，好像什么也没有想，静静地听着风吹树叶的沙沙声，看着远处的景色，有山有水有吱鸟的叫声，还有水塘里的青蛙声，相互依存动物世界都这么欢快交流，正当秦瑛很好奇地想象着的时候，余光让她觉得有人向她走近……

餐厅已经关闭了，酒店又走出了一位帅气而沉稳的男子，从走廊的另外一头也走到了秦瑛的附近，在秦瑛的视线里，两个人同时双目对视一眼，又自然有意散开，各自都看天空起来，最后还是这位男士忍不住也坐在秦瑛旁边，找话说："你是住在酒店开会的吗？我也是参加这次会议的。"

秦瑛先警惕地看着，然后才说："我是来这里看看。"秦瑛这回答等于没说。

男人开始自我介绍了："我叫邓诚，是来这里考察参加保险行业发展趋势会议，同行们去楼顶上泡温泉去了，我想静一下散步走走，这座城市，特别是这酒店环境卫生空气好。我们每次都选择在这里开会！你好像不是本地人吧？"

秦瑛："这个你也能看出来？"

邓诚微笑不语地点点头，然后邓诚委婉，小心地问："你是做什么职业？能说说吗？"

秦瑛没有正面回答，只是笑笑说："你不是半仙会猜吗？"

邓诚自嘲地地说："猜不出来！"

邓诚不知道是什么时候，把自己一张名片递给了秦瑛："这里有我的联系方式，希望加我！若是在珠海需要我帮忙的事，请联系我，后会有期！"

九月份的珠海气候宜人，虽是夜晚了，但是四周的宁静和大自然树叶散发出来绿色植物的味道，让秦瑛深吸一口气，望着已走进酒店的邓诚背影，将名片打开看了一眼，某保险公司集团邓董，顺手又放进包里。

从那之后秦瑛忙着看房，准备开一家"爱吧书吧"区域，又要请沈总夫妻俩装修房子，还兼写作，还为忙碌的谋生应聘理疗师工作奔波，经医美小霞推荐，终于稳定下来了，这行业在沿海城市最吃香！生活转动起来几乎都忘记了这位一面之缘的邓诚。

有一天，秦瑛正在珠海某高档会所理疗室工作时，走进了一位男士，此人正是五年前见过邓诚。四目相对，俩人又惊又喜。

前台正是秦瑛值班，也来不及躲开，只得笑着说："没有想到吧？咱们在这里又见面了吧？你需要理疗吗？哪儿不舒服？"

秦瑛的地盘，一连串的询问，让邓诚一时半会地不知怎么回答。

邓诚有些疼痛地支支吾吾说："我装修抬东西，把腰拉伤了！"

秦瑛没有多说什么，赶紧将艾灸红外线仪器打开，对着邓诚的腰部照射，那次邓诚临走之前又办理了治疗充值卡 6800 元。

再后来因为秦瑛自学又考取了专业理疗师职业教师证书，被另外一家医美诊所高薪聘用，最主要是只上白班，周末两天，逢年过节都有假期，从那以后就再也没有看见邓诚了，这是第二次碰见邓诚。

第三次偶遇邓诚正是前一周末，秦瑛像平常一样，逢周末会来到"爱吧书吧"自顾不暇地看书，做一些小说创作的构思提纲！忙碌起来已到了废寝忘食的地步，这就是秦瑛的业余生活的重要一部分。

近段时间秦瑛出版了两部书，正在手机回复购了书的读者们信息。秦瑛已经习惯了这种检测真伪鉴别朋友的方式，就像大浪淘沙一样，留下的朋友一定是值得秦瑛交友的底线和原则，对她虚伪之友进行淘汰制。

这种人多了去了，秦瑛很平常心态去面对现实生活中的人和事，所以也不会有太多的失望，因为不指望期待什么，生活就显得特别简单！秦瑛埋头看着书，手机如有信息就回复一下，突然一个熟悉的声音进入她的耳朵："真的是你呀？这么巧？我能坐在这里吗？"

秦瑛欣喜望着邓诚，不好意思地笑了！俩人这么有缘。秦瑛点点头，身体向里移了一点位置，邓诚并肩地坐了下来，随手拿起桌面上秦瑛看过的书，翻开一看，发现作者介绍图片仅是秦瑛的照片，紧接着翻着目录，看着开头和结尾，才用欣赏的眼光看着秦瑛说："这书是你写的小说，书吧有卖的吗？我想带回家好好读。"

秦瑛说："你是认真的，需要多少本？"

邓诚欣喜地说："先买十本，我可以送人。"

秦瑛看着邓诚这么支持，当然有些异外，没有想过谋面三次的邓诚，比某些交往了几十年的同学、同事、同行文友老师还靠谱。真的令她感到一丝丝温暖，同时也夹杂着各种难已说出的凉意，一种曾经被无数次怠慢，虚假的搪塞、敷衍、拒绝的悲伤，还有那些骨子里不希望她好的人，社会上什么人都有，形形色色的人物关系，真不是表面看起来的那样简单美好。哦，秦瑛这次出版书策划促销的活动中，一目了然地领悟到了什么是世态炎凉，冷暖自知罢了。

可真没有想到真诚的朋友还是有的，就像这位眼前的邓诚，一瞬间让秦瑛对邓诚刮目相看。看来两人之间的关系还有机会赢取更好的发展，秦瑛的心情现在好多了，世界上还是有人间真情，她想这几年多来，邓诚有没有找过她？这一刻，该是秦瑛对邓诚有些好感和好奇了，似乎也期待着什么？她告诉自己不要胡思乱想了，一切随缘吧！

没有想到一周之后又在爱吧书吧见到邓诚，而他竟然就是沈总和秋甜要介绍给她认识的朋友。邓诚坐在秦瑛对面，跟大家交代了这几年他的生活情况。

这几年来邓诚之所以没有打扰秦瑛，是因为他正面临着与妻子离婚判决，也就是说，正在结束婚姻生活状态。那时邓诚一门心思只想投入工作，用不停地工作时间来减压离婚后的孤独感！

离婚财产夫妻应各自一半，但邓诚将大套别墅和豪车都让给了妻子，一套市中心的公寓留给已是成人的女儿。自已则留下一套市郊很偏还没有装修的乡村农舍，这还是当年无意中在走村串户考察市郊住户村民，作保险市场调研时，发现了一处荒漠没有人居住带院子 1000 平方面积平层房。

村主任告诉邓董，这房子是他侄儿的，一家三口进城做生意发展很好，这房子一直空闲着，他们急于在城市里买铺面房，手上缺点钱，想卖掉这房子，可就是没有人接盘。那时正好邓诚想购买类似这样可以养老居住的房子，无心插柳柳成荫，邓诚接手花了 46 万元全款买下了这套带院子的乡村房子，房子里没有什么值钱的东西。村主任很感谢邓诚的及时相助，解决了侄儿的资金问题。

邓诚买了房子后也一直空着，直到离婚后，需要住的地方，才想起来这地方。每到周末就找沈总安排装修师傅将房子重新装修，将外墙保持红砖原样，将室内全部拆除了房间之间的墙板，将窗户改成采光更好的落地玻璃窗，他喜欢这种一眼看透底的简洁设计！院子也只是用买来村民的文竹栽在院子周边围成一个三面大圈，留下一面进入可以停下六台车辆的地方，又在屋角窗边设计增添几台石头和木椅子，两边对称地摆放着，有桌椅板凳供人休息的地方，顶部又架起了几根钢管混凝土结构架子，在视觉上又充分利用空间价值，整体打造后，像是一座乡村的建筑别墅。

屋子里暂无任何装修，只是用简易的普通吊扇在屋梁上方，地面全是用的水泥路面，墙面也是对应地抹着一层水泥墙面再涂上一层清油漆，增添了几分怀旧气息，浓厚氛围吸引了很多村民夸奖："这城里的人就是聪明，把这么破的一个房子整得像一座茶店，又有点像农家乐，还可以做民宿酒店，也可以当一个销售农副产品的展示店，花店。"因为空间大，可塑性高，可以根据未来的需要，添置做些项目需要的摆设柜子及软装饰。

说话间，大家都不想打断邓诚，都像听故事一样的听着，邓诚风趣谈起乡村风土人情世故。

秦瑛听着就暗自庆幸，这也许就是缘分的安排，合适的时间，合适的人，遇见了合适机会，还真有那么一种神奇的感觉，上帝借沈总和秋甜把邓诚带进了秦瑛的生活中。

今晚的爱吧书吧，因邓诚到来，两个人有了无限想象空间。沈总和秋甜俩比谁都开心，一个劲儿地向邓董讨喜酒喝："我看呀，你们俩就是有缘，看看我说过什么话？”

秋甜抢话说：“是啊，我们俩不知道你俩先认识的情况下，不约而同地想起了你们俩很般配哈，真的，那个时候沈总还没有说出你邓董的名字，说要给秦瑛介绍一位男朋友，我想到的也是你邓董，你俩太合适了！”

起初邓诚听到俩人不停推荐介绍女朋友给他，心里还很抗拒。没有想过原来仅是五年前见到的秦瑛。心中暗喜，幸好今晚被沈总强行拖来了，邓诚一直不好意思直接拒绝，推着再说吧。好像心里一直有秦瑛的影子常在脑海中浮现，生活中除了工作之外，再也没有其他女人了，他想往后的婚姻生活，另外一半一定要自己来选择，他不想再看错了人，也不想将时间浪费在无趣味的女人身上。

于是一开始就躲避沈总介绍的女朋友之事，所以根本没有问女方叫什么名字？哪里人？长得什么模样？什么职业？统统没问？

而沈总也想神秘给俩人惊喜，双方的情况就什么也没有吐露，沈总拍着胸脯说：“你看你看，这就是缘分吧！哈哈哈！”

邓诚解释着说出差点不来见女朋友的小插曲，一下子打开了秦瑛的心结，邓诚像知道秦瑛心思，赶紧补充今晚一见的原因。

邓诚：“明天专设宴请沈总秋甜俩，谢谢介绍牵红线之恩，并邀请秦瑛作陪一起去‘崖口人家’吃海鲜大餐。”邓诚脱口而出就说去“崖口人家”，那是珠海最有名好吃的海鲜城。

邓诚话一说完，沈总又差点惊掉了下巴：“我的妈呀，你俩吃也同样喜欢吃一样的食物，哈哈太有缘了！”说完眼睛都笑出来了。

这一晚直到九点爱吧书吧要关门的时候，大家才依依不舍，那晚是邓诚和秦瑛第四次特别的重逢。

沈总秋甜俩借故先走，临行前向邓诚使一个眼神，示意给邓诚机会，快开车送秦瑛回去，邓诚开着路虎吉普车，将秦瑛安全送到租住的海边小区楼栋门前，才放心地暗自乐了起来，像得到宝贝一样高兴地驾车离去！

第 4 章　半喜半忧

秦瑛让邓诚开车先离开，才再转身进了小区，这是沈总和秋甜积极推荐租住的高档公寓，因为自己新买的房子就在这小区里，还没有装修好！她不想过多地解释个人生活隐私信息，最敏感是具体住处！也不想过早地暴露自己的生活圈，当然包括自己开的爱吧书吧店！为此特别叮嘱了沈总和秋甜俩，对外不要说爱吧书吧她是背后老板，也别说在珠海这高档小区里有个人名下的房产。因秦瑛这两处房子装修都是经过沈总和秋甜安排妥当。

在珠海秦瑛只信任沈总夫妻俩，这两口子是秦瑛来珠海认识后，成为最值得信赖的朋友，生活中大事小事都咨询他们俩，夫妻俩在珠海可真是百事通。

秦瑛的个人婚姻问题，沈总夫妻俩挺上心推荐邓诚，今晚一见，原来是已偶遇过几次的同一人。其实第一印象给秦瑛也有那么一点幻想成为伴侣的感觉，只是这种念头在脑子闪现后，被强行制止了，那瞬间的好感被秦瑛的理性所替代，她不想再成为花痴，也不敢再随便对男人动情了，也就是这些性格敏感的原因，秦瑛可以静下来这么多年，她学会了与自己独处，平凡地生活着，她感觉到她一个的生活状态挺好，很充实独立自主。如果在决定选择伴侣这个终身大事方面，她得自己挑选把握，她也不能再看花眼了，一定得谨慎严格对自己未来负责。

婚姻对她来说这是一件很严肃的事情，第一段恋情已经让她心里产生了对男人多疑的心结，同时在这五年多的时间里，虽然和谁都没有谈过恋爱，但是她隐隐约约地感觉到，还有一个男人在向她示好，最近一段时间这位男人更加频繁地诉说着思念之苦，虽只是在微信网络上叙说对秦瑛的好感！但那些恰到好处的关心问候，在夜深人静的时候，也常常伴随她入眠。

只因此人不在一个城市，秦瑛与这位从未谋面的男士，也只有在微信上交流，男士说他居住在一个北方的城市，而秦瑛则已选择居住在沿海城市珠海，两个人已聊了也有七个多月的时间了，从没有实质性的进展。

　　这位神秘男人是秦瑛投稿在网上认识的名叫总编程默，认识这位总编程默，秦瑛以作者笔名加了微信，总编与作者沟通的方式，在微信传递。一来二去，秦瑛的文章在总编程默的帮助发表在省刊报纸上，后期逐渐被推荐上月刊，年刊出杂志。

　　记得有一次微信聊到关于出版书之事，总编积极地寻问秦瑛："你写的长篇小说能否先发给我看看，如果内容合适，我可以帮你推荐社出版。"

　　那个时候秦瑛都还没有见过这位程默主编，只知其名未见其人！在公证号，及省刊报纸杂志上主编是有程默电话号码，微信号，通过作家介绍，才知道程默主编是位文学大作家，有很多头衔，什么省作家协会主编，中国作家协会会员，精短小说会员秘书会长等等，秦瑛被这突然降临的好消息，有点惊喜不已，她怎么也不会想到，出版书有程默总编帮助推荐仅这般容易，此事咨询问到对的那个人了。于是秦瑛将刚刚写完连载过的书稿，整理修改好后，汇总发给了程默主编。其实在遇到程默总编之前，秦瑛已有两个出版社编辑老师预定好小说出版事项，只是想多比较几个出书方式，既然书稿完成了，就看选择那个出版社为宜的问题。

　　秦瑛一直与程默在网上微信上交流文稿之类的话题，后来渐渐熟悉了起来，可以聊到一些爱情婚姻的话题，再后来在程默鼓励下，秦瑛上稿频率很高，几乎每期都有一篇小小说上稿，由于程默主编是执行总编，作者上稿只要有程默推荐，都会直接上报纸发表，因此秦瑛成了多产作家，慢慢在文学圈内行业，站稳了脚跟，后面秦瑛与程默积极推荐的出版社合作，也是顺理成章的事情。

　　秦瑛的第一部以人物传记文笔，抒写了一部女人励志感人长篇小说，经过三审三校的修改，终于如期出书了！随着出版书后的喜悦分享，作家与主编两人之间有一种情感的共鸣，主编程默好像几次借着小说内容套话，判断小说中的人物有一些秦瑛的生活成长轨迹，从那以后，程默开始每天都会在微信上，谈工作、友情，及生活中出现的某一件事，在此程默引导了秦瑛很多观念。

　　两人聊天范围多方面，情感迅速升温，有时候秦瑛创作会忘记了时间，甚至在半夜凌晨突然想起写作中灵感，想聊点情节创意，程默也会耐心地听秦瑛说完故事线条灵感由来。就这样两人似乎都没有谈到爱，但是又总说不完的知心话。

　　程默三次有问到秦瑛："如果可以，你会嫁给我吗？"

　　类似这样的假设，这种试探的方式，近期秦瑛已感觉到了程默的明目张胆！有一天深夜，秦瑛微信有程默的十几条信息未读……

　　程默发给秦瑛微信语音声传出来打开第一条留言："哦，这近几天干吗去了？我天天在想你，你可以不想我，但你记住我可是天天想你，只有我这个傻男人，总是在想你，你记得我就好……"

　　第二条留言："你若是那一天，看见程默赤身裸体，蓬头垢面地，像个疯子一样，嘴里叫着秦瑛的名字，那就完了，记得我在想你都快想疯了。"

　　第三条留言："真的，我们可以视频吗？别不理我！但要记住我在想你！"

　　第四条留言："你记住我说过的话，你是一位精灵的作家，将来若是认定了我，我一定会使你成为知名大作家，一位多产曝光率高的作家。"

　　秦瑛听着程默发给她微信上的语音，有着欣喜，但又有些不可思议，心里在想，没有那么夸张吧？这才哪跟哪呀？两人连面都没有见过？唉！秦瑛叹了一口气，摇摇头沉默下来，并没有及时回复程默信息。

　　邓诚约好第二天请客，正是星期天在崖口人家海鲜城会面，秦瑛又见到了邓诚，还是原班人马，沈总和秋甜接秦瑛一起来的，因为同居住在一个小区。下午5点，邓诚早早地到了这里等候多时，餐厅位置都定好了！

　　这次和邓诚共进晚餐，餐厅中途邓诚对秦瑛大方照顾，做到自然体贴入微，恰到好处，一点都不做作，像是久违的朋友，亲人，反正那感觉让秦瑛踏实，秦瑛开始情不自禁地会把邓诚与程默比，这一比不要紧，在秦瑛的心里有一种莫名其妙的感觉，她一希望两个男人要是同一个人就好了，因为邓诚只是不温不火地对她好，也还没有给到她的任何语言上的表白，而程默虽然没有见过面，但微信上留下作家简介的那张微笑照片，从外观上看是一位很和蔼谦和之人，照片上笑成一条缝的小眼睛，长着很性感厚厚的嘴唇，一对酒窝，看上去很满足憨厚自信满满的一位男士，程默微信语音上留下了无数条热情关心的问候，句句动听。

　　秦瑛开始处处有意无意拿邓诚与程默比较，就好比邓诚是温火，而程默可以将火点燃。

　　秦瑛在半喜半忧之间徘徊，她在没有来得及去作任何取舍，毕仅两位男士还没有发动直接行动上追求，这个时候如果说要选择谁作终身伴侣，似乎太早了一点，秦瑛今天得好好地观察邓诚的表现，看看邓诚为她忙碌起来夹菜端茶倒水样子，心里一阵阵温暖。

沈总和秋甜偷偷地相互做鬼脸乐了起来，秋甜悄悄地对沈总耳根说："看邓董对秦瑛很喜欢的主动，他俩有戏了，是吧！"

沈总说："还得让邓董追紧的，男人就应该主动，我会让他加把劲。"

秦瑛看邓诚的目光也变得温柔了一些

邓诚温和而谦逊地为餐桌上的每一个人提供着贴心的服务，这海鲜大餐吃了两个多小时，每道新鲜的海鲜邓诚都让服务员推荐地上，邓诚在中途借故打个电话，把单买了，又不声不响地坐在秦瑛的身旁，秦瑛是位明白人，她从邓诚的今天表现看，邓诚对人对朋友们实在，那晚沈总说："让邓董破费了！定好下星期日，让秋甜在我们家烧三杯鸡给邓董吃，啊！还是原班人马，怎么样？"

邓诚思索了一下，将头转向秦瑛，邓诚的目光有种期待扫向秦瑛射来，意思是说："我们一起去吧！"

秦瑛笑着点点头，秋甜趁机上前牵着秦瑛手说："这次我还给你再露两道美食，你俩一定都喜欢！就这么定了，我和沈总先回了，邓董你可以陪秦瑛在海边走走，看看这小镇夜景，很美的。"

邓董从心里感激秋甜夫妻俩的暗中相助，笑着对所有人说："好的，一定照办，我乐意！放心吧！"

秦瑛随邓诚并肩沿着水边走着，看着远处灯火，像星星一闪一闪的夜色，秦瑛发自内心地说了一句："没有想到这里还有这么美。"

邓诚欣喜地说："等下星期天请你去我那乡村房子看看，那空气也很清新，很适合静下来全神贯注写作的地方，如果那天白天你有空，我来接你，先一起参观乡村房子装修，给我提提建议，晚上再一起去沈总家共进晚餐，你看怎么样？"

秦瑛收回远处瞭望水面的目光对邓诚说："你都想得这么周到了，我能不去吗？正好我也想看看沈总公司是怎样给你设计装修乡村带院房子。"

好奇心使秦瑛满口答应了邓诚的邀请。

邓诚接着话题说："我原先是想把房子装好了，把老母亲接来和我一起居住，可老母亲说住在城里习惯了，什么都方便，理发，买菜，生活各方面都很便利，不愿意来我这偏僻小村庄，还说老了喜欢热闹，所以这乡村屋子拖到现在才想着按照我准备度假居住创意设计装修，慢慢装，慢慢添置喜欢的家具。"

秦瑛听着邓诚聊起他妈在一起的故事，听着听着，感觉邓诚对长辈照顾得很好，母亲身体很健康，邓诚给母亲家里请了一个做饭打扫卫生的阿姨，生活上照顾得很周到，所以平时邓诚上班工作很安心，周末都会去乡村屋子看看装修进展，遇到情况或突发奇想，会临时自己动手做一些活。

秦瑛望着眼前的邓诚，有种感觉这男人很实在，而且敢想敢做，是一位动手能力很强的爷们。若是真和这男人一起生活，应该是秦瑛享福些？毕竟邓诚比她能干多了。想着想着秦瑛忍不住地笑了……

邓诚看秦瑛突然偷偷乐起来的样子，还以为是自己那句话说错了，紧张地问道："你笑什么？"

秦瑛看见邓诚这紧张可爱认真的样子，有意指着远处城里的方向逗邓诚说："你老妈听见正说她坏话呢？"

说完就咯咯又笑了起来。

邓诚反应过来的时候，秦瑛已走向邓诚停车子的地方，邓诚看看时间也不早了，是该送秦瑛回去了！两人迅速上车，吉普车上向前看的视线真好，秦瑛坐着副驾驶座位上，向着前方望去，车速驶过了一排排路边树林，一处处沿途风景，一直开向城市的中心，看着前方明亮高楼大厦，闪闪发光的万家灯火，邓诚用深情的眼神看着秦瑛说："我怎么感觉时间过得这么快啊？你不觉得吗？"

秦瑛害羞地用手指着前方车头说："嗯，你现在赶紧看前方，好好开车注意安全，好吗？"

邓诚马上回答："嗯，我眼睛正看路面，也看看你，不耽误！"

说完两个人都笑了起来！车上飘出轻音乐萨克斯曲子回家，一直重复地放着……

第 5 章　痴话撩人

　　秦瑛每周一白天工作在一家高档会所理疗室上班，忙碌起来就不会看手机微信信息，秦瑛职业已经习惯了一上班将手机设置成静音，等忙完了一天后，晚餐老习惯回到爱吧书吧解决，吃一个素菜团子加一碗小米粥，或者煮一壶水果茶，边品边看着书，有些时候没有写作更新了！

　　记得还是在出版书之前的三个月，整部完成的书稿已上线传给了程默总编，那段时间秦瑛创作灵感很多，刚刚完成出版书稿，受程默总编鼓励，让秦瑛写一部完美中年的爱情小说故事，甚至要求以生活中的原型程默男一号与秦瑛女主为题材，进行创作思路，故事情节提纲秦瑛都写好了 31 章节故事线条，中心思想，一切准备就绪，开头的第一至二章节内容都写得很顺利，那时正遇上春节临近，一切家里琐碎的事情太多就给耽误写作进程，这一放下就没有动笔写了，那种幻想的爱情婚姻美满幸福快乐故事情节，秦瑛在现实生活中好像找不到为爱付出追求的人物原型，小说创作没有实质性进展！秦瑛写不出来，也不想自欺其人地写下去，心里空空的，想想还是把写的开头两章后，暂时沉淀一段时间，给自己一个充电学习过程。

　　秦瑛继续看着手机后面几条程默以往的信息：“为了你的书稿在年底之前与出版社签约，必须打全款后，合同才生效，出版社才正式开始三审三校程序，我没等你三天后打余款，我已先垫付了这笔余款 3 万元，所以你不要担心出版书的进度。”

　　第二条信息：“反正你的事就是我的事，我一定会办好的！”

　　第三条：垫资的截图，还有程默与出版社编辑对话截图，还有程默替秦瑛代签的出版社合同！

　　听完看见这些，秦瑛心里一股暖流涌上心头，语言此时不能表达出来自己的心情，于是赶紧把手机邦定的定期银行账户打款还给程默，微信转账 3 万元余款，看到已经显示转账成功后，才立刻回复程默微信留言："谢谢你为我考虑这些细节，你没有说就垫付了这个钱，真的谢谢你对我的信任帮助，现在请你及时查收这笔款，另外，为了表示感谢你，我想给你邮寄礼物送给你！但又不知道你的身高体重，衣服规格大小，能够把你的衣服码数及地址全部发给我吗？"

没有想到程默秒回："看到了，出版垫的钱已收到，衣服就免了吧，咱们俩就不用说感谢的话了，我为你做事是应该的，我乐意，你呢就别跟我客气了，我是穷点，没有多少钱，但是我有一颗真心，喜欢你的真心！我吧什么也没有，就喜欢搞点文学创作这点爱好，再遇见你是位才女，帮你是应该的！"

秦瑛看后信息更是想还这个人情，毕竟还不是男女朋友关系，不能贵人贱用，这个人情不能欠着，得马上还，这是秦瑛做人做事的风格！于是秦瑛不加思索地又发了几条消息："请把衣领后的牌子拍照发给我，上面有你穿的码子大小标志，及时将地址也同时发给我！请配合！"

这一招还真管用，程默按要求将信息内容发给了秦瑛。

几天后秦瑛给程默买了九件各种款式的男装一线品牌衣服，同天办理邮寄手续后，截图发给了程默才心安理得接受了，程默为她办的这些事情，秦瑛在与男士交往中，最怕欠人情债，这样以后做事处理男女俩人关系，也轻松一点，她可不想给程默误会，这次程默主动为她垫付出资的事情，让秦瑛越来越放松了对男人示好的戒备心，她想象中的程默又亲切了许多！

临近春节就要到了，程默收到秦瑛邮寄给他的衣服，高兴地给秦瑛回话："衣服收到了，真的很合身，没想到穿哪件都合身，谢谢啦，另外今年春节如果你要守爱吧书吧不回来，过年我年三十那晚一定给你发个红包，记得接收啊。"已经习惯了，在外一个人过春节，因为特别的原因，创业也不容易，越是节假日爱吧书吧越是人多，初六就要开放！所以秦瑛也就不计划回去过年了，程默承诺这句语音留言，让秦瑛感到一丝丝的温暖，她自己觉得这个时候有一个人，想着她也就很满足了，虽然两人没有明确男女朋友关系，像这样有一个人关心暧昧语言，特别是在异地他乡夜深人静的时候，显得特别撩人。有程默时不时的温暖话语，像一股暖流撞击着秦瑛的心房。年三十红包转到秦瑛手机微信上，但是秦瑛看见红包并没有打开没接收，一直没有接收。大年初一都没接，她不想平白无故地接受程默的这些小钱，心意她领了。她不希望花男人的钱，虽然她不知道红包是多少？但是她没有接收打开，就是想告诉程默，俩人最好是在经济方面清清白白，而且俩人都还没有表明说过什么关系，这时候微信上很多信息沉默发过来："你红包怎么不接呀，赶快接受，这是我的心意钱不多，但是你一定要接，不然我会生气的。"没有收下的红包 24 小时就自动退还到程默的账户，因这件事情程默似乎还真有点生气，在微信上又给秦瑛发来很多条消息："我虽然穷，但这是我的心意，我记得有一个人在很远很远，值得我用这种方式来关心，我不管怎么说，我会在春节、你的生日，这两大节日一定会给你红包。你收下吧。"就这样程默又在劝秦瑛，如果不收就是瞧不起他等一些话，在初六又找了个理由，六六大顺给秦瑛发了一个 ¥600 的红包，非要秦瑛收下，说这可是图一个顺和吉利！这个数字好很好，程默知道秦瑛迷信这个数字就图个吉利吧，开门大发。六六大顺！心想以后找个机会再还回去。类似这种关心在意自己的人，还真没有。让秦瑛觉得程默是在礼尚往来，她心里清楚，那几件品牌的衣服并不便宜，价值几千元，所以收下 600 元红包，或许程默里坦然一点。那一天记得秦瑛正在看电视，突然程默发来消息："怎么了，在家干吗呢？"

秦瑛正在边看电视剧边泡脚回复："没干吗，放松泡泡脚。"接着程默回复："今后我愿意天天给你热水泡脚，真的，我会天天给你洗，我虽然穷，没有别的财富给到你，但是我一定会给到你最真的爱。我可愿意为你做这个事情。"此话微信中，逗得秦瑛有些想入非非心里暖洋洋的。她想，如果这就是生活，未来若遇上了真爱，也许会这样把平凡的生活过得像诗一样的浪漫，想着想着秦瑛不好意思地笑了起来，可能是热水泡脚的原因，全身发热，那种感觉就好像自己害羞做错了什么事一样，其实除了秦瑛一个人在房间里，没有任何人看见秦瑛心里在想啥？

程默还在继续用撩妹的话说着秦瑛听，此时耳朵传出程默描述那么热情话语："你咋不快来我这个城市啊，其实这种感觉我原来跟你说过，如果你来了，我见到你的时候，有可能是我眼里含着泪，你太不理解人了，我知道我自己想谁？我知道我自己稀罕谁？所以当你来见我的时候，我们一直在网上联系，从网上遇见到现在这长时间没见过面，这次我可以见到你了，我肯定会激动，肯定会心动，我眼圈肯定会红，我就是这样的人，我知道我自己，我不知道你是怎么想？我肯定知道我自己，我不会说谎，我也没有谎话可说，因为这是真情实感的流露。"一瞬间的爱，秦瑛顿感到脸红热燥。

　　秦瑛在爱吧书吧里，静静的看完程默发来的这些信息，心情很矛盾。望在窗外远处的星星，心里开始想起了邓诚的邀请，周日去邓诚郊外的乡村房子看看，一时半会的想不起来，自己那天穿什么样的衣服去呢？这好像是正式的第一次私下约会吧？

第6章　乡村之行

　　星期天的早上到了，这是秦瑛和邓诚的第一次私下交往，受邓诚上次邀请，秦瑛上午 7 点准时走到小区门口。邓诚已在吉普车上打起闪灯，提示秦瑛快点上车。沿途两人打开车里的音乐，打开了吉普车的天窗，沿途的风景是那么的美妙，空气中夹杂着青涩的海风，使人呼吸顺畅，明媚的阳光普照着树林间一闪而过缝隙，那光芒时亮时暗，阳光路过的地方，显得格外亮堂，邓诚开着车向坐在副驾驶的秦瑛脸上看去，在阳光照射下，显得格外动人美丽，车子飞奔在公路上两旁的树木花草房屋，飞速地在车头两侧移动，邓诚笑着问秦瑛："你喜欢这样的早晨吗？"

　　秦瑛说："我从来没有这么早，坐着敞篷的吉普车，像兜风"。

　　邓诚时不时地问道："你喜欢这里的空气和路上的这种海风吗？"

　　秦瑛边点点头，边看着邓诚说："喜欢啊，如果不喜欢就不可能跟你同行，正因为喜欢，真的，没想到我差点错过这样美好的清晨，早上的阳光真美。"

　　每天周末开车到乡村都是四十分钟的来回，邓诚熟悉地形地貌，兴奋地介绍着继续说："如果乡村这地方很适合居住休闲，想想这种生活，很安逸，没有事的时候就种上果树和一些花草，再将房子前后院变成鲜花盛开的地方，你一定会喜欢。"

　　邓诚情不自禁地乐了起来，今天只用了三十来分钟就到了，邓诚下车后逗着秦瑛说："我带了个便当，你也可以吃一点，垫垫肚子，尝尝我的厨艺，等到了乡村，我再弄点地道的特色小吃，咱们今天中午就在那里吃好的，你肯定会喜欢吃我做的鱼，还有村里的树上摘的果子，全是现在季节吃的果子，真的很新鲜，在这里生活成本真的很便宜，只要动手种果树，包你吃个够。"

　　秦瑛随意说道："我喜欢吃苹果、荔枝、橘子、樱桃。还喜欢桂花树、栀子花，是喜欢那种春天风一吹就闻到的绿色香气，那种大自然一年四季都有绿色的植物，我喜欢可多了，我喜欢小鸟的叫声，还喜欢吱吱小鸟唱歌，虽听不懂鸟语，但感觉它们是在说话，一样有趣。"

到乡村就开始忙碌了，但不知不觉时间过得很快，工人已经在那里了，没想到工人这么自觉准点在邓诚家前院等着，工人比他们还要到得早。包工头直接在院子开始做工，秦瑛跟着邓诚走进院子看到一片空地的钢筋、水泥袋、地砖等一些建筑材料，有水泥工，有油漆工，已在整理院子地坪及墙内施工刷墙。随着邓诚走进屋里，感觉正如邓诚所说第一次介绍的那样，自己乡村房子的大概情况，只是比他说的还要装着更实用，邓诚指着大厅说着未来的计划，然后走到二楼的时候说了一句："楼上有三间房两个洗手间设置，其中把中间变成一个大书房，设置两台大长书桌子，用中式的家具隔断屏风放在中间，可以像开放似的书房，开门给能见的两边的设计展示柜，书柜，所有的文艺作品都可以放在上面展示。"

邓诚昨天还指着书房窗户两侧继续边想边说："秦瑛，你如果喜欢可以在书房里写作，放两台电脑，做任何事互不打扰。"邓诚这样说的时候，悄悄地瞟了一眼秦瑛的反应，秦瑛听着心里莫名其妙的有种心跳加速的感觉，言语上没有回答，心里可开心了，然后就看着墙壁四周空空，放着准备打柜子的木材问："你准备做隔墙到顶的书架和展示柜吗？"

邓诚回答："对呀，沈总的木工师傅手艺很高，比买柜子实用结实耐用，而且这能充分利用面积，我想做起来一定很好看，我用原始原木，将大自然都搬到这里来，你应该喜欢。"

秦瑛真没想到邓诚的装修规划也把秦瑛喜欢的也都考虑进去了，把她当女主人一样对待。秦瑛的一颗心怦然心动，此眼前站着的男人看，就觉得邓诚真是挺实在，秦瑛想都没想到的安全感瞬间而来，有一种踏实的感觉涌上心头。不由自主地跟邓诚会意一笑，调皮地在想：你都安排得这么好，也没问人家还没嫁给你呢？

邓诚心里在想，不知道怎么会想到秦瑛，设计方案都安排得那么周到，考虑秦瑛习惯安静写作，避免互相打扰，这个邓诚将空间利用，设计风格中，又能随时看得见彼此，又互不打扰。

这正是秦瑛她也想要的那种空间，她不希望很拘谨，邓诚的生活过得像透明玻璃，一眼望去见底，这种安排正合她意，可是她又在嘀咕：我的想法，为什么邓诚会如此的了解，他为什么知道自己喜欢这些呢？难道他也这样想的吗？不然怎么解释？只是见了几次面就把我当生活女主人，连居住方式都考虑进去了。看来，这个男人是认真待她的。

秦瑛控制不住自己的思绪，走到二楼的阳台，向后院眺望看去，那里有远去的群山和乡村屋顶冒着炊烟升起，一股乡烧草垛子的味道，迎面扑鼻，真好闻，秦瑛闭上眼睛深呼吸着，耳朵听见鸡叫声，看见有村民们陆陆续续挑着箩筐进菜地，乡邻乡亲的那种场景像 80 年代的那种农村，这里人们纯真质朴，好安静啊，时不时的鸡叫声让秦瑛想象，这就是一个大自然的大农村，与喧哗闹市相比，能享受这般宁静，真是太难得了！

邓诚被工人叫下去问一个什么事情，秦瑛叫邓诚："你赶快去忙吧，我随便看看走走，随便逛逛。"在周边小村里还有小卖部，就是那种农村之间的摆地摊的那种小超市，秦瑛听邓诚来时介绍过，可以去看看，只要中午 12：00 之前能回到这里。

邓诚："中午我带你去一个村里农家乐，那里食物特好吃，就这样定了。"说完邓诚和沈总公司的工人去院子，将木材竹比画着，忙去了。

秦瑛很乐意这种安排，没有把她当成客人，就好像她的是女主人似的边走边看，然后跟邓诚用手指着外面意思，是告诉他我出去转一转，邓诚会意一笑说着："去吧，去吧，我就在这里。"

走在村庄外面，秦瑛看到这种屋子的前后院虽然不是很大，但能大门前院能停六辆车，还有两个石头桌子，四周围用文竹围着三方种的树苗，两颗果树分别在石头桌两旁，两边安置摆放着两个长凳。这样设置，将来长高了夏天可在树下好乘凉，可以坐下来喝茶，这是未来长期才能见到场景，这种安排真的很有意义。秦瑛会心地笑了笑，真的，没想到她把自己给带进去了，已经想象自己就是这里的女主人。从小超市地毯式走到村庄，有 30 多户人家，都是平平凡凡的生活，这里村街面上有很多古玩，地上摆着马铃薯，花生，季节的橘子，梨子和小苹果，山楂，水果应有尽有，秦瑛情不自禁地，蹲下来跟乡民大婶聊起来，去的时候空着手，结果回来的时候，收获满满，每一样买一斤也有够她提的，手上的东西变得越来越重了，还看到了远去有两所农家乐一是专吃鱼宴，地道鱼，还有一个叫烧土鸡炖汤的农家乐。

　　走到有一个凳子就在搭着棚子的那种路边草屋，秦瑛就感觉累了，坐下来买了一壶茶，大娘就是一个 50 多岁，拿着家里的花生、蚕豆、豌豆摆放三小盆，让秦瑛吃，一壶茶配上这些小吃，这是配套买一赠一，秦瑛不好意思地笑了，看相不好吃起来却很美味，花生和地瓜干都很甜，原汁原味不是油炸的食物，还有蚕豆炒年糕，小豌豆也是一咬就炸开花，满口香的感觉，在农村的小吃比城里的零食都好吃。从不吃零食的人，这一下觉得怎么嘴这么馋，看来这里的人好养活自己。她像是喝醉了，感觉到乡民们很亲切，草屋的大娘对着她说："你是外地来的吧，我们这常常有游客过来看，喝下午茶。第二次又带一波朋友过来玩，像你现在是上午不是很忙，到下午人可多了。"

　　再往前走就到了湖边，有老农在那里摸小鱼，秦瑛情不自禁地停了下来，看着老农是怎样抓鱼摸虾，因为喜欢吃这种小鱼。城里还买不着了，农民给秦瑛分成两袋，对包好，每袋有五六斤，一共有十几斤，加上来的时候还买了一些水果，她可拿不动了。正发愁的时候，没想到邓诚开着他的吉普车沿途找了过来。

　　"嗨，秦瑛你果然在这儿，我沿着每个地方绕了一圈，想到你肯定得逛到差不多了，应该到这里了。"

　　秦瑛高兴地说："你咋知道我在这里，快点来帮忙我拿上车，我买了喜欢的东西，要不中午可以做一些吃。"

　　邓诚把地上袋子全部放进车上，还边说："中午已经有安排了，这鱼放到院子去，等会儿我帮你处理洗净，带到城里放到你家冰箱里，够你吃一个礼拜，你要喜欢吃鱼，那我们每周过来，包你吃够。在等会我带你到菜农那里去，买点当季青菜，你这一个礼拜不用买菜啦，走吧，我接你去吃饭。"

　　老农："原来是你的朋友啊，这鱼是你的朋友硬是要买啊。每周来告诉我一声，我会上午给你们弄好，来了就取，不用久等！"

　　邓诚非常熟悉跟老农打了个招呼，嘴里还念叨说："很高兴你喜欢这里，我还怕你不习惯呢，这可是纯粹的乡村，今天咱俩跟工头们一起吃鱼宴，还有锅巴粥，可香好吃，我每次来要吃几碗，我今天请大婶特意加几道地道菜。这样好吗？沈总的工人特喜欢跟我干活，这个村里他们喜欢吃这里的鱼，说这比城里的盒饭好吃多了，所以你放心啊，工人们都很好，不要拘谨，我希望你爱上这个乡村，我这里还正缺女主人呢！我希望有跟我一样喜欢这地方的女主人，我就会把钥匙交给她。"说完调皮地看着秦瑛笑了起来："我是说的是真话，你可别笑我。"

秦瑛嘴上没有反驳，心里在想这邓诚人缘真好，跟他在一起无形中有种轻松，甚至容易把秦瑛带进未来想象的规划中，好像邓诚已经把她当那个最靠谱的女主人，想到这里秦瑛自己不好意思地低下头，提着路面上的小石子，对邓诚说："你可是这样说的哦，别到时候后悔。"

邓诚笑道："怎么会，我喜欢都来不及，开心死了，我也不知道为什么？周一到周五工作完成后，在公司很紧绷的神经，但一回到这里我特别放松，就好像几十年前我就是这里的人一样，村民几乎每家我都认识。以后跟着我一起走，你可成了名人。"

说完自己哈哈大笑，邓诚都不知道笑什么？感染笑声使秦瑛也笑出了眼泪，用手擦了一下说："真没想到你还有这么调皮，那你就在这里当村主任得了。"

邓诚抿嘴微笑着看着秦瑛说："你还别说，这里村主任说了，村里的建设方案，都要来请教我跟他聊，私下当兄弟一样的聊，其实他是长辈，但村主任对我每说一句话就是挣钱的精点子，这不以前在城里，从来没有人还知道买保险？结果在村主任认识我以后，这些村民几乎家家都买了我们公司的保险，我都没花力气就是村主任功劳！"

"这还得从有一家孩子生病了，问我能否理赔医疗费，经我当初劝着这家村民办的保险，只办了三个月就发生病，我们保险做了理赔手续，将钱送到村民家中，就这样大家一传十，十传百，结果一年内全村都买了我们公司的保险，而且还逐年递增保险项目，由原来一家只办一个老人，到结果又办小孩的，儿子办了，又办媳妇的，特别是万能保险，在这里老人孩子都办，现在村民几乎都拥有医疗保险，人寿保险以及意外保险。都把我在这里成了他们的救星，村民说我是贵人，我人生感触最深的是，只要去替村民想，把真心给他们。我从不提保险业务，但是村民都找我来买保险，你知道吗？这种成就感比中彩票还开心。"

看着邓诚肺腑之言讲村民的故事，秦瑛就好像是身临其境地感受到邓诚当时的喜悦。秦瑛被邓诚身上的闪光点所感染，喜欢他善良智慧朴实，以及任劳任怨宁愿自己吃亏也替他人着想的包容心。她觉得邓诚很有男人的魅力，还有一种亲切感。感觉有邓诚在的地方，气氛就很活跃。秦瑛已经感受到了，不仅仅沈总夫妇喜欢邓诚，还有今天眼见着的村民也都拥护向着他，难怪邓诚做事如此顺利，好像不成功都难。秦瑛也开始慢慢也对邓诚有好感了，开始产生了心灵感应，秦瑛脸变红了起来。

这餐村里的午餐让秦瑛吃得太饱了，秦瑛悄悄地对邓诚说："你别再加菜给我了，你自己多吃点，少喝点，晚餐还得继续去沈总家。"

邓诚："误不了，今天我们给秋甜家带一些新鲜鱼、土鸡蛋、青菜，他们俩也喜欢！"

午餐完后，阳光透过树叶洒在俩人的脸上，邓诚和秦瑛散步沿村边走进院内，指着一楼的一房间："你先去在沙发午休一会儿，我去把那些小鱼刺开洗净，用盐腌制入味，你带回家只煎一下可以直接吃了。"

秦瑛也真有点困倦了，点点头，没有客气，直照屋里走去！

也许休息好了吧，等秦瑛醒来的时候，发现院子里晒太阳的邓诚已把买的东西全部放好在车上了，两大类，一包是送给沈总的，一包留给秦瑛。这男人真的会照顾人，过日子一定是个好男人！

邓诚的表现，顿时让秦瑛想起了一位情感专家说过的话："没有行动的爱，什么都不是，对的人把你宠成孩子，错的人把你熬成疯子，满眼都是你的人才配得上你全部的爱，一生所求的爱，是永远的陪伴！"

邓诚迎着秦瑛说："我们可以去沈总家了，这些鱼得早送，放长了会不新鲜了，上车哟。"

秦瑛边上车边关心地问："你一会也没有休息，忙完这些，今天有点累吧，我来开车吧，你上车躺一会儿，眯一会儿！"

邓诚看着善解人意又体贴人的秦瑛，将手上车钥匙交给了秦瑛："那我不客气了，好，有点累，上车补一觉，到了沈总家叫我。"

秦瑛笑笑说："人是铁，饭是钢，身体健康要注意休息，做一个梦就到了。"

一路上听着轻柔音乐，邓诚真的做了一个非常好的梦！

秦瑛开得很慢，想让邓诚多睡一会儿，四十多分钟就到了沈总楼下停车场，看到后车座位上睡觉还在像笑的模样，秦瑛把车轻轻停下，下车伸伸懒腰，在车旁站了一会，可能是太安静了，反而邓诚醒了，打开车门不好意思对秦瑛说："怎么不叫醒我？你开车累了吧？唉，我刚才真舍不得醒啊，真做了一个好梦。"

两人提上要带的东西，按了沈总家的门铃，秒开门的是秋甜："就知道是你们俩，快进来，三杯鸡烧好了，就等你们俩开饭啰。"

邓诚把手上东西递给沈总："快放冰箱，都搞干净了，要吃的时候直接做就行了。"

沈总接过来说："就你了解我，知道我就爱这鱼，怎么没有休息好？像是没有睡好？"

邓诚不好意思对沈总笑着说："不是，我还在想刚才在车上睡着了，做的那个梦，像真的一样。"

沈总夫妻俩异口同声地问："什么好梦，快说快说。"

邓诚又瞟了一眼秦瑛，那我真说了："我梦见沈总在酒店大厅当我和秦瑛的证婚主持人，讲话的内容我还记得，无论世界上的那一种语言，唯有爱才是最永恒美丽的语言！追求真爱最要紧的是看行动。"

沈总听后笑着说："你听听，梦中沈总讲话，讲得多精辟啊，讲得好，像个领导吧！"

第 7 章　虚假难藏

　　时间过得真快，在秦瑛作品出版期间，程默的小小说也被秦瑛推荐到另外一个平台上报；这边秦瑛投稿也被程默积极推荐在省级刊物频繁上报，每期都有发表小小说。秦瑛感觉在程默鼓励帮助下，进入创作高峰期，两颗志同道合的心走得越来越近。虽然远隔千万里，但彼此之间有说不完的话题，就这样聊到东南西北，有一天却聊出了另一个话外音……

　　某天秦瑛打开程默的语音留言："今后你的事都是我的事，我早说过你是天才作家，你只要认定我，我一定能让你成为名作家，你一定能做到理想中的专职作家！"一个女人的声音夹杂带笑声喊出来："快出来吃晚饭啦！"接着程默提高了声音，似乎有意让女人听到："这样吧，你的这篇文章我先审核一下，下期再商量排版的具体内容，我先去吃晚饭，有问题给我留言就行。"程默说话的内容又像是正和微信通话的人谈论公事语气。

　　秦瑛开始有点纳闷了，为什么正在表白爱意话题会突然变成了公事公办的语气，而且电话语音那头传来女人的声音，程默是有家室的男人？

　　秦瑛又有些怀疑，那为什么有时候半夜他还可以随时回复微信，甚至于可以直接接听秒回信息呢？几个为什么把秦瑛自己都弄糊涂了。语音第二条传出一半，就被关闭了，她感觉程默那边一定有隐情。

　　秦瑛想了一会儿，回复了这样几条信息："听了你的语音留言，理解你的心意，但是我感觉你是有家庭的人，语音中有女人叫你吃饭的是你的妻子吧？我一直以为你没有妻子，是单身。如果你有家室，为何你又能在半夜随时回复信息？算了，也不好问你这些情况。但愿没有打扰你，真以为你是位自由的人！但现在我已经猜到了。你先安心吃饭吧，不用急回复。"

　　秦瑛从那一刻开始就想，只要程默是有婚姻家庭关系，就应该好好珍惜维护自己的家庭生活，不要多想一些有的没的事情！秦瑛骨子里恨小三这种女人，秦瑛在小说中没有少写这些插入别人家庭的女人，所以生活中的秦瑛是绝对不会去扮演这个角色，她的婚姻观里不允许发生这些事。

她想着在接下来的日子里会暗示程默看看她写的小说故事情节中发生的婚外情，作品表明了自己的婚姻观，世界观，人生观。她决不会去破坏别人家庭，也不会去接受已婚男人的求爱。她寻找的是唯一真挚的感情，好配得上自己这么多年的等待。

秦瑛是很有主见的女人，虽然渴望得到爱情，但是骨子里认为爱情就应该专一，选择男人的标准要求品质排名第一，事业经济方面也很重要，她不再是 18 岁少女的情怀，她得面对现实，生活教会了她很多判断人的敏锐思维能力，她不会被所谓的甜蜜爱情故事轻易地冲昏了头脑。

已经是夜深人静，若是以往程默会及时回复秦瑛的信息，甚至会说出"想你"的这些话。若是清晨散步的路上，程默会要求与秦瑛视频，但是这个要求秦瑛只配合满足了仅有的一次。

程默还不高兴，但是后来几次，秦瑛都拒绝了程默打开微信视频聊天的习惯，她要让程默知道，他们俩目前只是作者与编辑之间的关系，对比其他作者，程默对秦瑛只多一些好感和信任而已，他们还在相互了解试探中。她不想节外生枝的尴尬局面出现，但是今晚她却明显地感觉到自己曾经的猜测是对的。女人的第六感很敏锐，秦瑛也是超级敏感的女人，之前两人交流中的一些细节也透露出一些蛛丝马迹。

程默每次清早在外散步的时候会很放松地要求聊天视频，仅有的那一次视频聊天中，程默聊到很欢的时候，突然猛吸一口气随地吐痰，秦瑛看见了顿时感觉有点恶心，但出于礼貌，又是刚刚网上认识不久，秦瑛没有表露出厌恶的表情，只是找到一个简单的理由结束视频："对不起，水烧开了，我得做早餐，不能聊了，挂了！"

还有一次秦瑛打开程默发来的视频，那是他参加活动看山景红叶过程中拍下的，视频中显示出都是一些男性老作家，程默说类似活动全是和尚，没带女人，但却忽视了视频录音中出现女人的声音，当时有一个女人正在与拍摄中男人们说笑，气氛轻松愉快。不用说，那天程默是带着妻子一起参加看枫叶文友活动。

这些情景在秦瑛脑海里重复的出现，秦瑛顿时感觉程默还真不简单。前段时间，当秦瑛跟邓诚再次相遇，秦瑛还会将邓诚跟程默相比，也会考虑如果在他们之间选一位当伴侣，她要怎么选择。那时程默和邓诚在秦瑛的心目中同等重要，而现在她对程默产生了失望，有些反感和抗拒。

程默看到秦瑛在微信上，问到有关他婚姻实质问题了，想了想这样回答："是的，我有妻子，我们是一儿一女的家庭，但是我和她没有共同语言，睡觉都是分房睡，只在一个锅里吃饭，平时各搞各的。我每月工资卡都在妻子手里，我每月工资 4000 元，自己只留 1000 元零钱。我们互不干涉各自的生活和工作，房产证也只写妻子一个人的名字。"

秦瑛回复："那你们还是很有感情基础，应该珍惜自己拥有的一切，真正的爱就是能一直陪伴你的那个人，好好过日子吧。"

程默秒回："遇见你之前，我从没有对任何一个女人动心，我对你是认真的，如果你跟我走在一起，我会给你一个名分的。当然，为了爱我会净身出户，希望你勇敢坚定地向前走，相信我就是能给你未来幸福的男人，因为我有一颗善良和爱你的真心。"

秦瑛无语，也不想马上顶撞回去，毕竟才刚刚确认了程默是有家室的男人，想到程默几个月来帮助过她，在文学作品积极推荐中所做的热心帮助，不免有些伤感。为什么对他的婚姻不敢早点面对问个明白？现在多么尴尬，进也不是退也不是，左右为难。于是秦瑛在不知道怎么回答他的时候，只有保持沉默不语，想着放一段时间想好了再说吧！静观其变才是明智之举！

秦瑛不闻不问的态度让程默有些沉不住气了，接下来的几天里，又出现了程默的微信消息："一连几天没有你的信息，你都快把我逼疯了，我想你，我告诉你我想你，请你回复我。我想让你知道世上没有比我对你更认真的男人了。你最好坚定选择跟我走下去。相信我，我们在一起一定会很幸福，我一定让你成为最知名的作家，你想干什么我都支持你。如果你不想跟我一起走下去，那就当我从来没有说过这些话，我再也不会说了，我也理解你。答应过你的事，我还是会帮忙做到，你放心吧！"

秦瑛看到这个消息才有点放心，都是成年人了，经历了这么多的事情，程默应该明白自己应该做些什么，不该做些什么。秦瑛还能接受两人这样的关系——编辑跟作者之间的纯粹关系。

　　接下来的日子里，秦瑛为了报恩，也积极地托文学老师，将程默的书将推荐到国外的图书馆上架，供华人读者们阅览，对程默作品也起到提高宣传作用！让更多的读者看到程默写的书。在文学领域中，秦瑛也尽量帮助程默——只要不提个人感情之事，这种朋友关系还是很好。

　　时间一晃就过去了七个多月，秦瑛一直避免跟程默有过多的接触，如果没有文学作品上的探讨，就尽量不联系。

第 8 章　渐渐露馅

　　清晨起来，秦瑛很熟练地做早餐，一个煎蛋和煮了一个梨六颗红枣，加上一片柠檬煮了一碗水果茶，冲了包麦片牛奶！简单吃完早餐，慌慌张张了拿起随身背着包就去上班了。

　　到了单位正好是星期二，理疗的人就诊的比较多，秦瑛预约客人很多，进门换上工作服就投入工作忙了起来，这一忙就忙到了下班的时间。手上还有两个客人，今天估计要加班两个小时了，八点半钟才能下班！中途休息也只有半小时吃饭的时间，随便填饱肚子就继续忙去了，秦瑛感觉时间过得真快，这里是私人高端会所，工资待遇高，但是不会养懒人，全凭靠技术手法好，服务好才能胜任此工作，这里的客人都是高端人士！

　　工作时不能怠慢松懈！这就是民营实体公司发展根本！

　　秦瑛来珠海这几年在投入工作的时间，比别的女人要付出很多，不然的话，投资自住房，需要还银行贷款，爱吧书吧的租金及员工工资，都需要她自己来解决，一份工作收入要维护正常的住房装修还款开支，爱吧书吧自负盈亏，维持员工和租金的支付，每月有一些盈利。

　　另外，海景房的复式公寓投资是一次性付款，等待港澳大桥通车，这是秦瑛来珠海做的投资环境房地产业最漂亮的两次地产项目投资！唯有这样努力才能使秦瑛显得稳重成熟，这方面不输给任何男人，当然这也形成了她的实力，在今后的择偶选择伴侣的问题上，提高了自身的价值。随着年龄越大单身越久，选择男友同时，会比经济实力相当，这样更难与她有匹配条件，她是绝不会嫁给比自己实力差的男人！这也是为什么秦瑛这么拼的原因。

　　忙碌了一天，下班有点晚，秦瑛就直接开车回家了，感觉有点累，洗洗温水泡脚早早睡觉。醒来就到了星期三早上，还好六点起床，不慌不忙地准备老三样早点吃了，再看墙上时间还早，秦瑛感觉这两天除了忙工作，生活上很安静。这时才发现，是她的手机在房间里充电，于是赶紧打开手机看看。

"我的妈呀，有这么多来电显示未接，还有微信留言！"

秋甜微信留言："美女呀，知道你忙，但请抽空回复一下，有事跟你商量。"

秦瑛给秋甜一个回复："秋甜，忘了带手机，有事请留言！"

有 3 个邓诚的未接电话，秦瑛也给邓诚同样回复："忘带手机，有事请微信留言，看后及时回复，谢谢关心。"

程默有 4 条微信："我越想不想你，但是越想你。"

程默："我在外散步，很想跟你说说话。你知道吗？我又有一篇小说获奖了，很想与你分享，告诉你我的喜悦，我在想你。"

程默："如果将来咱们在一起生活，你带着车投奔到我住的城市，我学会开车后当你的司机。咱们一起办一份报纸，你负责拉业务联系广告商。凭你的聪明才智，咱们一定可以挣到钱，把这个报纸越办越好。到时候你肯定会实现理想的生活。"

程默："你怎么不说话呢？"

秦瑛抿嘴呼吸，感到诧异，不是已经彼此心照不宣不再"过界"了吗？为什么程默又提起这事？而且，程默的这些想法念头也未免太过分了吧，叫自己带车过去给他学车……

秦瑛想了想还是忍不住地回应说："如果你是自由单身，我才会考虑投奔你，你说能给我未来的幸福，我今天就快人快语地问问你，我若真投奔你，我住哪里？我们不可能将天当房，地当床吧？总得要有个住的地方。我们来实际一点，你说你能给我幸福，你现在都还有家庭，你还不是自由的人，怎样给我幸福？先声明，我决不会当小三。"

秦瑛从来没有像这样回答，猛然被程默的几条信息内容搞得气愤激动，她瞬间理解了程默对她的好是有所图。

秦瑛有意丢下这几句话，想让程默有自知之明，也是有意制止他再别说所谓的真爱，很明显，程默已有家室了，有妻儿子女，连谈恋爱的资格都没有，还能和秦瑛谈未来？程默连名分都不能给，还能谈真情？真不知道程默有什么底气说这些话。

接下来程默又解释，他不仅说自己穷，还说自己傻，自己笨，不会经商做生意，办报都倒贴钱，就想等秦瑛救急，用秦瑛的智商去把报纸这个平台办活挣钱。要等秦瑛来把文学报刊这个事业做大做强。

具体措施没有，都是一些大话空话，若是这事放在程默还没有对秦瑛说出那些暧昧情话之前，或许秦瑛冲着要干一番事业的意愿，还真的会投入人力物力资源，把这个办报平台实业做好。

可惜啊，程默没有耐心等待，把内心的意图渐渐露馅了，要不是当初语言聊天露出的破绽，秦瑛还真会跳进这个坑了。

现在秦瑛刹车还来得及，毕竟什么都没有发生。说实在话，那么有才华的男人，怎么会这般赤裸裸地说出这些话。而且好像还不明白他现在说的一切，都是非分之想。

秦瑛希望程默明白她的态度，她可是绝对不会接受一位有家室男人的情感，想都别想。秦瑛把球踢给了程默："没有自由身，什么话都免谈！"想让程默知难而退，把这个歪念压下去。

哪知道程默那边秒回："我就跟你直说吧，我原来跟你说过我是个穷人，如果要我现在给你这位，未来的新娘像年轻人那样，买房买车，我确实做不到。也许我的真心并不值钱，但是你要是认可我对你的爱，你可以去拼出理想的生活条件，而且你目前也有足够能力为我们买一处安身之所。如果你不肯付出，那就证明我们没缘分。"

程默一番言语自信到极致。秦瑛此时感觉好笑，对程默发给她的这些话感觉到无语。此时心里猛然蹦出一句话：何为真情？秦瑛倒还听出了话中更深层的意思。

秦瑛反复领会程默的语音意思，重复地听了几遍。开始以为是误会听错了，结果一遍遍地听得清清楚楚，秦瑛的心也凉了，她原以为程默是真的欣赏她的文才，后来是渐渐动了真情。真没有想到，这几个月网上的情感交流，原来是这样真实目的。

秦瑛若没有听过这些语音，也许会幻想着和程默走在一起，过着世外桃源的文人浪漫小日子。秦瑛不是嫌弃程默常挂在嘴边上说的穷，她最瞧不起的是一个男人压根儿就没有担当，没有想过要为爱付出一种责任，为事业去争取努力的决心。明明什么也没有，还说他很满足眼下的这种安逸舒适的生活。从头到尾都是说他要等秦瑛去闯去拼，他来协助。想的是真美，真是异想天开。

秦瑛脑子里带出来的一句话："真敢想！"

秦瑛真没有想到，程默不仅忘了自己还是有家室的男人，连爱其他女人的资格都没有，对秦瑛谈何是真心？而且怎见得与他一起就会幸福，幸福在哪里？

秦瑛小心谨慎地回复，不然会误解更多，到时候害人害己，误了他人的家庭关系。无论如何，自从知道程默有妻子之后，秦瑛以为程默会跟她一样，有些话不能再讲了，看来程默又忘了自己已经是有家的人了……

秦瑛想想，还是给程默一次做完美男人的机会，在没有真实确认程默的意图之前，还是想表达委婉一点，给程默一点面子，于是客气地回复微信："我知道你有家庭后，我知道我们不可能了，所以不可能往这方面去想了。我没有想过这些未来的事情，也不能去想！你应该懂得我的意思，希望你能理解，我们都是成人了，有的事情可以做，有的事情我们不能做。"

第9章　异想天开

　　秦瑛回复程默信息后，就想使自己冷静下来，她希望彼此之间都有一个过渡期，不希望太尴尬的局面发生。

　　秦瑛想，他们之间只当是文友关系就好，以后再不提感情这方面的事情，她可以装着两人之间什么事情也没有发生过。

　　一晃一周慢慢地过去了，这期间还真的很安静，秦瑛心想这样保持平静也好，彼此心照不宣，也可以在文学交流的这个圈子里维持友情，时间长了她与程默的微妙关系也会慢慢消失。他们两人本来就什么也没有发生，只是程默在情感方面表达已出轨，幸好还没有造成实质性影响。将这种感觉扼杀在摇篮中，是最明智的处理方式。

　　可偏偏事与愿违，有一天秦瑛在下班去往爱吧书吧的路上，听到手机不停地响，因为开车也没顾得上马上接听。到了爱吧书吧把店里事情处理妥当后，秦瑛坐下来静静地看下书，结果手机不停地又有信息提醒的声音——秦瑛设置为"梭子"的声音。

　　秦瑛斜靠在沙发上，看着微信上程默发给她的信息："这几天我一直在控制自己尽量不去想你，不看你的任何微信，但没有想到你根本没有给我发微信。你能做到不理我，可我做不到不去理你不去想你。我再也不会提那些事了，我越不想这些，就心里越难受，想着想着我还是有话想跟你说。近几天我想通了，我是癞蛤蟆想吃天鹅肉，我是痴心妄想，我知道这个事是不可能发展成我想要的更亲密关系，你也不会为我们走到那一步。我已看出来我在你心目中有几斤几两。就当我之前什么都没说，但该帮你的事我还是会照办，我还是希望你也能继续帮我推荐作品发表在报纸上，刊登我的小说作品，希望我们一如既往地互相帮忙。"

　　秦瑛看见程默说到这段话，无非是表达自己内心的感受。程默话语间对自己的冷嘲热讽。有些话秦瑛一直憋在心里没有说出来，秦瑛确实觉得程默的心思就是异想天开。程默在失望中用了"痴心妄想"的说法来自嘲。

秦瑛没有马上去辩解说什么，无论怎样，秦瑛知道只要过了这段时间，程默对她的那份感情随着时间流逝就会退去。因为秦瑛明白自己在程默心中其实也是一种错觉，那并不是真爱。

情感专家曾经说过这样一段话：当一个男人如果真爱这个女人的时候，他不会在女人面前哭穷，也不会在女人面前耍大男子主义，让女方将一切财富付出，来证明对他的爱。要不然，这男人根本就没有爱过这个女人，在男子心里这女人是一文不值，而且还要用爱的借口绑架女人为自己付出。

这种情感上的试探，堵塞在秦瑛的心中像一团火，燃烧的窝火。秦瑛心想，程默不仅没有与她有一点经济条件抗衡的实力，还冠冕堂皇地索求房和车，赤裸裸地要求秦瑛用财富上的付出来证明真心。

程默的每一句话都显示出大男子主义霸道，表现出莫名其妙趾高气扬的自信。秦瑛感到悲哀，程默其实一直以来就没有认真投入过。秦瑛想要寻求真爱会这么难？她必须通过舍弃财富才证明自己的感情是真爱？

秦瑛缺乏安全感，在情感中她显得谨慎小心，在没有确定爱情真伪之前，她的确是不会冲动。因为她挣的每一分钱都是自己靠智慧，勤奋努力得来的，她的人生轨迹就是要三思后行。如果说感情非要用经济钱去衡量的话，哪怕是自己怦然心动的感情，也会刹那间清醒止步。

她对感情要求专一，真诚，而且是要赋予实际行动，而不是只动嘴上说的甜蜜，她不再是 18 岁的少女情怀，她为了得到真爱，已经耗费了大半辈子了，都进入了大龄剩女的行列，但也不惜一切地等下去。她的性格注定要另一半，一定为之付出真挚的情感，她才能为之所动。

作为伴侣，程默达不到秦瑛的标准，若按照普通朋友的关系维持，程默不错了，反正也不会考虑和程默有更进一步的关系。

一星期后的一天，秦瑛正好将一部小说书稿修改完成，这是程默曾经答应负责推荐给出版社作品。

秦瑛不想再找程默麻烦，将作品发给了另外两位编辑老师，得到了两位老师的认可和支持。其中一位是秦瑛的同乡，编辑老师在审稿中给了点评和建议，将人物年龄改小，人物的职业设定得更高层次，将写出年轻化的爱情婚姻的作品。

这样一来整部作品是为了推荐给影视平台，这有些纯商业市场化，小说主题内容就失去了秦瑛的写作初衷。

秦瑛想了想还是想坚持自己的想法，不想作大动修改。如果一味地迎合市场需要那等于是失去了小说作品原有想表达的真实故事原型，失去了很多客观的东西，如果改变了真实性，秦瑛担心改得面目全非，脱离生活原本环境。秦瑛也认为，如果写出不熟悉的人和事，这部作品将一定没有生命力，对作品故事里的人物写不出感情。于是再三考虑后决定还是按照自己的意愿去写，除了在文笔修改以外，将故事主线条维持在原创主题上，这样下来就只能选择另一个可以接受作品原样的出版社。

此时秦瑛想从侧面听听程默的意思，顺便看看他是否愿意像以往那样帮忙出版。毕竟整部小说书稿内容程默清楚写的什么内容，更容易沟通。

微信上秦瑛将出版编辑老师关于出版问题罗列出来，程默谈出了自己的意见：

1. 让秦瑛还是等同乡的编辑老师建议，先修改，再等待出版。

2. 同行相忌，他不方便插手这次出版的任何事情。

3. 另外，既然选择不想发展成伴侣关系，程默也表明自己的态度，也不会去做知己。

程默的信息告诉秦瑛，他是不会再帮秦瑛了。当初程默这样跟秦瑛说："今后我该帮助你的，还是会继续支持你，该办的事一定照办！"如今证明这些只是虚假的客套话。

秦瑛听到这些信息，觉得有些话真不该说，试都不应该试。这次沟通下来，秦瑛对程默最后一点念想都没有了。

秦瑛有些失落，这就是那个对她"情有独钟深有好感"的程默？那个曾经热情洋溢说出过肺腑之言，对她如何如何有爱慕之情的男人？

程默的表现这前后对比，咋样都让秦瑛感觉是她自己太天真，还是程默太敢想了，真有些异想天开。

第 10 章　瞬间看透

秦瑛看见微信上程默的回复，心里早已想到是这样的结果，她只是想论证一下自己判断是否正确，再做理性的处理也不至于草率。

现在秦瑛劝慰自己该对程默死心了，她不愿意相信程默真的就此拒绝提供帮助。她一方面希望程默胸怀坦荡，对她怀着不带条件目的性的爱；另外一方面又有些担心是自己的一厢情愿。如果程默真对她无私大度的好，就不会说出那些赤裸裸贪念的话意，她此时心里很乱很复杂。

果然没有过三天，程默微信里发出了信息："我的意思是说，如果你联系的那位出版社编辑老师，还没有具体的签约，没有出版具体时间，或者没有出版具体计划，你就直接告诉我，剩下的出版问题，就由我帮你解决。我说不理你不管你，其实我是气你的，因为我知道你的作品写得很好，只是没有遇到好的伯乐。我发现你，欣赏你，可你又拒绝我。我指明的方法，你又不照着做，当我是你的备胎？"

秦瑛明白世上没有无缘无故的爱，也没有无缘无故的恨，她知道程默帮她是有目的性，而这个目的性已经很明显，她不能用未来余生的幸福，去赌上后辈子命运的主宰大权。她听过不少情感专家的节目，谈智慧女人的命运将如何应对生活中遇到这些问题，她了解相关的应对措施。

于是秦瑛很礼貌地回答："首先谢谢总编还一如既往的帮助和支持，也谢谢你的理解。关于小说出版一事，目前我还以全面修改为主，另外已将初改的版本发给了其他愿意出版发行的代理公司，已有此书合作出版的计划，我正等待对方回复。此次出版有你的关心我就心满意足了，这次出书就不劳烦你了，在此谢谢。"

看见秦瑛回复信息如此有礼有节，程默心里顿时五味俱全，程默心头又生一计。

　　程默有两个文学爱好写作的会员群，秦瑛一直沉默潜水，没有发有关自己的作品，一般从不与群里任何人互动交流，只看和学习。

　　这接下来的几天里，群里频频出现很多新的女性作者文章及作者简介，整个群里都是早上问好晚安祝福，群里成了作者向程默总编的早请示晚汇报现象。程默很享受这种像皇帝一样的待遇，那种精神虚荣的满足，已使他变得越来越自信满满，唯我独尊的心态空前活跃高涨。

　　唯独没有秦瑛的奉承讨好，一条信息也没有出现，这让程默又疑心了起来。

　　一天早上秦瑛打开手机微信，又看到程默发来的微信内容："从未谋面的微信朋友，如果有事相求，我愿鼎力相助，如果不愿待在群里，也可以自由退出。"秦瑛怔住了，这又是程默哪根筋搭错了？怎么总是出尔反尔，说好了一如既往维持现状，怎么又开始设防了呢？秦瑛想也没想直接发出六个字："啥意思？是劝退？"

　　紧接着手机响了起来，秦瑛一看微信语音通话显示是程默，接通听着程默怎么说也好，省得一句一句回复。

　　程默微信这头解释着："我不是那个意思，我在群里找不到你，我急了，我就想用这种方式问一下你到底是什么意思，你怎么悄悄退群了呢？"

　　秦瑛解释："你有两个群，我退了其中一个群，我记得早跟你说过。另一个群我没退，我只是沉默没有发声。你如果想让我退群，你直说。如果你在群里发一些内容不想让我看到，我可以马上退群，你可以大刀阔斧地做你想做的事情。群里最近有很多新的女作者出现，就当我什么也没有看见。我还是要强调两点，我为何还保持跟你联系，一是你的书正在邮寄的路上，你托我将书要放在图书馆里，供人阅读，提高你的知名度和宣传之用，如果我做好了这些，是要告诉你一声对吧？第二，另外我还有一篇小说原定在你的下期刊物上发表，如果你如期照办了，做了好事是不是也会告诉我一声？毕竟这是我们作者与编辑之间保持联系最适合的方式。"

　　程默听着急着辩解补充："我可不是这个意思，我不会要你删掉我的微信，我的意思很清楚，还是那句话，你的事，我会鼎力相助，你要退群由你决定，我可没有什么见不得人的东西。你看到的女作者是有很多，她们来自全国各地，都爱好文学写作，虽然作品没有你写得好，但是要给她们多鼓励，多给机会展示她们的作品。不瞒你说，确实有几个女作者对我有爱慕之情，甚至愿意在我的城市买房来陪伴我，我都没答应。还有一个女作家是在国外，有别墅和车，希望我投奔她，她什么都不要，只图我这一个人。你明白吗？你看不上我，可有好多女人喜欢我。你今天给一句话吧，行，咱们继续朝着这个目标努力处下去；不行，我就真的永远不提了。"

秦瑛瞬间看透了程默，逼着她表态，秦瑛停了几秒之后："我们不要再提这个话题好吗？投稿出书的事，我不想麻烦你，因为我给不了你想要的生活。有些东西是我们的共同爱好，比如你说的房子车子，但不同的是这些财富我靠自己努力奋斗来获得，而你却把这些东西跟爱绑在一起，要女人为你的所谓真心的爱去付出，来满足你所需，还以此证明这才是真爱？如果你一定要这样做，这样试探我的底线，实不相瞒，今天我也说句大实话吧，我们的关系是不可能再像当初那样单纯了！你是爷们，你在家庭生活中应该去为你的女人孩子付出，并提供这些财富。而不是向你爱的女人索取？

你口口声声说爱我、很想我，我倒想问问你，你为的'真爱'又做了什么呢？你连基本的生活条件都给不了，还能指望你能给予我未来的幸福生活吗？真不知道你为何还能有自信说得出口，你连一句承诺都给不了。你说目前你穷这是现实，唯一能改变的就是为了爱你以后会净身出户；而条件是我先必须为你的爱买房买车，才有你的一席之地的居所，是这样理解吗？"

程默发出了笑声，用自嘲的话地打断了秦瑛："好吧，我只是告诉你，只要你答应我可以向发展伴侣关系，我一定会为你净身出户。但是今天你让我觉得你不愿为了我们的爱做这些事情。好吧，我替你惋惜，你失去了遇到我这么一位好男人的机会，随你吧。"

秦瑛顿时感觉有些不可理喻，有些情绪直接把话说出来："总编领导请你别打岔，让我一口气把想说的都说完，免得彼此误会耽误了一生。我是认真考虑了才如实回答，咱们就此打住，再也不要谈论这个话题了，不然连微信文友都没法做。不谈了，我该忙去了。"

再过两秒，秦瑛尝试一下发图片回复代替要说的话，结果显示红色感叹号！此条信息发送失败。

秦瑛的微信从此减少了许多杂音，她自嘲无语，埋头把微信搞一个大清除，没有留下一丝她与这位程默总编曾经聊过的痕迹，眼不见为净，要拉黑就拉彻底干净。

秦瑛删除掉程默不止一次的深情表达。只可惜，话还没兑现，就已经彻彻底底断了联系。明摆着，程默心想你秦瑛不给予我想要的，白白帮你那也是不可能的。虽然程默总是信口满满的说过："我帮人，从无所求。"

这男人的嘴，说出来的话，女人们能信吗？更何况是秦瑛呢？秦瑛暗暗庆幸，这次宁可放弃所谓的名利虚荣，也得冷处理，识人真不能太讲面子了，该做减法就得果断放弃私欲杂念，无欲则刚。有的情还真不能接受，这婚外情更不能发展。她做人有底线，瞧不起这种对爱不忠的男人。秦瑛怎会倒贴这类男人，一旦被她识破，她自会有耐心看着此人，自动找到台阶下，体面地走远。

秦瑛庆幸赌准了程默沉不住气，先"拉黑"她，不然她还真不好说出狠话："拉倒吧！"

这文人有时候也鬼话连篇，有句名言说得好，"时间是检验真理的标准！"

天上不会掉馅饼，也不可能有免费的午餐。有些时候"有钱"就是好。无论男人女人，用钱就能识别是真爱还是假爱。程默知道与秦瑛不会有戏了，知趣地先溜。

秦瑛很淡然，关于程默的好坏，从未对任何人提起。她知道有的人就是路过，只能算是在她人生中的一位过客，到了点就该下站了，就当是起初认识的那份美好，是一次错觉。

第 11 章　拨动心弦

常言道"日有所思，夜有所梦"，秦瑛的梦境给了她一个很明显的提醒：程默出局了。程默给的并不是秦瑛想要的情感生活。梦里她记得最清楚的那句话"余生谁能陪你走？"也许就是暗示自己的爱情对象绝对不是程默，而是一个需要继续等待的男人，一个能够让秦瑛托付一生的男人。

在秦瑛焦头烂额的这段时间里没有听到邓诚的消息，邓诚在忙什么呢？秦瑛忽然想到已经半个月没有邓诚音讯，难道他发生了什么事情吗？

秦瑛在上班之前打电话给好友秋甜："喂，秋甜！问一下邓诚最近这段时间在忙些什么呀？快两个礼拜没有听到他的声音了，没敢冒昧地问他。想请你帮忙联系一下他，再告诉我一声。"

电话那头秋甜说："你俩真有感应，两礼拜前邓诚母亲突然脑出血去世，他忙着处理后事去了。因为发生这种事情太突然，他临时前只打电话告诉了我老公沈总，并交代不要告诉你，怕你担心。他说可能要将母亲骨灰带回老家山上，在老家待一段时间处理一些事情，至今还没有回来。听沈总说，他好像下个月会回来了，毕竟他公司有很多事情需要他做决定。邓诚交代过，如果你有什么事需要帮忙的，让我们尽量一定先告诉他。"

秦瑛静静听着，忽然电话那头又传来沈总的声音："秦瑛啊，正好我在秋甜身边，顺便告诉你一个信息，你要有心理准备，有关海边你租的那间爱吧书吧。规划部门朋友告诉我，那里是要拆迁范围之内，你签的租房合同就没有续租期了。你会在近期接到政府的通知，要作好相关的准备。但是你也别太担心，我已经把这些信息及爱吧书吧经营权实际情况跟邓诚说了——正好那天邓诚打电话关心你怎么样，我没有考虑就直接说给邓诚听了。邓诚叫你别着急，他会回来和我一起想办法解决。现在你得稳着，没有接到正式拆迁办通知，房东没有找你谈之前，你一定要像以前一样照常营业。"

秦瑛听完之后都不知道说什么好，看似平静的两周里却发生这么多变化，要不是有沈总和秋甜这两位好朋友，秦瑛真的不知道怎么办才好。城市规划部门幸好有沈总的朋友，不然的话，一旦拆迁安置爱吧书吧大件物品是一项非常困难的事情。

秦瑛能不着急吗？爱吧书吧往哪搬？还需要继续经营吗？放弃自己喜欢做的工作和生活方式吗？要知道这不仅仅是秦瑛的生活一部分来源，最主要是她的一部分精神寄托。

珠海附近有一个叫南朗小镇，正属于大湾区规划之中，国家给予了很多好政策措施，特别是近年来随着我国经济发展水平增长速度，港澳大桥建设项目建成，在南朗小镇寻找开发经营服务行业，应该还是有发展前景。秦瑛很看好珠海这座有发展潜力旅游城市，那么附近城乡旅游景点也一定适合发展配套的服务行业。有了这些大方向，秦瑛心里已经有目标了，她不再焦虑不安。

在精神世界里，秦瑛已经不再纠结与程默的关系，这个世界上没有爱情可以，但决不能没有事业，秦瑛明白自己想要什么样的生活。

秦瑛像往常一样，白天在会所理疗室工作，下班和周末都会在爱吧书吧打理一下经营事项，静静等待房东的正式通知，心里有数就不慌不乱——她也做好了最坏的打算，大不了暂时停业不开爱吧书吧，那也没有什么可怕，趁现在还有时间可以去附近找找适合开新店的地方。

又一个周末，秦瑛在爱吧书吧思索着哪些东西可留，哪些东西可搬，在备忘录本子上写着一项项要准备办的事项，一个声音打断了秦瑛的思路："一个人在写什么啊？这么认真，信息又不回。"

秦瑛惊喜地抬起头，看见沈总和邓诚一同来到了桌边。刚刚那句话是邓诚说的，他露出担心的表情。沈总补充道："我就说吧，秦瑛没有事，她会在这里，邓董还不信，非要拖着我一起来看看你。"

秦瑛指着桌子边的沙发说："快坐，来得正是时候，我这边还有两件事想请教沈总，这爱吧书吧里柜子，哪些部分可以卸下搬走再用？"

沈总笑着对邓诚说："还是由你自己说说建议吧，我来补充。"

邓诚胸有成竹地说："那天听沈总跟我谈起这个爱吧书吧是你在经营，得知政策将要将区域规划拆迁的信息，我就考虑到这是一个很大的工程，我跟沈总也商量了此事。我先说说我的看法，如果不同意你还可以提议。我的想法是咱们不要走费力的事情，争取一步到位安排，我把方案分别讲出来供你选择：

1. 如果爱吧书吧想继续迁移经营，建议迁入在乡村旅游发展潜力的区域，正好在我那里有一层楼空间，还没有具体设计装修。

2. 麦茶装修风格还是由沈总整体设计装修，因为沈总了解你喜欢的风格。

3. 这样安排就可以减少装修成本，降低资源浪费，还可以为长期从事这项工作环境创造条件，优势是这个行业发展在旅游景点区域会得到政策的扶持，也会有广阔的发展前景。

4. 我很看好，所以我永远支持你长期在此地经营下去，我也受益。你别以为我是帮你，其实也是帮我自己。

我说完了，看看你还有什么想法，说出来听听。"

秦瑛一脸惊讶，不知道说什么好。她知道这是邓诚想要帮她，但是她心里还是有点担忧，她真不想欠人情。程默起初也是积极地帮助秦瑛，后来知道没能成为伴侣发展关系，到最后连朋友都没能做了。她真不想让自己的情感生活变得越来越糟糕，她的要求其实也不高：只是追求找到一位能理解爱她的男人作伴侣，而不是把友情和爱情搞混淆。她需要冷静，一方面需要事业发展，一方面又不能接受无缘无故的友情支助。

秦瑛很纠结，目前她很愿意与邓诚成为很好的朋友关系，但她认为一定要吸取程默的教训。秦瑛求助地向沈总看了看，沈总很懂秦瑛的顾虑，马上解释说："秦瑛你放心，我作为你们的共同朋友中间人，我帮邓诚起草一份正式租赁合同，时间按照邓诚的心意，可以 10 年一签，前 5 年租金可根据营业额的百分之五交付，没有营业额可以直接免出租费用，因新地域经营可享受优惠政策。可赠送三个月装修时间，所有都按照正常程序签合同，这样你们俩看行吗？"

秦瑛听完沈总的补充，反而更不安，这哪是签合同呀？这分明是白送，而且是没有给秦瑛任何压力的方式，这样更不妥吧？

邓诚像是看出了秦瑛的顾虑："哎呀，秦瑛别多想了，我乡村房子如果装修好了，那么好的空间岂不是更浪费，再说我母亲去世后，我平时生活都会在城里那套房子里住，就是周末才回乡村那座房子里。哦，还有我只是选择留在二楼，用于我私人空间，并且沈总帮我考虑好了，从后院开门直接上二楼，不占一楼经营场所空间，没有任何影响，沈总设计布局很人性化，我认为这套方案对我们三方都有利。"

秦瑛看到邓诚和沈总两人都这样说了，也明白目前没有比这个更好的方法了，这主意也许是他们俩已经商量好的了，看见这份帮她的真心，一时半会她还真没有理由去拒绝这番好意。

秦瑛在外创业也很不容易，不能因为与程默关系处理不好，而怀疑任何好心好意的人。虽然邓诚跟秦瑛没有交往多久，但邓诚的每次待她友好都不是装出来的，而且感觉很踏实，就是帮秦瑛。

房子就是要用来住的用的地方，不然浪费了资源。邓诚就是秦瑛理解的那样，有意说出轻松，好让秦瑛同意。

沈总是个挺会办事的人，马上对秦瑛说："别再犹豫了，今天决定下来，我回公司把租房合同拟出来，明天还是在这里来签合同，我就好安排具体设计和装修材料准备了，争取在年底之前全部弄好，不然夜长梦多，这拆迁办的迁移时间不会太长，顶多半年时间，我们得抓紧。"

秦瑛望着两位那副认真的劲头，真不是开玩笑的样子，只好点点头不停地说："谢谢，真的谢谢你们为我考虑这么周到，好吧，我们明天在这里定下来。"

邓诚微笑对秦瑛说："这就对了，别再让我们大家为你操心了，我也喜欢有这么一个安静看书的好地方。"

沈总拍拍邓诚的肩说："咱们可以放心走了，去我公司具体拟草一下租房合同。"

秦瑛看着他俩走出爱吧书吧大门的背影，才收住依依不舍的目光，心里暖暖的，她背靠在沙发上，眼睛有些泛红。那是一份感激不尽的心酸，这份情只有她自己深有体会。

第 12 章　清澈见底

出门后沈总对邓诚说："邓诚啊，说实话，你知道今天这样决定意味着什么吗？别说租金收益半送了，你可考虑好了，今后这一帮就是十年啊！"

邓诚对沈总说："到公司后我再跟你说说心里话。"

车子开到了沈总的公司，下车进公司大时邓诚就开始问："沈总，当年你追秋甜的时候，不也是从给她安全感着手吗？你那个时候都买了房写上她的名字，不然秋甜怎么这么死心塌地跟随你创业呀？你们有多次艰难的时候，秋甜没离开你，这就是你找对的伴侣，就要给她有足够的安全感。我既然选择对秦瑛好，就不让她想东想西，我也想向你学习，我也要拿出我的诚意，默默地为秦瑛做点什么，不让她左顾右盼而忽略了我这份真情，我一定要用行动向你学习取经。"

沈总笑着说："你不知道当年创业搞装修公司多么艰难，秋甜一个女孩子家能跟我这个离异还带着一个儿子的男人一起打拼公司，默默跟随了最艰苦的三年，我能不给她安全感吗？当然你跟秦瑛情况比我们当初要好得多，财富这个东西，只要给对人，留给最亲近的人，让她心里踏实，跟随你一辈子，这财富还不是在你家里？我在这方面把财富看得很淡，只要心爱的人与你同甘共苦走下去，我的财富都是共享，因为只要爱的人在，财富只会越来越多，你说是不是这个理？"

邓诚："所以啊，今天我要沈总帮我一个忙，等明天签合同的时候秦瑛会留下身份证复印件，麻烦你给我留一份，我那边乡村大院房子马上也可以办一个分割产权证，我想把秦瑛的名字带上了，一层的名字都写给她，二层是我自己居住，我想让她在这十年安安心心经营爱吧书吧，但是我没办好之前还是瞒着她好，等到时机成熟，我再选择场合对她说，你看呢？"

沈总听完邓诚的心声后，沉默半晌才微笑地说："我相信你的眼光，愿你心想事成，我支持你。"

　　第二天爱吧书吧签租合同如期完成，此时对邓诚来说这只是让秦瑛安定下来的一种仪式，沈总是邓诚做好事的配合者。秦瑛并不知情！

　　这边经营时间要等待沈总乡村装修的速度而定搬迁时间。

　　沈总当众表态了："幸好三个月前秦瑛的高档公寓房精装修完毕，现在随时可以拎包入住了，接下来的时间，我会加紧进行乡村爱吧书吧设计装修方案，等装修设计效果图认可了，我们就可以再签装修合同。"

　　秦瑛："我好期待这个乡村爱吧书吧方案设计，我的理念就是一切崇尚自然风格，既少花钱又要不拘形式进行实用的设计风格，也可以将旧物改造利用，这可要给沈总增加难度了。麻烦沈总多费心，先谢谢沈总，你做事我放心。"

　　邓诚接着看沈总说："沈总可以将一楼前院全部设计布局爱吧书吧区域，我二层楼你就按先设计从后院直上二层楼，与经营范围不矛盾，可以自带两个不同的生活区域和经营空间，先装修所有一层楼的经营场所，我的二楼后期再装修。"

　　沈总接话说："我也是这个意思，先装修一层楼，也会考虑设计一间办公室兼休息室卫生间套房，可供居住。秦瑛若经营晚了，不想回城折腾，也可以休息在爱吧书吧。放心吧，我会把所需的功能发挥到极致。"

　　秦瑛："沈总，还要拜托你叫一辆搬家公司的车，我会在下周开始搬进你装好的房子 6-606，已经通风三个月了，房间里应该没有异味了。"

　　沈总："没有问题，你只需要叫一辆商务，装一些你的全部生活用品，其余的家具配套都有。"

　　邓诚自告奋勇地说："这好事我要算一个，沾沾喜气，乔迁之喜值得庆祝吧！我的车也可以带一些东西。"

　　秦瑛笑笑点了头，沈总说："那就定在下周日早上六点钟，在小区楼下见。祝我们乔迁新居大吉。"

　　此时的秦瑛在脑海里突然浮现程默的那些自以为是语音留言，跟站在面前实实在在做事的邓诚没法相比。邓诚是处处都替秦瑛着想，言行一致；而程默嘴巴上甜言蜜语，却也只是索取，人还没有见过，却把条件开给了秦瑛。

　　秦瑛很庆幸能够及时发现程默的私心小九九，及时止损，也是一件非常好的事情。她相信眼前看到的一切，生活还是要实在的经历，才能真正辨真假，同时秦瑛将这段没有曝光开始的网恋，彻底的放下，正是时候。

　　她得重新开始，不能错过身边的好人，感觉邓诚对她也是有好感的，她真的很期待进一步了解邓诚，男女都是单身，没有什么不可以去交往，比起程默，邓诚可真是钻石王老五。而程默连追求自己的资格都没有，有家庭还跟别的女人谈爱情。想到这里，秦瑛突然觉得自己有点俗气，物质了，但是这是秦瑛的真实想法。她容易吗？这一路为寻找真爱，从不计较个人得失，不仅付出了情感和金钱，还有这么多年的时间精力，就是当年从不和男人计较谈钱，结果还伤了自己，成了大龄剩女。都快 40 岁了，她不能再揣着糊涂装明白，一定把眼睛擦亮，好好跟想要做伴侣的男人，谈一场恋爱，谈钱，谈事业，谈生活琐事，要看是否真的适合。

　　她不想局限于表面的好，她要求一定要找一个能够包容她好和俗的人，她不想找一个让她不自在不舒服的人在一起，那种婚姻生活，她秦瑛宁愿不要。

　　秦瑛看时间已到中午，马上吩咐员工，端上从家乡带来的土鸡山药汤上桌，请邓诚和沈总两人吃，并还带有家乡圻春的土特产黏米粉素食圆子，还有邓诚上次乡村给秦瑛准备的小鱼，全部煎至两面金黄，让他俩赶快吃，还给秋甜准备了一些，也给邓诚准备了一些带回家中备好打包盒。

　　秦瑛对朋友们的关爱也是怀有一颗感恩的心，她没有在言语上表达说出什么感谢的话，她只能用行动上去尽心去回报朋友们对她的帮助和照顾，她是心甘情愿为他们多做点事。看见邓诚和沈总也不推让，吃得津津有味，秦瑛的心里有说不出的高兴，笑着说："你们爱吃就多吃点，以后我可以多为你们换着花样吃，最近邓诚好像瘦了很多，要多营养补补。"

　　沈总边吃边笑着说："哈哈，心疼邓诚了。"秦瑛不好意思地借顾在后厨拿东西走开了。

　　回到桌前时，秦瑛手上已有两提包装盒装好的食物袋，递给沈总和邓诚手上："放上冰箱里，想吃多少，拿到热波炉加热几分钟可以吃了。拿着吧，吃完后记得带着，知道你们俩还有很多事要忙。"

　　邓诚吃饱喝足了，满意地笑着说："这鸡汤是我这辈子喝过最好的汤，味道真鲜美，还有这素菜馅的黏米粉圆子，还有这煎的鱼，我都爱吃。沈总，我可比你吃得多。"

　　沈总还在低着头把碗中的汤水一点不剩地喝得精光："你看看我，全部吃完，太好吃了，这样吃下去我可真的要长胖了哟。嘿嘿，沾光沾光，谢谢秦瑛，那我不客气了，这替秋甜谢谢你。邓诚我们赶紧去乡村房子现场看看吧，把你要交代事项现场办公说说，我好准备装修下步落实了。"

秦瑛看着他俩吃饱离开的背影，心里乐滋滋地继续待在爱吧书吧，同两个员工一起忙碌了起来。这一天，秦瑛似乎有了盼头，一切的问题有了朋友的帮助安排，事情并没有想象中那么复杂，有这样能帮助办事的朋友，真是秦瑛修来的福分。她暗暗喜欢邓诚做事风格，办事靠谱有执行力，冥冥之中总感觉到邓诚是她的福星，总是在秦瑛很为难的时候及时出现，接着困难似乎就迎刃而解。在秦瑛的印象中，总是邓诚为她付出更多，此时的秦瑛心里暖暖的。她在想，下星期日搬家那天，一定要在新家做一桌更好吃的美味佳肴，把家乡的好特产都拿出来分享，露一手厨艺，给邓诚和朋友们吃个够。

想到这里，秦瑛满脑子已经装满了家乡的食谱。

这一星期秦瑛的心情格外敞亮，无忧无虑，一门心思三点一线理疗室上班，爱吧书吧，回家。每次在回家还准备打包生活用品，为搬家做好准备。人逢喜事精神爽，时间也过得真快，一晃眼这搬家的这天就到了。

快要入夏的季节，春满花开，高档小区的环境真好，一片片绿油油的草地和沿小路的树枝，飘散着淡淡的花香，小鸟飞过树梢间跳跃，空气中弥漫着浓浓的桂花香，阳光灿烂时隐时现洒落到每一处地方。

邓诚，沈总秋甜都早已来到秦瑛租住的楼栋门口了，当初买房就看中了这好小区，是因为社区环境成熟方便，也考虑到了新房装修好后方便搬迁安置。

换一个楼栋就是秦瑛选择的 6-606 号房，还真别说，一个小区搬迁，选择的吉日吉时 6 月 6 日 6 时，这叫顺顺顺。

秦瑛高兴地把大家迎进来，把已打包好的行李一一安排让大家搬进车子里，两台车就装完了，三个小时全部卸载安装到了新家，这房号金牌子 6-606 在大门中间，客厅大而敞亮，客厅露台正对着小区的绿化带，秦瑛和秋甜加爱吧书吧两位员工小雪和小贝，全在厨房忙碌做饭，秦瑛特定将爱吧书吧提前挂牌放假两天，安心地做一顿大餐给搬家帮忙的朋友们吃，今天来一个土鸡大火锅，最主要是在异乡打拼多年，还没有像今天这样有家的感觉，朋友们都在一起团聚，这好像是第一次在一个属于自己的家聚餐吃饭，放松没有拘谨的感觉。正午阳光明媚，太阳从露台方向余光晒到客厅里。厨房设计很大，四个人在一起忙碌打转都很应手，功能区域规划设计得非常到位。这可是秋甜和秦瑛的功劳。

不一会儿，秦瑛拍着秋甜说："这里没有你的事了，你快去负责拿酒，开始上菜吃饭了，这里马上就好了。"

客厅里，秋甜问大家："是喝红酒，还是来啤酒？"

只听邓诚说："我们还是选红酒吧，女士美女们可以一起喝。"

沈总笑着说："还是由女主人秦瑛发话吧，快来一起开涮，你说两句话。"

秦瑛招呼着小雪和小贝，一起上桌就座，随后压压嗓子说："就听邓诚的吧，我们大家喝红酒。这第一杯酒，我向大家表示感谢，感谢对我的帮助和友爱，我就先干为敬。大家喝好吃好，祝愿大家生活越来越好！干杯！"

这一天的午餐一直延续到傍晚时分，夕阳西下，大家都还在聊得热火朝天。邓诚看事做事，一会儿从客厅端空盘进厨房，一会儿将切好果盘放在餐桌上，一会儿又将泡好的青茶端在茶几上放着，供解酒润肺清火，看情景邓诚还特懂养生。

秦瑛看到邓诚没有把自己当外人，做起家务事比秦瑛还麻利。她此刻的心情真的想笑，邓诚这是为了帮她，替她收拾餐盘洗净一切，真像男主人，想到这里还是没有忍住笑出声，马上又克制住，向客厅张望。这里小雪小贝看着电视追剧"浪漫爱屋"，秋甜和沈总也好像聊着装修房子的事，邓诚陪着坐在沙发旁边，时而添茶水，时而给出一些自己的想法，谈到话题都是乡村的房子整体装修设计方案。

看着这帮朋友这么上心做事情，秦瑛的心总算放下了。有了这些好朋友，事业，生活，工作都一定会越来越好。

第 13 章　一心一意

秦瑛让邓诚周一开始，每天抽空下午来会所理疗室做艾灸调理身体，邓诚办的会员卡一直没有使用，最近做的事情又多，身体总感觉很容易疲劳睡眠不足。

秦瑛从邓诚近几次对她的帮助来看，她看邓诚没有顾上自己的生活，不免有些心疼，她只能提醒邓诚有了健康身体，才能更好地生活。

邓诚只要能见到秦瑛，他很乐意地听秦瑛的话，周一上午处理完工作事情后，下午一点敲响了秦瑛理疗室的门。

秦瑛已经准备好红色紫外线仪器，配上从圻春李时珍故乡艾叶贴，对腰背酸痛的部位分别进行温灸理疗。邓诚趴在理疗床上，很享受这种温暖的感觉，很快就睡着了。一个小时过去，仪表计时停止的声音把邓诚惊醒了。

邓诚伸了一下懒腰，拍了拍肚皮，蹬蹬腿，不好意思地说："这艾灸温得我身体发热，真舒服，这周我都会坚持来。睡一个午觉补充睡眠真好。"

秦瑛温柔地回答："是啊，身体健康是本钱，趁着我这两个月还在这里工作。我的培训讲师资格证考下来了，我会在下半年向公司申请辞掉这份工作，去当公司培训中心讲师的岗位工作，因为那里工作更适合我。工作时间一周只上三天班，工资待遇福利根据招收学员人数给予提成。我可以选择在家备课，工作时间灵活，这样就不会影响我的写作进程。"

邓诚高兴地听着秦瑛说话，他从心里更加佩服秦瑛的进取精神，秦瑛的励志勤奋，一直是邓诚对她产生好感的原因之一。她的文静和倔强是不同的两个面，有时会呈现在邓诚的梦境中，邓诚知道那是他想念秦瑛的原因。今天听秦瑛说出工作计划，他比秦瑛还高兴。秦瑛在努力向着自己理想目标改变，她做到了，她改变不了社会大环境和别人，她可以做到改变自己，做更好的自己。

正如邓诚见证秦瑛的那样，秦瑛身兼两职，一心想把自己生活过得更好，才能去帮到家人。秦瑛很自律，什么是当下最该做的事情，秦瑛很有主见。

就像个人婚姻问题，她不会再把时间浪费在像程默那样的男人身上，虚伪的世界里她没有时间去耗着。而且假情假意的程默也没有那个耐心，最后一次发给秦瑛这样的微信内容："给你的真心你不要，会员群你都退了，那你就把我们的微信删了吧！你不做情侣关系，那我们也别做微信好友了。"

看到这条信息，更加证明了程默内心深处的自负自私，没有一点程默曾经所说过的痴情痕迹，这男人变脸可真比翻书还快。幸好没有见过面，又幸好秦瑛还没来得及开始就结束了这段几个月的"网恋"。

邓诚的道别打断了秦瑛走神的比较，秦瑛陪送邓诚到楼梯口，看着邓诚离开后，转身向自己的理疗室走去。她得收拾整理好仪器，马上就有新的预约客户到来，在这医美行业，秦瑛已经成为公司的骨干成员。

秦瑛曾经也在乎过别人的眼光，毕竟自己喜欢以作家身份来面对大众，多体面啊，是有知识有文化的女人。面子都说得好听，可是在异乡发展，得必须要有养活自己的能力，思来想去还是听从女友的推荐学习考证。祖国的建设发展使这座海滨城市发展更加日新月异，这正是医美发展的好时代。

秦瑛为了挣更多钱，就要付出更多的努力，天上不会掉馅饼，只有不断努力付诸行动的人，才能收获财富和幸福生活。这是秦瑛最深刻的体会，女人的靠山就是自己。生命中可以没有爱情和婚姻，但绝不能没有事业和工作。

在没有实力的时候，没得选的时候，只有去做自己不喜欢的服务工作——当初选择这医美行业，也是为了解决养活自己，挣钱速度快，早日积累创业成本，再过渡到干自己喜欢的事业。

邓诚对秦瑛的好感逐日递增，邓诚心里已有更完美的计划了，他想把乡村的房子产权之事办妥，给秦瑛一个惊喜。他想把自己的心塞满秦瑛所需的未来。

人这一辈子总会遇到很多巧合，越想得到的，越是得不到。越不在意的东西，就会在不经意之间发生你的身边。生活就是这样想的，没有指望任何人的时候，只要朝着自己规划的人生意图方向努力，去学习去寻找商机，做自己喜欢的事，哪怕是离目标暂时很远，一步一个脚印努力奋斗，终究有一天就不知不觉地来到了身边。

秦瑛坐在理疗室，回忆着这几年来的生活经历，找工作，租屋开店创业，买房，还一直坚持写作出版，发表市级、省级刊物上有散文、小说及在文学世界栏目，已连载长篇小说三部作品。回头想起来都有些佩服自己的自律和坚持不懈，时光见证了秦瑛的初心开始生根发芽开花结果，这一天虽然来得有点晚，但是她相信女人事业上的成功，经济上独立，不怕遇不到好的伴侣对象，她相信这点，因为爱情是唯美传神的瞬间情感，而婚姻需要价值相互平衡才能走得长久，该来的一定都会出现。

邓诚经过这一星期的理疗，再加上秦瑛每天还带一些不同的营养餐给他吃——今天老鸭汤粉，明天猪肝汤，后天红烧猪排，每天换上不同样好吃的东西，还真把邓诚气色调好了，精气神又恢复了原有的样子。

邓诚在星期六下午临走之前对秦瑛说："我这一星期吃了你做的营养餐，体重都增加了。明天星期天咱们一起去乡村房子跟沈总碰头，装修方案我们当面商量确定下来。"

秦瑛听到这句话，立刻想起来了一件事情，让邓诚等一下，转身去办公桌前拿来一封信交给邓诚，是拆迁办的通知：请于今年 12 月 30 日之前完成搬迁。

秦瑛说："你不用太赶了，这个时间还来得及。"

邓诚说："这事宜早不宜迟，我们得先有准备好就不慌，明天我早上八点去你家门口接你。"

秦瑛心里也知道，乡村房子装修是一个大工程，是得抓紧，但她不想太让邓诚操心了。她能把这么好的地方租给她，特意腾出地方给她继续经营爱吧书吧，心里已很感激了。

自己喜欢这个环境！甚至居住养老！她都喜欢，还有小院，整个一层的面积，都给她租十年，这是帮了她多大的忙啊。这是最适合秦瑛喜欢的生活方式，一半烟火一半仙气。秦瑛能开爱吧书吧，还可以种下四季鲜花！那里交通条件好，又与城郊乡村搭界！年底能够搬迁到这乡村旅游景点，长期处于自己喜欢的生活环境，从事自己喜爱的工作，真是邓诚帮助她实现愿望。

星期天早上八点前，秦瑛提前几分钟到楼下小区门口等邓诚和沈总。做事业讲效率的人都很守时，秦瑛一下来就看到了沈总已坐在邓诚的车上聊着，顺手把做好的三个人的早餐递到沈总手上："你和邓诚俩人的早餐，家乡的黏米圆子，是肉馅的，还有自磨的热豆浆，还有我做的油条，鸡蛋，早上凑合吃点。"

沈总笑着说："我有意饿着肚子等你送吃的给我们。嘿嘿，邓诚我没说错吧，看秦瑛多贤惠，就知道一定会准备好吃的早餐。"

邓诚接过吃的东西，退出主驾驶座，秦瑛上车说："你们俩趁热吃吧，我来开车。"

这一路上两个爷们边吃边聊，秦瑛开车平稳，路上人少车少，微风吹过车窗，很爽！

40分钟很快就到了南朗小镇乡村，邓诚和沈总异口同声地说："我们先从院子布局开始说起。"

秦瑛跟着他们一起听着，邓诚拿出沈总设计的图纸，问一处，沈总就解释一下，没有意见就过，有更好的建议马上在项目上做出标记，中途如果秦瑛有更好的灵感思路，也会参与进来。

看见沈总设计的小院平面图，秦瑛兴奋地指着其中三个地方说："如果在这里种下苹果树、桂花树、橘子树，那就更完美了，八月桂花盛开的时候，浓郁香气四溢，前来的客人会享受外面阳光下看书喝茶聊天。还有当苹果和橘子结果的季节，我会将其制作苹果酱、橘子饼、桂花茶，将其果实成熟后充分利用。你们说可以吗？种植树的成本由我来出，算在装修预算中。"

邓诚听秦瑛这么说，顿悟过来："这个想法好，沈总我后院也要栽这三种树，干脆这种树的项目算在一起，都算我的经费，前院后院装修布局土建施工一体化都算我的，就这么定了。"

沈总知道邓诚的心思，邓诚想帮秦瑛，于是配合邓诚说："当然你邓董的地盘你说的了算。一楼所有室内算秦瑛的，室外算邓董你的，我装修预算这样分开公平吧？没有意见我就这样打预算了，如果现在确定这套大致的方案，今天晚上可以做出预算了。"

这一天三个人就围着平面设计图，绕着一层楼房子由外到内的转，商量着，探讨着，比画着，重点事项记录在平面图上，好像没有多久就到下午五点多了，项目也总算完成了核对，这现场办公的方式还挺效率高。

沈总说："好了，今天就到这里，剩下的工作就是我了，下次我拿装修合同来签订后，就开始实施了。"

邓诚一手叉腰说："走，我们可以去农家乐吃饭了吧？秦瑛的早餐真管用，一直坚持到现在才感觉到饿。"

秦瑛说："对，对，在装修期间，我来当生活部长，管吃管喝怎么样？"

沈总开玩笑说："那我可要多吃点，管饱。"

这餐点了一个大吊锅辣味菜，土鸡炖笋干，三个人喝了一箱啤酒，聊着吃着，直到月亮爬上了树梢天空，繁星闪烁着光芒，还是秦瑛说："该回家了，我来开车，你们可以在后座上眯一会儿。"

邓诚探着头向天空望着说："今晚的月亮真的好圆哦！"

沈总接话说："这意味着我们的事情都会圆满成功，今晚我回去加班把预算合同拟出来，放心吧，我不拖你们后腿，一定会提前在年底之前完成装修计划。"

沈总第二天十点钟就把室外装修合同送到邓诚办公室签了。邓诚说："室内装修合同可以给秦瑛签约，但是装修款写上装完验收付款。所有装修款由我先垫付，你只跟我结账。你对秦瑛只说这是你公司规定，让客户放心满意，做口碑宣传。"

沈总："那我跟秦瑛合同也给你一份，秦瑛只是走程序形式吗？"

邓诚看着沈总说："没有比你更能懂我的心思了，就这样吧，我既然选择了去呵护秦瑛这个好女人，认定了她，我得让她安安心心，等到她哪一天甘愿做我的新娘。我能够做到的就会都给予她。这些东西都比不上秦瑛重要，我应该一心一意去对她好，为她排忧解难。"

沈总不停点点头，边退出邓诚办公室边挥挥手中的合同说："那我去找秦瑛签合同了，星期天乡村见。"

秦瑛见沈总准备好的合同，只扫了一眼，立马签名，并直接问："装修款应该转给你，你得进材料需要资金周转，先转给你 20 万备用怎么样？"

沈总："暂时不用，我想装完验收合格付款方式。"

秦瑛惊讶张大嘴巴望着沈总："不会吧？都像你装修公司这样做生意，那得垫资多少钱啊？不行不行，我们可不能这样办事！"

沈总笑着说："你就给一次机会我公司吧，当是你帮我做广告宣传的，多介绍业务就可以了。怎样，这就是奖励你的福利待遇！走啦，我明天就开始准备材料动工了，放心吧！"

秦瑛看着沈总的背影，想到室外的装修合同都由邓诚揽着付钱了。她秦瑛何德何能，配得上朋友们这么大的恩惠对她。她真不知道怎样去报答这帮朋友们，此时又想起程默说的"他是真情，但不值钱"。秦瑛想了想，何为真情？

邓诚没有对秦瑛说太多甜言蜜语，但行动上却给予了能够依靠的肩膀。秦瑛从心里充满了温暖，她已经领悟到了什么是真情实感的爱情，她感觉到了谁是她余生可以依赖的人。那个人就在她身边，以前怎么就没有发现呢？差点又错过了这么好的人。

第 14 章　可见真情

接下来的日子里邓诚和秦瑛以一周一聚，只有在周末乡村的房子那里才有机会见面，沈总的装修进度按计划有序开展。

一晃眼三个月过去了，秦瑛通过了自学考试，公司批准了她换讲师岗位的申请。秦瑛成功华丽转身，将工作重心放在自己喜欢的写作中，同时可以有时间兼职赚点钱来解决慢节奏的田园生活。她爱上了这乡村里的生活状态，她心里有一种莫名其妙的感觉，这里空气、村民还有朋友们朴质的友情，她很喜欢这种放松的感觉。没有虚假敷衍，只有相互包容相互理解的支持鼓励，在这里她能敞开心扉地体验到做回自己喜欢的事情。

邓诚也没有闲着，周一至周五处理公司业务，周末两天都配合沈总为装修提供资金支持。

在快完成乡村装修最后一部分项目植树种草种花的时候，邓诚对沈总说："我把这乡村的房产权私有财产分割证办下来了，一层楼房产写上了秦瑛的名下，等爱吧书吧迁移搬家，我们选择一个好日子，再告诉秦瑛。办成这件事，我才踏实了。沈总替我先高兴一下，我们这几周都安排完成种树，树苗和草种子我与园林绿化公司选择好了，购买了移植后第二年就可以开花结果的树木花草。"

沈总佩服地对邓诚说："支持你，配合你，还有什么好事都说出来，让我高兴高兴！秦瑛终于等到了属于她的幸福，我和秋甜就想喝你俩的喜酒。"

邓诚笑着说道："这个千万别催秦瑛，我等她心甘情愿地嫁给我，我想等到这爱吧书吧前后满园春色、硕果累累、桂花盛开、鸟语花香了，那个时候最好。"

沈总看见邓诚对秦瑛如此上心的一番真情流露，作为共同的朋友，他也要好好地去帮助邓诚一片爱心。他站在男人的角度考虑，他也为邓诚的胸怀宽广而骄傲，可以说是佩服得五体投地，他相信邓诚一定能找到属于他的爱情和完美的伴侣，秦瑛一定会爱上这位能肝胆相照的爱人。邓诚就是那个能用实际行动证明真爱的好男人。

好事连连的日子，时间感觉过得飞快，一转眼已经到了年底最后两周了，这个周末意义非凡。

秦瑛、邓诚和沈总、秋甜一起相约乡村屋子会面，定一个搬迁吉庆好日子，策划一个隆重仪式，搞得热热闹闹，这些都是邓诚瞒着秦瑛所做的一切。

邓诚也把村主任请来了，到早上九点钟，村主任忍不住先宣布说："我代表全村村民乡亲们，欢迎你们把知识分享给大家，这份情谊我们永远都受益良多，谢谢大家给我们村带来的惊喜。"

接着由邓诚发表了肺腑之言："我就此感谢村主任及时村民的大力支持，感谢沈总对装修落实工程的鼎力相助。同时欢迎我们的乡村女主人秦瑛正式加入乡村振兴建设项目，经营爱吧书吧，将精神知识文化交流在贵地乡村落户。祝此活动圆满成功！"

这一天是 12 月 16 号 9 点 9 分，秋甜说："这寓意一切顺利，长长久久的幸福。"

秦瑛先听邓诚这样一番话有些蒙了，乡村女主人？邓诚喊声："下面欢迎我们的女主人讲话。"该轮到秦瑛女主人讲话了，这突如其来的场面，让秦瑛有一点吃惊和措手不及。幸好秦瑛有当讲师的经验，这对她来说也不是很难应对的事情。秦瑛立马先镇定了 3 秒钟，秋甜悄悄小声附在秦瑛的耳朵说："邓诚已经把经营范围面积产权写上你的名字，你是名副其实的女主人。"

秦瑛有些意外了，这些突如其来的幸福来得让她感觉太惊讶了，情不自禁地发出了真实的心声："我何德何能享受大家给予我这么多信任和恩惠？我不知该从何说起……这份信任和贵重的礼物，我只有在今后用行动来报答这份真情。在此我感谢所有的祝福和朋友们的陪伴，谢谢大家给我的帮助鼓励。我想要说的话都在心里……"

秦瑛有些说不下去了，嗓子有些哽咽，她不想在这喜庆祥和的日子里落泪。也许是感激的心情，对邓诚的爱无以言表，也许是庆幸自己终于等到了爱自己的那个男人。她再也克制不住喜泣交加，涌出泪水模糊了双眼。这情形瞬间被沈总眼尖看见了，迅速接过话说："大家现在随我一起来看看我们女主人的爱吧书吧，请大家一起验收吧！随我来参观。"

秋甜陪着秦瑛，用手轻轻地拍打着肩背说："应该高兴，这可是好事，邓诚这么真心待你，可真是实心实意相中了你，等爱吧书吧开始营业了，后期我们都要等着喝你们俩的喜酒。快擦干净脸上的泪痕，别让人感觉有人欺负你似的。"

沈总带着大家一伙人，从来乡村屋前院后开始介绍起，邓诚陪同参观走在前后左右，看到有秋甜陪伴在秦瑛左右一起时，就放心了，但邓诚时不时地向秦瑛的方向而移动关注。

秦瑛看见院子里已经实现了规划图上的美景，她感慨万千地说："谢谢你和沈总把我想要做的一切都实现了，真的好像是在做梦。这一切真的要好好地感谢你们，感谢你们为我和邓诚做了这么多的事情，我真不知道怎么报答你和沈总给我的帮助。"

秋甜大笑起来说："我和沈总说过了，要早一点喝上你们俩的喜酒，是我们最开心的事了，你知道吗？俗话说成人之美增寿七福之幸事。"

秦瑛点点头看着远处的邓诚对秋甜说："都听你们的，等邓诚亲口说娶我，再定吉日良辰吧！"

邓诚不知什么时候已经走到秦瑛身边问："是你想要的样子吗？还满意吧？走我带你先去看看室内的装修布局，有一点点修整，增加了一些生活空间。"

秦瑛拉着秋甜的手，一起跟着邓诚走进了爱吧书吧大厅内，一看就是秦瑛喜欢得不得了的田园怀旧风格，既朴实又自然，用的材料全是天然的石头和废弃的木头，墙面有红砖装饰也有水泥墙装饰，搭配在一起就是看起来特别舒服亲切，有一种温馨暖意，爱吧书吧两个员工小英小贝放着老唱片的轻音乐，向秦瑛说："秦姐，这是最适合爱吧书吧放的曲子，像是从很远的地方飘过来的声音，显得宁静，又不会吵到客人看书，冥想的曲调优美，全是大自然赐予的声音，像我们家乡。"

接着小贝也说："秦姐你快来看，沈总帮我们解决住的休息室，太好了，我们不用再来回跑了。你看我和小英住在一起，还有卫生间衣帽间，右边是我们的标准间，比酒店还好，左边是你的单间休息室，也是小套房，什么都有。"

邓诚赶紧打开水龙头说："这都是沈总和秋甜的功劳，秋甜怕你以后营业晚了累了不想回城里，特意给设计的这套房。"

秋甜笑着说："喜欢吗？沈总可说了，这都是像五星酒店拎包入住。"

秦瑛看见爱吧书吧将以前的精品柜体，能够用的东西都搬过来了，换上新油漆，刷新结果像新柜子一样，显得是那么协调，整体色调只有三种，咖啡色、浅灰，还有黑色系列。看上去时尚大气。沈总可真是当自己家一样节约装修成本。

沈总正好带着村主任一起的朋友们到大厅看着，这边秦瑛和秋甜商量好的事跟邓诚嘀咕了几句话，所有的人参观完毕后，邓诚向大家喊了一句话："现在大家请就近入座，我们秦瑛向大家说几句话。"

秦瑛在秋甜的鼓动下走向大厅的中央，向每一位到来的朋友们问好，紧接着说："为了感谢大家前来捧场支持，我今天作为经营者，正式向各位试营业，将我们原来爱吧书吧正式改名为'爱吧书吧'，向各位朋友们推荐我们家乡的美食小吃风味，及提供所有的书籍观阅，为读者带来愉悦的视觉享受，品尝美味可口家乡特色小吃。最后请大家吃好喝好，在爱吧书吧舒适环境中度过一个美好愉快的周末。"

大家入座后，小贝小英在秋甜的指导下，分别给入座后的朋友们端上了早上准备好的茶点，及家乡的黏米粉圆子、筒子骨汤米粉、水煮花生、水煮蚕豆、卤鸡蛋、卤鸡爪、八宝粥、桂花糖糕、青茶麦茶、桂花茶、茉莉花茶及当季节新茶。

小贝在吧台上竖着一牌子写着今天的活动项目："如果有喜欢的特别品种，今天可办理打折优惠卡活动，欢迎大家后期光临、惠顾、预定各类品种。"

这次免费试营业的下午茶时间，从中午开始延续到下午六点，办理优惠活动充值卡 1 万 8 千元。

没有想到试营业是如此的成功，并受到众多朋友们的喜爱。大家都说好，在这里不仅能放松看书休息，也可以选择带朋友来室外太阳伞下喝茶谈生意，和朋友一起聊天聚聚。室外只有三桌石凳、三桌老防腐木椅，还真是这里气候宜人，一年四季如春，邓诚帮秦瑛作了详细走动人口普查数据显示，室外的座位将需发展被预订座位业务。

六点过后，等朋友们都离开了，秦瑛让沈总和秋甜留下来，把装修款的账结清。

没有想到沈总说："邓诚已经全部结清了，室内的装修部分只有工人工费、拆迁安装购买新的小电器设备等费用共计人民币共 16 万元邓诚全垫付了。"

秦瑛看着邓诚说："你还想不想让我安心经营这乡村爱吧书吧了？"

邓诚笑着说道："不影响，你看看我们签了十年合同，这才刚刚试营业期间，等你经营进入正轨了，有收益了再付款给我，也来得及。我现在也不等着钱用，你开店需要资金周转。"

秦瑛看着眼前的这个邓诚，心里涌入许多突如其来的暗中比较，此时她能说什么呢？

经历过三段不同时期不同形式的恋情，秦瑛满脑子闪现出模糊青涩的初恋，画出与程默一闪而过几个月虚拟网恋，再回过头想到邓诚为她做了这么多实事，默默地替她分担所有的问题。站在邓诚面前，秦瑛从心里感觉到的踏实，安全感原来是邓诚的真情实感，没有一点花言巧语，全是实质性地为她排忧解难。

处处是真情可见。

第 15 章　隐居乡村

当被爱出现的时候，秦瑛体会到的是快乐、充盈、保护、接纳、平静、关注、轻松。这就是被爱的感觉。这些感觉都是邓诚给予秦瑛的，她也想要把这些平凡而又美好的温柔传递给邓诚，她已懂得如何去珍惜现在拥有的爱，她想要让宠爱自己的男人心安。秦瑛当着在场的沈总和秋甜俩媒人面前，深情地问："邓诚你这样做，是想好了娶我吗？"

邓诚毫不掩饰地看着秦瑛说："是的，但是我会等你心甘情愿的那一天，我给予你的这些还不足够，在我的心里你比金钱重要。"

秦瑛向邓诚走去，望着窗外的景色意味深长地说："你知道吗？你是给了我一个干事业的平台，我很喜欢这里的一草一木。你帮我提前实现了创作文学的梦想和灵感，我一生都为之付出，现在你终于使我提前拥有了这一切。我做梦也没想到这美好的一天就这样提前到来，所以今天向在场的朋友们表态，愿意同邓诚白头偕老，过上隐居乡村的生活。这里有你，有我们共同营造的爱吧书吧。同时感谢我和邓诚的媒人，感谢你们把邓诚介绍了我，这是我三生有幸。"

沈总秋甜看到他们相互表达爱意的温馨场面，立刻鼓起了掌，将邓诚推向秦瑛，大声疾呼地说："邓诚冲上去，快说嘛！"

邓诚认真激动又木讷地告诉大家："我早就想好了，等待桂花树开了，橘子、苹果树丰收结出硕果满园的季节，我在这里娶你，举行我们的婚礼仪式。"

爱吧书吧设在乡村这里，有得天独厚的自然资源环境，西靠五桂山延绵苍翠山脉，东望伶仃洋海面，天然海洋温泉、300 亩天然红树林生态区和大片湿地公园。周边交通便利，有京珠高速、西部沿海高速、深中通道、东部外环广珠城轨、省道、小区直达公交车。这里靠近珠海唐家、位属于翠亨新区，置业一步到位。

秦瑛想好了，邓诚在这里已经把创业的根基都铺好了路，房产证都办在她名下了，她不能就这么接受，她得为邓诚的付出做出诚信。

于是她拟好了爱吧书吧两套经营方案：

一，是将合同经营十年所有的利润都按照 5:5 分成给邓诚，把邓诚出资买房及装修的钱作为投资成本。她作为经营技术及管理人员投资入股的一种合作形式。

二，将每年的经营收入 5:5 分成部分全部作为还给邓诚购买的地产所投资的成本，作为自负盈亏，除掉员工薪资，及所有水电费用开支外，将十年收益纯利润先用于还清房款方式。总而言之她不能白要邓诚的无偿支助。两种方式任选一种都可以使爱吧书吧正常发展。

她也知道写作目前养不了自己，但爱吧书吧有了这块土地使用权，能使她安心打造自己的创业和文学梦想的发展平台。相信自己一定不负众望，她会将爱吧书吧经营好，成为她和邓诚未来共同事业谋划幸福的港湾。

目前写作只是丰富秦瑛的生活，但边经营爱吧书吧，就会使秦瑛实现当专职作家的文学梦想。在那个时候也分不清是写作养活了她，还是她用写作的快乐成就了美好的人生。

秦瑛没有直接回答邓诚心愿，将这项补充条款交给邓诚过目，指着自己和邓诚的共同银行账户那一栏空白处既正式又调侃地笑着对邓诚说："看后请把你的账户号码、名字、填写上去，这样你就会定期收到入股分红利润进账了。我同意你刚才说的婚礼设想，我想那个时候场面一定收到更多祝福。"

邓诚看了补充合同，心里一阵忐忑的心情，他不想与秦瑛算得这么清楚。沈总看到僵在原地等待不知如何回复邓诚，顺手接过来看一下补充项目，其中还有沈总见证人签名一栏，正好也要签名，这份合同补充很正式，对邓诚有经济利益好处。

沈总似乎明白了秦瑛的良苦用心，她不想欠邓诚太多，她想把情和钱分开算清，这样各自都没有压力，她不想让众人误解她是爱上的邓诚的财富，还有她自己也有挣钱的能力。

当然作为女人，在邓诚心目中她是唯一就心满意足了。秦瑛想着，等她跟邓诚真正成为一家人了，什么事都可以一起分享，但现在还不能接受这么大的厚礼。如果照单全收了，她会感觉浑身不自在。她希望婚姻一定要给彼此足够的平衡价值，她一向崇尚男女平等，经济独立，你有实力，我也优秀，彼此都有挣钱的潜力，还是有门当户对感觉，才使她更有踏实感。

沈总看到此补充条款后，打了圆场："拿笔来我先签字，邓诚你就填上你的信息和名字吧。这是好事，还发什么愣啊？你签字了，才能证明你认可秦瑛有这个实力，经营好爱吧书吧。"

邓诚在沈总和秦瑛的示意下，乖乖地把自己银行账户写上去了。沈总开玩笑说："这样多好，你每个月都可以分红获得利润了。你看看有共同账户了。"

邓诚把房产证拿出来递给秦瑛，秦瑛笑道说："我明白你的心意，还是你先保管吧。"

秋甜笑着对秦瑛说："我那个时候跟你一样，其实只要爱你的人有这份真心，我们女人就乐意了。我们女人要的就是男人的这份一心一意的爱，把将你当成是他唯一的女人。说到你心坎里去了吧。"

秦瑛不停地点头："是这样想的，只要对我是认真的，所有的财富我都愿意一起与爱人分享。"

邓诚看秦瑛很有主见，此时说什么都不会改变秦瑛的决定，还不如去接受。他懂秦瑛此时的内心深处的想法，他更愿给秦瑛一辈子的安心。看着眼前站在身边的爱人，邓诚明白这辈子找对了爱人。秦瑛也回想往日经历过情感对象，他们都只是过客，眼前的邓诚才是她等待多年的真心爱人。

秦瑛心中像明镜一样，看得清清楚楚，谁是真情，谁是假意。她会好好珍惜这位实心实意的好男人邓诚。

等沈总说完玩笑话后，邓诚自然地签了补充协议。心里想就当是给秦瑛预存幸福，给予秦瑛的储备金吧，这笔收益账户密码，后期会设置成秦瑛生日加上开店的日期数字，到时再把密码告诉她。这样也好，秦瑛有创业责任或许更能挖掘开店潜力，让财富增长无限，任其发展。

多给予秦瑛随心所欲的自由空间，这也许是秦瑛最适合接受的爱，也会使秦瑛毫无压力，为她的文学梦想打造更大的人生舞台。

邓诚想，只要秦瑛愿在这乡村落户，踏踏实实干番事业，秦瑛提出什么规划，任何补充协议他都会全力配合，做到永远支持紧跟。他和秦瑛的爱情就会在这片炽热的土地上播种、开花、结果。

想到这里邓诚签字的笔尖，刷刷刷一气呵成地签完，庄重地双手将补充合同交给了秦瑛："交给你了，我想签你一辈子。"

邓诚这句话，逗得在场的所有人都笑了，秦瑛很害羞地说："好呀，你等着。"

第 16 章　浪漫满屋

　　如果生命中出现了等待已久的爱，你会觉得生活中的一切都是那么美好。秦瑛感受到了邓诚对自己是真爱了，她也义无反顾地选择相信。每星期一三五到城区里完成讲师工作，余下的时间她将全部重心放在爱吧书吧的经营上。

　　秦瑛一有空就带着小贝小芹制作天然植物工艺品，利用废旧物，添加漂亮的五颜六色防水油漆把乡村屋子全面装扮。外面墙面，地下的大小石头，还有三面环绕圈子树干，院子拱门柱子等等，只要眼睛看到之处，秦瑛都会把对生活的热情，用色彩搭配作画。那怕只是路过的人，都会被这片浪漫温暖所感染。

　　两个家乡带出来的女孩小贝和小芹已经深深体会到什么是有意义的事情，她俩从心里感谢秦瑛把她们当成乡村爱吧书吧的主人，她们打心底里佩服秦瑛的才能，跟着她学会了很多生活方式。她们从来没有感觉到秦瑛以高高在上的姿态教训她俩，她们自愿参与这些改造工作。一开始只是觉得有趣好玩，体验下来发现自己是真的喜欢做这些事情。能够在这一年四季都美丽如画的地方生活和工作，她们无比庆幸，因为时常心情愉悦，感觉时间过得特别快。

　　秦瑛几乎到了痴迷的程度，每一天都有一点点意想不到的惊喜改变，触发了秦瑛更多的想象力，不停地折腾出自己喜欢的设计理念。秦瑛从内心到骨子里都感谢邓诚给她这么大的空间施展人生舞台。秦瑛已经领悟到了，一个真正懂自己的人，才能给予她最快乐的爱情。这是她对生活充满信心的力量，也是她陶醉其中的真谛，她真的找到了属于自己的真爱，对生活的热爱是一切美好事物的本质特征。

　　邓诚还是周一至周五的时间全心赴在公司的工作中，一到周末就主动来做秦瑛的助手，邓诚很乐意被秦瑛支使开车去城里，带买清单上写好的各种油漆和画笔等工具，再配合秦瑛对乡村屋外植物再造种植，进行体力劳动，对地面不平进行施工整理，确保水电都能正常使用。

有了邓诚和沈总的帮忙，乡村屋子外景改造进展更加顺畅快速。转眼已经到了第二年秋天，小树做好的围墙已慢慢长高，周围开满了鲜花，移栽的果树已枝繁叶茂了。

看着这慢慢变美的乡村风景，越来越像电视剧看到的浪漫满屋一样秀丽，那挺拔的几棵果树，桂花树，已长出新的绿色叶子。秦瑛经自己亲手打造的家园，让她更加喜爱这个地方。秦瑛常常站在苹果树下祈愿，希望来年的秋天能实现邓诚和她的愿望：我们会在这里等着硕果累累，丰收在望的季节，天公作美，大地作证，我们一定会越来越好，幸福快乐一辈子。

又是一个周末，沈总和邓诚神秘地交谈着，趁着秦瑛和两员工都还在爱吧书吧里，送走最后一桌客人后，邓诚开心地笑着说："秦瑛，我们今晚可以看到奇迹时刻，你一定要真实地告诉我们你的感受。"

小贝小芹拿出已准备好的员工餐食物放在桌子上："秦姐快点坐下来，邓总和沈总还有话要说呢，快一起吃吧。"

秦瑛被拥簇着推到桌前坐下，沈总说："现在我们先吃饭，忙碌几个月了，今晚可以看看效果了，等会我可要秋甜多拍几组视频。秋甜在车上拿好摄影机去了，等会就好好欣赏我们的杰作。"

邓诚也只笑说："快点吃饭，吃完了等你按开关通电进行剪彩仪式。"

在秦瑛一门心思地创作墙画的时候，沈总和邓诚也没有闲着，为了给秦瑛一个惊喜，特意在要换位置放灯线的时候，让秋甜把秦瑛支开。整个屋顶花园外面的路灯光设计，都是邓诚想好的要给整个爱吧书吧增加夜晚的魅力。邓诚比谁都期待着这刻的到来，这是他给秦瑛献上的最浪漫的礼物，他希望她会爱上这里的一切，也包括他自己这么一个人。

秦瑛和在座的每一个人一样，一下子就把东西吃完了。大家异口同声说："我吃完了。"随即大家哄堂大笑。大家都神秘地请秦瑛快出去，站在苹果树下，握住邓诚递过来的一无线按钮。大家齐声喊道："123！"秦瑛按下开关，首先是小院的路灯沿着脚下亮起来了，接下来屋顶上像星星一样闪闪发光灯泡亮起来，再接着沿墙边到树上的枝杈上满满的星星闪烁。一眼望去沿着小院围着栅栏的树苗都布满了绿色红色的灯泡，小树上看上去像是一群萤火虫在跳跃闪着光芒。整个看到的是亮闪闪的世界，这里的夜景被热爱生活的人们包围着。秦瑛被震撼了，她只随口对邓诚说过，想要的童话世界里的美好事物。那只是她写出来的小说情节，真没有想到邓诚却记在心里，在她不知情的时候低调完成这些事情。前后实干了几个月，邓诚今晚总算可以好好休息了。

沈总说："秦瑛这是你写的浪漫满屋吧？为这，邓诚常常念叨着你小说中的话，邓诚都能背诵全文了。"

秦瑛还沉浸在幻境中，没有答话，只是傻傻地笑着望着天空，一会儿扫一下树枝头，一下又摸摸围着小院树苗栅栏上的灯光，仿佛身在童话世界里。秦瑛感动地说："谢谢你邓诚，谢谢大家给我这么好的厚礼，我好喜欢好爱呀……"

秦瑛落泪了，是高兴的泪光，邓诚木讷有点心疼地抱住秦瑛笑话道："你猜我又看到一个什么光了？"

秦瑛马上克制自己情绪问："在哪里？什么光？让我看看。"

邓诚开心快乐大笑："我说你还真信了，你的泪光呀！"

在场的人全部被邓诚的回答逗笑了，笑声在这里飘在空中。在这片土地上，垒起了又一间星光灿烂的乡村屋子。

第 17 章　创作巅峰

邓诚因每周星期一要召开公司会议，今晚和沈总完成了小院电灯线路，晚上也试行正常通电，看到灯光照明已达到预期的浪漫效果。一切就绪后，虽然说有些依依不舍，但当晚还是得和沈总夫妻一起回城。

而秦瑛的工作安排是每周二、三、四、五共四天则在公司做培训讲师，周末两天加星期一都可以留在乡村爱吧书吧。自从搬迁移居乡村为主日子里，秦瑛待在乡村生活空间大于城市的环境。看见宁静的乡村景色，空气中弥漫着浓浓的清香，秦瑛待邓诚走后，怎么也睡不着觉，灵感来了，那晚突然又一气呵成写出了另一部小说的开头。

秦瑛自从在乡村屋里静下心来的时候，便很快进入写作状态。一连几个月过去了，秦瑛有许多散文和小小说都被精短小说杂志录用发表，同时进行的第二部长篇小说书稿整理也快完成，并注入新的内容章节。第三部小说在陆续连载更新中。

一晃眼已经又到了下半年，秦瑛已进行创作巅峰时期，几乎接二连三都有出版社编辑预约谈出版事宜。秦瑛真没有想到，自己的小说没有程默的关照，也一样被其他出版社编辑老师推荐看好。写了五年的第二部长篇小说通过了审核书稿，正在进入出版校对之中。秦瑛的第三部小说已完成创作，在纸媒上已连载到结尾章节，现有三个出版社的编辑跟她预约书稿，洽谈出版具体谈事项。

这种创作效率是秦瑛所想要的生活状态，她喜欢灵感来了就去写，秦瑛的工作和生活忙碌而有序地进行着，愉快的日子就感觉过得很快。

秦瑛有时候会在小院木椅上休息一会儿，看着碧蓝的天空，闻着花草散发植物的清香，总会让眼睛闭上养神一会儿，享受着发呆一阵子，脑子会像放电影一样闪现出小说构思故事情节中，某一段想表达精句或灵感，这个时候，秦瑛将随手带的小本子和笔，打开并记录下来某一段话、某一个场景。秦瑛保持着勤奋持之以恒的文学创作的好习惯，除了公司培训备课以外，留一些时间用在经营爱吧书吧，余下所有零散的时间，全部是秦瑛自由发挥写作的黄金时间。经常会在凌晨三四点醒了，就开始写着梦见清晰故事思路，会有意用手机一句话，录下来，待写作时有章有节地向小说中故事激情创作，有着充实丰富的备注素材，这就是秦瑛的小说内容接地气的原因，好的文学作品来源于真实的生活，又结合了作品中想表达人物思想观点及教育意义，将正确的三观融入感动读者，又必须高于生活效果，秦瑛在文学创作这方面已深深地爱上了，这已是秦瑛生活中一个重要部分，写作已割舍不了的生活状态，秦瑛也分不清，是在生活需要她写作，还写作使她明白了活着的意义。

有时候会又睡到自然醒，马上向小院花草和菜苗洒下水，走过几圈，伸展身体，戴上耳机听歌和音乐运动十分钟。随后又自由自在行走一遍，摸摸大果树、桂花树、又看看菜苗、欣赏自己种的花。花枝上有许多的花蕾，闻着那种淡淡的植物的清香，随着风儿迎面扑鼻而来。她很享受这雨露滋润大自然的味道，迎来来清晨的阳光，送往迎来的夕阳黄昏，真的很惬意。创作灵感的源源不断来源于这里的美好时光。她喜爱的这种浪漫小屋，充满了花香。

回到书房一坐上桌前，端上一杯咖啡，还有一壶提神醒脑的浓茶，秦瑛在这一待就是一整天。中途只许小贝或小芹送一份午餐套餐，全天门上都有挂着免打扰的牌子。这个牌子还是秦瑛自己亲手用一块小木片制作的，用彩色颜料画出一朵花瓣写上"免打扰哦！"四个字。

小贝小芹都知道送餐之时是不用敲门的，每次轻轻地把装满吃的食物托盘放在指定的沙发茶几上放着即可，有时候小贝会留下温馨叮嘱的小纸条提示：秦姐趁热吃哟，汤趁热喝哟。

已是秋天的季节，从窗户向外望去，桂花树上结满了黄色的桂花。香味扑鼻而来吹拂着秦瑛的头发，写了几万字的小说内容，眼睛有些胀痛，秦瑛会习惯的养成做一些眼保健操，揉揉眼睛周围肌肉放松。随后打开轻音乐，闭上眼睛靠坐在沙发上，听完两首歌曲后，顺手撕开编辑老师邮寄给她这季精短刊物上发表的小小说，说是已被列入上封面提名了。能上头条文章的作者，算是优秀作品吧。

秦瑛很欣慰地将杂志打开，入选封面上就看见了那篇小小说《上楼下楼》，这是很早就想写的一篇关于在职场上的微小说故事，以前在职的时候就想写，一直忙生存没有顾及文学创作爱好。也不知道为什么，到了乡村生活的环境中，总会不经意想起以前的点点滴滴，有些灵感来源于以往的情感故事。

片刻之间看完这些自己已创作一篇篇作品，吸引了更多广大读者的喜爱，秦瑛有一种莫大的幸福。她悟到了什么是适合自己的另一半，这个人很重要。不是有很多情感专家说过这样一段话吗："婚姻里的女人，如果选择男人作为伴侣，女人一定要选择一个能成就你完美人生，给予你所爱世界，灵魂自由，能够懂你的爱。"

秦瑛感觉她遇到了，想想邓诚这个好男人，秦瑛心里就会莫名其妙地笑起来：邓诚你听好了，我秦瑛非你不嫁。这种心灵的感应和创作的动力真好。

在那段时间，秦瑛自己都不敢相信，作品能接二连三发表。这些时期的创作源泉全来于邓诚给予的支持理解。秦瑛发现邓诚最懂她的心，邓诚常常在周末跟秦瑛一起自驾游，在珠海和中山周边历史景点参观游览。邓诚充当导游，走到哪里就解说到哪里。在游览孙中山故居时，秦瑛站在大厅前，看着博学多才的邓诚耐心地跟她讲解孙中山革命的故事。秦瑛对邓诚又多了几分崇拜和敬重。

在乡村屋子居住的那段时间里，邓诚和秦瑛清晨约好跑步爬山，一起去当地小镇品尝风味早茶，一起在海边鱼女景区散步，一起偶尔也像年轻人一样看一场电影，再一起驾车回到乡村爱吧书吧喝下午茶。

在属于他们的阳光窗户桌前小息，望着窗外果树慢慢已长满新叶及开满五颜六色的花朵，正在迎着阳光静静盛开，地面种下的绿色草坪铺盖在树的周围，一直延续在屋子外周边。秦瑛喜欢和邓诚在这里一直看看书，喝喝茶，聊着说不完的话。直到晚上外面前院路灯和树灯全部亮起——童话般的世界，正是这片乡村书屋的亮点。开业近一年多来，被村民一传十十传百地引来了许多慕名而来游客。当游客逛累了，会在此休息一会，喝杯茶吃点农家风味小吃黏米粉圆子，临走之时还不忘了多买几份打包带走。

礼盒是秦瑛特意定制的，上面印着乡村爱吧书吧特色简介、微信号、整个乡村屋的外景、星光灿烂的夜景图片。客人们都很喜欢这种包装袋，宣传效果很好，有很多客人通过加微信扫码网上预订了农家特色小吃。这些宣传也带动了当地乡村的土特产集市的交易，还有餐饮的生意。有些游客打算在乡村小住几天，于是又带动了乡村农舍发展。秦瑛为了扩大销量，以营养全素食为卖点，设计了简易加热就可以吃的半成品黏米粉圆子。这种产品符合当时的健康饮食生活观，产品受到顾客的认可。

这是一段美好的日子，是秦瑛文学创作的巅峰期，也是经营爱吧书吧的高峰期，同时还是爱情和财富的增长期。

秦瑛每月都会按照合同的条款的约定，向邓诚的账户上存进全部所得利润，存进去的不仅仅是财富，还有她对邓诚爱的回报。秦瑛很喜欢这种如愿布施爱的过程，她很享受这些给予的快乐，她感觉女人爱情的延续，也一定要拿出价值诚意，回应邓诚对她的真爱。想想有一天能和邓诚走进余生婚姻的情景，相心相爱平衡而轻松自在的生活节奏，那不就是秦瑛所理想的爱的场景画面吗？

秦瑛美美地想到这里，自然会意地笑了，她和邓诚这样的相处方式真的满足了她对爱情的期望，没有制约，相互信任，时时念想着彼此。这种行动上的爱比只用嘴巴吐出来的三个字"我爱你"胜过百倍。

邓诚感觉到秦瑛的爱和善良，每次邓诚看着眼前身旁秦瑛的脸，都会有种说不出的幸福和满足。"秦瑛，咱们可以结婚了吧。"这话几次差点说出口，又被克制住，只是望着秦瑛傻笑。邓诚把持住自己的激动，他想给秦瑛最好最完美的婚礼，他要给秦瑛一个浪漫的惊喜。

第 18 章　　出乎意料

邓诚不温不火地在公司忙碌着，所有业余时间都用在装修乡村别墅整栋二层楼，他很想在不影响公司工作的同时，跟沈总带的装修队伍一起把装修活干完。有邓诚在场，沈总遇上事情可以就地解决，这样工期顺利进展。

装修期间，秦瑛爱吧书吧专为装修员工提供工作餐和服务，在小包间伙食标准按照沈总要求，让体力劳动的工人吃好吃饱，两荤一素一个汤还有一点下饭菜。

在一年多的时间里，别墅安装了中央空调系统，买进了洗衣机和烘干机等现代设备，定制了全木质家具。二层居住房间设计得温馨舒适，两主卧次卧都按套房设计，两张大的洗手台面，延长添加衣帽柜两侧，大间侧面的客厅带一间敞开式书房，两套次卧可以自由进出使用，还不会打扰主卧房主人。

邓诚这期间从没有因工作的事情延迟乡村别墅装修进度，真是挣钱创业和家庭建设两不误。装修接近尾声的时候，邓诚感觉最近容易疲惫犯困，他打算去医院做一次全面的体检。

星期一开完晨会后，邓诚驱车来到珠海的一家大型医院做了全面检查，结果被一位权威专家叶医生叫住："你家有癌症患者吗？"

邓诚想都没想说："没有癌症亲人，父亲是自然病逝，母亲是心肌梗死突然离世的。"

叶医生说："从检查中发现，你已患有二期胃癌，赶紧治疗应该还是可以改善转良。你得抓紧时间治疗，不然不好说，也许病情会恶化，癌细胞扩散转移。你可以选择化疗或者选择中医调理，建议你尽快决定治疗方案。"

邓诚蒙了，这段时间他感觉不舒服没有胃口，他以为只是身体太累了，没有想过竟是得了二期胃癌。邓诚看着体检报告单上写着的诊断结果，有点站立不稳。邓诚从来没想过的自己也会患上不治之症，医生的话似乎暗示他还能再活两年，也许积极治疗还有救？他和秦瑛还没有去享受美好的生活，难道就这样等死？

邓诚不想在化疗中痛苦挣扎等死，想象中头发掉落直到秃顶，身体骨瘦如柴，他不想以这样的样子在秦瑛的面前出现。那种场面太残酷了，没有给到秦瑛的爱，反而就这样一命归天，他心里很不甘心。

邓诚没有回答医生的问题，拿着那份体检报告默默地走出医生办公室。他无助地拖着沉重的步伐，不知走了多久，在医院花坛的座椅上坐了下来。这事情发生得很突然，他一时间接受不了，也不知道能跟谁说这事。

邓诚刚从母亲去世的低谷中走出来，遇上了能共度余生、能给予他欢乐和爱的女人秦瑛，幸福还没有开始，又遭遇了这样沉重的打击。邓诚不时想到和秦瑛在一起愉快游览观光的情景，那样的画面温馨又浪漫。他答应过秦瑛余生要给她美好的生活，他答应了要陪伴她一生，他不能就这样被胃癌断送了生命。

慢慢冷静下来的邓诚又想到，如果自己的病真的治不好，他在去往天堂之前一定要好好珍惜与秦瑛相处的宝贵时光，而且他也要让秦瑛的余生不用为生活而发愁。邓诚打算要将所有事情处理好，也为秦瑛做一些事情，让她能幸福下去。

邓诚心里有了打算，他打电话给自己公司聘用的律师。律师严大明是邓诚长年聘用值得信赖的好朋友，邓诚公司和他自己的私人律师事务工作，他都会全部交给严大明律师办理。

这电话来得急，还约在医院附近的公园见面，严大明心想一定有什么重要的事情发生了。他接到电话后马上赶来，见邓诚坐在公园椅子上，一副心事重重的样子。

下午的太阳光猛烈又刺眼，珠海这座城市的秋风夹杂着海洋潮湿的气息，吹在邓诚的脸上显得他格外憔悴苍老，看起来像是没有睡好觉。

严大明直奔主题："邓董事长是不是有什么急事需要我马上办？"

邓诚的嗓音有些沙哑："对的。有三件事要办，需要你做一个公证。一是公司保险受益人添加一个人名，她叫秦瑛，是我此生最爱的女人。二是将我个人公司应得的分红利润总额比例50%分给秦瑛。第三，将我乡村房地产业的所有权，包括二楼整层楼房产权证，也添加秦瑛的名字。"邓诚交代完这些事后显得轻松了许多。

严大明小心谨慎地问邓诚："发生了什么事情？能给我讲明原因？"

邓诚严肃坚毅地说："我刚刚检查出二期胃癌。秦瑛是我准备要共度余生的女人，我们本来计划十月一日国庆节举行婚礼。现在婚礼看来不可能了，我想以这种方式去爱她，让她替我好好活着。"

邓诚有些哽咽说不下去了，眼睛红红地看着严大明，有些话题又咽回去了。

严大明律师沉思片刻后说道："我有一个建议给邓董，公司不是要在九月在三亚举行一年一次高层精英人士的会议吗？入会可带一名家属或者一名高端保险客户。我建议这次先邀请你的未婚妻一起来三亚陪伴你左右，共同见证公司成立以来的发展历程及取得成果。另外也是想让秦瑛好照顾你。办理转让公司个人纯利分红总额的事情，还有乡村房子产权之事，我想到公司年会举办结束后再议也不迟。"

邓诚不加思索地说："好的，我答应会议结束后再办此事，但是一定要先拟好文字报告出来，我好在清醒的时候签字。另外麻烦你办理预定两张飞往秦瑛老家湖北的机票，我想在举办公司会议之后，去一趟秦瑛的故乡。那里是李时珍的故乡，我会以养生之名去那边找一些有名望的中医看病，做保守治疗。我想争取和秦瑛多待上一些时间，一边治疗休息一边多陪陪她。公司的事情有你把关，我很放心。"

严大明律师认真地说："好的，我就按邓董的意见去办。您去李时珍的故乡寻找中医名方，我也认为是好主意。我有一朋友患有严重胃病靠中医治好了，邓董体质好，看中医治疗也能除病根，恢复健康一点问题没有。相信您这次和秦瑛去李时珍故乡，一定会有收获。"

邓诚突然想起稻盛和夫书中说的一段话，关于结婚的意义是什么，这是他听过最认可的答案："不是拖垮彼此，而是生活中给对方鼓励。遇到事情，有个人可以一起商量。在生活累的时候，彼此相互安慰，相互鼓励。下班了，能有个人一起吃饭。在外受了委屈，回到家可以有个温暖的拥抱。一生太漫长了，总要有一个相伴走完余生的人。"

邓诚想到这里，他更想调整好自己的心态，积极开始中医治疗。如果想娶秦瑛这个好女人，给予完整的爱，自己必须倾出所有。首先是要好好活着，他心里放不下秦瑛，他想好好地陪伴她余生。

　　严律师看见邓诚满眼都是秦瑛那份情浓意真的神情，此时此刻很希望能在公司三亚会议见上秦瑛一面，看看那是怎样一个女子能让邓董事长把全部的爱都给予她。在严大明律师的眼里，严大明律师分明看见了邓诚那份对秦瑛爱的挚诚，在这病入身体的危急时刻，邓诚想的不是自己，而是首先考虑解决秦瑛的后顾之忧。年龄何干，相貌何顾，家境何妨，直到现在严律师才相信人间自有真爱。

　　严大明律师心里还在想，若是自己得了癌症，他是绝对承受不了，也不会第一时间想着如何利用最后的时光照顾好自己所爱的人。他为邓董事长为人和博大胸襟而感到惭愧，甚至不知不觉地涌出感动的热泪。他为邓董事长遇到真爱痴情而感动，邓诚对秦瑛如此真情相待，严大明这一生单身，是从尚不恋爱的独身主义者，都如此动容。

　　严大明律师怕邓诚看见他这般泪洗面的狼狈，转头不敢正视邓诚，顺势转身挥挥手，从喉咙里发出了一声："好，放心，我去办。"

第19章　真情相拥

　　邓诚公司在三亚举行的一年一次高端会议的时间快要到了，邓诚隐瞒着病情处理完公司的工作安排后，决定亲自对秦瑛发出邀请。

　　这是一个特别的周末时光，邓诚自从获知自己患癌症后，看着眼前的熟悉的风景，感叹人生曲折，他多想能平安无事地活着！他感觉自己身体十分虚弱，但不知道如何跟秦瑛说。他很想以旅游休假的名义邀请秦瑛一同前往三亚参加公司年会，向众人宣布他和秦瑛的关系，他多想和秦瑛生活在一起，将所有的美好都给到秦瑛。

　　乡村爱吧书吧屋外的院子里，邓诚踱着步子四处转悠，最后选择了木椅静坐下来，望着这亲手打造的浪漫满屋的一切美好，心绪难以平静，阳光的照射顿使他感到温暖，此时邓诚放松身心地闭上眼睛，想着秦瑛笑容、一幕幕浮现在脑海中、挥之不去。

　　秦瑛最近也意识到邓诚精神状态不好，话变少了，一副心事重重的样子。每次邓诚周末回到乡村忙碌的时候，心里就很踏实有安全感。这个周末秦瑛有半天没有看见邓诚的身影，忙完活后就跟着找进院子里，见到邓诚坐在院里。

　　秦瑛悄悄地从屋内走到邓诚的身后，看着邓诚累坏消瘦的脸庞，邓诚闭着眼睛养神的样子，真的可爱，但是细心的秦瑛感觉到邓诚有点不对劲。因为最近看他吃得越来越少，感觉他总是很疲惫。秦瑛一直担心是邓诚工作太繁忙累坏了。

　　秦瑛心里越来越爱眼前的这个男人，很想拥抱邓诚，于是轻轻地走在邓诚的身旁，双手蒙上邓诚的双眼。此时邓诚感受到那是秦瑛的一双柔软细腻光滑小手，在抚触间传递出一种爱的温暖。邓诚的情绪像翻江倒海地涌上心头，他不想睁开眼睛，他就想秦瑛这样捂着他眼睛，他很享受这种感觉。与秦瑛恋爱后，他还从来没有如此亲密的身体接触，他和秦瑛都在有意克制自己的欲望，特别视线相交时眼神中透露出来的那种喜欢和爱。

邓诚想只要能看到秦瑛他就心满意足了，因为他知道要给秦瑛最美好的生活，不只是男女之欢那么一点点的触碰。他知道秦瑛是好女子，他明白秦瑛的自律和坚守的感情底线，更知道他们俩都属于成熟稳重的人。正因为如此，所以他们才能彼此理解到对方身上优点，走得越来越近，身心愉悦地享受着那份宁静致远的快乐。

邓诚感受着秦瑛手心的温暖，又想睁开眼睛看看秦瑛。顺势抓住秦瑛的手抚摸着自己的脸颊两侧，像是捂着自己的心一样。邓诚心里想对秦瑛说："亲爱的，我真想永远这样下去，我在你的世界里，我在你的心里，每一天每一秒，都有你在我的身边。"

秦瑛的手被邓诚亲吻着，禁止不住地拥抱着邓诚，缠绕着附在邓诚的耳边轻轻地说："今天怎么会这么安静这么乖呀？有什么心事和话跟我说吗？"

邓诚对视着秦瑛肯定地点头说："说你是才女吧，你还不信，猜猜看，我会给你说什么好消息呢？"

秦瑛甜蜜地笑道："亲爱的，还真的有好消息呀，那你快说说给我听。"

邓诚卖着官腔，高兴地说："有两件好事。一，我正式邀请你参加公司的高层会议；二，随后立即带我去你的故乡，拜访你的家人，另外替我的一位生病的朋友寻找名中医救治的方子。顺便我们也放下繁忙的工作，在你家乡的公主山庄酒店休闲度假，享受大自然的风光。你接受任务吗？"

秦瑛又惊又喜地问道："你怎么突然答应陪我回老家？我以前邀请你一起去看看，你可是忙不完的工作呀。这是什么风把你吹醒了？还有什么事都说出来。不会这么简单吧？"

邓诚害怕秦瑛纠缠打破砂锅问下去，于是对着秦瑛说："没有了，赶快做好准备回你家乡。就要见到你家的亲人了，你怎么介绍我啊？"

秦瑛不好意思傻傻地笑着说："我呀，就说你是我的大管家，你想怎么介绍？说出来听听？"

邓诚没有想过要怎么在秦瑛家人面前介绍自己，只想先让秦瑛答应下来他的邀请。后面就随遇而安见机行事，能隐瞒病情多久就瞒多久，走一步看一步。眼下的时间对邓诚来说真的太宝贵了，他感到生命脆弱不堪，他必须与时间赛跑，把要做的事情做好。

目前他就是想能为秦瑛多做一些事情，在心里默默祈祷着奇迹降临，坚信中医能治好自己的癌症疾病。医生也说过，调整好乐观开朗的心态，会对治疗产生好的影响。而且严大明律师的朋友不也是治愈了吗？邓诚此刻安慰自己，只有相信，积极行动起来，早些寻名医专家尽心尽力治疗，之后就顺从天意吧！

秦瑛看在邓诚身上真的问不出什么事了，就用手指头点了一下邓诚的头说："你不说是吧，看我要是发现了你的秘密，我一定要好好地收拾你。"

说完，秦瑛将邓诚的缠绕得更紧了，头发被风吹到邓诚的脸上，正好遮住了邓诚已发红的双眼。邓诚克制住自己的情绪，他知道自己是不会撒谎的人，前面是他全身心爱着的女人，他看见秦瑛天真无邪的笑容，更不能让秦瑛知道自己患有癌症。他不忍心看到秦瑛为他伤心难过，他想他还有机会去与癌症拼搏，还有中医治疗的最后机会。不到万不得已，以邓诚的性格，他是无论如何也不能对秦瑛说病情，他希望有奇迹发生。

有了这样的想法，邓诚又收回了内心深处悲伤无奈的情绪，迅速转头反身从背后抱住秦瑛，紧紧温柔地依偎在一起。趁着秦瑛看不见的瞬间，邓诚把泪流满面的脸庞，深陷在秦瑛的衣背上。他小心地擦拭干净泪水，直到平静恢复淡定，才慢慢放开手。真怕秦瑛看见他脆弱一面，不敢想秦瑛会是怎么面对这样的事情。邓诚虽然是爷们，平常什么事都能沉思找到答案，当事情发生在自己身上时，也会表现出惊慌失措。他担心那心事重重的样子，会被细腻的秦瑛瞧出什么。秦瑛本身又是作家，有一双在现实生活中捕捉素材的智慧眼睛，而且思维敏捷。为了逃避秦瑛的追问，邓诚还真费了不少的心思，他一直矛盾地扮演应付躲避着秦瑛长谈，害怕时间长了装不下去露馅。

最近发生的事情真让他有点措手不及，还好有严大明律师的配合，不仅替自己打理公司的一切业务，还守口如瓶地替他办一些重要的私事，几乎是他的私人秘书了。这位独身主义者的严大明，在邓诚身边工作待了二十多年，崇尚不婚的他看见邓诚对秦瑛这样痴情，他也开始相信人世间还是有真情存在。

邓诚最放心信任严大明律师，有了严大明的朋友通过中医治愈癌症的先例，邓诚就有了慰藉和活下去的希望。他明白要腾出时间治疗，还要从自身的心态转变，事业、工作、挣钱的重要性都比不过生命。谁都知道除了生命是自己的，其他的什么也带不走，财富都是零。

　　若是命运不眷顾邓诚，他也做好了接受现状的心理准备，他会做好两手准备，在有限的生命里多陪伴着秦瑛，把快乐给到她。所有关于财富转让的事情叫严大明去办，在邓诚看来是正常不过了。他要照顾好自己心爱的人，让秦瑛幸福，即使他真的没救了，真的要走了，去天堂里他也会祝福秦瑛能幸福快乐地生活。他相信秦瑛永远会记得他的真情，一定是任何人也替代不了的爱情，让她此生无悔。

　　被宠爱的秦瑛越来越感觉到邓诚细腻体贴的照顾，她也越来越依赖邓诚的这份刻骨铭心的爱情，他们俩就这么静静地拥抱，静静感受拥抱爱人的幸福。

　　他们两人在乡村院子里待了一个下午。直到黄昏落日之时，太阳余光躲闪退去，闻着桂花和青草树叶的清香，他们俩陶醉其中，你中有我，我中有你，两个人在院中椅子上并肩而坐，紧握住手，欣赏着他俩建成的浪漫满屋，两个人时不时欢笑着。

　　这个下午邓诚手机设置静音状态，严大明打了很多电话和发给邓诚的信息他都没有注意到，不知道那边是不是发生了什么棘手的事情。

第 20 章　不离不弃

严大明见邓诚没有接电话，只得在微信上留言："邓董，急事面谈，我已找到了那位能治好胃癌的高人。建议你在公司会议召开当日晚上就飞去湖北，从三亚飞往湖北的机票我已帮你和秦瑛定好。我现在把名医的详细地址发给你的手机上，请保存好。秦瑛是当地人，我建议你还是对秦瑛讲明已患癌症二期的情况，便于配合名医及时制定治疗方案，不能延误时间。特请做好先参加三亚会议，再飞往湖北的行程准备。"

邓诚看到手机信息的时候，正在爱吧书吧中与秦瑛就餐。秦瑛见邓诚近期胃口不好，特意煮了土鸡炖汤，想给邓诚补充营养。秦瑛见邓诚拿出手机看后又是心事重重的样子，不知道又发生了什么，就说道："别再看手机了，快安心喝汤吧。什么事比你现在吃饭还重要？"

邓诚马上回过神来："秦瑛，正好公司发信息告诉我，已安排好了你同我一起去三亚开会的机票，后天就出发，让我们准备行李。因为时间紧，会议当晚我们还要一起飞到你的老家湖北，已安排人员到机场接我们直接去酒店。我今天就回城里去准备一些会议需要的资料和个人行李箱。你也别忘了做好准备，开会那天我会开车接你。"

秦瑛心疼地说："知道了，还有两天呢。现在你要好好地吃饭喝汤，休息好，吃饱喝足了还来得及。看你平时不急，怎么这点小事就心神不宁了，太不像你了。快先喝汤，再不喝就凉了。"

秦瑛的话让邓诚意识到自己乱了方寸，马上调整好自己，装着若无其事的样子，很给面子地吃了起来。一副狼吞虎咽的模样，逗乐了秦瑛。邓诚看见秦瑛笑开花高兴的样子，似乎都忘记了自己的病。如果这样一直有秦瑛在身旁，邓诚的病好像好了一半，人的精神支柱多重要啊！邓诚心里就是这样想的，开始对中医治疗有了期盼，那种想与秦瑛一起生活的动力，形成的一种强烈的求生欲望。他想着自己一定要与癌症抗争，积极配合治疗。有一种强烈意念要尽快使身体恢复健康。

三天后，参加会议的高端精英们准时集中在机场候机大厅。一大早邓诚就去接到了秦瑛，两人已在公司的人群中，邓诚安排秦瑛坐在就近的座椅上。离安检还有半个小时的时间，邓诚把手中的包塞进秦瑛的手中，看看手表上的时间："你看好机票和证件包，我先去趟洗手间。"

大厅里人很多，秦瑛向着邓诚熟悉的背影望去，直到看不见了才收回目光。这个时候邓诚包里的手机响了起来，秦瑛左顾右盼见邓诚还没出来，手机铃声已响过三遍了，似乎是很急的事情。秦瑛怕误了邓诚的重要事情，于是顾不上那么多，赶紧打开包取出邓诚的手机按下键接听电话。秦瑛还没来得及说话发声，电话另一端的声音传了过来："邓董啊，我担心你忙忘了，我把你在医院拿回的专家确诊你的癌症报告和拍的片子都放进你的文件资料袋里面了，资料袋里面还有圻春名医的联系方式和详细地址。我们公司一行人已在三亚安排好会议场地的布置工作，就等参加会议的人员到达。这边您放心，快要安检了吧，你手机里有我发给你这几天的信息，我看到没您的回复，我就打电话给您说说……喂喂喂？邓董您在听吗？那边怎么这么吵，我怎么没听见您的声音？喂，邓董，是手机信号不好？是在安检了吗？"

秦瑛听到听话那头传来声音，她不知道是谁，但是知道了邓诚最近很不正常的原因，原来邓诚患癌症了！怎么会这样，怎么我一点都不知道，只是觉得他瘦了，我没有照顾好邓诚，我还忽略了他，怎么办！我现在该怎么做？邓诚还瞒着我！

候机大厅已开始检票排队了，秦瑛赶紧挂掉电话，并看到落名为严大明律师发给邓诚短信内容："另外邓董您交代转让给秦瑛的乡村房产权证书，还有您公司分红保险受益人秦瑛公证书，我都拟好法律文件也带上了，到会议空闲时请您过目签字即可。请邓董放心，目前首要任务就是好好放下工作，积极配合中医治疗调理身体，一切都会好转。"

秦瑛扫了几眼就看清了信息内容，赶紧把手机放回邓诚手提包里，眼睛向卫生间方向焦急地张望着。秦瑛此刻心情像过山车一般，悬吊在半空中，她心里慌乱，甚至都不知道见到邓诚后能说出什么。是责备他隐瞒真相？还是能为他做些什么，比如明明白白地告诉他：癌症不可怕，有我在你身边，无论发生什么事，无论今后怎样，我都会对你不离不弃。亲爱的邓诚，我会自始至终永远爱你，这是我想要对你说的话。记住，你还有我在。只要你能好起来，我宁愿什么也不要，我只要有你就足矣，你比金钱财富更重要！你怎么还这么傻呢？都这个时候了，还想着我。我秦瑛何能何德在异乡遇到了你，此生我只选择你，我愿这辈子和你在一起。

这些话在秦瑛的脑海里不停地浮现，秦瑛想要找个合适的机会向邓诚表白，她的心里只有邓诚，她不在乎应该是谁主动求婚，她只知道她要给邓诚信心，邓诚会好起来的。不是说过吗，好人一生平安！

邓诚去洗手间的时候，秦瑛机缘巧合地听见并看到了严大明传给邓诚的信息，秦瑛发现事情比她想象的严重得多。邓诚似乎不愿意将这个消息告诉她。

此时邓诚更需要秦瑛在身边，秦瑛下定决心和邓诚共度余生，陪伴他积极面对生活。心情对癌症患者的影响极大，许多人面对自己患癌的事实，被现实的压力给压倒。秦瑛想努力照顾好他。邓诚从洗手间回来，依然尽力表现得如平常一样，秦瑛也装着没有发生什么事情。两人都藏着心事。

排队快要到秦瑛的时候，邓诚才赶上队伍中。秦瑛已让三对公司的人先办理安检手续，秦瑛看着冒出汗的邓诚，忙心疼地拿出纸巾，帮忙擦掉邓诚脸上的汗水，克制自己的内心波澜，安抚地调侃邓诚："我怕你掉进卫生间了。还来得及，不用这么匆忙。你拉肚子了？还好吗？"

邓诚笑着说："还不都是你害的，天天喝汤，一定是太吃好了。没有事，现在轻松多了。"

两个人顺利登机，并排地坐在头等舱。坐在前往三亚的飞机上，他们总算可以好好休息一下了，一路上的追赶，邓诚感觉有点累。此程像是两人在度假，享受一趟浪漫之旅。两人在飞机上望着对方，邓诚发现秦瑛这身白色运动装打扮是如此的阳光健康，他思绪万千：自己这生病之身能给予秦瑛幸福吗？这样瞒着秦瑛，还想娶她为妻，这样合适吗？邓诚心里矛盾，不知道该不该向她求婚。命运如此荒诞，好不容易遇见了她，可自己可能不能陪伴她下去了；不过会有可能经过治疗后完全康复，就当患病这事没有发生，他再理所当然地勇敢向秦瑛求婚。

秦瑛发现邓诚脸色精神黯淡了许多，身形也消瘦了。她望着窗外广阔的天空，飞机在蓝天白云高空中飞翔。此刻广播响起空姐的声音："尊敬的旅客们，请大家系好安全带，飞机遇上了热带气流，进入了有雷雨大风天气，请不要随地走动，卫生间停止使用。"

机舱内顿时有些骚乱，大家突然一下子喧哗了起来。"怎么办？怎么回事？怎么这么倒霉呀？"此时广播里又传来空姐的声音："大家不要惊慌，请大家安静听广播指示。"

大家都屏住呼吸静静地听空姐讲解逃生知识和气流影响，每个人的脸部表情都显得格外严肃。就像飞机即将要爆炸坠机一样，此时飞机的顶部传来与气流的撞击摩擦声，大家都清楚地听到唆唆的声音。在意外来临时，人会显得那么的渺小，生死之间的距离以分秒计算。

此时秦瑛和邓诚的双手紧握在一起互相凝视着对方，同时情不自禁地脱口而出："亲爱的，我有事想对你说。""秦瑛，对不起，我有事也要对你说，我对你隐瞒了一件事。"

秦瑛用手捂着邓诚的嘴唇，看着邓诚深情地说："我先说，我不想在意外之前没有把话说清。我爱你，无论你怎么样了，发生了什么事情，我都永远爱你，我要永远和你在一起，永不分离。"

邓诚也抢着对秦瑛表白："亲爱的，我也爱你，我可以用我的余生来你陪伴。若是没有意外，我一定把所有的美好和爱都留给你。有你在我身边，我感到没有什么惧怕的了，死也要走在一起。这是天意吗？我此生无憾！我还有一事相瞒，现在说了也不晚，我本想隐瞒你一辈子。现在我患有胃癌二期，我一直不想让你为我担心，我只想给你留下欢乐和幸福。所以瞒到现在你不怪我吧？反正在生死之前，我什么都跟你说了，没有秘密心里轻松许多。你还要对我说什么？你说吧，我听着。"

秦瑛已泪流满面，邓诚反过来去拥抱她："亲爱的，别这样，看你哭，我心里难受，快哭花脸了。不知道的人，还以为我欺负你呢？"

秦瑛用小拳头捶打着邓诚的身上，泣不成声，哽咽地说出："你是一个大坏蛋，最坏的大坏蛋，我恨你瞒着我一切，我恨你宁愿一个人撑着这些精神压力。我要你娶我，我要嫁给你，今生今世，我们永远都不分开，好吗？答应我！"

邓诚被泪水模糊了双眼，他替秦瑛抹去眼角泪水，欣慰地笑了笑说："我答应你，我一定娶你。我们会没有事的。"

也许是他们俩的情真意切连上天都感动了，飞机颠簸了 15 分钟后穿过了暴风雨气流，系统显示已恢复正常运行状态。广播里又传来空姐说话的声音："大家好，我们已穿过了暴风雨气流，一切恢复正常，但是大家不要随地走动。还有 1 小时 40 分钟就要到达目的地海南三亚这座美丽城市。"

机舱内顿时爆发出欢呼声，邓诚紧紧抱住秦瑛，他们俩经历了生死考验。看见依偎在怀里的秦瑛满脸泪珠的狼狈样子，两个人相互破涕而笑。他们就这样缠缠绵绵地静静等待着飞机安全着陆。

第 21 章　心心相随

这趟飞机终于有惊无险平安着陆在三亚机场，邓诚和秦瑛一出检闸口，就看到严大明律师在那里等候接待邓诚。严大明惊讶地看了一眼邓诚身边的知性优雅大方的女人，很有礼貌地点头微笑，走在邓诚旁边悄悄地说："这就是未来的嫂子秦瑛吧？难怪邓董念念不忘，现在我理解了。我们直接去酒店吧，都安排好了。"

邓诚毫不掩饰地对严大明说："你不仅对上号，你还跟她通过了电话，这还得谢谢你呀我的严律师。这就是我的未婚妻秦瑛。"又向秦瑛介绍道："这是我公司的律师严大明，你们好好正式认识。"

严大明律师马上岔开话题说："先到酒店休息，早上 10：00 准时召开会议，在酒店的 16 层楼会议室。到时候我会提前 10 分钟通知您。"

邓诚接过严大明手中酒店的房间卡，递给秦瑛一张，两人跟着严大明来到了接送车前，上车紧接着就问："沈总和秋甜夫妻到了吗？酒店安排在哪个房间，我们得先去看看他们，有事要说。"

严大明笑着说道："就知道邓董不会忘了朋友，已安排好了，就在对门 107 房，您是 106。房间都是套房，一个规格。"

秦瑛忍不住笑出声说："别急，慢慢来，有的是时间。我也正好有事跟秋甜说，我们爱吧书吧后期几个月就得让沈总和秋甜两人多操点心。疫情防控期间实体店不对外营业，做好网上销售特色熟食产品，靠小芹小贝两人就可以了，只做当地老熟客生意。店铺以网上外卖服务为中心。"

严大明一脸茫然不解地看着邓诚，那意思分明在问："秦瑛知道了您得病的情况？"

邓诚拍了拍下严大明肩背说："你打我电话时我上洗手间了，电话是秦瑛接听的。真的好好谢谢你呀，终于让我能透透气，不然憋着我心里难受。"

严大明这才敢正面回应秦瑛说："不是有意想要瞒着你，是因为我有朋友也是得这个病，人家通过中医治疗真的康复了。我们邓董也是好心，怕你知道后又多一分担心，想等治好了再跟你说。是吧邓董！"

秦瑛平静地接受现实，对严律师说："谢谢你，严律师。邓诚身边有你这位朋友，我很高兴，也很放心。公司能有你在，邓诚可以去我的家乡好好休息静养调理身体，一定会康复的。"

一路上 20 分钟的路程在聊天中，很快就到了，车子在风景秀丽的别墅酒店门口停下来，这里每一座别墅阳台直通天然的游泳池，一晚上的酒店住宿费用是 3600 元，一座别墅分六个大套间，大家可共用大厅、厨房、酒吧台。室内配套设施完善，一应俱全。

来到酒店休息了片刻，冲过澡出来后两人精神状态好很多，秦瑛和邓诚换上出席会议的衣服，然后敲响了沈总和秋甜的房间。三下声响，房门就打开了，秋甜以为是服务员，还没反应过来，看见站在门口的是邓诚和秦瑛，惊喜地喊着："老沈，是邓董和秦瑛来了！快进来坐坐，还有半个小时就要开会了。"

沈总笑着迎着邓诚说："这次的会议住宿规格比我们家还舒服，我刚才还对老婆秋甜说，我装修一辈子的房子，可从来没有享受过这么高档酒店，这是沾邓诚你的光哟！"

邓诚："你和秋甜满意我就放心了，这样吧，时间不多了，我们边去会议室，边说话。有事情要拜托你们俩。"

一行四人一起走向会议室，邓诚跟沈总说着男人们要交代的事情，秦瑛把爱吧书吧放不下的事情都交代给秋甜。当然，秦瑛实话实说了陪邓诚回老家休假一段时间的原因。她不在店的时间里，让秋甜多陪伴照顾着店里的小芹小贝，两个女孩需要互相有个照应。

秋甜感慨地说："看见你们能这样乐观地去面对，我真的替你们高兴，一切会好起来的。没事，这边的事，你放心吧，有我呢。我就把那店当成我家，有事没事我都会去天天陪伴她们两个。"

秋甜再不能说了，后面说出来的话，一听就知道嗓子哽咽了。虽然秦瑛语气好像很轻松的样子，像是安慰自己也是在安慰秋甜，但是秋甜的内心是有些惊恐和悲伤。她想着邓诚这么好的朋友，怎么会得上胃癌二期呢？这对情侣是她和沈总一起牵线搭桥的，他们准备要在秋天收获爱情，举行婚礼仪式。这样一来，又不知道要等多久。秋甜担心他们还能够如愿结婚吗？

秦瑛看见秋甜偷偷要哭泣的样子，忙拉着秋甜的手说："你心里怎么想的，我都知道。别担心我们，我和邓诚都想通透了。这次回老家什么都不想，就是在山清水秀的家乡好好调养身体。配合中医治疗，一定会好起来的。我老家有一个名医，已经有朋友在他那里治愈了。所以放心啦，别担心邓诚，我会安心陪伴他，照顾好他。等他康复就回我们的爱吧书吧举行婚礼。"

邓诚不知道几时走到了秦瑛身后，望着自己深爱的女人，听见秦瑛劝慰秋甜的那番话，猛然发现自己是世界上最幸福的男人。邓诚满眼爱的女人，一点都没有看错，秦瑛是个好女人，真的值得拥有得到幸福。他必须好好健康活着，一定兑现承诺，永远爱秦瑛，给予她一生的陪伴，不仅仅是财富。秦瑛需要爱的人陪伴，那么这个男人就是我邓诚。

邓诚没有惊动秦瑛和秋甜的谈话，听着声音，自己的鼻子已酸楚了。准备转身离开的时候，严律师挥手向邓诚喊道："邓董，可以入座了，马上开会了，等你第一个发言，快请大家进会场吧！"

这一喊把秋甜和秦瑛带回了现实，这个时候两个人才发现邓诚就在她们俩靠着的柱子的另外一边。秦瑛心想，她说的话一定都被邓诚听到了，不然邓诚眼睛怎么红红的？

这可怎么办呀？等会还上台讲话，这样精神状态下的发言能够讲好吗？秦瑛有些自责，不该这个时候对秋甜说出这些令人难过的事。

进入会场后大家很快就安静下来，主持人简单说了几句之后请邓诚上台说话。秦瑛从没有参加过邓诚公司的会议活动，这是第一次在台下看见邓诚在台上讲话。秦瑛有些痴痴地看着她心中的王子：邓诚一身合适的深蓝色的西装，配上红色的领带，临时吹了头发。虽然消瘦了不少，但身材挺拔，一股男人绅士风度恰到好处地展现出来。秦瑛看着台上站着仪表堂堂的心上人，就感觉邓诚走向台前的第一眼就看向自己，还在自己身上停顿了三秒。

邓诚首先向台下嘉宾表达谢意，感谢大家多年以来的支持和信任，并祝福大家在公司举办的新的保险项目上，找到保驾护航新险种。这个险种能够使被保险人享受一生的平安保障。最后他祝愿大家在会议期间玩得尽兴。

邓诚娓娓道来的发言把会议的气氛都调动起来了，接下来会议气氛非常热烈，不知不觉就到了午餐时间。这是宴请宾客最高档次的海洋自助餐，有百种食物花样，向所有客人提供红酒、白酒、啤酒，还有各种冷饮热饮供客人享用。

秦瑛在用余光搜索着邓诚穿梭在人群中的身影，回味着邓诚从台上讲完话后，就直接走到她的身旁，寸步不离守着，看得出邓诚不想让秦瑛感到陌生。庆幸有好朋友沈总、秋甜和严大明律师几位陪伴左右。秦瑛能感受到邓诚的照顾，他的细心体贴温暖了秦瑛的心。

宴会厅里邓诚悄悄地告诉秦瑛："你今天多吃点，这个是你最爱吃的螃蟹，公的蟹肉多，你多吃几只，还有多喝点乌鸡汤。"

邓诚只留意秦瑛喜欢吃的东西，全部带着秦瑛走了一圈，介绍说着美味佳肴的菜名。秦瑛盘子放满了，邓诚才动手去拿自己喜欢吃的食物。沈总和秋甜依次排列坐在秦瑛桌前。

窗外阳光明媚，那绿色的植物和五颜六色的花朵怎么看都觉得好美。秦瑛知道只是停留一天，但感觉自己很熟悉这里的环境，像是在梦里见过的场景。她感觉有邓诚陪伴，到哪里都会觉得亲切，备受关怀，根本没有邓诚害怕的陌生感出现。秦瑛喜欢这里的一切，因为这里有无话不谈的好朋友，跟朋友们待在一起没有一点孤独感。

在这宾客满座的场景里，秦瑛忽然轻松了许多。看到邓诚阳光明媚的笑容，她打心眼里喜欢并佩服这个能让她心动，能够陪伴她这一辈子的男人，她庆幸自己算是等到了疼爱自己的好男人了，有了邓诚的痴情，秦瑛心早已有归属感了。

秦瑛此刻心情很好，她为爱邓诚而疯狂，怀着少女的情怀，怦然心动，谁说少女不怀春啊，是美好的情感都会令小女子珍惜，只是以前不太好意思说出来。秦瑛抬起头，看到邓诚也在直愣愣地看着她，眼神坦诚又勾魂，这两个人四目视线已电上了，躲不开了。

第 22 章　蕲艾之都

　　下午的会议邓诚只露了一下脸。为了不惊动其他参加会议的人，邓诚患癌症的消息没有透露，公司只有严大明律师知道这事。若有人问邓诚为何离开，他会配合邓诚作出合理解释。

　　从会议大厅出来后，邓诚直接在别墅门口跟秦瑛汇合。沈总和秋甜已经帮秦瑛将邓诚的行李箱放在去机场的车辆上，见邓诚出来后赶紧安慰地说："放心休假吧，好好玩，这边有我和秋甜。一路平安，我们等着喝你和秦瑛的喜酒呢！"

　　秦瑛依依不舍地和秋甜道别，上车后秦瑛把头埋进邓诚的怀里："路上休息一会吧，咱俩总算是可以好好休假了，一定好好养好身体。"

　　邓诚握着秦瑛的手轻压着说："我们马上要去你的家乡，那也是中医国宝李时珍的故乡。我那不是病，喝喝中草药汤，保证把我治愈好。放心吧，我有这个信心。"

　　秦瑛顺势借此话题，对邓诚说："我讲一个故事给你听，有个老人叫斯塔拉克丝，他在 1976 年的时候，就美国为医生确诊为肺癌晚期。医生都对他说，他的生命只剩下九个月的时间。考虑在美国医疗费太贵了，他执意要回乡下老家度过最后的日子。他拒绝了所有化疗治疗。回乡下后，每天睡到自然醒，该吃的吃，该喝的喝，心态乐观。每天在晒太阳的时候，做点钓鱼养花种菜的小事，和当地村民聊聊天，散步做些好玩的农活。一晃眼度过了医生被判决的九个月时间，活得好好的。这样一直活到了 104 岁高龄，成为当地的长寿老人。

　　家人把这位老人送到医院检查全身，结果发现身上的癌细胞都消失了，反倒是那些给他确诊的医生都已经早早过世。老人没有吃过任何的药物也没有做过化疗，他只是在享受日常的生活，忘记了时间，忘记了自己是一个病人。这个真实的故事，网站能够查得到。其实我们很多人不是死于癌症本身，而是对癌症的这种恐惧和抗拒让他们失去了希望，也失去了生命。

　　科学家走访了这个老人的老家迪卡，查不出了结果，只知道老人家吃的都是天然的未加工的食物，最便宜的食物却是最健康的饮食疗法。老人家还有好的作息规律，他有午睡的习惯，当身体想要困就睡，这是很重要的。这个例子说明了一切，健康取决于自己内心，看一个人以什么样的心态生活。要少生气，多宽容别人，才是放下自己。只记好事，就能够在平凡的生活中找到自己人生的意义。我想你一定也是在患者中活到 100 岁的人，我们一起怀有愉悦心情，好好享受大自然美好氧吧时光，你定会越来越好。你那不是病，你可是答应我了，要陪我一生一世。"

　　邓诚听秦瑛说完故事之后，还真从低迷中悟出了很多道理，心里轻松多了。是啊，别担心太多了，糊涂虫似的过日子，放手一搏，就当每一天都是最后一天，后面活下来的时间就是赚到的好日子。邓诚劝自己，没有什么不可以的，我体质好，那老人家是晚期都活到了 104，我还年轻，还只是二期，没有理由不好好地活着。

　　秦瑛听见邓诚这样说，压抑在心里的担忧没有了，秦瑛对中医药调治好邓诚的病症很有信心。沿途说话中，不知不觉就到了三亚的飞机场。这里太阳高照，蓝天白云下的风吹到脸上都是热的。时间刚刚好，排队安检顺利拿到登机牌。严律师真周到，帮两个人定的还是头等舱，宽敞舒适。这南航的服务还真好，上来后空姐就递上两件毛巾毯，起飞前秦瑛叮嘱邓诚说："起飞后，你就好好睡一觉，别胡思乱想了，做个美梦我们就到了。家乡那边已有酒店专车服务接我们俩。"

　　邓诚真听话，飞机发动起飞后，盖好毛巾毯闭目养神了，不一会儿就打起小呼噜了，睡得很香很实。

　　秦瑛可没有闲着，做好蕲乡艾草的功效资料搜集整理。当看见蕲乡李时珍故乡简介的博文，看着看着更加坚定了信心。

　　秦瑛全神贯注地盯着电脑上的内容：世界艾草看中国，中国艾草看蕲春，家有三年艾，郎中不用来。《本草纲目》记载蕲艾"灸百病"。

　　提起这千年药草，蕲春人豪气十足，短短的十几年，蕲艾产业链从无到有。多种蕲艾养生产品，包括艾条、艾绒、艾饼等传统原料；蕲艾灸贴、眼贴、足贴、颈贴、腰腹贴等各种灸贴；蕲艾精油、蕲艾足浴、蕲艾日化等产品，在蕲乡已普及百姓生活中，在大健康这片蓝海里一定能找到调理治疗邓诚胃癌的好方子。

　　蕲春艾灸疗方法源自医圣李时珍的《本草纲目》，是以地道的蕲艾为灸材，流传蕲春地区四百余年，是有明显地域特征的一种地方性灸法。蕲春以蕲艾为主导的大健康产业蓬勃发展，传承好蕲春艾灸疗法，传播中医药文化，深受国际患者的赞誉。

中医特色治疗：灸中之皇——督脉灸。人体后背的正中线上，也就是从颈椎到尾骨这段距离，贯穿着总管一身阳气的督脉。古人称之为"阳脉之海"。脉如其名，就如同汪洋大海，汇聚了全身经脉的阳气，并把这些阳气输送、布散到全身体表的肌肤腠理之处，发挥温煦机体，抵御外邪的功能。

督脉灸是灸中之皇！在督脉上艾灸，借助督脉总督阳气的作用，激发出人体自身的阳气，又将这种温热，通过复杂有序的经络系统层层传递到全身，恢复人体的自愈力。

艾师傅鼎灸宝，微烟艾灸，艾灸面积大，控温方便。一宝在手，可以灸督脉，也可以灸任脉，非常方便。患者通过艾灸可以驱逐出身体湿气，因为艾热进入人体后，能促进血液循环通经活络，去除湿气，可以舒缓腰酸背痛以及身体各种不适。《本草纲目》有这么一句话："蕲艾灸百病。"

一路上秦瑛查阅了不少中医救治患者的各种真实故事，更了解了中草医学文化给人们生活中带来的帮助，拯救过无数患者的病痛折磨，救活过被已诊断为时间不多的癌症患者，他们中有战胜了病症活到 100 多岁的人，这就是蕲艾中医博大精髓。秦瑛看着这些家乡对艾草的文化传承事例，一丝丝的安慰给了她信心。

秦瑛耳边响起空姐广播的声音："旅客们，飞机还有 20 分钟就要着落了，请大家系好安全带。"

邓诚被广播声惊醒，这觉睡得真沉。看见秦瑛刚好合上电脑，关心地问："你没有休息啊？又写小说吗？"秦瑛温情脉脉不语，意思是你猜猜看。

不一会飞机如时安全着落，一出大厅就看见酒店工作人员举着牌子，写着他们两个人的名字。严大明办事安排真到位。工作人员接过邓诚和秦瑛的两个大行李箱子，两人会心一笑，跟随酒店工作人员走进停车场。

一路上秦瑛看见家乡日新月异的变化，感到既熟悉又陌生。这就是她要奔赴的蕲春，人们称这里为蕲艾之都，是秦瑛小时候成长的地方。

车程不到 1 小时，很快到了蕲春公主山庄酒店，这是当地最适合养生的有名酒店。

秦瑛在飞机上做了不少关于中医艾草功效的记录，也有了行程计划，她向酒店工作人员请教："请问明天早餐后，能带我们去这几个地方吗？"

秦瑛一点也不想浪费时间，直奔做事主题。

邓诚则不同，他想借这次机会首先拜见秦瑛的家人。邓诚善解人意地对秦瑛说："不差这两天，还是先看父母和家人吧。"

秦瑛愠怒地瞪了一眼邓诚坏笑着说："在我的地盘上，我说了算哟，听我安排好吗？明天包车去这几个地方。如果找到名医咨询顺利，接下来会有足够时间，我们可以顺道去我家，满足你的好奇心。让你这位未来女婿尽孝心，哈哈，这样安排可以吧？"

邓诚理解并佩服秦瑛的处事能力，在这里好像自己也只能听从秦瑛的安排了，没有理由拒绝秦瑛，好像秦瑛说的都很有道理。

这天晚上，秦瑛和邓诚在酒店的精心安排下，在酒店院子外面选择了一桌家乡的菜肴。有温补的土鸡山药汤，还有一些地方特色小吃。两人慢慢品，慢慢和言细语地互诉衷情。

晚饭后他们又在酒店室外一起散步。家乡清爽的晚风，吹打着两个人的脸。邓诚仰天呼吸道："这里真是天然的有氧空气，真香，你闻到了吗？"

秦瑛在那瞬间已闭目养神地享受着家乡的美妙声音：小鸟吱吱声，风吹树叶的沙沙声，还有月亮偷看他们俩，透露出柔和光源，映衬在她和邓诚相依的身影，这情景真美……

第 23 章　忘我境界

　　第二天清晨的阳光照进秦瑛房间，白色窗帘上透过的光刚好照在醒来的秦瑛脸上。秦瑛看看床头柜上的小闹钟，整六点过五分，是该起床了。不知道隔壁主卧室内邓诚休息怎么样？为了让邓诚休息好，她特意提出自己睡在酒店套房侧卧室。

　　昨天他们说好了，接下来邓诚听从秦瑛安排。秦瑛收拾好自己后敲响邓诚的房门，没想到邓诚早已洗漱好了，就等秦瑛一起去一楼东侧餐厅。

　　餐厅中有丰盛的早餐品种，有牛奶、鸡蛋、水果、米粉、面条、炸酱面、油条……

　　秦瑛只要了最清淡的小米粥加一小碟咸菜和蔬菜煎饺，给邓诚端上了一碗豆腐脑加一碗瘦肉馄饨。

　　天公作美，这一天的天气很不错。在酒店门口，包车的石师傅已等候多时，见秦瑛和邓诚的两个人向车子走来，忙热情迎了上去："你们俩就是去向桥镇昙树岭避暑山庄寻找名医看病咨询的吧？请上车。"

　　秦瑛看着说出熟溜家乡话的来人：一脸被太阳晒红的肤色，结实健壮和蔼随和的样子。秦瑛亲切地回应道："是啊，您就是当地有名的万事通石师傅吧，这几天都要请您当导师了，谢谢您石师傅。"

　　秦瑛和邓诚上了石师傅的车，石师傅边开车边沿途介绍，并说已预约好了与名医就诊的时间，排第三号就该邓诚就诊了。

　　石师傅接着说："你俩不用着急，只要见到名医就诊了，保你们心踏实。一周七服中药，喝完后再复诊，根据病情调治情况，再开七服中药，喝完再看看。经我送来的患者都医好了，高高兴兴地回去了。要不说大家都来找这位名医呢？这名医也怪，从不做广告，甚至姓名都不说。患者被医好后传出名了，百姓都叫他艾神医，我们也这么称呼他。"

　　说着聊着，不一会的工夫就到了石师傅所说的艾神医的院子门口。艾神医就住在离太平山庄附近山里边的小村庄，只有十几户护林村民居住着。后来是因为艾神医名声在外，络绎不绝的患者前来就医会诊，结果让这个十几户的小村庄也一起出了名。很多人知道这里住着一位菩萨心肠的艾神医，一位善良的老人。

　　艾神医看病从不收费，只给诊断结果及治疗的土方法，用中草药成分配方调理身体。这个村子还有一个特点，几乎每家院子和田埂地边都会种植成片成片的艾草。那艾叶在风中摇曳的时候，从远处就能闻到艾草的芳香，那种纯植物的香味扑面而来。

　　艾神医家的院子，就长着整片整片的艾草，从院子的门口四周围的艾草一株株排列生长，组成的一道艾草艾叶的风景墙，从远处望去，真是天然的美丽风景。

　　邓诚和秦瑛欣赏着院子里各种中草药花草，院子里每一个角落都可晒到太阳，随地都有石头凳子、木桩树凳子供患者及家属朋友们就座等候，有时候有很多来自不同地方的人，大家互不认识，但最后从病友变到朋友。大家同病相怜，相互安慰，共同克服病魔，走出癌症阴影。

　　这时艾神医身边的娃儿小超向院子里喊了一句："3 号邓诚请进。"

　　秦瑛想陪同一起进去，结果被小超挡在门外："艾爷有规矩，为了拿脉相准确，不让患者分心，定下神拿脉看病因，闲人免进。"

　　就这样秦瑛只好在外等了 1 个多小时，走出来的邓诚表情似乎很凝重，手上拿着一个汤药罐子和一袋子里装的中草药。药方中还有些草药要去县城中药铺抓药，按照方子所说煎好喝完，一周后再来诊断调理情况。

　　艾神医并没有直说多严重，只是告诫邓诚："不吃生冷辛辣食物，不要暴饮暴食，也不要饿着。吃清淡，少吃多餐，睡到自然醒，平常该干吗就干吗。看淡一切，但又要热爱生活，把每天都当成世界末日的最后一天，去做自己喜欢的事情。忘掉自己，多想他人，关心他人，这病根就去得快。只要每天醒了见到早晨的太阳，你就是赚到了。"

　　秦瑛迎上前去，让邓诚先上车等她，自己问一件事情就出来。

　　艾神医一看便知道秦瑛想要问什么，连忙制止："你也别问邓诚病因情况，你只需要好好陪伴他就行。每天喝药都叫该喝茶了，不要对他说喝药，你要带他多去乡里走走看看，陪他玩好，吃好，休息好，总而言之开心就好。"

艾神医的话给了秦瑛精神上的安慰。秦瑛见在神医这里再也问不出什么问题，想想既来之则安之，接下来就是去按艾神医开的方子配中草药，回酒店熬药。

上车后秦瑛对石师傅说："我们去县城中药铺吧，按方子配置中草药。石师傅这道你一定熟悉，辛苦你了，咱们尽快去。"

石师傅接着建议："抓好中草药后，顺便就在中药铺里把 7 天的中药煎成袋装，带回酒店冰箱放着，每天三包，热开水烫几分钟，就可以喝了。以前的病人都是这样做好的，可省事了。"

秦瑛兴奋地说："还有煎药房吗？太好了，需要等多久煎好呢？"

石师傅立即回复："排队编号等两小时左右，没有关系，等待的两个小时，我带你俩在太平山庄转转，看看还能不能调到太平山庄别墅酒店住。这样步行就可以走去艾神医那复诊，不用来去折腾，这样安排好吗？"邓诚听后觉得这个建议好。

到了中药铺抓好配方上的药，石师傅直接带着秦瑛和邓诚将中草药交给煎药房，作了登记，拿到取药的号码纸条。两小时后，再来取药就好。

真亏有石师傅，不然的话哪有这一环套一环的顺利，要不说在外有个朋友是个宝。

石师傅将车开到太平山庄酒店，在大厅咨询台一问，便知还有套房房间，今天可以办理入住手续。就这样秦瑛让邓诚就在太平山庄大厅休息等候，她和石师傅去原酒店办理退房手续，将生活用品让石师傅转运到太平山庄。这一系列操作弄好，刚刚好也到了取中药的时间了，一切进行得有条不紊。

邓诚看到秦瑛为自己忙完这些本该由他来做的事情，心里感到很温暖。石师傅在旁边看到秦瑛忙完之后有些累的样子，忙对两人说："今天喝完药后，早点休息吧，我明天早上九点钟来这酒店接你们，去徐家湾秦瑛的姨妈家是吗？"

秦瑛和颜悦色地说："对，我们明天把一天的药包带上，让邓诚去乡下陪我姨父钓鱼，放松放松。我有几年没有探望这家好亲戚了，还真想他们。昨天我已打电话给他们了，说这几天要去看他们。他们知道我们住酒店，非要我把酒店房间退了。我不想给他们添麻烦。"

邓诚欣喜地说："真的吗，明天可以去乡下看看钓鱼？那师傅明天上午见。"说完就迫不及待地拉着秦瑛一起向酒店房间走去。

这一晚上，两人可能是精神作用，睡到自然醒，休息得很好。在酒店大厅吃完早餐后，看时间还够，又在附近水库散步走走，呼吸着新鲜空气。

邓诚主动说："我昨天诊断后还有很多想法，艾神医也没有说任何保证的治疗方案，只说患者得上这个病，有两种不同结果。关键是取决于患者的心态，放下任何压力，坦然面对，积极调理身体，那病就不医都会自愈。若把病太当回事，那就会吓死自己。一晚上我什么也不想，则是算我想通了。艾神医不是医病，而是在医我的心里头的疾病。"

邓诚说这些话时，手指着自己的心，意思是我放下了，我不能把自己吓死了，"艾神医都说了，每个人身上都有癌症细胞，战胜病魔就是学会与癌细胞相处，互不侵犯，和平共处。这话听起来有点意思是嘛！"

秦瑛和邓诚坐石师傅的车子去徐家湾附近的李时珍酒厂，买了一箱中药补酒和街道上的当季水果，给姨妈姨父带上礼物。邓诚还让秦瑛封一个大红包 1 万元，那是秦瑛的心意。要知道这家亲戚是秦瑛老妈同父异母的亲妹妹。

秦瑛早年从小就听妈常念叨过，她自己的母亲在参加革命的时候被汉奸杀害了，那时秦瑛母亲还只是一岁。后来组织上就为父亲安排一个生活上能给予照顾的小脚村女，这个村女就是组建新家的女主人，秦瑛母亲的继母，也就是秦瑛姨妈的母亲。秦瑛的妈妈自小从 16 岁就离开村庄到城市参加了工人阶级队伍后，就很少回老家了。结婚成家有了秦瑛后，每年春节前后或者清明，都会带秦瑛来看这位同父异母所生的亲妹妹，秦瑛叫她少珍姨。

少珍姨的丈夫叫徐忠家，是一个孤儿，在家乡农机厂当医生，与少珍姨在农机厂工作相识，自然恋爱，结婚后生有一子。少珍姨和姨父徐忠家在蕲艾之乡退休务农，现在三代同堂和谐地与儿孙生活在一起，盖了一栋五层楼的乡村别墅房，过上幸福美满的田园生活。

远远地就看见少珍姨和徐忠家姨父在门口迎接，秦瑛和邓诚一下车走进院子大门，就听见身后鞭炮齐鸣，响个不停。少珍姨说："今天来了贵客，小瑛儿，你姨父说要放长长的鞭炮，让你们长长久久幸福快乐。"

秦瑛听完少珍姨这番话之后，突然看见少珍姨和姨父满头白发，那双粗糙的双手，都冒出血管精道，一条条显现在手背上，穿的那身衣服还是秦瑛几年前给的。秦瑛说："现在日子过得这么好了，都盖了楼房，少珍姨咋还穿这么朴素的衣服，快丢了吧，换新的。"

少珍姨大咧咧地笑着说："没事没事，这农村乡下穿好的，也没有什么人看我们，我干农活还真喜欢穿这身衣服，舒服挺贴身，柜子里还有很多小瑛你给的衣物，每天不重样，都穿不过来，你可别再买了，浪费。"

邓诚已坐在大厅高背木椅上，也静静地看着为他们的到来忙前忙后的徐忠家姨父：在风中吹过头发还乱着，但是黝黑的脸庞泛着红光，满面的精气神，让邓诚立刻感觉这位男主人的和蔼可亲。徐忠家姨父朴实忠厚，处处为他人着想，见他不停地见事做事，忙着抓鸡又忙着端出一竹篮子刚摘下的水果。

邓诚心中涌出很多感动，情不自禁地上前拉着走徐忠家手说："请别再忙了，难怪秦瑛常说很想你们，说你们是她家乡最亲的亲人。我今天一见，我都喜欢你们了，就像一见如故，这种感觉真好。"

秦瑛打断邓诚的话，抢着说："姨父啊，我这次带邓诚来，可能要多待上一些日子，这往后姨父钓鱼，下农活摘菜种地，也教邓诚做一下，他喜欢这里氛围。瞧瞧邓诚眼睛都红了，他比我还激动啊。"

说这话的秦瑛何尝不是说自己呢？她有意转移目标，掩盖不住自己内心的乡思和对亲人的热爱，眼泪早已流出来了，只有借说邓诚才使自己破涕为笑。

邓诚抢话继续说道："你天天想念少珍姨他们，爱他们。现在来了，当着面，你要把心中的爱大声说出来啊！少珍姨，姨父，我说真的。秦瑛不好意思说，她就是这么一个人，跟你们久了，变得也特别实诚，所以我很想守护她。"

徐忠家凝视着邓诚，说了意味深长的一番心里话："此时我非常理解你的心思，你很爱小瑛，那你更要好好陪伴守护着你所爱的人。放下压力，珍惜眼前人，把每一天开开心心地活好。我们要活明白，做到忘我的境界。你无所不能，阳光会滋润着你的生活，把每天的迎晨观落日当作幸福，你就是生命中最快乐的人。"

第 24 章　利他忘我

邓诚接过徐忠家姨父手中的钓鱼竿、网兜、一双雨鞋，还有一件全棉面料的深蓝色工作布兜！邓诚换上这些行头打扮，穿着跟当地村民没啥区别。邓诚感觉一身轻松，愉快地向秦瑛眨眼睛，意思是说："我去钓鱼去了，回头见。"

秦瑛也开开心心地挥手说："你今天跟姨父多钓小参子鱼和小龙虾，晚上我想吃虾球。另外我跟少珍姨学做黏米粉素食丸子，将来在珠海爱吧书吧自制自销，省去邮寄费成本。这主意不错吧？"

邓诚刚开始钓到鱼就马上兴奋地用手抓鱼尾，结果鱼儿溜溜地滑走了。徐忠家姨父手把手教邓诚，邓诚上手很快，后来钓鱼的数量都快超过了姨父。这下邓诚可乐坏了，笑个不停，他很久没有这样开心了！

秦瑛这边寸步不离地跟着少珍姨，一会儿去菜地里挖地菜，这是做黏米粉丸子馅需要的一种天然绿色野菜，很多人都喜欢吃它，用来当饺子馅主配菜或者下火锅都好吃。

秦瑛从东头走到西头，在地面土埂上不停地挖野菜，两个小时的工夫，秦瑛已满头大汗，挖出了满满的竹筐子。秦瑛从来没有出这么多汗，以前总是闷在空调书房内写作办公，这下全身上下活动，一站一低头瞅着地里野菜挖，她越挖越起劲。秦瑛紧跟少珍姨，追上去一看，少珍姨的竹筐里装的野菜比秦瑛的还要多一半。秦瑛不服输地说："少珍姨你怎么这么快呀，我都没有停下，都赶不上你，有什么窍门能又快又准的挖到野菜呢？"

少珍姨边继续挖地菜，手不停着说："没有什么窍门，就是熟能生巧。你农活干得少，哪能跟我这天天在地里干活的人一样？这是最好的天然氧吧运动，空气清新，早上起来我最喜欢的是到菜地里来摘下一天家人要吃的菜。有时候菜多吃不完，就多挖点又驾着轻骑摩托车送到菜市场卖掉。我租了一个固定的小摊位，我的菜很新鲜，往摊位上一摆不一会儿就卖完了。买菜的基本上都是我们的熟人，我会跟他们说好一周两天上午摆摊的时间。我家种的菜都不打农药，全绿色环保健康新鲜菜，谁都知道好。"

秦瑛又说："你知道吗？我昨天晚上做梦，就梦见你带我去捡鸡蛋。接着看到满眼都是地菜，我不停挖呀捡呀，可高兴啊。后来鸡叫声把我的美梦吵醒了！"

少珍姨笑着说："你是日有所思夜有所梦，像小时候一样，还那么喜欢我们这农村乡下里来玩。"

秦瑛看着红光满面笑着说话的少珍姨，皮肤是阳光健康色，没有化妆的全素颜，汗水都粘着脸上，脑门头发被清晨的微风轻轻吹拂，在早晨阳光的照射下显得很美。秦瑛情不自禁地说："少珍姨真好看，你别动，我用手机给你拍一张相片。"咔嚓咔嚓几声，秦瑛成了跟拍摄影师了。

"哈哈哈哈，我这是老阿姨了，还美？别拍我了，多拍点自然风光吧。瞧瞧那片果园，还有你姨父包的后山天然养鸡场，相信你更喜欢。走，我们该回家做黏米粉丸子了，你待会一看就能学会。"

秦瑛也感觉在乡村做农活像是玩似的，干活出汗都不觉得累，还不愁没吃的东西。土灶烧菜做饭真好吃，没有城市里各种调料和讲究，但炉子上炖的汤都好喝，怪不得退休后少珍姨和姨父都没生过病，身体还比以前好了。他们干活累了就歇歇，到了晚上还用艾草热水泡脚。粘床就睡着了，一觉睡到自然醒。

少珍姨在家里一边烧火一边说："小瑛你和邓诚说好，把酒店房退了，搬到家里三楼住，上面有新的居家用品，比你们住酒店还舒服方便！"

秦瑛心想她自己一点问题都没有，每次来乡下踏青过春节拜年的时候，都是住在少珍姨家里。最早的时候还是住在徐家村的平层房屋里，冬暖夏凉，在乡村居住从来没有安装过空调，最热的时候也只是小电吹风扇。夜晚静静地听着风吹树叶上沙沙声入眠，很逸闲，有一种自得其乐的满足。

午餐时间到了，徐忠家和邓诚一前一后走进别墅的院子里，换上拖鞋，坐在木椅子上，围坐在石头大圆桌边，等着少珍姨的黏米粉丸子和纯正宗的土鸡汤。饭菜还没端出来就闻到了香味。

秦瑛在灶炉旁，一直看着少珍姨是怎么做好吃的午餐。今天黏米粉丸子算是学会了，秦瑛还想学做锅巴粥，她非常喜欢吃这个乡下才能吃到的锅巴粥。

少珍姨把米饭全部添出来，装进饭盆里，这时看到锅里焦黄色的锅巴米饭。

她抄底抄开再加几瓢水，将锅盖焖煮开，利用灶的余火温煮好。揭开锅盖后，那锅巴粥的香味闻起来就很香，想想吃过锅巴粥的人，都忘不了这道美食的诱惑吧。这么多年来，秦瑛只要回到乡村这里，喝上锅巴粥配上当地时令蔬菜，能够吃两大碗。

少珍姨的贤惠勤劳和朴实乐观的生活心态，能够感染到周边的人。徐忠家就是看上了少珍姨的善良和真诚。邓诚这一上午学会了钓鱼的技能，还学会了耐心，更是读懂了做男人的担当。他也在徐忠家的身上看到了朴实无华，默默为家庭付出，不求回报。这种人格魅力吸引了邓诚，他瞬间发现原来男人身上的闪亮点，不是长得多帅多好看，而是他内在的人格魅力。这两口子真是模范夫妻，是邓诚和秦瑛心目中崇拜的朴实而平凡的偶像。

邓诚突然觉得自己以前是白活了，他现在悟透人生哲理。邓诚在心里面问自己：还来得及吗？

邓诚不能闲着，一闲下来就想到自己的病。秦瑛懂邓诚的感受，看出他的内心深处的担忧。秦瑛装着没有察觉的样子，大大咧咧地向邓诚喊一声："好烫呀，邓诚快来帮我一把，快点过来拿炖的鸡汤罐，我端锅巴粥。保你两样都想吃，真的好香呀，闻闻味道不错吧！"

邓诚赶紧起身帮忙着接过秦瑛手上的盘子。少珍姨体贴地说："没有做多的菜，今天就吃些简单的主食，糙米锅巴粥，黏米粉丸子，土鸡汤炖蘑菇。"

徐忠家接话说："晚餐更简单，大碗鱼汤炖全素馅的地菜饺子。邓诚一定得吃，美味可口哦！在我们乡村生活，没有高档的珍馐百味，但是这些土生土长的东西都有，保你吃得好开心，吃得营养丰富，身体健康得很。你瞧瞧我退休后，这么多年从来没有感冒过，还越来越结实了。你看看像钓鱼这样的活，就当是在阳光下补钙，不需要吃什么保健品。"

秦瑛走近邓诚身边帮助挟着菜，放在盘子里，逼着邓诚先尝尝味道。看着邓诚先咬一口菜丸子，接着喝口鸡汤，那仰天微笑调皮的可爱神态，让秦瑛放心了，"好吃多吃点，这可真是美味佳肴。"

邓诚刚刚开始还保持端正的坐姿，后来都顾不上形象了，也学着徐忠家端着碗筷，一会去看院子长的花儿，一边吃着碗里的食物。不一会工夫吃完了，又去添一碗锅巴粥，还真吃不腻。

秦瑛轻言细语的声音在邓诚耳旁响起："我少珍姨让我们把酒店房退了，别花冤枉钱，来这里长期住，你愿意吗？"

邓诚想想说："你决定吧。不是钱的问题，如果不听从亲人的邀请，就等于看不起这么好的亲戚。再说我理解你们之间的感情，你以前都住这里。我不能当恶人，我想让你亲上加亲，我同意客随主便，我乐意退酒店搬迁到这里长住，嘿嘿！"

秦瑛听邓诚这么说，高兴得跳起来就打一拳邓诚的腰："我真开心你没有把我的亲戚当外人，你喜欢我的亲人，我真开心呀。今天吃饱喝足了就去退掉酒店房间吧，两点之前不算今天的钱。"

邓诚开玩笑说："你多打几拳，就当给我捶背捶腿好吧。瞧你那么抠门，还想省一天的房费。"

秦瑛手舞足蹈地跑在少珍姨面前笑嘻嘻地说："少珍姨，他答应搬到家里住。没有想过他这么快就把这里当成自己家了。少珍姨你说邓诚靠谱吗？如果你觉得他人好，病好了我们就准备结婚了！"

少珍姨表达自己的想法说："邓诚这男人很好，他生病后把自己的财富安排到你名下了。他这样对你是讲感情的，唯有真爱真情才能做得到这些。我相信邓诚的病会医好的，就让他在这里生活，配合中医调理养好身体。让他学习你姨父利他忘我的境界，一切都会好起来。"

秦瑛点头表示认可，"当初就是感觉他好傻，自己都患有癌症二期了，不赶紧看病，却第一时间想到我的往后余生怎么办。就在那一刹那，我感觉财富对我来说就是一个数字，邓诚好好活着比什么都重要。那个时候我心里就想要嫁给他，陪伴他照顾他。我对他说，积极治病才是真正爱我。"

秦瑛的激将法给了邓诚一颗定心丸。在挫折艰难的日子里，他们愈发体会到真情可贵之处。

秦瑛和邓诚在少珍姨家里一住就是七个月，这段时间里邓诚看到中医治疗的效果渐渐显现出来，邓诚的精神状态一天比一天好。这样的成果真的有赖于乡村的天然氧吧环境，还来源于秦瑛亲戚家人无微不至的照顾。在饮食方面，邓诚吃的是纯天然绿色食品，再加上每天都服用中药调理身体，邓诚的体质慢慢改善，精气神也恢复过来。邓诚养成了少吃多餐的饮食习惯，身体以前的胃酸、胃疼、胃胀打嗝都没有再犯了。

最近几次，艾神医看到邓诚前来拿脉就诊时谈天说笑，当秦瑛陪伴左右的时候他显得心情更好。有一次他们看完病，临走之前艾神医夸秦瑛说："邓诚兄弟能在这短短的时间内恢复过来，你有很大的功劳，邓诚在心情愉悦下身体自然就能产生对抗病魔的能力。"

对一个病人来说，心情很重要，身边亲人的关怀是邓诚好转的重要原因之一。

在少珍姨家住下之后，邓诚就没有把自己当作病人了。徐忠家每天都带着邓诚去一趟山里的养鸡场捡鸡蛋，把鸡赶到草地上放养，让它们自由地吃虫吃草。下午在果园里摘下当季的果实，有柑橘、桃子、苹果、梨、山枣，这些跟城市里买的水果不一样，虽然看相不好，但味道特别好。

邓诚每周钓鱼一次，午饭后在阳光下暖暖地晒着，眯着眼睛，享受着午觉半小时。到了晚上，大家会在小院子里坐下来聊聊天，扯嗓子学鸣叫，哼着小曲小调。

元旦将近，秦瑛收到了小贝小芹俩的祝福和爱吧书吧经营情况报告："瑛姐，这里一切都好，真的感谢少珍婶婶寄给我们的素菜馅黏米粉丸子、土山药、花生以及 100 公斤芋头。这次礼盒销量比上次多三倍，网上买的客人真多。这几个月网上销量都比上几个月翻倍了，销售额突破 2 万多，还有一部分礼盒可以卖到年后，不会断货。卖出的货款我明天转给你。在此，祝邓诚哥早日康复，我们想瑛姐和邓诚哥了。

这边实体店爱吧书吧周末忙一点，都是附近海湾小区的业主熟人，他们会在周末来爱吧书吧吃点特色小吃美食，看看书。沈总和秋甜姐他们两个都会在周末帮忙。这边请瑛姐放心吧，替我们谢谢少珍婶婶，邮寄的礼盒及时到货了！感谢乡亲们的支持帮助！"

秦瑛拉着邓诚看完全部信息，邓诚明白了，少珍姨和徐忠家两口子把秦瑛给他们的一万元红包买了农产品寄到爱吧书吧，事情办完了也没有吭声，做了这么多实实在在的好事情。秦瑛和邓诚相互看了一眼，心想这个人情可怎还啊？

两人抬头看着远处灶台前后忙碌的少珍姨的身影，在柔弱暖黄色灯光照耀下，少珍姨麻利地收拾着柴火。徐忠家递上一杯水，让少珍姨喝。少珍姨抹去身上的蓝色布兜，接过杯子一口喝下去。徐忠家拿出一条手巾擦掉少珍姨脸上的水珠，那种疼爱的眼神，看着就让人羡慕不已。

秦瑛在邓诚耳边透露说："姨父是孤儿，自从和少珍姨结婚生子以后，心甘情愿为这个家付出。姨父对我少珍姨说，他这辈子都是倒插门的女婿，但他还是爱这个家，见到少珍姨家的亲戚朋友来访，对人实诚招待。没有一个人不说徐忠家姨父好，个个都夸他勤劳致富。平日里他跟少珍姨从不为自己花钱买衣服穿，穿的都是亲戚朋友送的衣服，一件衣服可以穿很多年。他们总说穿着太好的衣服别扭，干活怕弄脏了。走访亲友时才穿上新衣服。"

邓诚眼睛没有移开，静静望着可敬的亲人。夕阳的余晖洒进小院，秀丽的乡村风景像画一样美丽。风透过敞开大门的厅堂，吹动着少珍姨的衣角。那身衣服正是秦瑛五年前送的生日礼物，没有想过少珍姨到现在还穿着。少珍姨的身材依旧那么苗条漂亮，真不像是乡村的妇人。即使穿着粗丝棉麻混纺面料，看上去依然纯真善良温婉可人。难怪姨父徐忠家常说："少珍是我这辈子遇见的最善良的女人。"

少珍姨的美丽不仅是容颜的美貌，走近她的人都能感受到她内心世界的温柔善良，这才是她的魅力所在。跟她接触的人都觉得很舒服，她会善解人意地对待别人，用行动去表达出来。

邓诚想起那一万元的红包，本意是给秦瑛亲人一些恩惠，没想到少珍姨和姨父免费供吃供住，毫无保留地爱着他们，照顾他们。为他们做了那么多的事情，连爱吧书吧的进货礼盒包都替代办好了，做好事不留名。

邓诚自愧不如地对秦瑛说："我们太自以为是了，总以为用钱可以解决每一件事情。我真羡慕少珍姨和姨父，他们心中有爱，比我们想象中富足，精神上充实。人缘也好，在乡村里好得每位村民都是发自内心夸奖他们。有点难事，立马有肝胆相照的乡亲们来帮忙。这真叫牛啊，我们能有他们一半，我就满足了。"

秦瑛脑子里一遍遍想着法子，不想让少珍姨吃亏。秦瑛忍不住把想法说给邓诚听："你看我这样做行吗？后期爱吧书吧的所有特色小吃黏米粉丸子，我们就让少珍姨作提供投资入股，网上销售的收益都归于少珍姨。我们还免费为少珍姨打造乡村美食提供销售平台，这样就可以让少珍姨多劳多得了，而不只是挣点人工手工制作费。我想让少珍姨在当地也可以带领闲时的村民劳动力，利用当地丰富特色文化食品形成产业链，将农副土特产品能做多大就做多大。这事我们可以试着做，为少珍姨和村民做点实事项目，你看怎么样？"

邓诚听秦瑛这么一说，瞪眼看着秦瑛笑着回答："真没想到，你比我脑子转得快。这办法好，能帮到他们，他们俩听到对村民有利肯定会同意。"

邓诚稳住自己的心跳，拉着秦瑛的手放在自己胸膛，感受他的心跳。邓诚没有骗秦瑛，他是想让秦瑛知道，他也会像徐忠家姨父那样对爱忠诚。去了解秦瑛所想，爱秦瑛所爱，能够为秦瑛亲人带来快乐的事情，他邓诚都会全力以赴支持。

邓诚此时忘记了自己，想到的都是秦瑛想要做的事情，他要义不容辞地去做利他人忘我的事情；从小事做起，从行动上去做实事。这是徐忠家姨父影响邓诚的精句哲理，走这条利他忘我的路，人生的道路就会越走越宽广。

第 25 章　良辰美景

　　春节临近，每家每户都开始准备年货了，乡村人特别看重春节，大家都想把这个节日过得热闹喜庆。

　　这天早上，少珍姨用糯米制作糍粑当早餐，特意让邓诚尝鲜解馋。这道菜她做出了三种花样：第一种，下在鸡汤里面放了几条糍粑，加了几块山药片，味道鲜美又不油腻，配上咸菜萝卜菜叶，做出秦瑛吃不腻的锅巴粥。第二种，将糍粑煎至两面金黄，撒些白糖粘着吃。第三种，把切好一长条块的糍粑用灶的余火慢慢烤熟，外壳烤出金黄色的锅巴。

　　邓诚看见桌上摆放着三种吃法的糍粑，胃口大开，他笑着对少珍姨说："我们在这里住着都不想走了，顿顿吃得好，没有一餐重样，就连糍粑都能做成三种吃法！"

　　少珍姨端着一碗汤放在邓诚面前："先喝土鸡山药汤，再尝其他的东西。春节快到了，有很多唱戏的场所都搭好了小舞台，每年初一到十五都有戏班子来镇上的公园门口唱黄梅戏表演。你姨父跟我商量了，邓诚还是在年前去艾神医那就诊拿脉，让他多开点调理身体的中草药巩固一下。今年你们就在我们乡村家里过年，体验了一把我们乡村跟城市不一样的年夜饭，然后也可以去镇上听听戏。"

　　邓诚说："好哇，我正有此意，想看看农村怎么个热闹。我想体验一下放鞭炮的感觉，尝试各种好玩的、好吃的，还看看戏。秦瑛你同意留下来过年吗？"

　　秦瑛用眼神朝着少珍姨递了一个秋波："我当然愿意呀，这些接地气的生活素材可记录下来当写作素材。"

　　秦瑛从珠海回来蕲艾故乡后，写作灵感更多来源于这里的人和事。秦瑛走到哪里都不停下写作，在乡村生活这段时间，秦瑛已将第二部长篇小说全部书稿完成了，第三部小说也陆续发表连载中，作品还没有写完就已经在制作有声小说。秦瑛感觉有写不完的好故事。

秦瑛说："我可没有想过在春节期间走，我当然赞同留下体验乡村的良辰美景，过不一样的春节。"

徐忠家姨父拿出两条红色围巾，往邓诚身上披上一条，一条递给秦瑛说："你少珍姨前两天和我一起到孙女的学校参加家长会，小孙女又考全班第一名，校长奖励给我们这两条红色围巾。这可是图个好彩头，我们送给你们。就这么定了，在我们家过一个红红火火的春节。春节珠海小贝小芹也要回家乡，咱们可以在这里团聚见面。我还在想，农村在初二后可以开始拜年，到时候我请她俩来我们家一起吃年饭吧。"

邓诚接过这条红色围巾，心里很温暖，突然徐忠家姨父把他当做自己家人和孩子一样照顾，给出无微不至的关爱。邓诚回想起从前过年的欢喜记忆。现在父母已不在了，回珠海也是一个人的生活。要不是认识了秦瑛，估计春节期间还是过着公司到家两点一线的生活。

邓诚变得脆弱，此时像小时候一样，见到亲人就委屈矫情，眼泪突然就掉下来了。邓诚这一流泪不打紧，可吓坏了少珍姨："邓诚哪不舒服啊？是吃坏肚子了，还是撑得胃难受？快让你姨父瞧瞧！"

邓诚知道自己是怎么回事，看大家误以为他身体不适，赶紧用手挡住眼睛说："没有事，是被糍粑噎住了，我去趟洗手间。"

邓诚够机灵，连秦瑛都蒙过去了，真以为他是糍粑吃得快噎住。小时候秦瑛也有过这样的经历，被食物噎住直流眼泪。秦瑛扶着邓诚小声说："像小孩子一样，悠着点儿，现在好些了吗？"

邓诚走进卫生间门里，停下脚步回头看看秦瑛说："你还跟进来吗？你看我，我怎么也没法尿尿啊？"

秦瑛看邓诚这副憨厚可怜的模样，一下子笑了起来："那我就在门外等你出来，真逗，我可要收卫生费的呀。"

邓诚不想在节日期间，让大家知道自己的世界里还有这么多年情感的积压。他这感觉就像是小孩子见到自己的亲爹亲妈才有的情绪释放。已经有很多年没有长辈把他还当成孩子一样疼爱了，这一天他又感受到那种逝去的欢乐童年和父母健在的情景，仿佛回到了以前的幸福时光。

邓诚这么多年来，没有遇到这么质朴的亲人，纯粹的亲情使得邓诚倍感亲切，秦瑛在身边陪伴也让他感受到幸福。他想到自从得知患病之后，秦瑛对他的关心从情感上已超越了男女关系的责任。在他们还没有正式结婚的情况下，秦瑛一直陪伴守护他医病治疗，甚至敢在亲人面前表明自己心意，要跟他永远走下去。

虽然他和秦瑛还没有过真正的夫妻生活，但是他们已公开恋爱关系，在众人眼里已是事实婚姻男女关系了。秦瑛为了爱，放弃了女孩子们讲究的矜持和颜面，一门心思到处为他寻求名医治疗方案，全身心地为他治愈病根，发动亲戚为他提供优质居住环境，让他无忧无虑地安心住下来，战胜自己的心病和身体上的疾病。秦瑛给了他莫大活下来的信念，是凭着爱的意念，让他看到了活着真好的信心。秦瑛是他一辈子可遇不可求的好女人。

邓诚想到前妻背叛他的那段无情无义的婚姻生活，这与他患上胃癌有着直接的原因。在那些生气郁闷的灰暗婚姻日子里，他总是饱一餐饿一餐，回到家里经常是吃冷菜冷饭或者泡泡面。那个家根本没有家庭的温情。

每逢过年过节，邓诚大包小包送一大堆礼物给前妻娘家，而且是全程揽下厨房做饭做菜的活。做完年饭，从没有让他上桌吃过团圆饭。那个时候邓诚认为只要他真心爱妻子，爱她的家人，就会得到同样的情感回应，但是没有。在年轻干事业的好年代，前妻却因他长年出差的原因在外面有人了，而且出轨对象是邓诚最信任的大学同学，那是一段不堪回首的往事。

邓诚看着卫生间镜框中的自己，气色红润，脸都长圆了，两眼炯炯有神，这些都是秦瑛带给他的福气。邓诚沉思默想许久，他没对秦瑛说过跟前妻之间事情，心里像明镜似的知道两个女人没法相比，秦瑛的善良及她娘家人的好品质，正是他向往的婚姻爱情氛围。他此时一条心珍惜眼前人，那就是秦瑛，当他病好后，一定给秦瑛最幸福的生活，他要给予这位无所求却能在他万念俱灰的时候陪伴左右的爱人。

门外秦瑛的喊声，打断了邓诚的思绪："嘿，这么久，你掉在洗手间里了吗？快出来，姨父姨还在大厅等着你呢！等会少珍姨还带我们俩去逛小镇选春节对联红纸呢。今年多买点，由你给村民写对联，你不可推卸哟。"

邓诚整理完毕开门出来，牢牢抓住秦瑛的手，在她耳朵边轻声说："你是上天赐给我的好女人，我一定要好好照顾你一辈子，等过完春节元宵节后，一回珠海我们就结婚好吗？我不想再往后拖了。"

秦瑛摸摸邓诚的头："你没发烧吧？我要看你的表现，我们亲戚都同意呢！那就听你的。不然的话，你就在这里养着，天天当农民多好啊！"

两人一笑一搭地坐回桌前，姨父和少珍姨都没动筷子，等着邓诚上桌后才一起吃完这顿早餐。

邓诚本不想对比在前妻家吃饭时的情景，可瞬间姨父徐忠家和少珍姨对他这般善待尊重，让邓诚又情不自禁地涌起感激之情。他将心里面想的话脱口说出来："亲人啊，我一定好好地爱你们，往后我就当自己的亲戚走动，每年陪伴秦瑛来看望你们，千万别嫌我烦。"

说完这些话后，邓诚装作轻松的样子，掩饰自己的内心酸楚，将刚刚泛起的心凉情绪压下去。今天他不能哭出来，他应该高兴，过去的全让它过去，今后再也不会承受那样的痛苦了。

乡村的春节正如秦瑛所介绍的那般好，邓诚和秦瑛在自家院子里，摆开二张长桌子，倒上黑色墨水，给乡亲们写对联。乡亲们在书中选出自己喜欢的对联，邓诚写在红纸上。

这不隔壁刘胖叔选了这一副对联，横批：新春大吉，上联：春风入喜财入户；下联：岁月更新福满门。余老爷是村里最老资格的爷辈分的老人，选择了这一副，上联：阅卷清风能识字；下联：思情明月也读书。少珍姨选了一副对联是这样写的横批：吉祥如意；上联：一帆风顺家业旺；下联：万事如意全家福。邓诚在写的过程中，也感受到中国文化传承，赋予着节日的喜气和智慧，横批：万事亨通，上联：平安如意千日好；下联：人顺家和万事兴。徐忠家姨父猛说好："给我儿子超超来一副对联，横批，恭喜发财；上联，金玉满堂家兴旺；下联，鸿福齐天富贵长。"

不知不觉就忙了一整天，这种自选自写对联真有意思，人人参与，个个献艺。别看这来自乡村农户们，文化风土人情的句子对联张口就来，真不愧是新型的社会主义新农村。

邓诚和姨父忙完后就把红色的门联贴在家门口，从进大院子的大门就贴上了，窗户上还贴上剪纸红色窗花图影。院子正门两边挂着小红色灯笼，喜气热闹，一片祥和。

　　村村户户都将挂满了红包彩带系在家门口的院内树枝上，据说是留给那些来向长辈拜年的小孩子，作为压岁钱红包。钱数不等，但都是年前去银行特意换的新钞票，从 1-10 元都有。这纯粹就是图个热闹欢迎的祝福，拜年叩拜互谢的风俗，一直延传下来。这次让邓诚长见识了，现在更理解秦瑛为何总是念念不忘这里的乡村。现在邓诚都爱上了这里的人，这里的一草一木。

　　邓诚第一次这样的年，相信会让他终生难忘。他想可能是因为他爱的人在这里，这份被爱包围的亲情之中，他享受着被纯真无邪的大爱。邓诚把亲人们对他的好和不求回报的爱，收在眼里，爱在心里。

　　年过月半，邓诚在少珍姨和徐忠家姨父亲自陪同下，在农历十六的那天去拜访了艾神医。艾神医看这一大家人来访，看着邓诚神采奕奕的气色，还是忍不住职业习惯，拉起邓诚的手，拿脉听诊说："脉搏很稳，身体已经很好了，但是为了巩固，我这次多开些调胃方子，还是多备些温和中草药带回去，间隔一周只喝三副中药即可。回去后，等三个月药喝完了，再到大医院拍片彻底检查一下，结果出来后报告我一声就行，好让我老夫放心。"

　　邓诚提高嗓门回应道："那是一定的，我还得亲自来看望艾神医。"

　　艾神医却仰头大声爽朗地笑着说："那个时候我不希望你再来找我了，这是我的心愿。"

　　邓诚向艾神医行了一个九十度弯腰的大礼，连续三次叩头拜谢。邓诚感激之情无以言表，邓诚有些激动地从喉咙里发出哽咽的声音："谢谢艾神医妙手回春，给了我再生的信念，您不仅是用中医治愈我身体上的疾病，您同时治愈了我的心灵。"

　　艾神医握住邓诚的双手："兄弟啊，是你的亲人们救了你，不要谢我，要感谢他们。感谢这片土地，是这生生不息大自然眷顾你。我们都要感谢这番良辰美景劳作下的乡亲们啊，是大家给予了我们的爱，凭着爱，我们的日子越来越好。"

第 26 章　爱情天梯

邓诚在心里面有许多话想说，可就是说不出口，望着秦瑛这一家实诚的好亲戚，邓诚不知道自己现在能说什么好。秦瑛看见邓诚的嘴角微微颤抖起来，似乎很难说出一句完整的话来，憋了半天还是从嘴里蹦出来重复说的话："谢谢，谢谢。我这辈子第一次感觉像家。"

邓诚依依不舍，那眼神足以代表邓诚此刻的心情，那是无比喜悦和感激。这种哽在喉咙里情感，不能只用几句话能表达他的心声。他强忍着背过身向徐忠家姨父走去，先双手合十敬了少珍姨，再双臂迎着徐忠家姨父拥抱。此时邓诚的眼泪哗哗哗地流出来，他不敢抬头，只得把头深深地埋在姨父的肩膀上，久久不能平静下来。

向艾神医道别后，邓诚木讷地上了徐忠家的私家车，七座大车可以放秦瑛和邓诚的两大箱子及艾乡的土地特产。秦瑛本来不想带这么多东西，可少珍姨说："这是顺便送给我姐的，我们也一起去省城看望你妈呀，要不是你们乘飞机航班还有两天，我们还下不了这个决心，我晕车。"

秦瑛来的时候只是为了抢时间给邓诚治病，这春节过月半了，回珠海的飞机非得从湖北省武汉市机场乘机，只有这机场离蕲春最近。

秦瑛的母亲退休后一直居住在省城，那里还有秦瑛母亲老一辈的亲戚，他们有的在省内担任省级领导的重要职位，但每逢佳节，再大的官也会看望秦瑛的母亲，因为秦瑛母亲辈分最大。一大家人都会一起团聚，今年相聚的日子正是今天农历十六，少珍姨和徐忠家姨父不会缺席，每年会带一车的土鸡蛋、土山药、土鸡、红薯、花生、青菜，送给省城的大小亲戚们。

徐忠家姨父说："是我们沾你妈的光，这些东西，你能带上飞机的就带回去；不能够带的东西，我们都送给你妈安排。亲戚多，一分就没有多少了。"

秦瑛补充说："我们就是这样安排的，在省城看看母亲和亲戚们，另外邓诚与家人也该团聚见面。而且这座城市有名的肿瘤医院就在武昌东湖旁边，既然来了就顺便在这里做一个全面检查，回珠海心里也有数。"

邓诚在车上比平时话少，他心里七上八下忐忑不安，他不知道突然一下要面对的这么多秦瑛亲人，不知道大家对他的第一印象会怎样。今天他才知道秦瑛大家庭里还有这么高级别的大领导，心里难免会有些不安，想到见面后会不自在。

两个小时左右，就到了秦瑛妈妈家小区楼下。大家把车上东西搬了下来，紧接着就直接把秦瑛妈妈接上车，前往家庭聚餐的地点——洪山广场大酒店豪华餐厅。省城的亲人们都在这里等着秦瑛和邓诚这一车的亲人，大家早就在这里等候多时了，这是年后月半的一次大团聚。

午餐开始的时候，大家都忙着打招呼，邓诚第一次见到这种场面，本能地觉得自己是局外人，他很自觉地坐在秦瑛的旁边，没太敢主动与亲人打招呼，微笑的脸庞因紧张而略显僵硬。

邓诚见到了那位领导亲戚，他身高 1 米 8，长得像电影老演员王心刚，他一脸和蔼亲切友好说道："亲人们，大家今天好好聚聚。照顾不周，但要吃好喝好，随意。"说话功夫像没事一样，一双手搭在邓城的肩膀上，小声亲切地对他说："你就是邓诚吧，早听家人提起过你，多吃点啊。家人多，没有时间个个照顾好，若不周到，你也别放在心里。"

邓诚想从凳子上起身感谢这位平易近人的大领导亲戚，对方用一双温暖的大手轻轻按住他，示意他不必见外。邓诚只得坐在位子上说"感谢感谢"，有些激动地不停点头。

这餐大家庭的饭局前后吃了两个多小时，愉快地结束后，大家还是像往年的老规矩一样，全部到秦瑛妈妈家，坐在一起品尝乡下送来的新茶，然后再各自将少珍和徐忠家带来的土特产分一分。大家像蚂蚁搬砖一样，想拿什么就拿什么，大家都很随意，彼此也不计较。大家都喜欢吃带来的地道土特产，以往每次都是这样分光。

秦瑛妈妈说："你们喜欢的东西都可以拿回去，多余的留下就是我的了。别客气，这都是少珍和忠家的心意啊，每年都想着咱们大家，从大老远提供这些我们最喜欢吃的东西。我们能吃上这就是福气啊，这让我常想到从前年轻时候，你们小时候吃的年味饭。"

邓诚看到秦瑛的家族是这么大，大家和谐友爱互助，就连大官亲戚也没有一点官架子，看上去就像是为大家服务的和善长辈，红光满面地随时照顾每一个亲戚。

邓诚发现自己越来越没自信，此刻他突然有一个念头，似乎他高攀了秦瑛，他配不上秦瑛这种好女孩。说真话，秦瑛凭这样的家庭条件，在家乡肯定能找到比他更好的人，更适合她的门当户对的爱情婚姻。他邓诚没能给予秦瑛更多的东西，反而觉得会是秦瑛的累赘。

邓诚沉默的一刹那，还是被敏感的秦瑛有所察觉，这就是她一直没有带邓诚见家人长辈的原因之一，她怕邓诚有顾虑想太多。但今天这场面真是赶上了，一些事情不得不接受现实，这丑媳妇也得见公婆！

由于人多，秦瑛也不便多问。这一天下来真忙碌，从早晨的赶路到省城的团聚，又到了亲人的寒暄和分开。各自回各家时已到了傍晚，月亮已经升起，秦瑛与邓诚静静坐在阳台的椅子向外眺望。

邓诚傻愣愣地看着天空自言自语说："这样一下子安静下来，又想起你和我在珠海的情景，那天是你的新居搬家，咱俩也是在阳台静静坐着。其实只要爱人在一起，生活都会有这样最好的感觉。"

秦瑛感觉邓诚有点累疲惫，就说："你今天早点休息吧，咱们明天还要按时起床，姨父安排好的司机要来接我们，可不能耽误了，这是我们的重要事情。医院的专家可不等我们，我们只能提前到达。"

第二天早上秦瑛简单收拾东西准备出发，带上洗净的苹果——因为要检查有的项目要求空腹，不能吃早餐。秦瑛陪着邓诚也没吃早餐，检查完以后咱们一人吃一个苹果，平平安安。这句话是秦瑛小孩子的时候听妈妈说的话，后来成了一种习惯。无论出远门干什么事，最好兜里揣着苹果，这寓意是向好的方面想，平平安安健健康康的意思。秦瑛多年来习惯了身边总是带着两个苹果。

果然姨父联系的司机很守时，邓诚和秦瑛到了楼下见到楼道就停着一辆黑色的国产老牌车子，知道肯定是等他们司机来了。果然不错，司机向邓诚他们闪了两下灯光。

上车后就直奔中南肿瘤医院，虽然是上午 8 ∶ 30，没想到却人满为患，排队的挂号的真的多如牛毛，男男女女老老少少，没想到才刚过农历月半就有这么多人来医院看病。

司机很熟练地将邓诚和秦瑛领到专家门诊的门口，把病历放进去排队。坐着等了半个小时，专家叫了邓诚的名字。专家挺仔细地前后看了半个小时，开处方开检查单和化验单，一下拿了七种项目的体检单，拍片子、验血、验尿液，还有其它项目。

后面就一直幸亏是这位司机带着他们穿过不同的楼道，在不同楼层穿行排队等候取样检测，不然那么多人，就是一个人等候拿检查结果报告，也不知道要等多久。一天都不见得顺利做完这些事情。

已经是中午 12：00 过了才做完几样，还有两项已约在下午检查。需要空腹的检查已经完成了，秦瑛和邓诚一起请司机在医院的对面小餐馆吃饭。这小餐馆很干净，菜式也挺简单，瓦罐汤配几个家常菜。

司机说："我习惯就点一份汤下面。"邓诚也来一份汤下米粉。秦瑛本来想让大家吃好点，没有想到时间还是有点紧，还得抓紧时间，于是也叫了一份汤下年糕和猪肝粉。三个人吃三样，都挺营养，很清淡。汤不油腻配点小泡菜，这中餐吃得舒服。可能是大家饿坏了，早餐没吃，一下吃得精光。司机说："我们吃完就赶快去分头排队拿做完的结果单。我先陪邓诚去做下午的几个项目，拿拍片子的结果，秦瑛可先去排队看看，我们弄完了就回头去找你。"

就这样一项一项地检查，拿结果。邓诚在等待取验血结果时在窗口看电脑屏幕上显示自己的名字和号码，结果发现隔着屏幕下两行出现了前妻的名字。"难道是她？"邓诚四处张望，看到旁边一个熟悉的身影，果然是前妻！

邓诚一愣一愣地看着对方，还以为是幻觉，想躲避但忍不住抬起头盯着她看。彼此都神色惊讶，谁都没想到会在这里遇见。

邓诚心里不知所措，嘴巴微微张开，却没有开口说话，呆在那里打量着眼前的人，心里有点乱。"几年没见了，怎么瘦成这样？似乎也是生了病？在拿什么结果呢？没有人陪伴？"邓诚脑袋飞速转动，他从前跟这个女人共同生活过十年啊！怎么会这样？她不是跟相好偷情跑了吗？怎么会落到这般境地？到底发生什么事？

好奇和心痛一下子涌上邓诚的心口，堵得慌，他虽然是做好了所有的项目检查，自己的情况也还不知道是好是坏，但看到前妻这个样子，明显前妻的病比他要重得多。

前妻也看到了邓诚，躲是躲不开了，她不好意思地低下头。窗口护士已经喊到了前妻的名字"叶小兰"。她没办法，只得硬着头皮到窗口拿到单子。接过之后，没看一眼就走了。

邓诚看着前妻瘦得不成人型的背影，加上那种病号服穿在身上，知道前妻一定是病得不轻。他找到自己的单子，马上以最快速度跟在前妻后面，他怕前妻发现自己，没跟太紧。邓诚只想看看前妻走向什么病房，了解她得了什么病。

即使她曾经背叛了他，但到这个时候，好像邓诚心中全然无恨，他只是想能不能帮到她。邓诚也不知道为什么会突然对她恨不起来，这明明是他以前想要看到最解恨的结果。怎么此时看到前妻这般模样，却没有那种痛之快，仇之恨的感觉。他真想上前直接问个究竟，他要给这几年心里的窝囊找到一个答案，要一个结果。

叶小兰走到肝病患者的那栋楼，邓诚跟随着追到了 4 号房间，4 号病房门上面写着叶小兰的名字。邓诚没有跟进去，在护士室门口问了前妻的病因。护士问邓诚是她的什么人，邓诚如实回答是前夫。

护士很同情地将病人情况告诉了邓诚："她是肝癌晚期了，她家人一个也没有来看过她，所以我们把结果告诉了她，让她有心理准备。她挺可怜的，什么事都一个人扛着。这肝病要是早发现早治疗就好了，她拖太久了。她得病后，丈夫就跟她离婚了。她没吵没闹，每次都是一个人来化疗。这次怕撑不了多久。她这病根是气出来的，堵在心口里。肝脏是人体重要排毒器官，这肝癌晚期，真的救不了她了。她现在主要是疼痛难受。你们曾经是夫妻，现在她都这样了，你还是多安慰她吧！半小时后，我们要给她化疗了。"

护士忙去了，邓诚忍不住转头直接走到 4 号房门前，敲门响了一声，妻子便回头一看："怎么是你，我以为是护士呢！"

邓诚："这里说话不方便，病人需要休息，我们在走道说几句话好吗？"

叶小兰跟了出来，随手把门关上，轻轻地说："你今天怎么会在这个医院，你还好吗？没想到我会成这个样子吧，我这是自作自受。你今天是给自己看病拿结果吗？"

邓诚说："我没拿到全部的检查结果。"

叶小兰："你都看到了，那男人是骗子，看到我检查出有肝炎就躲得远远的。

我与你分开第二年他就跟我分开了。他在外面有别的女人，我知道不能全怪他，我这是得的传染病。我也知道那个时候检查还是早期，但我没脸去找你，就让你恨我吧。但没想到天捉弄人，偏偏怕见到的人，偏偏碰见。这就是嘲笑我。我就那样了，医生跟我说了这病是气出来的，要养着。我心累，是命啊！你留下的房子还是你的名字，我没有办理过户。你给我的钱一半在治疗花了，还有一半加上退休金也够花了，还有医疗保险，但是像这种没有质量的生活……与其这样活着，我真不如早点解脱。快了，我的日子不多了，今天既然见到你了，这也是天意，我都跟你说了吧。"

邓诚默默地听着，恨不得把这几年的信息都一股脑地记下来。这来龙去脉总算是听明白了，此时他心里无比纠结和悲凉，本想着会恼怒地刺激一下前妻，却发现五味俱全的感觉同时袭击着他的胸口，他有一点快支撑不住的感觉。面对愁苦的前妻，他不知道是恨前妻还是在恨自己无能为力解救她。

难道真的没有办法了吗？就这样看着她等死吗？护士都那样说了，他还能做些什么呢？怎么会这样？怎么会这样？邓诚即使得不到前妻的爱，但也不希望前妻等死。他突然一下有种怜悯心，导致他忘了自己来医院是做什么。他恨不得再尽最后一点力，帮帮前妻。

叶小兰很冷静，示意邓诚别太靠近她，会传染。邓诚这才止住了向叶小兰靠近的脚步："你需要我帮你能做些什么吗？"

叶小兰："谢谢你，不需要了。我现在一个人都习惯了，常年在医院，我这是第三个年头了。一直没敢跟你说，几次想找你，对你交代一些事情。我想着走之前要跟你打个招呼，你给我婚前名下的房子，我都还是留给你，这本来就是你的，我没改过来。我当时是有点小九九，跟那个男人结婚之后，我留了一手。如果他对我不好，离婚了也得不到一半，所以所有的财产还是你的名字。我想着房子写你的名字还有保证。果然他嫌弃我走了，我们离婚简单，这财产物归原主。你只要不恨我就好，我不请求你原谅，只怪自己傻，是我看走眼了，我把你这么好的人搞丢了，是我对不住你。我知道你现在也有个好女朋友，你好好爱她吧！我中途有几次忍不住偷偷去看看你了，当时你在谈恋爱了，于是我就只能远远地退出了你的生活。像我这样的女人不配得到你的原谅，我只能选择不打扰你。这就是最好的惦记，最好的爱。真的对不起，是我错了，希望你现在越来越好。真的真心地祝福你。快走吧，我马上要打针做理疗。再别来看我现在这个丑陋的样子，我都嫌弃自己。"

邓诚有些僵硬地认真听完叶小兰的这些话，也不知道是为自己哭，还是为她命苦而哭。邓诚幼稚地有过报复前妻的念头，当恶果今天来了，此时邓诚听着前妻不停地道歉。他从悲凉中释怀出来，叶小兰对他来说了这些悔过的话，已经让善良的邓诚泪流不止。他本以为听到这些消息会痛快，却没想到自己哭得稀里哗啦，不知道说什么安慰的话好。

邓诚结结巴巴地说："不要说了，谁都有错，我也有错。我对你关心太少，我忽略了，我对不起你。现在什么也别说了，安心治病吧。现在医学发达了，应该可以救的，对，试试中医治疗怎么样？"

前妻也泣不成声地说："傻呀，别犯傻了，我这边治不好了，医生已经给我下诊断书，我熬不过三个月。这也是天意，在临走之前能见到你挺好的，我满足了。我把房产证和所有值钱的东西，都放在原来那个柜子的抽屉里，你知道的。存折还是你设置的那个老密码，我没改。如果真到了走的那天，你一定要去我们以前的家拿回那些东西。现在都对你说了，我心里无牵无挂了。我有点累了，我回病房躺一下。你走吧，我想休息了，真的别再乱花钱给我看病了，我已经没有任何希望了。"

叶小兰边向病房走去，边又回头不放心地对邓诚说："我现在好疼，活着还难熬，我现在就想早点上天堂。我要走了，该说的说了，你再别来了。"

此时，只听到走廊医生护士在喊叶小兰要去做化疗了，这个时候所有探望的家属都要退出去等候。没法，邓诚被护士长往外赶，邓诚双脚瘫软在走道角落里地上坐了好一会儿。想到还要取结果单子，只能走出那栋传染住院大楼。此时邓诚边向外走，眼睛从未离开他前妻的那栋楼的方向，脑子里全是叶小兰弯下腰的身子，那瘦下来的背影。

走出大楼后，邓诚猛然想到，得赶快回到去取结果窗口，不然秦瑛找不到他的人，会着急的。他跌跌撞撞，进电梯出电梯转楼下电梯，几个楼道里穿梭着，主楼次楼错层，终于到了一楼取单窗口。他看到秦瑛果然焦急地在那里找他，看了他好像哭了的样子就马上问："你哪里不舒服啊？你上哪去了？哎呀真把人急死了，这长时间，快快把单给我看看。还有几项等会儿司机帮我们去取，他让我们在大门外凳子上坐着等他，叫我们俩再别乱跑了。"

邓诚像小木偶一样听秦瑛指挥，但一句话也没有听进去，只是跟着她走到门诊外的椅子上坐下来。思绪有点混乱，邓诚不知道自己该如何对秦瑛说。他不能瞒着她，肯定要跟秦瑛老老实实交代。但是他不知道怎么说给秦瑛听，这对秦瑛又会带来什么样的影响呢？

邓诚思索着有什么样的法子跟秦瑛开口。首先说出留下来不回珠海的理由，随后今晚再跟秦瑛单独的时候，全盘托出？还是先来编一次善意的谎言呢？

邓诚脑袋不好使了，他感觉生活总是跟他出难题，让他不得安宁。邓诚想着秦瑛那么单纯善良，他不知道该不该隐瞒秦瑛，他只知道这是不对也不妥的愚蠢办法。那该怎么做才好呢？邓诚急着仰望天空，此时太阳西下的光芒正好斜照在秦瑛的脸上，邓诚眼睛里看着这么美的秦瑛，像是在风景中的画，情不自禁地用手抚摸着秦瑛的脸颊，将风吹拂在耳边发丝，一根根的收拢。此时邓诚什么也没有想，只是本能地重复着动作。

第 27 章　依依不舍

夜慢慢黑下来了，少珍姨和徐忠家姨父与亲人团聚之后，只在秦瑛妈妈家待了一个晚上，第二天就赶回乡村蕲春了。他们每次都只待一天，心里老惦记着乡下的农活，鸡要照管，菜园里需要浇水，反正每次到来就是为了送农副土特产品，完事就马上赶回家。

秦瑛妈妈已早早睡下了。邓诚怕吵醒秦瑛妈妈，两个人坐到阳台外面，静静地望着窗外天空。邓诚想对秦瑛说出白天医院发生的事情，但一时间不知从何说起。邓诚感觉今天的夜晚特别难熬，他几次看着秦瑛就是不敢张口，堵在心口上却无法诉说。

邓诚深情地看着秦瑛，深吸一口气后才说："你知道我今天在医院碰见谁了吗？"

"谁？别卖关子了，快说嘛。"秦瑛靠近邓诚催着。邓诚吞吞吐吐说："我见到了前妻，她得了肝癌，住进了这里的肿瘤医院，已经快不行了。我本应该恨她，但看到她那情形，却恨不起来。不知道为什么，心里觉得挺难受。她的日子不多了，她向我忏悔，她告诉我她这些年过着落魄的生活，我听着有种莫名的心酸。她后悔的时候来珠海找过我，发现我和你正在交往，她自认不配再来打扰我的生活，又悄悄地回到了湖北。我也不知道该不该在这个时候跟你谈前妻的过去，但我想跟你说一件事，我想在她走之前，让她心里好受些，少一些遗憾。毕竟她是快要离开人世的人了，我不忍心让她走得那么悲凉，你懂我的心吗？我不强求你要理解我，为什么会原谅背叛过自己的女人。说实在，我也不明白自己为什么要这样做。我打算明天不跟你飞回珠海，我想留下来陪伴前妻最后一段时间，小瑛你同意吗？"

秦瑛被这突如其来的真实事件打乱了阵脚，她是写小说的作家，经常写别人的爱情故事，却没有想过她和邓诚之间竟会发生这样的生活故事。此刻秦瑛想到的不是自己，她沉默了一会儿，心里升起一阵一阵的心疼："我理解你的难过，我只是心疼你，不知道怎么才能帮到你。"

听到这番暖暖的心里话，邓诚很惊讶，没想到秦瑛跟他一样，表现出来的是对前妻的同情。他被秦瑛的善良大度而感动，不知道怎么表达自己的心情，只是默默地转身。秦瑛拿着一杯温水递给邓诚说："我理解你，不用考虑我，你留下来吧。只是明天我们不要对妈妈说详细情况，免得长辈担心。我们可以在医院附近找个酒店暂时住下来。我可以陪你去医院看望她吗？到时候再看情况决定行程，也许我独自飞回珠海，处理一些急事，你留在这里随时照顾前妻，你看行吗？"

秦瑛的话让邓诚无比感动，邓诚没有想到秦瑛有这般情怀和大气的胸襟，他感觉此时说什么都无法表达出自己的情感。秦瑛大度地分担了邓诚内心的痛苦，也让邓诚释放出压抑在心底的情感。邓诚发觉自己更爱秦瑛了，他再次坚信秦瑛是他此生最值得守护的女人。邓诚默默地将秦瑛搂在自己的怀中，生怕别人抢跑了的感觉。

这一夜，两人就这么呆呆地坐在阳台望着天空。他们静静地靠着，相互拥抱依存，很久很久没有松开，这将是一个无法入眠夜晚。

第二天早上，秦瑛向妈妈说明离开去机场前先和邓诚去探望一位病人，随后直接去机场飞往珠海。秦瑛妈妈是善解人意的长辈，妈妈只给两个人说了几句："你们都是成年人了，我相信你们会处理好一切。有些事情，按照自己的意愿去做，顺其自然，水到渠成，你们以后会懂。"

秦瑛妈妈再没有说什么，长辈心里很明白，只是没有明说而已。在家人团聚的那一天作为长辈代表就说过宽心的话："你们创业也要注意身体健康，只有健康的身体才是真正人生最宝贵的财富。"

秦瑛懂得妈妈满满的叮嘱，老人家是希望年轻人能幸福生活，不只是为了挣多少钱。老人希望儿女们以健康为主，在力所能及的情况下去努力发展；在情感上要对得住自己的良心，对得起自己的初衷。

邓诚很感激秦瑛的妈妈，并深深鞠躬道谢。邓诚已感受到秦瑛妈妈的认可，这是对他最好的肯定。秦瑛的妈妈是最受人尊敬的长辈，能得到秦瑛妈妈的支持，这是邓诚与秦瑛走进婚姻殿堂的定心丸。

飞往珠海的飞机是在下午 6：15 起飞，现在是早晨，很多事情还来得及处理。

秦瑛和邓诚匆忙地告别了家人，马上赶到医院附近的连锁酒店，订了一间标准间。秦瑛安排好邓诚住的酒店后，准备和邓诚一起，买些营养品去探望邓诚的前妻，就在这时邓诚手机响了，邓诚接通后传来焦急的声音："喂喂！你是邓诚吗？我是昨天医院你见过的护士长，能请你马上赶到医院急救病室吗？你前妻快不行了，但是一直喊着你的名字，想要见你最后一面。你快来吧！"

邓诚不能理解为什么护士长能打通他的电话，想必前妻在紧急联络人那一项填写了邓诚的号码。这时邓诚有点慌乱，手脚冰凉，反应迟钝，不知所措。对他来说太突然了，昨天见面还看到的前妻，突然就说不行了，这也太快了吧？不是说还有几个月的时间？

幸好秦瑛在他身旁，连忙对邓诚说："赶快去医院看看，我陪你一起去。"秦瑛将重要随身物品马上收拾好，牵着邓诚的手连跑带走赶到了医院急救中心病室。

医院重症监护病房里，护士长指引邓诚来到前妻的床边，秦瑛随即跟了过去，站在邓诚的身后。

前妻看到邓诚火速赶来，她心中百感交集，眼泪不由自主地从眼角沿着脸庞流了下来，有点泣不成声。她在尽力控制着自己有情绪，有种喜泣交汇的感激。她想支撑着身体起床，邓诚马上抓住她的手说："你躺下说，我听，我们会一直守护在你的身边。"

邓诚的前妻叶小兰比秦瑛大两岁，本来还年轻，根本舍不得这么离去，看见邓诚后，她似乎平静了许多。她指着枕头下放的一封信和一套房门钥匙，亲自交到邓诚手上，这才慢慢地平静地躺了下去，眼睛一刻也不离开邓诚，微笑轻声说道："你能帮我梳理头发吗？我想打扮整理一下自己，你帮我吧。就算是走进天堂，我也想美美的。"

秦瑛松开握住邓诚的那一只手，让邓诚去帮叶小兰梳头盘发。自己则同医护人员，悄悄退出病房，在门口外的窗口默默祈祷。

邓诚满含热泪一边帮前妻梳头发一边看着前妻的脸颊，像是说：你要是肝疼痛，就喊出来，别忍着，有我在，你别再有轻生的念头。

叶小兰不想活，有她的道理，她不想浪费这些无谓的治疗费，所以情愿在最后离开之前见邓诚一面。

叶小兰好像回光返照，一下子精神起来，跟邓诚交代着一项项重要事："记住，你一定要好好地把我写的信看完照办。拜托你了，我只有你这么一个亲人，可我辜负了你，你别恨我。"

说完后叶小兰有些依依不舍，对着邓诚平静微笑安详地说："我想休息了，你快去办事吧。别再担心我了，好好爱她，她真是一个好女人。是我这辈子没有福气。我要休息了……"

邓诚看着前妻不说话了，好像平静地睡着了。再过几分钟，仪器屏幕上显示心脏脉搏已经没有了跳动的信号，只听见发出滴答滴答的声音。整个病房一片沉默，几分钟后大家自觉地慢慢退了出去，只有邓诚像欣赏一幅画一样，守在前妻的身旁。

秦瑛被邓诚在前妻临死之前的痴情善良之举而感动，她亲耳听到邓诚前妻的话："你要好好地爱她，我真心祝福你们幸福。"

秦瑛想让邓诚一个人静静地陪前妻一会儿，强忍着眼泪对护士们说："我们不去打扰他，他此刻最好的安慰是安静。"

护士长轻声自语地说："要准备后事了。"

邓诚在一旁守着，感觉叶小兰只是睡着了。邓诚心里对她说："我已经原谅你了，我不恨你。有谁没犯过错呢？放心吧，我会按照你的想法，把你安葬在山上，葬在我们曾经种下的那棵树下，这叫树葬。可以埋掉所有的烦恼，让树陪你吧，你在天堂想到这棵树，就像到了家一样。"

邓诚想到这里，已泣不成声，有一种难以言说的悲伤，眼睛涌出无数的眼泪，他不停地用衬衫袖口去擦。邓诚为叶小兰如此伤心地哭泣，可惜这一切她已经看不到。秦瑛看见，并被邓诚善良深沉感人的场景而触动，她又悲又庆幸自己，遇到了值得托付终身的痴情男人。

邓诚突然想到身边还有最值得他疼爱的人。秦瑛在哪呢？邓诚轻轻抚摸了一下叶小兰的脸颊，慢慢地将白色的床单盖上她的脸。邓诚在护士的陪同下退出房间，这时护士长带着工作人员拿着担架将叶小兰抬起放入担架上，转移到医院的太平间。

邓诚看着前妻被搬上担架抬走太平间的方向，眼泪包含着无尽的忧伤。秦瑛扶着邓诚，感觉他好像站立不稳，邓诚需要休息一下了，身心极速疲惫不堪。

秦瑛只好陪着邓诚回到酒店，想好好跟他聊一聊，让他不要那么难过。邓诚平静下来后想到不能耽误秦瑛回珠海的飞机。他强装着坚强，强忍着悲伤，很理性拉着秦瑛的手说："瑛子，把我的机票退了。我送你去机场，你一个人先回去吧，我留下来把这些事情全部处理完。这些事情可以不用告诉你妈妈，不要让你的家人为我们担忧，你理解我的意思吗？"

秦瑛说："你不用送我。你这边不需要我帮你做点什么吗？"

邓诚说："不用了，我能处理好，你专心处理自己的事情就好。你那边也有一大摊子的事情要忙，你为我已经耽误了很长时间，那边不能没有你。我留下来就可以了，我把这边的事情处理完，你放心吧，我可能要在这里停留一段时间，因为我要按她的意思卖掉房子，把她用过的东西全部处理掉。这些事办完之后我会找你。在这段时间中，我可以等到自己的检查结果报告。到时候看情况再做进一步打算。"

秦瑛明白如果她留在邓诚身边只会让他分心，不能安心处理一切事情。她同意了邓诚的方案，一个人飞往珠海。

邓诚想送秦瑛去机场，秦瑛看邓诚这种心事重重的状态，理解地给邓诚一个拥抱，附在他耳边轻声说："好好照顾自己，我会等你回来，再见，保重。"

邓诚只是点点头，闷出一句话："我想送你上车，这总算可以吧？"

邓诚跟秦瑛手牵着手向酒店大门走去，邓诚把秦瑛的大旅行箱子搬上车，跟司机打声招呼说了几句话："这是打车路费，你拿着。开车慢点，安全第一啊。"随后走到后座位，向秦瑛说了道别的话："到机场后，我安排沈总去机场接你。到家回信息给我，我会每天惦记你的。"

司机发动车辆，邓诚无奈地后退，向秦瑛依依不舍地道别。载着秦瑛的车辆驶向城市的主干道上，直到看不到踪影，邓诚才向医院方向走去，该了结过往的一切陈年旧账，邓诚方可彻底释怀。

第 28 章　花晨月夕（大结尾）

三天之后，叶小兰的遗体进行了火化。邓诚按照她留下信的叮嘱事项一一执行，最后一项是将她的骨灰安葬在老家山上两人合种的大树下。

邓诚遵从叶小兰的意愿，树下不留名字，不竖牌坊。他在大树下挖了一个小坑，把叶小兰的骨灰盒放进去，又将那封信点燃，灰烬与树下泥土混在一起将骨灰盒掩埋。

邓诚深深舒了一口气，对叶小兰说："你安息吧，你要我做的事情都完成了。我会好好地替你活着。"他沉默地靠在树干上，轻轻闭上眼睛，脑海里浮现出叶小兰微笑的神情，像是告诉邓诚"我已经到家了，你去忙吧！"

邓诚睁眼望着蓝天白云，耳边响起一阵阵树叶摇动的沙沙声。邓诚的心情平复了很多，他想到中国古语"人固有一死，或重于泰山，或轻于鸿毛"。经历过前妻去世后，他已经不再害怕死亡，他认为有生之年不要留下遗憾就好。

邓诚想起稻盛和夫说过的话："我们终其一生，都在寻找两个东西，一个是价值感，一个是归属感，价值感来自被肯定，归属感来自被爱。人这一辈子千万不要马虎两件事。一是找对爱人，二是找对事业，因为太阳升起时需要投身事业，太阳落山时要与爱人相拥的。你是谁，便会遇见谁。或许最好的人生，就是有能力爱自己，有余力爱别人，有时间去完成想做的事和梦想，有情怀去探寻诗和远方。"

将叶小兰骨灰葬好之后，邓诚将叶小兰留给自己的房产挂在中介代理出售。他回到医院拿检验报告，一些指标还显示＋号，表明身体还未完全康复。医生对邓诚说："要完全治愈，还是要继续吃中药。"

邓诚结合目前的情况，跟秦瑛提议暂未返回珠海，继续留在这边治病，以及处理好卖房的事。艾神医看过检测结果，肯定了邓诚的身体已经有明显的好转，但还需要继续调养。他又给邓诚调配了一周的七服中药。艾神医对邓诚说："看来我们这里的气候很适合你，如果你要彻底治愈，需要长期住下来，不知邓兄有何想法？"

邓诚向艾神医说出了自己的顾虑，秦瑛要在珠海发展自己的事业，如果他因为治病跟秦瑛长期分开，会对秦瑛不公平，毕竟自己曾许下诺言要尽快回珠海与秦瑛结婚。另一方面，邓诚也希望在养病期间还能做一些有益大众的事业，邓诚事业都留在珠海那边，留在这里邓诚隐隐觉得在浪费宝贵的生命时光，发挥不出自己的人生价值。

艾神医想了一下对邓诚说："结婚这事你问过秦瑛意见吗？不如让她决定在哪边结婚。"

艾神医的话一针见血提出了问题关键，邓诚想了想说："我会考虑对秦瑛说明一切情况，但又觉得自己都没有想好，不想让她担心误解。"

艾神医突然想起一件事情，又对邓诚说："我前天看过一个病人，好像提到过他们乡镇正在对绿色环保发展有些政策，对外开放承包荒山开辟绿色通道，可以发展植树造林和培植果园基地。你若是想在这里长住并发展新事业，可以考虑一下这个方向。我可以帮你问问打听联系方式。"

邓诚高兴得跳了起来："我有兴趣！这件事非常有意义，我想留下来将荒山改造成果林。我愿意在有生之年干一件为子孙后代造福的事。这是一个千载难逢的好机会，拜托艾神医帮我联系一下。您不仅治愈我的身体，还打开了我的心结。"

邓诚一下子有了精神支柱，他兴奋地向艾神医匆匆告别，直奔少珍姨家跟他们说了这件事。邓城是一个敢于挑战的人，无论是对待爱情，还是对待事业工作，说干就干。几天后艾神医联系邓诚，并为他引见负责承包荒山的主管领导张局长。

张局长认真听取了邓诚的建议及草拟的策划方案，要求邓诚在一周后拿出可执行的具体方案，并确定承包多少亩荒山荒地。

邓诚虚心请教徐忠家的建议，走村串户向村民收集意见，及了解气候变化，对各种情况深入详细调查分析，将人力、物力、财力的分配都备注在文案中。经过一周时间的充分准备，邓诚将改造荒山变成绿色果林的方案顺利交到张局长手上。

张局长举行了专门的会议讨论这项工程，项目重要负责人一致通过邓诚承包500 亩荒山的方案。乡镇领导特别批准邓诚有权使用六亩荒地作为生活宅基地。方案通过后，邓诚当即表示自己投入 1000 万元开展前期的基础设施建设。

事后徐忠家姨父和少珍姨问邓诚是否需要他们出资赞助，邓诚很欣慰，体谅拒绝了他们资助："资金问题我来解决，我正好将一些房产出售，有足够的资金用到这个项目上。我相信秦瑛知道这件事后会很开心。这里就是我们将来的家，我们可以一起享受蔚蓝天空，可以地老天荒地住在一起，将来墓地也不用选了，我们会在这里落叶归根。"

邓诚高兴地彻夜难眠，心想秦瑛听到消息后不知道会有什么反应。他迫不及待地要把这好消息告诉秦瑛。

秦瑛回到珠海之后就忙碌起来，每天打理爱吧书吧，一直都坚持写作，跟沈总和秋甜忙起来就没完没了。还好两个员工小芹小贝都很熟练书吧的管理和经营，帮秦瑛分担了不少工作。

秦瑛回到珠海的最初几天没有过多打扰邓诚，让他安心处理前妻的事。从他对待前妻的态度上，秦瑛看到了邓诚的善良，更加深爱邓诚。尽管秦瑛已经是邓诚的未婚妻，可是她不会给邓诚束缚，她希望邓诚能幸福健康快乐生活，爱他并非占有他，两人彼此相爱，不时思念对方就已经足够幸福。

待邓诚处理好前妻的事情后，秦瑛才像以前那样跟邓诚保持频繁的联系。但最近秦瑛感觉邓诚好像在处理着什么重要事情，有时一连几天都无法联系上。邓诚最后一通电话告诉秦瑛他有事要到山里去考察，那里没有网络信号，可能联系不上。秦瑛疑惑着邓诚会在老家做什么重要的事情？

这一天，当邓诚终于向秦瑛坦白说出自己接下来要做的事业后，秦瑛果然如邓诚所料的那般惊喜激动。

秦瑛认真回复邓诚信息：我对你承包荒山开垦种树这项目十分支持，在这里你可以改善乡村经济促进家乡发展，并且还能继续与癌症抗争，逐渐康复。相信这片土地会滋养你的生命。你做到了我想要做的事情，你喜欢的生活方式就是我理想中的生活。

亲爱的邓诚，这辈子能遇到了你，我很庆幸，也很知足。你不用担心我们婚礼的事情，那只是婚姻过程中的一个仪式。我爱你并非只是一时冲动，是你真心对我，让我自然感受到浓浓的爱意。真爱在哪里，我的心绪就牵挂在哪里，在我的心里，有三处可以与日升月明共度余生美好的宝地：我的家乡——中医之都圻春李时珍故乡；还有我们相识相知的中山和珠海，我俩在那里交集相遇，一座生机勃勃的城市，我们的第二家乡。最好一个家，是因你而拥有心灵存放，最踏实安全而又温暖的港湾，是我余生可以托付终生的定心丸。

就像我很喜欢《凭着爱》这首歌，它的歌词也是我此刻的心声：

曾踏遍刺脚的弯路

疲倦了　谁来倾诉

遇过几多痴情　怎会不知道

但我深知总有一日

定会找得到更好

凭着爱　我信有出路

凭着爱　情怀

在这一刻跟你　终于可拥抱

就算始终失意倒运

人生已再没苦恼

曾在这高高低低　弯弯曲曲中跌倒

才骤觉开开心心　简简单单已极好

最美丽仍然是爱　带泪尝仍然是好

未惧怕一生的波折伴到老

凭着爱　我信有出路

凭着爱　情怀不老

在这一刻跟你　终于可拥抱

就算始终失意倒运

人生已再没苦恼

曾在这高高低低弯弯曲曲中跌倒

才骤觉开开心心简简单单已极好

最美丽仍然是爱 带泪尝仍然是好

未惧怕一生的波折 伴到老

曾在这高高低低弯弯曲曲中跌倒

才骤觉开开心心简简单单已极好

最美丽仍然是爱 带泪尝仍然是好

未惧怕一生的波折 伴到老

凭着爱只管一生 磨炼到老

后记

关于这部作品的写作初衷，我是想写一部当代大龄剩女择偶标准的爱情婚姻故事。

小说记录了女主秦瑛跟三个男人交往的过程，通过三种不同的经历对比，秦瑛深刻认识到爱情和婚姻的真谛，最后她选择了能懂她的爱人，选择了能给予她一生一世陪伴的爱情。这是一部弘扬正能量婚姻观的小说，唯有真情实意换真心的爱情，才将能走进爱人的心里。

这部作品最先取名为《定心丸》，原来的故事主线是秦瑛跟程默之间互相帮助，两人感情渐渐深厚，最终修得爱情正果。写作到了中期，我发现程默的原型人物是个不靠谱的人。我是一个习惯于从真实生活中提取素材的写作者，现实生活的变化影响了我的写作方向。于是我修改了故事的走向，将作品名字改成《异想天开》，写出生活中一些虚伪男人的两面性，一方面隐藏自己的私心贪婪，一方面又表现出极好的人缘，热情主动，施人于善。在写作后期，我收敛了批判的锋芒，对程默这个人物没有加入太多个人主观分析，更偏向于真实地展示程默的所作所为，让读者自己去评判这个人物。

后来我又将作品的名字改成《何为真情》，并在某周刊报的"文学世界"栏目连载发表。作品完结之后，我又重新品味了一遍，发现作品后来的主题立意比最初的设想提升了不少境界。我想通过这部作品弘扬正确的爱情观：真心对待爱你的人，才会得到真爱的回馈。在作品出版筹备阶段，与老师共同探讨和斟酌，又将作品改名为《凭着爱》。

由于国际读者的需求呼声，现将此部作品书名为《春风吻上我的脸》以中英文版出版双语书，供广大读者能以中英双语阅读。

　　写出一部好作品并不容易，一部作品能出版成书需要很多人的热心帮助。感谢写作过程中所有帮助过我的朋友，感谢汇文书联各位编辑老师的专业指导和帮助！

作者：赵舒娴

2024 年 3 月 2 日